Tracks In the Sand

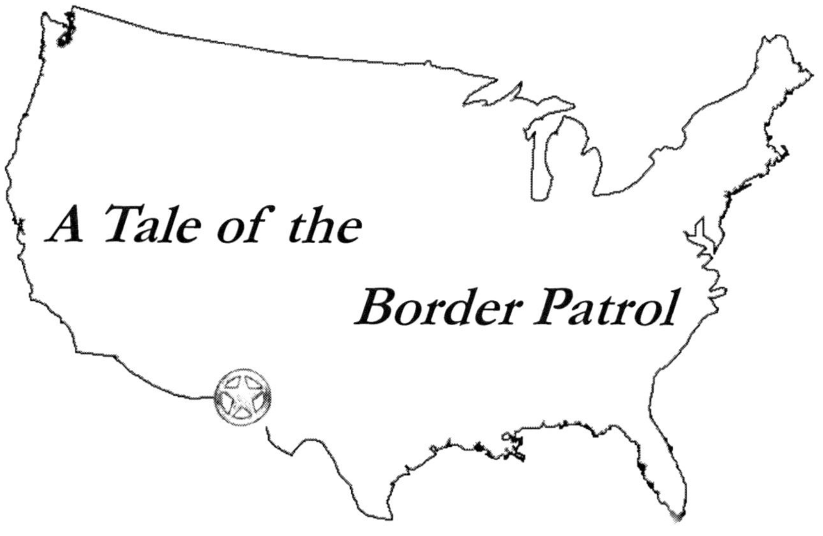

A Tale of the Border Patrol

It didn't all happen just this way—

but it could have.

Tracks in the Sand – A Tale of the Border Patrol is fiction. Characters, incidents, and dialogue are creations of the author. They should not be construed as historically real, but they portray a reality that existed in the time and place in which this book is set. Any resemblance to actual persons living or dead is mostly coincidental—but if you were there in those days you will recognize bits and pieces of people you knew. That's how fiction works.

Signcutter Press
4001 Summitview
Suite 5 – 106
Yakima, WA 98908
or
editor@signcutterpress.com
http://www.signcutterpress.com

ISBN 978-0-6151-8430-2

Dedication

Most of all for Sherrie, who's always there.
And
for all those who wore the green shirt,
and for those who do today,
and for all those who will—
and especially for those who have fallen.

Honor First.

For Kerri,
One of the really
good people we love,

Author's Note

The U.S.-Mexican border area is a strange place, not quite the United States and not quite Mexico. English and Spanish intermingle and a society exists containing elements from both sides of the border. Some would say the synthesis contains the best of both societies. Others would say it contains the worst. Both would be correct.

But that is the border area. "The border," however, is a line that divides two very different countries. The reader should understand that Mexicans and Americans have fundamentally different views of that border and what it signifies. Without going into historical detail, it is most easily said that Mexicans believe they were robbed of vast territory north of what has become the border. So, when a Mexican crosses the U.S. border illegally he has no sense that he is doing anything wrong; he believes he is simply overcoming an inconvenient impediment that does not belong there.

The U.S. Border Patrol has existed since 1924 to correct that notion. They have not been notably successful in recent decades in doing so—the presence of 20 million or more illegal aliens in the U.S. testifies to that sad fact. That is not the fault of the Border Patrol—it is largely because of ambiguous feelings on the part of Americans about whether the border matters or not. As a result, until about 2004, the Border Patrol was perennially resource-poor and undermanned by a factor of ten to what it needed.

Historians say that the Mexican War ended in 1848. They are wrong. The last shots have not yet been fired.

In 2003, in the aftermath of the terrorist attacks of 9/11, the Border Patrol was placed within the Department of Homeland Security, where it became part of Customs and Border Protection. Before then it had been a part of the Department of Justice. Before even that, at the time of its founding, the Border Patrol was part of the Labor Department.

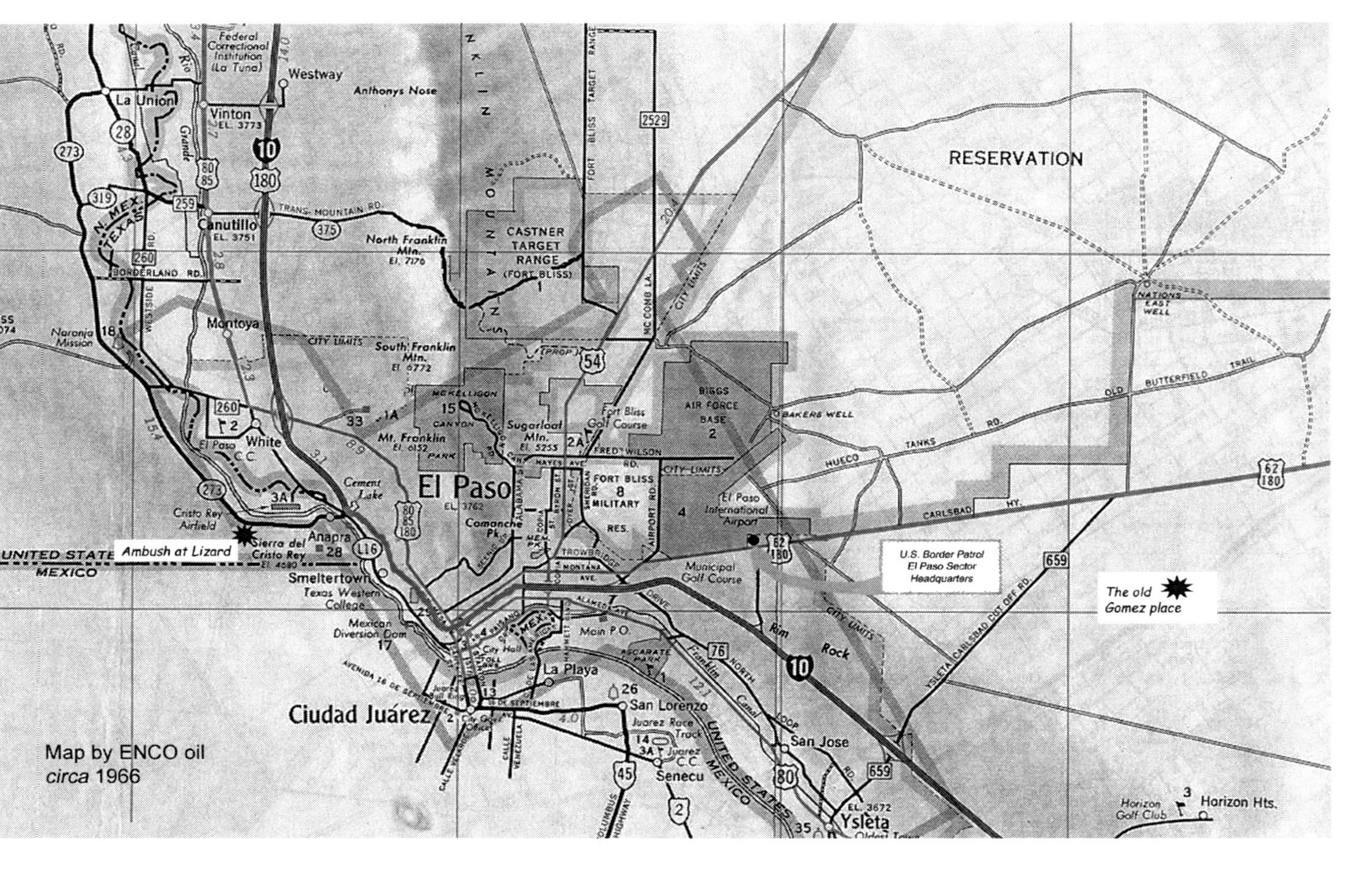

Map by ENCO oil
circa 1966

In The Beginning . . .

The battered Jeep Station Wagon rolled to a stop at the gate in the fence. Three strands of barbed wire hung in long, irregular sags between crazyleaning wood posts; the fence looked as though it had been there since the Apaches left. The Jeep, too, had been aged by the desert. Its pale green and white paint was faded by years in the southwestern sun and the round blue and gold decals on its doors had been scratched and torn by thousands of miles driving through the thorny borderlands of west Texas. The cloud of dust it had been dragging along the desert track rolled forward to add yet another layer to the rig and its occupants.

The tracks of five people continued on the other side of the gate. They shone like faded mirrors as the sand, pressed smooth by the feet, reflected the dawn sunshine into the Border Patrolmen's faces. To one side, the wire was pressed down where the walkers had climbed over it.

The balding man in the driver's seat squinted into the dawn glare with eyes the color of old denim, bleached out in the raw climate. The wrinkles around his eyes and on the rest of his hatchet face betrayed a lifetime of sunglare and hot wind.

"Open the gate, kid. We'll find feet in these tracks pretty quick."

Ken Travis stepped out the door of the old Jeep. He stood for a moment looking around before he reached high over his head and then bent from the waist and touched his toes. He stretched his six-foot frame to straighten out the kinks put in his back by hours of rough riding on the desert trails. His stiff, new gunleather creaked in protest at being reshaped. He didn't like being called "kid", but at twenty-two and looking eighteen, brand new to the Border Patrol, and on probation for another eight months, he didn't think he was in a position to object to anything somebody wearing tin wanted to call him.

After an hour of promise the sun was above the horizon at last. Now it lit the surrounding barren mountains clear to their bases on the desert floor. Ken had watched as dawn pinkened their crests, then as the light grew brighter and brighter it flowed down the mountains like paint splashed on a wall. The countryside, wrinkled and torn as a discarded bandanna, was lit in outrageous shades of purple and gold and red that would look gaudy if done by any hand but God's.

The passage of a cold front in the evening had brought showers that washed away the dust and smog. At dawn, now, the sky was a deep, unrelieved blue and the air was chilly. Later, the heat would return, the sky would look like a sheet of polished stainless steel and the sunglare would sap any beauty from the scene. Now, though, this late September day of 1968 was gorgeous.

He shivered quickly in the dawn breeze. It had been in the 40's overnight and the sun had not yet warmed things. He unsnapped a ring full of keys from his gun belt and opened the Border Patrol lock on the chain that secured the gate. After sliding a wire catch loop up off the post he walked the three strands out of the way while the jeep passed through.

How the hell does he have any idea of how far behind those five we are? He'd wondered a lot of things like that since he had come back from the Border Patrol Academy a couple weeks before, wearing his shiny, new Patrol Inspector's badge. This was his first day on the sign cutting detail, but he'd heard about how "The Real" Diehl could track a snake across a rock ledge.

At the Academy he'd learned some of the basics of tracking men across the desert but there had been nothing there that would explain much of what he'd seen in just a few hours with Diehl. The instructors had told them it wasn't a skill you could learn in class; you had to be out there and do it. He hoped that despite Diehl's reserved attitude he'd pass some of the information along, but Ken didn't want to be pushy with his questions or too talkative. Diehl seemed given to silence, so it had been quiet in the vehicle since the shift started at 2:00 a.m.

God, but it's beautiful out here this time of day. The Jeep passed through the gate. He closed it and locked the chain, and then got back in.

"That's one of the few good things about working with a trainee, not having to get out and unlock gates." Diehl said. "Did you lock it again?"

"Yes, sir." Ken had been raised to be respectful to his elders, but even allowing for that, "sir" seemed a word you'd naturally use to Diehl.

The old slab-sided Jeep ran along the sandy trail, bucking and rattling as they followed the footprints. A haze of dust hung constantly in the air in the vehicle, brought up from the sand and dirt on the bare steel floorboards by the pounding of the trail. Dust was a fact of life everywhere in the southwest, Ken had noticed. It sure was around El Paso and he hadn't even been here yet for the spring dust storms that arrive in April and May.

They'd found the tracks about 3:00 a.m. just north of Interstate 10 as they drove slowly along the drag road, looking for fresh footprints headed north. About midnight the evening shift had pulled a drag along that dirt road. He'd seen the drag when they turned onto the road; a gadget made from an old set of tractor tires chained side-by side together and laid flat. When pulled along the sand road by a jeep it knocked out all the old sign, marks left in the dirt by whatever passed that way, leaving a fresh, smooth surface for intruders to leave tracks in as they headed north. Like everything else that moved in the desert, the drag generated vast clouds of dust. They inevitably blew forward into the rig, too thick to breathe but too thin to plow.

Let's see . . . the drag was pulled about eleven o'clock last night and the tracks are on top of the drag marks, so they must have been made sometime after then. That means they were no more than three or four hours old when we found them.

Applying what they'd told him at school, he guessed that meant the group probably had developed as much as a seven or eight mile lead by the time he and Diehl got onto their trail. Maybe more, though. Usually, the larger the group, the slower they went, but this one was moving right along, not real fast, but steady. There had been no sign of stops to be found in the sand, beyond a place or two where one or another of them had stopped to take a leak.

For a while the tracks had wandered back and forth through the brush, heading generally north, then they hit this sand trail and lined out, headed northeast . . . to what? From the beginning, Diehl had leapfrogged ahead on the trail, not looking for tracks every inch of the way, but just looking now and again. Ken was sure they must have gained quickly on the group by doing that, but he wasn't sure how Diehl knew they continued from one place to the next.

"Goddam rigs" Diehl growled. "Somebody's gonna get killed in one if the outfit doesn't get us some new stuff. And some decent mechanics." The steering gear was so worn and loose on the ten-year old Jeep that that Diehl had to saw the wheel back and forth in quarter-turns just to stay between the bushes on either side of the trail. They were a thrill a minute to drive on the highway.

Suddenly a roar filled the Jeep, accompanied by a hard 'thud" on the roof. Ken ducked away from his window and Diehl swerved violently off to the left, bouncing over a mesquite bush, launching Ken up against the roof. A manic laugh, followed by "Gotcha, gotcha, and gotcha" came over the two-way radio as a small green airplane flew away, low over the brush. Diehl snatched up the mike, twisted the freq knob on the Motorola two-way to the local channel and said "Wagner, you sonuvabitch, I'm gonna shoot you down for that some day!" Then he hung the mike onto its dash clip with a grin, the first emotion he'd shown all night.

"Kid, that's 'Wings' Wagner, the craziest man in the whole Border Patrol." He braked the Jeep to a halt. "Get out and have a look at the roof."

Ken opened the door and stood on the sill, looking across the dull white roof. There, just off center, was a black tire mark a couple feet long, obviously left there by an airplane. And it wasn't the only one; the roof looked like the landing threshold of a runway. He'd wondered why so many of the desert rigs' rooftop antennas were bent forward; now he knew. His determination to stay quiet was blown away by his shock.

"Jesus H. Christ!" he swore aloud as he got back into the vehicle. "What's he trying to do, kill us and himself too? That's the craziest thing I ever saw!"

"What's the matter, kid? 'fraid you'll be in an airplane wreck? He's been doin' that for years and so far he hasn't hurt nobody. Could, I suppose, but it don't worry me. He's as good as they come, but he does think he has a license for crazy."

The radio spoke up again as Wagner sang out "Here they are, boys! I can't see 'em, but the tracks stop in this old adobe *jacal* about a mile ahead and off to your left. I'm staying a ways out so they'll think I'm still looking and not take off outta there running, but you oughta be able to see the busted windmill in the yard." Ken saw the pale green Super Cub flying a low, lazy circle a half-mile away.

"Do you mean to tell me he can actually track them from the air?"

He got no reply, just a glance that said "dumb shit" in all capital letters and he kicked himself for asking a question that had such an obvious answer. *Sure he can. He just said that's what he was doing.*

When Diehl had said earlier that they'd have an airplane at dawn Travis had assumed that it would just fly around looking for people walking in the desert. It never occurred to him that the pilot could read sign from the air, actually tracking the aliens himself.

Diehl cut off the trail, and bouncing cross-country, they quickly came to an abandoned adobe shack. Out back was an old corral. Its posts still stood like rotted teeth, but the rails had surrendered to gravity long before. The rusty, tin water tank was as dry and sandy as the desert around it and the windmill's fan was a crumpled mess of sheet metal and wire in the tank.

As they drove into the yard Wagner flew in low and fast from the north, the 150 horsepower Lycoming roaring as he pointed the Super Cub's wing at the ground and pulled the little two-seater into a tight orbit a hundred feet up. As the jeep slid to a stop four Mexican men and a boy fled, running in different directions for the brush from the shadows on the west side of the building.

Diehl ran after two of them, an old man accompanied by a youngster. He yelled, "Don't get stupid, Travis! We're miles from the border and they got nowhere to go, so they'll lay up pretty quick." Ken picked one out of the group and headed after him, drawing his gun as he ran. Then he remembered his Academy training and put it back, losing time while he snapped the holster's safety strap over the hammer

He dropped into a long-legged lope, the sun warm on his face. Through the brush ahead he could catch glimpses of the fleeing alien. He'd catch this one and then he and Diehl could go round up the other two with the airplane guiding them in.

Overhead, Wagner continued his orbit, closely watching Travis. He didn't like how the chase was shaping up. He picked up the microphone and switched it to broadcast over the P.A. horn mounted outside. "Watch it! He's doubling back on you!"

Ken heard it, but he was unaccustomed to voices from the heavens. He didn't understand a word. He stopped for a moment, puzzled at the voice, and looked up at the plane. Wagner waved and pointed, but Ken could make no sense of it.

"Where the hell did he go?" he asked himself aloud. He hadn't seen the runner in the last minute or two. The tracks had wandered, and then began to curve back toward the *jacal.* He looked back and forth, wondering.

WHAM! He was violently bowled off his feet by a stunning blow to his back. As he flew face-first to the ground events seemed to go into slow motion and his senses were suddenly sharp. He could see each individual grain of sand in front of his nose and taste the dust that rose from the impact of his body on the sand. He could feel a weight on his back and hear harsh breathing near his ear, and he could smell stale tobacco and onions on the breath. His neck hurt and he had lost his breath at the impact. And he could feel hands fumbling at his holster.

The mind takes a moment to decode a sudden, shocking sensory overload and sometimes a man dies while his brain deciphers all the new signals. Other times, through training, or experience—or sometimes dumb luck—he responds to the right signal, and quickly. Ken was lucky that day.

With a strength fueled by terror, he arched his body and rolled onto his right side, shielding the revolver with his body against the sand. He swung his left arm back and clubbed his assailant in the ribs with the point of his elbow, drawing a gasp from him. Another spasm of effort and he found himself lying on his back, free of the weight he had borne. Then he scrambled to his feet ready to fight for his life and saw the Mexican who had attacked him yards away, running once more.

Ken set off after him, this time determined not to lose sight of him and give him another chance at ambush.

He lengthened his stride and began to overtake the runner. Closer and closer and finally he could reach down and slap one of the man's feet sideways, crossing his running legs. The runner continued with a couple of stumbling steps, but balance gone, he took his turn with his face in the sand. As he slid to a stop Ken dropped knees first onto his back, drawing his gun and screwing it hard into the man's ear. "*Paraté, pendejo!* " he screamed, using without thought some of the gutter Spanish he'd learned already. His chest heaving from running and the adrenalin brought up by a brush with death, he said: "Twitch and I'll kill you right here!"

The threat sounded credible even to someone who didn't speak English and his assailant went limp as a sweaty sock. He was just a teen-ager, no more than eighteen, acne-ridden, skinny and short even for a Mexican. But bold, bold enough to attack a man carrying a gun.

Ken placed a knee on the back of the boy's neck, drew one of the boy's arms up behind his back, then holstered his ancient Colt .38 New Service. He placed a cuff on the wrist and then hooked up the other arm. He jerked the youth to his feet.

As they walked back toward the Jeep he was still breathing hard from fright and exertion. *Holy shit! I'm lucky he didn't get my gun and shoot me. Or have one himself. I won't let that happen again.* It had been his first brush with violence on the job and it scared him.

It was a cheap education in the realities of law enforcement work—the tuition could have been much higher. The Border Patrol was dangerous work. Many officers had been murdered over the years, but most of the people they arrested were harmless Mexicans looking for a job. That contributed to the danger though, because it was so easy to get careless when dealing with them. Out here in the desert the people they were after were guys willing to walk sixty miles across the sand and mountains with two tortillas and an old Clorox bottle full of water so they could live six to a room, pick somebody else's lettuce and send their wages home. You had to respect them, and generally, relations between them and the officers were amicable, if not outright friendly.

But, as Travis had just discovered, not always. *Oh, man! Back home no kid this age would even think of jumping on a cop. It's a different world out here.* He'd already decided, having spent three months at the Academy outside of Brownsville and a month here in El Paso, that it wasn't like any other part of the U.S. he'd ever been in. It was as much Mexico as the United States.

He found Diehl waiting patiently, lighting a home-built he had just rolled while sitting in the open back end of the Jeep, legs dangling. All four of the other aliens were seated in the sand at his feet and Diehl was conversing easily with them. Wagner still circled overhead.

Ken tugged on the cuffs, telling the boy that he should take a seat, too. Diehl stood up and pointed high at the aircraft, gave a circling motion with his arm and pointed straight out east. It was a sign to Wagner that all was done for the time being and he should continue with his patrol. The airplane rolled out of its turn and headed toward the sun climbing in the eastern sky.

"Where the hell you been, kid?" Diehl asked, eyeing Ken's uniform, the dark green cloth sweaty and faded by a thick coat of dust, face covered with sand. "I figured maybe you'd stopped off for a short beer somewhere."

"No," Ken said as he brushed himself off, "our rabbit here got a little *bravo* on me and I had to calm him down. No big deal and no harm done." He didn't mention the way he had let the man ambush him and how lucky he felt. His neck ached from the whiplash of the impact, though, and he'd probably have a headache later.

"Right." Diehl replied in a short tone. "Did you search him after you hooked him up?"

Without speaking Ken stood the boy up and patted him down thoroughly, the way he'd been taught at the academy: waistband, pockets, up and down the arms and legs, chest and back of the neck and a final pat of the front of the pants and crotch. The shoes came off and were shaken out; there were no socks and his hair was too short to conceal anything.

He found a knife in a hip pocket, a switchblade with a shiny black handle and chrome end caps. He took it out and tossed it on the front floor of the Jeep and made a mental note to himself about making sure to search these guys right away in the future. And he gave a quick, silent prayer of thanks that he wasn't dying out in the sand with that knife buried in his kidneys.

"Good search, Travis. Hope you learned something. Load 'em up and call Station One for pickup; tell 'em to meet us at the FINA gas station. They'll know where it is. Hope we got a Detention Officer on duty this morning so we don't have to take them all the way back to the station to process them." He threw down his cigarette and got into the driver's seat. By eight o'clock they were on their way down the highway once more, their day's catch in the back of the Jeep. The air through the open windows was noticeably warm now, signaling the onset of the day's heat. It would reach over ninety degrees before the September day was half through.

"Mr. Diehl," Ken said as they drove away "can I ask you some questions now?" Ken had come to the conclusion that Diehl wasn't going to pass along anything he wasn't asked for and it was too important to let go. He wanted to establish some sort of relationship with him and he was willing to go out on a limb for it.

Diehl glanced at him and appeared to think it over. A long silence followed as he looked back at the highway. He'd been watching the kid closely since the shift began, as you must with a new guy, appraising him, wondering if he was worth the trouble.

Diehl was a veteran of the Korean War; the fighting there had shaped much of what he had become, for good and for bad. He'd spent his youth on an Oklahoma reservation reading war coverage from overseas during WWII. The warrior in him wanted to get into the fight but it had ended when he was 15, before he was old enough to join the Marines, even by lying about his age.

He enlisted right out of high school, though. Straight from boot camp he was sent to the First Marine Division in Korea, where things were heating up. He arrived in November of 1950, just in time to get trapped in that frozen hell of a retreat from the Chinese invasion the newspapers called the Battle of Chosin Reservoir—the Marines called it "Frozen Chosin". He'd fought on through the rest of the war, too, and was wounded twice.

Even now, 18 years later, nights working alone were never peaceful for him. Sitting in the rig looking out at the dark there was too much time for things he'd seen and felt and done to pass across his mind's eye. Sometimes he thought he saw ghostly men moving out there in the night shadows. They wore quilted jackets and fur caps with a red star on the front and they moved low and slow from bush to bush, sneaking in on his position. Sometimes he even thought he could smell them, the heavy odor of kimchee and shit that permeated their clothes, that seemed to permeate everything in Korea. He knew they were in his imagination, but that knowledge never soothed him. He would have to get out of his rig and patrol cautiously in a circle around it, crouching, creeping through the dark, assuring himself that no one was there. All the other officers knew he did it but only a few, combat veterans themselves, understood why. It was a harmless quirk tolerated by other officers, but the object of some laughter when he was not around—laughter shared only by those who had never been shot at in anger.

He'd served through the war, then another peacetime hitch. He'd left the Corps in 1958, having made Gunnery Sergeant and having run a platoon of Marines for a couple years. He knew men and he knew war and he was a hard man by some estimations. Certainly he was one who did not put up with fools or foolishness since he had seen good men killed by fools and their decisions. That was a big reason he had left the Corps. The peacetime Marines had just too many fools around, what with nothing going on to cull the turkeys out of the outfit.

After he left the Corps there was no point in going back to the reservation in Oklahoma. His white mother had died and his Cherokee father had just disappeared. Having grown up running wild in the open spaces he needed room, big skies overhead and horizons far off.

He glanced at Travis again and then back at the road. Ken noticed the look and hoped for an answer, but was disappointed; Diehl remained silent.

In the U.S. Border Patrol he'd found what he sought. Now he'd been working the border for ten years, most of the time out in the sand. During that time and his Marine Corps years he had seen all kinds: the hotshots and the heroes, the bigmouths and the braggarts and, mostly, the guys who were just ordinary Joes trying to find their way through life. When it looked like one of them was going to be worth the trouble, you invested in him. Otherwise, forget it.

"This one might be a keeper," he thought of Travis. It was too soon to say for sure yet, but the signs were good. He believed you could tell a lot from the way people responded to silence. Some had to run their mouths all the time, even when there was nothing to say, like silence would make them swell up and bust open. Others just sat there like a turd on the sidewalk, seeming like they were afraid to say anything at all for fear they'd sound stupid. They were the hardest to teach. At least you could tell a motor mouth to shut up, but what did you do with someone that just didn't respond at all?

Being an eager probationer was not easy. Diehl silently recalled his own time, when for a year a valuable job hung on the weekly appraisals put together by the senior officers he worked with. "Seemed like every goddamn thing I did or said was wrong. Or at least somebody was quick to tell me it was."

It had been hard not to put on his Gunny's attitude and get up in the face of some of the pissants who supposedly knew what they were doing and who tried to tell him what was wrong with him. "Tell me what I'm doing wrong, but don't try to tell me what's wrong with me", he'd thought many times during his probationary year.

But he'd gotten through it, as most who graduated from the Academy did. It seemed there were always just enough guys who gave a damn about developing a probationer to teach him the tricks of the trade and keep him out of trouble and from getting killed. It had been a long time now since anyone had had to tell him anything about his job.

"I was borderline rude to him all night," Diehl thought about his hours with Travis, trying to provoke a reaction. "He just sat there and took it, but I don't think he was intimidated worth a damn. He was polite, even when I could see the steam rise in him."

Then, too, although the kid didn't know it, Wagner had called Diehl over the Jeep's radio when he'd gotten back there with the first two he caught. He told Diehl it looked like the kid might run into trouble, that his alien was doubling back and setting him up. With no walkie-talkies he couldn't call the kid to warn him and he didn't seem to understand the call from the airplane's PA system. It was too far off for Diehl to do any good and he still had an alien to run down, so he just had to leave Travis to work it out himself, as an officer often had to do out there.

Fortunately, it hadn't gone badly; in fact, the kid had handled himself well, from what Wagner said. Even after he'd been attacked he hadn't whipped on the wet after he'd cuffed him, like some are prone to do to play catch-up for the fright or pain.

He finally decided to open his personal door a crack and see what kind of questions the kid asked. "Sure, kid. Fire away."

Travis was pleasantly surprised. The long silence had made him think that he wasn't going to get an answer at all, just stony silence.

"Well, sir, right after we picked up the tracks this morning, you looked close at them, but then you took off driving. Didn't seem like you were really watching them, but every time we'd stop, there they were again. How'd you do that?"

Diehl slowed for the Ysleta exit off I-10 while thinking about how to answer. He swung into the lot of the FINA truck stop and parked beside the green and white Dodge van that was waiting there for them. It was the first new Border Patrol rig Ken had seen in El Paso. A rotund, middle-aged Detention Officer with a Pancho Villa mustache and a big bald spot tossed a butt to the ground as he climbed out of the driver's seat and walked around the other side to open the batwing doors. All the windows in back were covered with heavy screen and there was a screen wall behind the front seats to protect the driver.

"'bout time you pansies got here, Real," he said as Diehl and Ken stepped out of the Jeep. "Shouldn't keep us high-paid civil servants waiting like this, wasting the taxpayer's money."

"Travis, have you met Manolo Barrios here yet?" Diehl said. "He's oversexed and underhung and it makes him cranky all the time. But you can count on him when you need him, as long as he's not in a bar putting his moves on some scaly-leg."

Neither man had cracked a smile during the exchange and Ken was uncertain of how to respond to what sounded to him almost like fighting words. So figuring it's hard to go wrong with a handshake, he stuck his hand out to Barrios and said "Howdy." Barrios grinned at him and took his hand in a firm shake.

"Man," he said, "looks like you just took the pins out of that shirt. You just get here?"

"A couple of weeks ago. Still trying to find my way around," Ken replied. He stepped to the rear of the Jeep and opened the doors. They emitted an obnoxious squeal.

"You ready?" he said to Barrios.

"As I'll ever be."

Ken brought the old man and the boy out of the Jeep and pointed them at Barrios. Diehl stood a few steps away to discourage any thoughts of flight from the others. The two walked over to the van and Barrios loaded them up. Then one at a time Ken took the other two men out and passed them over. Finally, only the boy who had run was left. Ken took him out and Barrios noticed that he still wore handcuffs.

"What's with that one? He a runner?"

"Yeah, he is and he carries a pig-sticker, too" Ken replied as he walked him over. "Don't take anything for granted with him, either. He jumped me from behind when he could of kept running."

"Uh-huh," Barrios replied. He spoke rapid Spanish to the boy as he put his own cuffs on him and then took Ken's off and handed them back. Ken couldn't understand what Barrios said, but it didn't sound friendly at all. Barrios loaded the boy in with a hand on the back of his belt, lifting hard enough that his pants wedged firmly into the crack of his ass. He scrambled up to relieve the pressure. Barrios grinned, slammed the doors and said, "See y'all later."

"Thanks, Manolo," Diehl said; Ken echoed it.

"Come on. Let's get a cup of coffee." Diehl walked back to the Jeep, leaned in his door, picked up the mike and said: "Station One, H741, 10-7." A quick "10-4" came back and he turned off the engine.

"Uh, sir, I don't want to sound like a know-it-all, but aren't we supposed to say where we're out of service?" Ken asked, sounding a little nervous for the first time.

"Hell, yes, we are," Diehl replied, "but unless we're working a trail we all stop in for coffee at the same place about this time of day all the time. That's old "Banquet" Banks on the other end. He knows where we are and he'll call Dixie on the phone if they need us. She'll tell us to get out to the car and call in. Maybe someday we'll have walkie-talkies, but we don't have 'em now."

Radio procedures had been drilled into them at the Academy, but Ken had seen right away when he got back to the line after school that not everything he'd learned about anything was gospel all the time. In fact, hardly anything he'd learned, except to speak Spanish, seemed like much use so far. What Diehl said made sense though: *As long as they know where we are and can get in touch, that's the big thing.*

*****

They walked inside and Ken followed his nose to the men's room close by, the smell of the cake in the urinal providing an easy scent trail. He dusted off his uniform, splashed the sand off his face in the sink and took a leak. As he stood there, it occurred to him to check the condition of his revolver. He zipped his fly, and then pulled the gun out of his holster. It was old enough, he thought, to have seen duty in World War I. As a matter of fact, a check of the serial number would have revealed that it had.

He thumbed the cylinder latch with his right hand and then with the fingers of his left hand that were wrapped around the bottom of the revolver, he shoved the cylinder open. He found that it was stiff, the crane full of grit. He dumped the six round-nosed lead .38 cartridges into his right palm and then dropped them in his pocket. Then he closed the cylinder and cocked the hammer. It came back, but slowly, with a feel of roughness and grinding. Sand had packed into the hammer slot when he fell. When he pulled the trigger, the hammer moved, but only slightly. The gun would not have fired if he had needed it. That was a frightening thought.

He looked down into his S.D. Myers holster and saw an inch of sand in the bottom. The Jordan-style holster had been designed for speed of draw and at that it was good, but the very thing that made it a fast holster to draw from meant that it offered little protection for the revolver. In fact, it had acted like a scoop when he went skidding across the sand. He inverted it and dumped the sand on the dirty floor. Holsters made by some other outfits had an open toe; Ken could see the advantage of it. The gun would still gather sand, but at least the sand wouldn't stay in the holster. He turned the revolver upside down over the sink and tapped it to knock out as much sand as he could.

He reloaded the revolver and shoved it back into its holster. When he left the bathroom he saw Diehl sitting in a booth by the front windows that overlooked the fuel island. He walked over and took a seat.

"We'll sit here and observe traffic for a while," Diehl said.

"Seems like a good idea to me" Ken replied agreeably. "Do we ever actually catch anyone here while we're doing it?"

As they talked a waitress strolled over carrying two cups of coffee. She was tall and buxom, with suicide-blonde hair pulled up in a bun on top of her head. While she carried a few extra pounds, they looked good on her. She was still on the happy side of 40, but barely, and the lines on her face reflected a good disposition. She was one of those women who pour endless cups of coffee, have a talent for banter, call the patrons "honey," and make each guest feel he has a special place in her heart. They make it worthwhile to drop in. The nametag prominently displayed on her ample chest announced that she was Dixie.

"Morning, boys" she said. Then, looking at Ken, "You look to be a new one, huh? Is this old grouch going to let you stay around?"

"Yes, ma'm. Brand new and green as grass, but I'll get over it. Don't know yet if I'll get to stick around, but I'll die trying." He was not embarrassed at being new on the job; everybody had to start somewhere, sometime, he knew. Unlike several of his classmates, he didn't try to project an unearned, salty, experienced appearance. He didn't dirty up his hats or leave his uniforms outside on the clothesline, hoping they would quickly fade.

"Well, honey, don't we all get over it! And I hope it don't come to dying." She set the cups down, then turning to Diehl, she said "You be good to this boy, now, hear? He's mighty cute."

With a wink to Diehl and a touch on his shoulder, she turned and walked back to the kitchen with a lot of motion in the backfield. Ken's face burned with a crimson blush.

Diehl burst out laughing, his reserve gone for the moment.

"Dixie loves to throw a little embarrassment around and she'll really lay it on somebody puts a foot wrong with her. She's friendly, but she ain't easy. A year or so back half a dozen of us came in here about six in the morning on the way back to the station. Wasn't anybody here but us and her and the cook. One of the guys, you'll find out who he is in your own time, thinks he's mighty cute himself. He had just transferred in to the office and hadn't been in here before."

"Anyways," Diehl continued, "he was at the outside end of the booth. When she came up he turned his head and there were those magnificent tits just a foot from his face. He looks at the nametag, then up at her face, winks at her and says "Dixie, huh? Mighty nice. What do you call the other one? "

"Well, she gave him this look, something between bedroom eyes and a rattlesnake's. She grabbed his head by the handles, bent it back on the top of the seatback and laid a big, wet kiss right on him, a long one that looked like there might have been some tongue involved. Told him right then, while she held his head back, that he'd better have enjoyed it 'cause that was all he'd ever get. Then she just let him go and took all our orders like nothing had happened. He said it gave him a hard-on that stayed up for a week, but it embarrassed the shit out of him, too. He don't admit that part of it, but you can tell. He'll still come in here now and then, but he's mighty careful about how he talks to her—next time around she might just call him "Shorthorn" to his face. She don't take no prisoners. I generally got no use for women, you can't rely on 'em for anything serious, but Dixie's OK as they go."

Ken noted that first insight he'd gotten in Diehl's private personality; he wondered about it. It seemed to paint with a pretty broad brush and Ken thought there must be something in Diehl's background that had brought about the attitude about women.

Going on to answer Ken's question that had been interrupted by the arrival of the coffee, Diehl continued. "Never have caught anybody fueling up right here, but over in Deming there's a truck stop that it happens. Drop in for a cup or a meal and it seems like it no more than hits the table when some load of wets rolls in coming up from Columbus or off of I-10. Some of the guys keep on eating, ignore them, but it ain't in me to do like that."

Ken took note of the attitude, admiring it. He'd already seen more than enough burnt-out or just plain lazy officers who wouldn't go after a wet if he tripped and fell in front of them. He knew intuitively that when you are young and new on the job you don't have a real personality yet. You would become, in time, like those whom you choose as your models. He'd probably never become a high-flyer in the Border Patrol and he didn't care, but he was determined to be an honest, competent officer. Diehl seemed like that kind of man.

According to what he'd heard, Diehl was also one of the best damn trackers in the Border Patrol; after watching him during the shift Ken was ready to subscribe to the idea himself. Sign cutting was a skill Ken really wanted to master, for the good trackers got to work the desert most of the time, away from the city and roads and other people. It was just you and maybe your partner, or an airplane if you had one, and the guys you were after. The idea of being a man tracker appealed to him, it was a natural step beyond being the hunter and outdoorsman he'd grown up as. Plus, and he was almost embarrassed about it, it seemed to make him part of the western story, the latest in the long string of western lawmen of lore and legend. It wasn't something he talked about, though—it sounded pretty corny.

Diehl spoke as he picked up his cup.

"Manolo there is one of the best Detention Officers we've got, Travis. We were smokin' and jokin' outside, but he is. I've known him for years and he's never let me down. He used to be a cop over in Lordsburg, and like a lot of those guys do, he tried for the Patrol but didn't make the cut on the entrance test. Took it three or four times, but just couldn't get past it. So he signed up for what he could get and now he hauls 'em after we catch 'em. Some of them are guys who got in, but couldn't make the Academy or probation. Mostly, those guys are too embarrassed to hang around, but a few will take whatever job they can get. Some of 'em try again and sometimes they make it. Anyhow, we've got a few duds, but don't you ever underrate a good D.O. They'll save you a world of nuisance and will be right there to back you up if things get tough."

Trying to get back on track and get some answers before the shift was over, he said: "Mr. Diehl, about that group we followed . . ."

"Oh yeah," Diehl replied. "You wanted to know how I kept finding their tracks. I clean forgot you asked."

"First of all, it ain't no secret why I found their tracks every time I stopped. It's because I didn't stop until I seen tracks. In fact, the only reason I stopped to look was to make sure it was still their trail we were on. I was sure it would be, but it don't hurt to take a look to make sure. Take too much for granted and you can wind up switching from one group to another, maybe even an older set of tracks."

"Anyhow, these old boys don't come over here blind, you know? Back home, they've talked to guys who've been up here before and know the route. Or they've hung around the plaza in Juarez or Zaragosa talking to men who've been over, or maybe they even paid somebody to guide them. People think of wets crossing the border usually just imagine somebody in the water and don't think beyond that. That's the short, easy part of the trip here; they can cross lots of places and not even get damp above the knees."

"No," he continued, "they tend to follow more or less the same routes, all the way from home to wherever they're going, Chicago or Denver or wherever. They know the way, mostly, or at least have heard about it."

Dad used to talk about guys, you ask them what time it is and they'll tell you how to make a watch, Ken thought. *But it sure is good information.* He sat back comfortably, ready to soak it up as long as Diehl was willing to talk.

"Once they get across the river they'll look for the landmark they'll guide on. During the day it might be a mountain on the horizon. They'll sometimes do that on a bright night, too, but usually after dark it'll be a light somewheres, or a star. If they're headed straight north it'll usually be the North Star, like the slaves used to do when they were headed north on the Underground Railroad to be free. You know; they'd follow the drinking gourd."

Travis was surprised by the knowledge implied by the historical reference. He'd supposed that Diehl was a smart enough guy, an expert in his field, but uneducated and probably not a reader.

"The lights up on towers are pretty popular, too; that's what that bunch was walking toward. They were lined out on the radio tower out towards the Hueco Tanks. All I had to do was figure out what landmark they were lined out on, then just keep running ahead and cutting across that line. Them being on a trail made it even easier, as long as they didn't cut off of it. The time I look and don't find tracks, well, I know we're ahead of them, or they changed direction on me. Then we just go back, pick up the tracks, and follow them till we find feet in them. Or set down alongside the trail and wait for them to show up; that can be fun. That's all there is to it."

Ken thought it over and then said, "So sometimes when you're tracking, you're not tracking at all, you're figuring. Right?"

"Exactly." Diehl responded, pleased at this perception in the younger man. He pulled the makings out of his shirt pocket and began to roll a smoke. He curled the paper between his thumb and finger on one hand and then carefully tapped the tobacco out of a bag of Bull Durham into the curl. He pulled the drawstring on the bag closed with his teeth and dropped it back in his pocket.

"You're trying to put yourself in the man's own head" he went on and then he ran his tongue along the edge of the paper.

"And sometimes something don't seem just right, too. Like why did they head straight north on that sand road when they hit it?" Displaying dexterity that Ken had to admire as he watched the process with interest, Diehl rolled the smoke up into a smooth cylinder with one hand. He twisted the ends of the paper slightly and then fished around in the same pocket, coming out with an Ohio Blue Tip kitchen match.

"They were headed east toward that light for miles and then turned north along that road that ran up to the old adobe place. My guess is they expected to find that road, knew it runs over to the Carlsbad Highway. If they were going there, then I reckon they expected to meet somebody along the highway and get picked up. It happens, but why would they get picked up before our checkpoint on the highway and then have to go through it?"

He put the cigarette in his mouth, popped the match into flame with his thumbnail and lit the homebuilt. As he shook the match out he brushed a couple shreds of tobacco from the table to the floor, drew the smoke deep and then continued as he exhaled. Ken pulled a Chesterfield out of the pack in his pocket, flipped open his Zippo, struck it and lit his own cigarette as he pulled the ashtray over.

"What really don't make sense to me though, is why did they stop before dawn at the old Gomez place? They'd been there a while when we got them, judging by the cigarette butts laying around. They could have been clean out to the highway and gone by a little after dawn. We usually set up the traffic checkpoint out at the Dell City cutoff. They might have gotten there at change of shift when there's nobody there. We might not ever have caught them if they'd kept going, but they couldn't count on that. It's a puzzle."

They drank their coffee, not talking much, Ken not wanting to push his luck. Dixie dropped by and poured some more coffee, placing her hand on Diehl's shoulder again as she did so. They still had a few hours to go on the shift; maybe he'd have the chance to ask more. Diehl was still not chatty, but the sense of cold reserve was not so obvious any more. One thing, though, still bothered him.

He spoke up. "Uh, Mr. Diehl—I need to do something about my gun. It's full of sand from when I fell down chasing that tonk. Can we go back to the station so I can clean it up?"

Hearing a sidearm called a "gun" still grated on Diehl's nerves, but he'd long ago quit trying to explain to guys that what you carried in your holster was a pistol or a revolver and that your gun was behind your zipper. Not everyone had been a Marine, unfortunately.

"I'll show you what we call a "field expedient," son," he replied. "Come on outside." He stood up and dropped a dollar bill on the table, saying "I got the coffee this time."

Ken noted the promotion from "kid" to "son." He still wasn't crazy about it, he'd respond just fine to "Ken," but it seemed to be a step up for him from "kid."

They walked over to the Jeep and Diehl pulled out his tricky bag, an army surplus tool pouch big enough to hold miscellaneous gear like a transistor radio, fence pliers, a box or two of ammunition, all the odds and ends that an officer needs from time to time. The word is "*triques*" in Spanish, "stuff," but like many words in the southwest, it had been corrupted a bit when it was adopted from Mexican into American. Now it was "tricky."

Some guys carried .50 caliber ammo cans, while others made do with something else, but everybody carried something that was generically referred to as his "tricky bag." That, and an insulated gallon jug of water that began the day as ice, were the standard equipment every Border Patrolman brought to work. By the end of a hot day shift the ice would be melted and the water would be gone.

Diehl pulled out a small screwdriver that had come with his Smith and Wesson Model 19. Officers were allowed to buy and carry their own choice of weapons once they got off probation and the most popular choice was the Smith .357 Magnum. Diehl had bought his years before. Unlike most officers though, who opted for the four-inch barrel for comfort when sitting in a vehicle, the longer barrel dug into the seat and pushed the holster up, Diehl had bought the six-inch model. He believed that the increased sight radius made him a better shot; there was evidence on the qualification records to support that outlook. He was willing to trade comfort for accuracy, for one was survival.

"Give me that revolver," he said.

Ken unloaded the old Colt, muzzle pointed at the ground, and handed it over. Diehl popped the grips and side plate off, and then quickly removed all the internal parts, placing everything in Ken's hands as he did so. He'd learned weapons in a very hard school and would never be around one he couldn't strip to its smallest parts.

"Come on," he said, walking over toward the fuel pumps.

He pulled a rag from his tricky bag and laid it on the cement. "Set everything down on that."

When Ken had done so, Diehl lifted the gas nozzle off the pump and elevating the loop of the hose above the nozzle, he squeezed the trigger on the nozzle. That dumped a pint or so of fuel left in the loop on the parts at his feet.

"Now shake them off and wipe them down. When we're rolling again hold that rag out the window and dry it off."

Ken did as he was told, saying, "Thanks a lot."

"Ain't nothin'," Diehl said. "Keeps us from having to go back to the station to do it. No telling what shit we might run into there. End of shift's soon enough to go back."

They walked back to the Jeep, Ken with his hands full of parts wrapped in the rag, Diehl with a sly grin on his face. He expected that the next question would be if he'd put the thing back together.

Instead, Ken spread the rag on the hood. Then he neatly laid the parts out on it, checking each for any remaining grit. Reaching into his own tricky bag, he pulled out a screwdriver identical to Diehl's.

Diehl watched, pleasantly surprised as Travis carefully put the pieces back together. His eyes opened a bit wider as Travis opened his tricky bag and got out a small bottle of oil, from which he squeezed a drop or two onto the appropriate moving parts inside before replacing the side plate. Nearly as quickly as Diehl had stripped the revolver, Travis had it together. Putting the grips back on, he snapped it through six times, noting that all seemed smooth again.

Then, holding it in his left hand with the cylinder open over his palm to catch any rounds he might drop, he reloaded it swiftly, two cartridges at a time, from the loops in the carrier on his belt, his smooth motions showing hours of practice. With the revolver reloaded, he placed it in his holster and snapped down the safety strap. Then pulling the six cartridges that had been in the gun from his pocket, he filled the loops on the carrier once more. There was nothing of the show-off in the actions, just a man using a polished skill.

"Thanks again, Mr. Diehl," he said.

"Son, if you could strip that thing, why didn't you just do it instead of asking me?" Diehl was chagrined; he'd expected to play a little joke on the kid, leaving him with his revolver in pieces halfway through the shift.

"Mr. Diehl," Ken replied, "they told us at school not to ever do anything to our pistols but clean them; just do the barrel and chambers and wipe down the outside. Most particularly, they told us don't ever take off the side plate or do anything inside of it. I wasn't about to do something like that and put you on the spot by breaking rules right in front of you. And besides," he went on, "I'd never seen the gasoline trick—you just dumped it out of the hose."

"Where'd you learn to do that?" Diehl asked. "Most guys are scared to death of the inside of a weapon. All those parts just make their eyes glaze over and their minds quit working."

Looking Diehl in the eye with a level gaze, Travis said, "Mr. Diehl, I've messed with guns all my life and I wouldn't ever trust my life to something I couldn't fix, especially this old piece of shit."

Diehl looked back at him with a different look in his eyes than had been there before. "Son, you'll do. Call me "Real"." Now let's head back out to the Gomez place. I want to look it over again. Something ain't just right."

*****

Back at Station One another young trainee went to the lockup, the transient detention cell. Looking at the field data slip in his hand, he called out a name: "Salinas! Rafael Salinas. *Ven'te p'aca.* Come here."

An old man responded by arising and approaching the officer standing in the door. *"Soy Salinas.* I am Salinas," he said with dignity, speaking Spanish slowly for the benefit of the young man. Rafael Salinas was not his real name, but it would do for this occasion. He had lived on the border all his life and had used many names before. He would use others, no doubt. He had encountered Border Patrolmen many times and he knew them in all their variations.

He was accompanied by the boy who had been caught with him. "This is my grandson," he continued in Spanish. "May he accompany me, please?" The processing had begun. Both would be back in Juarez in time for a late lunch.

Chapter 2

Diehl pushed the rig hard out the narrow two-lane extension of Zaragosa Road, running north from Ysleta to U.S. 180, the Carlsbad Highway. He was wrestling the wheel again, cursing the cheap outfit that would make men drive a vehicle with 100,000 miles on it, especially 100,000 miles like the Border Patrol builds up. Most of the Patrol's sedans had even more miles on them than this old Jeep and all had seen hard use being driven at high speed across miles of western highways.

Before getting to the junction he turned off to the east on an unmarked, unimproved road. After following it for a mile or more he turned right onto a sand trail. Very quickly they were back at the Gomez place, having come in from the north this time. Ken realized that if they had turned left at the last corner the trail would have led them north, out to the Carlsbad highway, just as Diehl had told him earlier. They stopped right on top of where Diehl had slid to a halt a few hours before.

"Ken, when you get out, stick close to me; don't wander. I didn't look at the sign around here this morning after we caught those old boys and I don't want any more tracks laid down to confuse things for me." Diehl stood outside his door, gazing around. He walked slowly around the rig. His tracker's eyes took it in and his tracker's mind absorbed it all. He climbed up on the hood of the Jeep and looked some more.

"Somebody has been here since we left," he announced. "Come with me."

He walked over to the *jacal* and went inside. It was a jackstraw jumble of collapsed *vigas,* the heavy beams that had once supported the ceiling and the *latias,* the smaller sticks that had lain across the *vigas.* Chunks of the mud brick walls had collapsed inside at several places

"When I brought them back here this morning I never did anything but look in the window to make sure there was nobody else hid out here. I set them down in the shade of the wall and then we just loaded them up and drove off. That was dumb."

"Why do you say that, Mr. Diehl?" Ken asked, deciding it wouldn't hurt to keep being overtly respectful for a while. Maybe someday he'd be agreeable to a statement like that, but not yet, not by a long shot.

"Looky here," Diehl said. "Just inside the door. You see where them old adobes that fell down have been disturbed?" He pointed to a pile of mud bricks on the floor at the foot of the wall by the door.

"There was something put under them I'd bet, and whoever came out here after us picked it up. You can see where it set on the ground for a while. Looks like it was kinda small and wrapped in plastic. See the wrinkly marks it left in the sand? And see how there's no weave marks, like fabric would leave?"

Knowing what to look for by having it brought in front of his nose, Ken said, "Sure do." The marks were plain to see in the sand, which was still slightly damp from the adobe blocks being turned over. Desert sand often has moisture trapped in it and where the sun can't get to it that moisture is close to the surface. Something laying atop the sand will often draw the moisture up.

"Now," Diehl asked, "How do we know that whoever picked it up was here after us? And how did he get here?"

Ken thought it over, then said "I expect he came on that dirt bike that left tracks out there on the trail that came in the way we did. I didn't see his sign until we turned onto this trail, so I'd bet he came in all the way down the trail, not on the sand road like we did. You told me this morning the trail goes out to the Carlsbad Highway, so I expect he came from there. Whoever was on it might have been here yesterday evening, but I don't think so. That track is over the top of the ones we left this morning, isn't it? He rode on in close, but never came into the yard. He stayed out of the area we were in."

Ken pointed to the northeast corner of the yard and said "It looks to me like he parked out there a ways, but when he took off he ran over the tracks we left over there where we turned around and drove out. Do you think that the guys we caught put that package under there for him?"

"Not bad for a newby," Diehl said, smiling with the remark to take the sting out of it. Then, not yet ready to answer Ken's question, he posed his own: "But if that's how it happened, how come he didn't he leave any footprints over here at the house picking up the package?"

Ken looked around and then asked if he could walk the area now. Diehl told him to go ahead. Ken walked over to a point near where the bike had been parked, taking a looping path that would keep him away from a direct line between the house and where the bike had been. He stopped close to where the bike had parked and looked around, checking out the ground before he actually walked on it.

After a minute of looking, he said "Mr. Diehl, it looks to me like maybe he took his boots off over here. I don't know why he'd do that; what with the sun overhead I can't make out much more in the way of sign, but that's what it looks like."

Diehl was mildly impressed. Travis apparently had a good eye for sign. He was looking like a better investment all the time.

"Come on over here and I'll show you why" he called to Ken.

"You're right. With the sun overhead it's damned hard to pick out tracks, but if you have some idea of what you're looking for and where it might be, it's easier. It also helps to change your angle, so get down here on your knees, scooch down so your head's maybe a foot off the ground and look back towards the place he parked."

Travis did so, and there, very faintly, he could make out impressions in the sand, spaced out like a set of footprints would be.

"See," Diehl said, "he didn't want to leave a set of tracks right up to the door here. If we wasn't looking for them, if we hadn't come back this morning, we'd have never known he was here at the house. What he did was take his boots off and walk over here in his socks. With no sharp edges to shape the sand it don't leave that much of a track. A little breeze and it's gone. That kind of thing tells us something its own self, don't it?"

"Yessir," Ken replied. "It tells us that he knows about sign, or at least that we look for it and that he didn't want us to know that he'd been here. Does that mean the guys we caught brought something for him?"

Diehl gazed at the horizon with a thoughtful look, then said, "I sure to God don't know for certain. But I'd bet they did. Whoever wanted that package dropped there probably wouldn't have wanted to leave it laying around for long. Yeah, I think they probably did. Have a look at the boot prints he left over yonder.

Remember them and the ones the motorcycle left; sketch them in your notebook if you have to. We may see them again. Now, let's go."

Ken walked back to the parking spot to look at the tracks once more. In a dusty spot under the overhang of a mesquite bush the boot had left a clear partial track. It had a flat sole, distinctive in a land where cowboy boots were the favored footwear. The sole had some concentric circles, like a target in the center of the front portion, with grooves running from it out to the edges of the sole.

"Hmmm . . . looks like maybe a motorcycle racer's boot," Travis thought.

The tire tracks showed the bike was running a full knobby, designed for maximum traction off road, but dangerous on the highway. He noticed that when the rider departed, he had planted a foot for stability, then nailed the throttle, spinning the rear tire and letting the bike make a donut, pivoting around the front tire until it was pointed in the right direction. The foot came up and the bike dug out, headed back up the trail the way it had arrived. Ken thought that he was dealing here with a real rider, not some hotshoe pretender with a new bike.

He told Diehl what it looked like. He grunted in acknowledgment. "Yep. We'll see 'em again."

Chapter 3

Across the river in Ciudad Juarez a young man stood at a wall phone surrounded by years of handprints in the Cantina Rio Bravo, just off Avenida Juarez. "*Bueno*", he said, and then hung up.

The place was only a few blocks from the Santa Fe Street Bridge between downtown El Paso and the city of Juarez. The barroom was dim, lit only by two feeble bulbs in the ceiling and a late afternoon shaft of sunshine that beamed through the open front door. It struck sparks as it fell on the oddly clean and polished mirror and glasses on the back bar.

The two-tone walls were a dirty cream color and faded posters for bullfights long over were plastered here and there. From waist-high to the floor they were dark brown to hide the dirt left by feet propped against them. A set of steep stairs against a side wall led to crib-size rooms upstairs and a fan overhead stirred air that smelled of ancient sin. Two professional women long past their youthful dreams sat at the bar showing fat, lumpy thighs up to the hip. Bosoms gone bad pushed up, overflowing the tops of their dresses. Good-looking women didn't work the day shift in the Cantina Rio Bravo.

The man walked across a small, wooden dance floor to a table in a corner in the back of the bar. A fiftyish fat man with a full head of silver hair was seated there just out of the shaft of sunlight; he looked as though he had been poured into his chair years before. He had the corner to himself and he did not look as though he would welcome company. He belonged there—it was his bar. His name was Marcos Ayala.

The messenger said, " *Está hecho, tio. Hay éxito.* It's done, uncle, successfully."

"*Suelta la mujer*". The man replied. Release the woman.

The younger man walked back to the phone and dialed a number, then spoke briefly.

At a *rancho* miles south of Juarez in the mountains west of Carretera 45 a man hung up and then went to a bedroom and unlocked the door. Inside was the hostage, a young woman of about sixteen or seventeen years. As women often are, she had been used by the men who kept her there but their brutality did not leave marks that showed. Her eyes though, told the tale—they would never look the same again, or look at the world the way they had before.

The man blindfolded her. She shrank from his touch, making sad, frightened little murmurs as she did. He led her to an old Pontiac outside and placed her on the back floor. He covered her with a blanket and told her that if she valued her life she would not make a sound. She believed him. He started the car and drove off toward the border.

In an empty garage downtown he took her out of the car once more and removed the blindfold. He shoved her, barefooted, out the door onto the street without a word. She was free to find her way home, back to her grandfather, whose performance had been guaranteed by her life.

Going to the police never crossed her mind—in Mexico the law was not for such as she. It was there to help *los ricos*, the rich, those with money enough to buy the law they needed. No, she would tell her *abuelo* of her treatment but grandfather was old now, and weak, and could no longer avenge the insult. Or so she believed.

The driver walked a few blocks north along Avenida Juarez. At first glance he looked like someone's middle-aged uncle, with a round face and slicked-back black hair that was going gray at the temples. An ample belly preceded him and his shambling walk offered no challenges. The harmless appearance was deceptive, though. He was tall for a Mexican, and despite his late middle age he still had broad shoulders and muscular arms. Over the years he had murdered a dozen men or more, and while he took no particular pleasure in cruelty, torture was a tool he used if he thought it necessary. His thoughts and his deeds had left their tracks on his face and the street peddlers and beggars who approached him quickly shied away when he turned his flat, black eyes on them. His name was Ramón Diaz and he was Marcos Ayala's lieutenant.

He entered the Cantina Rio Bravo. He walked to the rear corner and said to the fat man, " *Está hecho, Patrón. Ella está libre.* It's done, boss. She's free." He pulled out a chair and sat down.

"*Bueno,* Ramón," Ayala replied with a satisfied look. He took a drink of his Dos Equis and smiled broadly as he took a cigar from his pocket.

Chapter 4

The old man, Salinas, wasn't really so old. A lifetime on the border doing some of the things he'd done had aged his face, and he walked with a bit of a stoop brought on by years as a *bracero,* doing contract farm labor on row crops in *los estados unidos* when he was much younger. Now, he was just sixty, but he looked ten years older. While certainly he was past his physical prime he was no weakling and his mind worked just fine.

He walked along Calle Lerdo with his grandson, having just left the Cantina Rio Bravo. He had gone straight there to be paid after the Border Patrol had put them back across the Santa Fe Street Bridge.

He cursed to himself as he walked along the dirty, broken sidewalk in the sunshine with his grandson tagging along a step behind. He was wondering why they had chosen him. He had retired from the smuggling business after years of exceptional success taking *pollos* across the border and to the jobs in the north. They weren't chickens, really, of course, but humans headed up to the insatiable labor market that is the United States, where a man could earn as much in a day as he might in a month at home. At first he had just led them those few miles to the safe houses and the highways of Texas, where he turned them over to men he'd never met and would never see again. As time went on and he became bolder, he turned the desert guiding over to others and began to do the driving himself, taking truckloads of twenty-five or thirty at a time to points as far north as Washington State and Ohio. He knew the business of smuggling and, he supposed, that meant that he could smuggle anything, but if one kept smuggling long enough, one would certainly spend time in jail. He'd always been very careful and very lucky, and so far had never been in any jail except Border Patrol detention facilities for a few hours.

"No," he thought, "I'm too old for *el juzgado.* And, the children need me."

These new ones in town though, the ones of the *heroina,* did not know the Texas desert, so they were forced to hire those who did. They didn't care if he did time in jail, he knew. If they didn't want him to get caught it was only because they would lose their drugs.

He tried to tell them no, that he no longer did such things, that he had never run drugs and didn't want to. But they made it clear that he had no choice—they took his granddaughter to ensure his cooperation and to show him he had something to lose. Then they paid him well for the trip when he had done it. And told him there would be other trips. The threat was unspoken, but clear; it was the old choice in the drug trade of *plata o plomo*: silver or lead. There was really no choice to be made.

And now, $500 richer, he was walking home. He could have refused the money, certainly, but to what point? He wouldn't do it for money, but as long as he had to do it anyway, he might as well profit from the work; *verdad?* They were fair men, he supposed, but he didn't doubt what they were capable of doing.

He turned off the sidewalk and unlocked a steel grill set in one of the small arched gateways through the wall that ran along the sidewalk for blocks. Inside the bars was a small courtyard, a place that provided a pleasant place to sit when the day cooled off. There was a small tree and a few rustic wooden chairs in the shade. It was, in effect, his front yard. His earnings over the years had allowed him to buy this modest place of his own, a place for him to live with his granddaughter and grandson and to care for them.

It was a source of deep sorrow to him, the loss of his wife and daughter and son-in-law when the bus they were on was forced off a cliff by a cattle truck while on the way to Chihuahua City to visit his wife's sister. It was only by the grace of God that the children were with him when it happened, the boy sick with a fever and the girl staying behind to care for him. They were all he had left now and they were as precious to him as the breath of life.

He walked across the packed earth to his front door and unlocked it. As he stepped in he was immediately struck by the sound of quiet sobs. He knew instantly who was crying and why the tears were shed. His fears were confirmed when he looked into his granddaughter's eyes as she stood and ran to him, her bare feet whispering quietly across the tile floor. He had seen the look before, too often in fact, on other women who had the misfortune or bad judgment to associate with *them* and those like them. Her face showed a desperate fear, for she'd found that hell doesn't always wait until death.

They had told him she would not be hurt if he did as he was told. He knew that by their standards she hadn't been. After all, there was no blood. There were no bruises. There were no missing teeth. There were only scars so deep that they would never be erased. *They* couldn't conceive of such things as scars on the soul, though, so they'd never even think they had lied to him.

As she sobbed against his chest he petted her head in sympathy and murmured softly to her. He knew that he would extract a revenge. He didn't know what it would be, or how, but revenge there would be. He would think for a while.

*****

The old man lay on his back on his hard, narrow bed in a small room that was little more than a monk's cell. A small, low chest with a kerosene lamp on top held personal effects. His meager clothing hung on hangers suspended from wooden pegs driven into the adobe wall. A crucifix hung on the whitewashed adobe over his head, the only decoration in the room. He lived simply so that the children could go to school.

As he looked at the dark ceiling above him, he listened to their soft breathing in the other room and thanked God for many things. He thanked Him for giving him those children for his old age, and for a youth and middle age of his own, and cunning that let him earn the money that brought them safe to this house this night. They had eaten well and now they were behind strong walls with a good roof over their heads instead of living in Colonia Alta Vista on the hills along the river west of town. There, even in winter, they would be sleeping in their clothes on cardboard in a shack made of cardboard and water would run across the dirt floors when it rained.

And he thanked God most of all at this moment for his memory that was still strong, that could remember names and faces and places and things done all those years ago. The name came back to him now: Pope. He would find *Señor* Pope and together they would make these sons of diseased whores pay for harming his *nieta.*

But he would have to be cautious, for *los malos*, the bad ones, would kill all of them without thought or mercy if they even suspected he was trying to do anything against them. They must believe he was just a tired old man, under their control.

There was a loud crash as two freight cars coupled hard in the yards across the river and he was asleep.

When he awoke, the old man knew how he would find Pope and how he would approach him, if Pope were still in El Paso. If he were still in the Border Patrol. If he were still alive.

He rose and washed himself in a bucket of water he fetched from the yard, and then scrambled an egg in a black iron skillet over a single gas burner. The pan had been an important wedding present to him and his Dora all those years ago. What a woman she had been, what a wife. How he missed her still. He added *chorizo* and some chiles and red peppers and made a small pot of strong coffee. His memory still worked and, *gracias a Diós,* so did his stomach. It would be very hard to give up good food. An old man's pleasures are few and food compensates for other pleasures long gone.

With his mud-colored pottery cup in his hand he came out into a bright day, just barely warm in the middle of the morning. The sun lay gently across the little courtyard of his house, illuminating the west wall and the hard-packed dirt floor swept clean by Angelita that morning before she left for school. Slowly, he walked over to the bench placed in the morning sun, sat, and leaned against the adobe wall, feeling its warmth against his back. He put his coffee on the small wooden keg that served as a table, dropped his hands into his lap, closed his eyes, and thought.

Later he would go to the old bars where he knew that some of the *coyotes* hung out. He knew that some of those smugglers still heard information that they passed to the law across the river. A few always thought it was good for business to inform on their rivals to see that their rivals' loads got caught. That occupied the Border Patrol, perhaps leaving things open for one's own load. The competition's customers would be sent back across the river, perhaps to seek out someone more capable. Someone like oneself even, if he was waiting in the plaza when they came.

He would see if any of the old *soplones,* informants, were still there. They could talk about old times and he could plant some seeds. But the old ones were no real matter. He knew if he spoke the right words aloud in the bar the information would make its way to Pope, to make him alert and waiting to hear from his old source, *Halcón.*

Chapter 5

The shift had come to an end at noon with no further activity. Diehl and Travis had returned to Station One, gassed up the ratty old Jeep, and turned the keys over to the next shift. The general lack of vehicles meant that they were in continuous use and didn't get the maintenance they needed. All were in some stage of falling apart.

Worst of all though, the shortage meant that the line was uncovered for an hour or two at each change of shift. Officers had to return to the station to turn their vehicle over to the next crew. Many of them stopped for coffee on the way in or the way out, or both. The practical effect was that aliens flowed freely across the border during the changes of shift.

Diehl called to Ken as he was in the door, leaving to go down to the pistol range. "Come on back here, Travis. Let's drop by the Anti-Smuggling office and see if "Padre" Pope is in yet. I want to run something by him."

As they walked down the hall to the Anti-Smuggling Unit office Diehl explained: "ASU ain't what it used to be, Ken. A few years back they had guys working in plainclothes across the river all the time, hanging around the plazas and the whorehouses and cantinas, listening to what was going on and talking to the wets. Most of the guys spoke perfect Spanish and a lot of them could pass for wets themselves. Had some good informants, too. In fact, there were even cops working for us. They'd collect *mordida* from the *coyotes* who smuggle the wets in, then collect a reward from us for the information about when and where the bunch would cross."

They stopped at a locked door. As Diehl knocked, Ken asked, "What happened? Don't they work like that any more?" He'd heard tales about the old Special Detail operations and officers that he didn't fully credit.

"I'll tell you more later" Diehl said, as the door opened.

"Real, you old sonuvofbitch! How they hanging?" The man who opened the door was tall and gaunt to the point of emaciation. His voice sounded pleased to see Diehl, but his appearance didn't show it. The skin of his face was stretched tight over the bones and the shape of his mouth was not like any human smile Ken had ever seen—if he had lips they didn't show. The last bit of meat on his body had long since burned away. His thin hair was gray and his gray eyes, set deep under pale brows, had dark blue circles beneath them. He looked like a man who had sneaked through hell's back door to do a story on Satan, then stayed a while.

He shook Diehl's hand and then turned from the door and walked back to his desk, setting his feet down flat and gently, as though he had sharp stones in his shoes. Diehl and Ken followed. The room was rank with the stale smell of too many cigarettes stubbed out in overflowing ashtrays. A light brown film of old nicotine covered the green file cabinets and gray desks. The janitorial crew had no access to this office.

"Padre," Diehl said, "you look worse than ever. The Undertaker can fix you up to look better. Why don't you get him to do that?" Diehl grinned as he referred to another anti-smuggling agent who had in fact been a licensed mortician before joining the Border Patrol.

"Goddamit, Diehl," Pope said, "don't be calling me that! " Unlike most officers, who gave in to the inevitable and accepted their moniker, Pope always protested the use of his. Diehl, his old friend, persisted with equal fervor in using it.

Many of the officers had nicknames. Ken had wondered about it during the week he was at the station before being sent to the Academy. He had found later that one of the officers was prone to hang nicknames on his fellow officers. The nicknames usually commemorated an event in which the officer had been involved, or memorialized a personal characteristic or quirk, or perhaps it was just some weird, unknowable, association in the foggy recesses of his mind. In response, some officer whose name was lost in the mists of station consciousness had hung "Spaceman" on him in recognition of his addiction to cheap science fiction novels and magazines. It had been shortened, appropriately, to "Spacey." Among the station's officers that abbreviated nickname was thought to be a stroke of genius.

However, no trainee had ever been granted a nickname. In his opinion, they weren't worth wasting the thought on.

Pope's nickname had come about, not because of the religious association of his surname, but because Smith had walked into the station's bathroom one night years before and found Pope hunched over the toilet on his knees, apparently in prayer. In fact, he had just returned from a forty-eight hour stint in Juarez, hanging around bars and drinking with whores and cops. Those assignments were always very wet undertakings; you can't hang around a *cantina* looking for information without drinking. Drinking on duty in Mexico had destroyed many good officers and whores had taken their toll, too. Drink had very nearly killed Pope.

"Jim," Diehl said out of deference to his friend and because he wanted something from him, "I'm looking for information, or to give you a heads up, or something. I don't know just yet what's going on. We came across something this morning that makes me think there's a new operation in town, though." He went on to lay out for Pope the morning's events and what the tracks showed. He closed by saying, "Have you heard about anything moving across the river besides wets?"

"Nothing solid," Pope replied. "But we did get a whisper that there's Mexican Brown heroin showing up in Juarez. They don't use heroin much over there. If it's in Juarez in any quantity then it's headed over here, so we passed the info on to Customs. I doubt they'll do much with it, any more than they usually do. We've still got a few informants over there. I'll tune them up and tell them to get back to me. You in a hurry for this?"

"Naw" said Diehl, "any time last week will be OK."

Then he turned to Travis, who had been watching quietly, hip perched on the corner of an empty desk, thumbs hooked in his gun belt, listening while Diehl and Pope talked.

"Ken, this here's Jim Pope, the oldest man in the U.S. Border Patrol. He goes by 'Padre'."

He grinned at Pope as he said it. Jim Pope was by far not the oldest man in the Border Patrol, but his appearance said he might have been. "Jim, this is Ken Travis. He's fresh out of the box, but I think he might make a PI if he's brought up right."

Pope stuck out a hand that might have come off a medical school skeleton. "Nice to meet you, Travis. You ever call me 'Padre' and you won't draw another breath. And don't pay any attention to anything else this old bastard tells you, either. We worked the other side together and he just couldn't cut it. Got no sand in him at all." He smiled almost fondly at Diehl as he said it.

In fact, Diehl had literally saved Pope's life when a rolling surveillance south of Juarez had gone sour. They had been led into a trap, an ambush on a lonely dirt road on a steep mountainside in the forest. They'd had to shoot their way out of it but the bad men were betting into a stacked deck; Diehl and Pope were both combat veterans with gun smoke in their backgrounds. As he hit the ground rolling out of the car Pope killed one bandit. The man had made the mistake of looking around a tree he was behind for a little too long as he tried to line up a shot. Pope put a round through his forehead as a reminder that in a gunfight there are no second place winners.

From his place in the ditch across the road, Diehl killed another man who came up through the cedar trees on the cut bank above Pope as he crouched behind the fender of their car. With his partners down after just twenty seconds and two deadly shots from the officers, a third bandit fled down the mountainside.

But the one Diehl killed had put a slug into Pope before Diehl killed him. With Pope bleeding heavily and stretched out in the back seat of their shot-up Plymouth, Diehl drove through Juarez and then back across the Cordova Bridge at high speed. He blew through a closed inspection lane, scattering orange cones and setting off alarms and pursuit as he drove straight to the emergency room at Thomason General Hospital. Pope's gunshot wound and broken hip were repaired. He underwent a long convalescence, but he survived—mostly.

The *Judiciál,* the Mexican Federal Judicial Police, never tried very hard to work out what had happened, especially after word got back to them unofficially what the story was. Certainly, there was no international incident, nor was there an investigation by U.S. authorities. It was just life along the border, good guys versus bad guys, with some men playing both parts.

"Diehl," Pope said as he opened the office door for them to leave, "Laura and I got to have you over for supper sometime soon. Maybe even invite somebody else over to keep you company. Eat too much of your own cooking and you'll go belly up on me someday and I don't have enough friends any more to let that happen. In fact, we ought to roast a goat in the back yard again or something, make a real *pachanga* out of it. Travis, you're invited too. "Real will let you know when. If he thinks you're OK, you're welcome in my house."

"Sounds good to me, Jim, the grub'll be good, but you can tell Laura to forget all about that matchmaking idea of hers. If I want another woman, I'll go find one. But it ain't likely."

They stepped out and Pope closed the door behind them. As they walked out the back door to their cars, Diehl said "Travis, I'll see you in the morning."

"No sir. Training day tomorrow; I'll be in class all day."

“Thursday morning then” Diehl replied. “And I told you: you can call me ‘Real’”.

“Yes, sir. I’ll try to get comfortable with that. See you then, Mr. Diehl.”

Chapter 6

Still intent on practicing his marksmanship, Ken went out to his car and grabbed two boxes of Remington wadcutters out of the trunk and then walked down to the indoor range at the back of the lot. The sun was hot in his face and the draft created by the fans that extracted the powder smoke and lead dust from the range felt good as he stepped into the lobby.

"*Hola,* Hector," Ken said as he came into the lobby and found Hector Solis there. "How'd you do?" Among the guys who were interested in the skill, the subject was paid closer attention than ball scores.

"Ain't started yet, *compa.* Want to join me? I'll coach you and you coach me."

"Good idea. I keep throwing a round down and to the right now and then. Cost me five points out at fifty yards the last time I shot for record."

"Always down and to the right, Ken? That sounds like you're jerking the trigger."

They walked into the range and took adjacent booths. The place was dim, except for a bright light over the shooter in each booth and another shining on the target from overhead. Ken clipped his target, a ten-ring bullseye, to the carrier and pushed the button. A motor ran the target all the way out to twenty-five yards. Ken called out to make sure there was no one in the shadows downrange before he put an empty .38 casing in each ear to muffle the sound of the shots. Later, much too late, after he was mostly deaf, he would discover that it had been pointless.

"I'll go with the high-tech solution every time," Solis said with a grin as he screwed a filter from a Marlboro into each ear. "Let me have your gun."

Solis unloaded the cylinder, then put back two rounds, not next to one another. Then he spun the cylinder, closed it, and handed it back to Ken. "There you go, Ken. Now let's see you do some slow fire on that target."

Standing sideways to the target and with his left hand in his pants pocket, Ken brought the revolver up to eye level and cocked it with his thumb. Carefully aligning the front sight in the center of the rear notch and balancing the circle of the target on top of the front sight, he slowly squeezed the trigger. Finally, the hammer dropped with a "click" onto an empty chamber. The sights did not jump, which told him that he had not jerked the trigger. He lowered the weapon to his side. "Damn, but this trigger creeps before it lets off," he complained.

"I ain't seen your whining license, boy, and excuses don't put lead in their guts, so shut up and shoot," was all the sympathy he got from Solis.

"Well, shit," Ken said as he brought the revolver up to eye level, thumbing the hammer back as he did. He squeezed the trigger slowly, feeling the internal parts moving across one another before the sear let go and the hammer dropped. It fired.

"How'd it feel, Ken?" Solis called as he looked through a spotting scope from the next booth.

"Looked pretty good when it went off. Mighta been a ten, but probably a nine off to the right."

"Barely a nine, almost an eight, at five o'clock," Solis told him. "Pay attention to your sight alignment, bub. Keep that front sight centered in the back one."

Ken lined up another shot as Solis peeked around the wall of the booth to watch his technique. He saw Ken, steady as a rock, begin to squeeze the trigger. It seemed to take forever for the revolver to fire.

The hammer fell on the empty chamber. When it did, the revolver twitched slightly down and to the right.

"Ha! Flinch! You're getting in a hurry at the last second and jerking the trigger a little, I bet. Squeeze that trigger a little faster so you don't get impatient. Once you get it started, keep it coming. Your sights are gonna waver a little, but just keep squeezing while you make your corrections."

An hour later they were cleaning their guns on bench in the lobby.

"How's it feel to be off probation, Hector? Didn't you guys take your ten-month exam last week?"

"Better than first day of sixth grade summer vacation, man. I feel like I can make some real plans now, instead of just thinking about the next exam. Now I know I got a job, I can bring Brenda out here from New York. She's gonna hate it for a while, it's so different from Puerto Rico and New York, but she's tough; she'll do it.

*****

Later, Ken sat on the deck outside of his second floor apartment, feet propped up on the rail, chair leaned back against the white brick wall that was close behind him. He had come home this afternoon and gone to bed for a nap. It had been a long time since midnight, when he had arisen to get ready for the 2 a.m. to 10 a.m. shift he'd worked with Diehl. He woke up from his nap to the shrieks of kids in the pool about an hour ago. They were gone now, in bed he hoped, and tranquility had settled in. He could go to bed late tonight since he didn't have to get up until 6 a.m. tomorrow. Time enough to press a uniform, polish up his leather and brass, get some breakfast at Sambo's Restaurant, and still be in class by eight.

He took a pull from the Miller High-Life in his hand and then reached to the round table by his elbow and pulled a smoke out of the freshly opened pack. As he struck his Zippo he looked around with appreciation.

Damn, but I was lucky to find this place. A good part of town, and only a mile to the office. He glanced down at the pool in the courtyard, one floor directly below him, where a couple of girls were still hanging around the pool, nipples popped up and prominent through their bikini tops as the light breeze chilled them. *A view, and privacy too.* He was at the end of the wing, which meant no one walked by his place on the way to another apartment.

The sunset was violent shades of red and orange and pink over the Franklin Mountains that run down from the northwest, cleaving El Paso like an axe blade sunk in the earth. Giant dark rays fanned high into the sky overhead, shadows cast by the peaks themselves as the sun dropped below the horizon. The lights on the antennas atop the mountains were just beginning to stand out against the gloaming and a solitary 727 was drifting in out of the dark eastern sky, landing lights bright, on final for touchdown at El Paso International a mile west of where he sat. It was cooling down, the temperature dropping from the day's high in the 90's into the 70's already. It would be chilly overnight again.

The radio inside was tuned to KHEY and Glenn Campbell was singing about a lonesome lineman. The TV in the apartment below told him that the Red Sox had beat the Orioles earlier in the day. Didn't matter, since it looked like Detroit and St. Louis had the Series sewed up anyway.

Somebody in the place was toking up, for the smell of burning, old, wet leaves was a minor presence in the evening air. *Hope that's not gonna be a problem; I can't even be around that stuff.* He'd never done drugs and didn't intend to start. *Maybe smartest to just hang around with other officers or something. But I hope not.* He knew there were a couple of Army officers in the place, part of the cadre for Army basic training out at Fort Bliss. *Maybe they'll be straight.*

Sometime he'd have to go down and see if he couldn't establish some sort of meaningful relationship with one of the girls for a few hours. So far, he'd been way too preoccupied since he got back from school to pay much attention to glandular issues, but Mother Nature can only be ignored for so long.

Although he didn't think of it in precisely those terms, he was very aware that he was in the early stages of the rest of his life. He had a job that was more fun than a man ought to be allowed to have—and he got paid well for doing it. A good car and a nice apartment, and two days a week to do what he wanted. *Life is good,* he thought, and all things considered, the future looked good, too. *However, the job's only temporary if I don't get through the training. I'd better hit the law books.*

His Spanish was already passable, or at least functional for Border Patrol purposes, but every time he opened an immigration or a nationality law book, he felt like he was Alice in Wonderland. Nothing was ever cut and dried like he'd always thought the law probably was. The Academy had been an education for him in more than the facts of the law; it had also shown him just how flexible the law could be, especially when there were powerful interests to be satisfied.

The job was a surprise and a blessing. He'd always felt trapped back in New England. It was a pretty place at times, but it just didn't ever feel like home. He'd been west as a kid on vacation with his parents and he knew that's where he wanted to be.

He'd left college at the demand of the Dean a year ago. They weren't pleased with his grade point average; told him to come back when he was a serious student. He had been on the verge of just picking up and moving out west but the draft hanging over his head made it hard to make any plans.

So he'd just hung around, awaiting the "Greetings" from the President that he knew would come, followed by a trip to Viet Nam. Most of the guys he'd been in college with who weren't married had been called up, so he knew it would be just a matter of time. For that same reason, he'd never hooked up seriously with a girl back there. No point doing that and setting himself up for a "Dear John" letter while overseas.

Then he'd heard a recruiting spiel on the radio, announcing that the Border Patrol was hiring for positions along the Mexican border. He knew the border was out west, so that was a big attraction for him. He'd never thought of law enforcement as a career, it had never crossed his mind. In fact, he hadn't had any idea what he wanted to do, but at least this would take him where he wanted to be.

The work sounded interesting. After the clerk at his draft board told him if he got the job he'd get a deferment as long as they didn't hit the bottom of the barrel otherwise, he called the contact number and asked for a brochure. To top it all off he'd read in the brochure that his pay the first year, counting overtime, would be over eight thousand dollars, far better than the five grand a year he'd been making as a hand at the paper mill.

So here he was. And here he wanted to stay, so he'd better hit the books.

Chapter 7

They were all back in class again after a two-week break from training following graduation from the Academy. It was the first of their post-Academy training days; from now until they got off probation one day a week would be devoted to training in Spanish and law.

At 8:00 a.m. sharp the training officer walked through the door. He strode straight to the blackboard at the front of the room, where he turned and faced the class. In his late thirties, of medium height, he was lean and fit. His creases were sharp, his brass and leather glistened, his hair was neatly trimmed and his face so closely shaved that it shone. Some men seem born to wear a uniform well; he was one of those. As were all the others, he was in dress uniform, less firearm, but he managed to make it look better than they did.

He stood erect, feet apart, hands clasped behind his back, as he stared at the class for a time, looking at each face. His gaze was stern, but it was not hostile. "My name is David Lopez. I am here to teach you what you need to know to become Border Patrolmen. I am good at it and I will work hard at it. And you will work even harder. Or you will depart—I will see to it. Work hard at it, though and I will get every break I can for you." He paused. "Are we all clear on that?"

A few heads nodded. "Come on, guys; let me know you're here, would you?" He broke out with an engaging smile that drew the hoped-for responses reflecting understanding of this basic rule—work hard or leave. His appearance reflected his intelligence and character and those things reflected well on the agency he worked for. Lopez was one of the first Mexican-Americans to enter the Border

Patrol and he had paid expensive dues, in terms of hard work, for the privilege. His work and abilities, and that of others like him, had opened wide the Patrol's doors to the hundreds of Mexican-Americans who now were found in the uniform. The outfit had more Latinos than any other federal law enforcement agency by far. Born and raised in Santa Fe, New Mexico, he was fond of pointing out to the occasional foolish individual who might be contemptuous of "Mexicans" that his family had been in this land since 1650. "When," he would ask, "did your grandfather get off the boat?"

"Let us begin, gentlemen, with me asking a few questions to develop a sense of your knowledge." He picked up a pointer from the chalk tray and held it in both hands horizontally across the front of his thighs. He freely used it to point at the blackboard, but as a matter of courtesy he did not use it to point at people—unless, as they came to discover, he was displeased.

"Mr. Hastings," he said, with a look at Lonnie Hastings, "give me a verbal sketch of how deportation proceedings are instituted." The class wondered how he knew already which of them was Hastings. In fact, he had reviewed their training and personnel files and had associated their names with the photos in the files. He was, as he had told them, good at what he did.

"Uhhh, by arresting an alien?"

"Mr. Hastings, that answer is correct, if a bit more elementary than I wanted. For our purposes in the Border Patrol that's usually the case, but not in every case do deportation proceedings begin with an arrest. Sometimes they begin with a written notice to an alien at his place of residence. However, . . .", he looked around the room, " Mr. LeClaire, can you expand on that?"

"Sir, we begin by advising the person of his rights to silence, to counsel and to a hearing. Then we advise him of the fact that we believe that he is an alien and that we believe he has committed certain acts that make him deportable. We send him to a Special Inquiry Officer, where one of our Trial Attorneys presents the evidence. He may have an attorney. If the evidence proves that he did what we claim, the SIO can order him deported. In most cases he is entitled to post bond and be out of custody."

"I note that you said the SIO "can" order him deported, not "will" order him deported. Why is that? Wait, Mr. LeClaire, let me direct that question elsewhere." Lopez looked around the room again. "Mr. Scott. Can you tell me why Mr. LeClaire might have put it that way? It makes it sound as though deportation is optional."

Scott thought for a moment. "Because lots of times a deportable alien can be allowed to go home on his own—if he's not a criminal or something. He can ask the SIO to let him do that, sir."

"Exactly right, Mr. Scott. There are certain criteria he must be able to meet, such as being of good moral character and being able to pay his own way home, but an SIO may allow an alien who is deportable to depart without being formally ordered deported. It is called Voluntary Departure: correct?"

Several heads nodded in agreement as he walked across the room, heels clicking on the linoleum. Then he went on.

"Which leads us to what we do here with aliens every day. We, here, can allow the alien to leave without going to a hearing if he wants. We call it VR, or voluntary return. Why do we call it VR, when the proper term is Voluntary Departure?"

He paused, awaiting an answer. Nothing came, so he went on with the punch line. "I presume it's because we would prefer not to say out loud that we just gave an alien VD." He waited while the class caught on and then he laughed with them.

"Instead of making every alien we arrest go to an SIO, with all the nuisance that would entail for us and for him, the law allows the alien to make his application for Voluntary Departure to us, rather than to an SIO. He admits that he is an alien who is illegally in the U.S. and says that he is willing to waive his right, and it *is* a right, to a hearing before an SIO and to go home by the first available transportation. Unless we are particularly annoyed with him for some reason, such as having a long record, we usually grant the request and he goes home that day."

"Mr. Travis. Why might that be important to the alien? Why would he give up his right to a hearing?"

Ken was caught by surprise; he was still thinking about the VD joke as he looked at the wall above Lopez's head. "Uhhh . . . I don't know, sir."

Lopez aimed his pointer at Travis like a gun barrel and said, "A moderate amount of thought is called for, Mr. Travis, but it's neither hard nor painful. Proceed."

Ken gathered his thoughts for an eternity. His mind raced and his stomach churned. The rest of the class sat silent. "I'd guess because it allows him to get home sooner and he knows he's going to lose anyway if he goes to hearing?"

"That's your guess? Well, at least it addresses one point. Yes, Mr. Travis, it is more convenient in many cases for the alien. He avoids being detained for several days pending his hearing and it puts him back in Mexico more quickly, so that he can try again sooner."

"But more important from a legal standpoint is this: an Order of Deportation serves to bar an alien from coming back legally to this country for seven years. A VR does not have that effect. And since most illegal aliens harbor at least some small, fond hope of immigrating to this country legally someday, they do not want to jeopardize that chance by being formally deported. Furthermore, although it very seldom happens, an alien can be prosecuted for coming back here after he was deported. It is a felony. While the risk of jail time is small, why take it at all? Now, let us get on with the day's lesson."

To avoid disillusioning the new officers, he omitted certain other unfortunate aspects of VR, things they would discover on their own in time.

For the alien, the process offered tremendous advantages. Chief among them was avoiding time in detention pending his hearing, which would give the Border Patrol time to find out by fingerprints who he really was. For the Border Patrol, it allowed far quicker handling of each case but at the cost of overall effectiveness. Like much of what INS and the Border Patrol did, effectiveness was sacrificed to expediency. Unfortunately, in an agency without much budget and with nearly no political support in Washington, expediency, not to be confused with efficiency, was a necessary evil. Experienced officers knew it and resented it, for they could see how ineffective it made them. In some of the men the knowledge bred apathy and sometimes contempt for the agency.

Chapter 8

Travis reached to the bed table and slapped the alarm into silence Friday at midnight. This would be a Saturday morning 2 a.m. to 10 a.m. shift. Add on the Uncontrollable Overtime from scheduled quitting time until noon and he was looking at a ten-hour day, at least, and if they got onto a hot trail it might stretch on for hours beyond that. *UOT's a nice benefit,* he thought as he arose and showered.

Now he sat at the small, cheap kitchen table polishing his brass nameplate, its pins stuck into the back side of the Styrofoam cartridge rack from a box of issued ammunition. Polishing brass and leather was a big part of a trainee's preparation for his shift.

He gave the brass plate another buffing stroke, then held it at angle to the light to look for any remaining tarnish—and found some, a faint, dull cloud on the metal.

With an exasperated sigh he shook up the can of Brasso, put some on the already tarnish-blackened rag, and went back to buffing as his mind wandered. Uniform upkeep gave you lots of time for thought.

Average nine hours a week of unscheduled overtime for six weeks and for the next six weeks they'd give you twenty-five percent extra premium pay. It only amounted to slightly better than straight time, but that was better than having to work it for free like a lot of cops did. You just stayed on duty when you had to, or wanted to. If they assigned overtime they had to pay time and half for it and they didn't like that. Instead, they tried to force guys to work UOT, but of course if it was directed it wasn't uncontrollable. There had been grievances filed over it, but he wasn't going to get mixed up in union stuff as long as he was on probation. All they had to do to get rid of him while he was a trainee was kiss him good-bye and give him a shove out the door, so until next June it would all be "Yes, sir", "No, sir" and "Whatever you say, sir".

When he'd told Diehl on Tuesday evening that he'd see him Thursday morning he'd forgotten the shape of the shift, that he was off duty on Thursday and Friday. He'd called Diehl at home after class Wednesday to tell him; he hoped Real wouldn't be mad about it. He'd sounded OK with it, though.

Ken wanted to make sure he got to the office early when he went back to work so he could pick the best vehicle out of a bad lot and make sure it was clean and gassed up, ready to go when Diehl showed up. Some of the other trainees called it ass-kissing or brown-nosing, but Travis didn't mind doing it. It seemed fair that the junior guy should take care of it. His turn would come, but for now he had a job to keep.

He thought back to his days off as he pinned the nameplate and then his badge to a fresh shirt and then picked up a boot to begin work on. Nobody even tried to keep a spit shine on boots they wore to work; the duty was just too rough on them, but his Justins always gleamed from a good buffing when he showed up at the office.

The "weekend," had been good, very relaxing. In fact, it'd been better than good.

He'd walked by the pool in his dress uniform after class Wednesday, Sam Browne belt and all the leather polished and brass shined and Smokey Bear hat tipped low over his eyes, just to see what the reaction would be. These days, with the war in Viet Nam going on and all the goddam hippies protesting, you never knew what sort of reaction a uniform would bring.

A couple of girls at the pool had given him a smile though, so he'd changed into his trunks and gone back down to check things out.

It was early evening when he got there, but the cement still radiated the sun's warmth and gave off a dusty smell when water splashed out of the pool. The sun had set spectacularly a few minutes before; there'd been a few high clouds in the west to bring fire to the sky. Now the area was in the deep shadows of the cabana on the west side of the pool deck. He set his beer and cigarettes down, dropped his towel on a chaise and then dived smoothly into the water and swam a couple laps before pulling himself up onto the deck. His college days as a lifeguard made him look good in the water, he knew.

He'd noticed the girls pointedly ignoring him as he'd walked over to his chaise, but giving him surreptitious glances out of the corners of their eyes as they carried on a quiet, unintelligible conversation. He was no expert on female behavior but he'd been around enough of them to know when he was being checked out. He was satisfied with what he knew they saw; a tanned, blue-eyed, sandy-haired man, a little over six feet tall, lean and supple as a whip, and still in good shape from the workouts at the Academy.

Within just a few minutes the short, round brunette stood up, wrapped herself in her towel, and walked out of the pool area, leaving the taller one there alone.

He knew a signal when he saw one, but he decided to wait her out. Finally, after sitting by herself for five or ten minutes, she came over to him asking if he had a match or lighter with no hint of coyness at all. Silently, he'd fired up his Zippo, lit her Winston as she leaned over, and then he leaned back in the chaise again as she sat down in the deck chair next to him.

He recalled the straightforward way she'd introduced herself. "Thanks. I'm Kate Toole. Dot and I live in the place below you. You're awfully quiet, aren't you?"

She was a redhead as near as he could tell in the flickering light cast by the tiki torches, about five-six, slim, and pretty in an unconventional way—mouth a little too wide, nose a tad too short, but striking in spite of the flaws. And he couldn't help noticing that she had big feet, at least for a girl her size, but it didn't matter; there were other attractions to draw the eye.

They passed the twilight time easily in the idle chitchat of two people getting acquainted, neither anxious to be liked nor eager to leave. She was from Ohio, but had come to El Paso a year before when she got a job as a stewardess for Trans-Texas Airlines. He told her about growing up in rural Maine. There had been no sense of compulsion to talk; the silences had been easy.

At one point she went inside. He'd enjoyed the view as she walked away from him with a graceful stride, her bikini making the view all the more enjoyable. The torches cast a pattern of dancing light and shadow on her back. Although she must have known he was watching she made no effort to enhance or diminish the effect of her walk. She didn't pick up her towel and wrap it around her waist, as many women would have done, conscious of their bodies. A few minutes later she came back with a beer for each of them.

She was comfortable to be with, he thought. Finally, he asked her if she'd like to do something the next day, Thursday. She'd said yes and when he asked if there were anything in particular she'd like to do she'd said, "Surprise me." He liked that.

So he'd washed and polished up his GTO early the next morning, bought food for a picnic and picked her up at ten. They'd wound up in the New Mexico mountains near Ruidoso, a hundred miles and more northeast of El Paso. They ate lunch on a blanket spread on the grass by a small brook, then spent the afternoon walking around the hills in the bright, autumn sunshine. They examined some tumbledown adobe buildings, wondering how old they were and what had happened there and making up stories for each other about what it might have been. The sky was bright blue with a few puffy cumulus clouds growing high. The aspens on the mountains had changed to gold and crimson in the cold fall nights. It was warm in the sunshine, but walking into a shadow brought a shiver as the mountain's autumn chill took over. He dropped an arm across her shoulders and she came close in response. It was a beautiful day and they laughed a lot.

On the way back they'd stopped for supper at a *posada* in Cloudcroft. A fire of *piñon* wood snapped in the adobe fireplace by their table in the corner, casting a warm glow on them and making a pleasant scent. A lone guitarist played quiet, mournful Spanish tunes from a shadowed corner across the room. They sat, not across from each other, but around the table's corner from one another. That way, they were close enough to feel side-by-side, but still able to look at one another easily. It had been the middle of the week and they had the place nearly to themselves.

As he buffed a boot, he recalled how several times during the meal she had reached over to touch his wrist as she made a point and how intently she watched him as he spoke.

They'd driven back home in a companionable silence in the dark, the dual exhausts rumbling and the big four-barrel carburetor making a low moan as he cruised along at eighty. He could faintly smell the tequila on her breath from the two margaritas she'd drunk, but it wasn't unpleasant. She looked languorous, utterly relaxed in her seat, hands in her lap, breasts rising and falling under her soft sweater as she breathed gently, eyes almost closed. The moonlight painted her face softly. It was an appealing sight; he'd wished he could absorb it rather than having to watch the road. One time she turned her head to him and gave him a soft smile that all by itself made the trip worthwhile. The day had been completely without tension, which seemed rare to him when dealing with women her age.

It was late when they got back. They'd lingered at her door facing each other and holding hands, she seeming to expect him to ask if he could come in, he wondering if he should. Finally, they parted with a brief kiss and she thanked him for a good time. She sounded sincere. They'd made no arrangements for further dates. Ken figured they'd run into each other again soon enough; there was no point in rushing things.

Coming back to the present, he snapped the shoeshine rag one last time on his right boot, then stood up and shook his pants cuffs down over the top of the boots. Walking to the dresser, he picked up his pocketknife, lighter, and wallet and dropped them in his pants pockets, and cigarettes in the right shirt pocket. They had to go on that side or they made a bulge that made his badge hang crooked. He put six extra rounds by themselves in his right front pants pocket; you never knew when the six on your belt wouldn't be enough. The twelve-round carriers worn by some officers, although permitted, weren't official uniform items.

Then he took his gun belt, holster, and cuff case from the doorknob where he'd hung them. He swung the belt around his hips with his left hand, caught the end of it with his right and then quickly buckled it in place atop his trousers belt. He picked up the five small leather straps with two snaps each, called "keepers," and ran each of them around both his gun belt and his trousers belt. He snapped them in place, anchoring his gun belt to his trousers belt. One went just forward of the holster and another back of it, with two others in the similar location over his left hip on either side of his cuff case. The last one he placed centered on his back. Although the snaps gleamed decoratively, the keepers' purpose was serious. If he had to draw his gun quickly they would keep the rig from rising with it if the pistol bound slightly in the holster. As it had been explained at the Academy, when you're being shot at you want to grab a handful of gun, not of gun, holster, and gun belt.

Stepping to the closet, he took his .38 off the shelf, opened the cylinder and dumped the loads into his hand. He recalled the story one of the older PIs had told at the coffee shop. Unknown to him, his wife had unloaded his pistol and put it back in his holster because she feared having a loaded weapon around the house. Not being the cautious type who looked to his revolver every time he put it on, he'd carried it around unloaded for days before he discovered the problem when he went to shoot a jackrabbit out in the sand hills. Ken was amazed at the number of officers who were utterly uninterested in such an important tool as their gun.

"Satan's ears'll be frostbit before I get that stupid," he thought to himself with the unconscious arrogance of youth. He pulled the trigger six times before he went through the process of loading the revolver quickly from the cartridge loops on his belt half a dozen times. Skills, he knew, were maintained with daily practice. Finally, he filled the loops once more. After thrusting the revolver into his holster he snapped the safety strap over the hammer, settled his hat on his head, and walked out into the night.

Chapter 9

Travis arrived at the office at 1:30 a.m, a half hour early. Most of the guys came in a few minutes before two, just before the shift started, then there was wrangling over who got what car. The Senior Patrol Inspector, the shift boss, always assigned the work areas but left vehicle assignments to a free-for-all among the officers. He didn't feel like dealing with the grief and recriminations that arose if he made the vehicle assignments himself, so he just left it to the officers. It seemed to Ken like a dumb way to do things because it delayed the PIs getting to the field by fifteen or twenty minutes. It seemed like pretty weak supervision, but nobody seemed to care.

By showing up early though, Travis had his choice of vehicles. He snatched the keys to one of the newest rigs, a two-year old Scout, off the board, put his and Diehl's names and the unit number on the Station One sign out sheet and headed out the door. The desk officer didn't say a thing to him about it since he, too, was a trainee doing his stint on the desk and he knew the score about new guys and the vehicles they usually wound up with. He'd made a note to himself about Travis's technique though; he would use it himself.

Travis walked out to the lot, straight to the rig. The number decal inside the windshield on the passenger side confirmed that it was the right one. It may have been only two years old but it had a lot of miles already and the pale green paint was faded to dull chalkiness. It was still the best-looking one there, though. He got in, started it up and noticed that the gas gauge registered full. Someone, God bless him, had done what he was supposed to and filled it up after it was used last.

He drove down to the service island to check the oil, water, and tires. Officers working in the sand hills frequently had to let a lot of air out of the tires to avoid sinking in deep when it got soft. They'd drive back to the office and forget, or simply neglect, to bring the tires back up to the proper pressure. Driven very far that way, or very fast, it was a dangerous thing if you didn't notice it.

Sure enough, he found that the two rear tires were half flat, so he pulled up to the air hose and filled them back up. Then he popped off the radiator cap and pulled the dipstick to check water and oil.

Awww, Goddam it! Both were low. *Why in the hell can't the dumb sonofabitch take a minute to finish a job instead of throwing it off on someone else?* Travis was not yet old enough to have become inured to this unchangeable element of human nature—it pissed him off, not a good way to start a shift.

He walked over to the locker, uncharitable thoughts on his mind, to get a quart of oil. Taking the spout in hand, he punched it through the lid of the can and upended it into the filler hole on the engine. While the oil glugged its way into the crankcase he turned on the wall faucet and took the hose over to top off the radiator, the glanced at his watch.

Hmmm, ten 'til. Diehl ought to be here any minute now.

Even as the thought crossed his mind a set of headlights flashed across him as Diehl's old Ford truck turned into the employee parking lot. Diehl gave the horn a tap to let Ken know he'd seen him and would be down.

Ken put the cap back on the radiator, pulled the spout from the oil filler hole and capped it. As he tossed the can into the trash Diehl strolled out of the dark, looking fresh and ready to go. That was something else Travis had noticed; Diehl never came to work looking anything but neat. He might finish up the shift looking like he'd crawled across the desert in the heat on his hands and knees, but when the shift began his clothes were pressed, his leather and boots were clean and his brass, if not gleaming, was at least bright. Some PI's came in wearing pants that showed last week's dust, and shirts with sequential sweat rings—almost like growth rings on a tree; you could estimate how long it had been worn by the stains under the arms. It was, he thought, a pretty sorry way to present yourself.

"You drive tonight, Ken," Diehl said as he threw his tricky bag and water jug into the rear compartment with Travis's. All their gear sat atop the extra spare tire that lay on the narrow floor between the wheel wells.

The security screen behind the seats made it impossible to reach your tricky bag back there; you had to stop and walk to the tailgate if you wanted something, but there just wasn't enough room up front for two men's gear and water. During the day, when it was hot and water was needed minute to minute, officers usually kept at least their water jugs up there, but not tonight.

"We've got the east sand hills again. Let's go have a look at the drag road first thing, see if there's been anything across yet."

Ken cranked up the little four-cylinder engine, dropped the three-speed manual into first gear, and pulled away from the service area. As he turned left out of the station onto US 62 he started to say, "Mr. Diehl . . ."

Diehl cut him off, saying, "Ken, you did good the other day. I like you and that doesn't happen very often with a new guy and me. It could change if you fuck up seriously or get stupid on me, but for now I want you to call me Tom. I'll teach you anything I can and help you when you need it. This outfit needs good officers; God knows we got enough fuckups here in El Paso but that's the price we pay for this being a disciplinary station. You'll work with them, and I'll bet you'll pick up pretty quick on which ones they are. Don't let them lead you into places and things where you know you shouldn't go. If you have serious problems with anyone, something you can't work out on your own, you come see me. We gotta start with good people and make good officers out of 'em. I ain't gonna say all this again, once is enough, so put it in your head and keep it there. I'll tell you if I see you start doing something wrong."

It was a long speech for him. He reached into his shirt pocket and pulled out the makings for a smoke.

"Now head down to I-10 and off at Zaragoza Road. We'll get on the drag road there and go east on it down to Horizon City. If we don't cut some sign we'll come back and get a cup of coffee at the FINA and maybe some breakfast. I didn't eat supper. Go on."

They drove east on Interstate 10 under a star-filled sky for another ten minutes. Ken was persistently amazed at how bright stars and the moon were on clear nights here—at four thousand feet, El Paso was above the general haze layer that was increasingly covering the rest of the country.

Getting off at Zaragoza Road, they turned left at the foot of the ramp and headed north, away from the border. A few hundred yards north of the Interstate Ken turned right onto the drag road. The drag lay beside the road, tow chain laying loose in the dust where the evening shift had left it when they quit at midnight. Usually, it was the last thing you did before you headed in and you tried to let the incoming shift know about what time you'd done it.

Travis dropped into granny low gear and let the engine idle, carrying them along as he looked for footprints on the drag road's smooth surface. The slight breeze through the open window was chilly. The headlights cast long, deep shadows behind the brush alongside the road, while the full moon cast usable light into the open areas.

After a few minutes of poking along, Diehl spoke up.

"Ken, at this rate I'll starve to death before we get to the Horizon City cutoff. Speed up some, maybe ten miles an hour."

"OK," Ken replied, "but I'm afraid to go too fast or I might miss seeing a track."

"Here's a lesson for you. Pay attention. When you're cutting sign you are not looking for tracks, you're looking for something out of place. When you find something that doesn't look right, that's when you slow down and start tracking."

"As you drive along your focus should be in front of you, but your peripheral vision should be working too, seeing what's happening along the edge of the road. Not everything leaves a nice, neat sign in the road itself. Sometimes you gotta see what happening around the edges of something to understand it. You chisel that on that rock in the back of your head, too. It's true more places than just sign cutting."

Five minutes later Diehl said, "Stop!" Then, "Back up about fifteen feet." Ken did and then Diehl said, "You didn't see it, did you? What were you looking at?"

Ken had to admit that he had seen nothing. He thought he had been looking at the road.

"C'mon, look, dammit! Don't you see how the surface texture of the sand in the road has changed? How it's not as smooth as what we've been looking at since we started?

With that prompting, Ken looked again, then said "Yeessss, I think I do. It looks like fine lines running longways in the road for a few feet. But I don't see anything that looks like tracks."

"Well, glory be, he's got eyes," Diehl said sarcastically. "This means I don't get breakfast, 'cause it looks like they ran a goddam herd of elephants through here. Now let's get out and have a look at what's around the edges. You do remember what I told you about looking at what's around the edges, don't you?"

Ken, face aflame with embarrassment at missing the sign, then the chewing out, said, "I do. Let me look."

"You check that side," Diehl ordered, "see what you come up with as a count. I'll look over here."

Ken took his issued tin two-battery flashlight out into the desert a few yards, then, as they had taught him at school, sank into a crouch and shone the light at ground level along the trail beaten into the sand. He could see no individual tracks in the bunch and didn't have any idea how he could tell how many there were. So he followed them further on.

Finally, by seeing tracks from time to time where someone had stepped out of line and left an identifiable single track, or had stopped to take a leak he came to the conclusion that there were four to six of them and one was a woman or small boy.

He heard the Scout grinding along in low gear behind him, turned, and found Diehl a short distance back. He walked back and Diehl got out of the driver's seat.

"Well?" he said.

"I make it four to six," Ken said.

"Close. There's eight of them and I read them to be cherries, too, because they don't look like they know where they're going. I backtracked them a ways and they seem to be just wandering around, not lined out on anything I can see. Let's just follow them up; we can't be too far behind 'em."

Ken got back in the driver's seat and pulled away.

"Do you know what you saw back there, Ken?" His tone had softened; he was educating now, not chewing out.

"Well, sir, I had a chance to think about it while I was walking their trail. I figure it was a brushout. I never saw one before, but they told us at school that sometimes they'll have the last man across sweep out their tracks with something like a blanket or piece of brush."

"That's right," Diehl replied, "that's exactly what it was. The lines in the sand were left by the branches on the mesquite branch he used. He backed up, sweeping side to side as he did. I found the spot on the bush by the trail where he broke the branch off and I'll bet you saw the branch on your side when you were following them up. That's what I meant before, talking about *anything* out of the ordinary, not just tracks. That brushout stands out at least as well as tracks crossing the road."

Ken didn't recall seeing a branch by the trail, but then, he had been looking for tracks, not stuff like busted branches laying around. He knew he'd have to broaden his focus if he was going to become a good sign cutter.

They drove north, following the tracks slowly, crawling along in low gear, dodging around mesquite bushes, seeing the occasional snake or scorpion or other night creature. A jackrabbit burst across the trail in long bounds, scared from its bed by something. The desert is a far livelier place at night than it is during the day.

Again, Diehl said, "Stop!"

Ken hit the brakes and clutch, stopping quickly. Diehl got out with his flashlight, a strong three-cell Kel light made of black aluminum with a knurled surface. They were fairly new devices, expensive, and not every officer had one yet since they had to buy their own.

Diehl shined his light down onto a looping line in the sand and began to follow it. After a few yards he stopped, then stepped quickly forward and bent over to pick something up from beside his boot. In the near-dark, Ken couldn't see what it was, but he was afraid he knew.

Diehl stood up and in his hand was a rattlesnake about two feet long, writhing with fury, wrapping around his lower arm. He walked back to the Scout, stopping in the headlights. He smiled at Ken and held the creature out into the headlights' beam for Ken to see and then came to the passenger door and stopped by the open window.

"How are you about these scaly critters, Ken?" he asked.

"Doesn't bother me being around them," Ken replied, "long as I know where they are and they're under control. I don't care if you get in with it, but you drop it in here and all you're gonna see on this side of the rig is asshole and elbows as I go out the door and it won't matter how fast we're going."

"Yeah, I hear that," Diehl said with an evil smile so big it wrinkled his brow as he got in. "I got him for a reason." He continued to grasp the snake tightly behind the head and the snake continued to make his objections known, hissing and dripping venom from his fangs.

They rattled and jounced on across the dunes and ditches for another mile. Finally, the tracks came up to a large clump of brush, spread around it, and went no further.

"Does that tell you a tale, Ken?"

"Yeah. They must be in there. And that's nasty stuff to crawl around in."

"Well, Ken, we're not gonna, 'cause I don't like it worth a damn myself."

He stepped out of the Scout and called out for the group to come out of the bushes. There was no answer. He called again. Finally, one lone girl of about sixteen years came out, followed by someone who might have been a slightly older brother. Ken locked them in the back of the Scout.

"Call Station One for a D.O. to meet us in a half hour out at the Interstate; let's get 'em on the way out here now. There'll be more of these guys soon and if there are as many as I think we'll have to haul 'em out in two loads."

He stepped forward into the lights and announced in Spanish, "In a moment I'm going to throw my tracking snake into those bushes and he's going to hunt you down. And he won't be happy when he finds you. So come out now with your hands up." He stood there in the lights, the snake now half-strangled and dangling from his hand, swinging back and forth as Diehl twisted his wrist from side to side.

Two men came out of a hole in the bushes on their hands and knees, eyes wide, never taking them from the snake. They made a big circle around Diehl, back to Ken, who hooked them up and then put them in the back of the rig.

"You go around the other side and get ready for the explosion."

Ken did so, taking up a position where he could see both the rear escape route and Diehl, too. Diehl gave them one more chance to surrender and then with a quick flip of his wrist, he tossed the snake into the bushes.

As Diehl had predicted there was an explosion, one of men in the bushes. The branches began to rattle and whip, as though driven by a tornado. *Hijo de puta! Chingado!* and other Spanish expletives flew, as well as shouts of *Vibora!* and *Culebra!* announcing the presence of a snake, real or imagined, underfoot. Suddenly four men burst out on two sides of the brush, two of them straight into Ken's arms, the other two falling into the sand at Diehl's feet.

Ken, chest heaving as he tried to concentrate on the job, could barely contain himself enough to cuff his two together. That finally done, he gave in to a guffaw that brought tears to his eyes and left him sitting on the ground, hiccoughing helplessly.

Finally, he fell back onto his elbows. "Oh, my God! Your tracking snake!" he said, overcome once more by gales of laughter. Finally, weakening for lack of breath, he gasped, "'He's gonna be mad!' Oh, Lordy, I'll take this one to my grave, I will." Still giggling, he pushed himself to his feet. "OK, Tom. What now?"

"Neat trick, ain't it? Back in the Corps I'da used a grenade, but this works just as well and it's a whole lot more entertaining."

"We'll sit here together until the D.O's call to say they're close. When they are, you'll drive the first four out to them while I sit here and keep these boys company. I'll amuse them by trying to whistle up my tracking snake. They think he's out there somewhere and you couldn't get them to move away from here for ten dollars a foot. It'll be OK. You come back after me, though, hear?"

Chapter 10

Ken awoke to the ringing of his alarm at five in the afternoon with thoughts of Kate on his mind. The tinfoil taped over the windows of the spare bedroom he slept in during the day blocked all the light but for an errant beam of sunshine that crept through a gap at the edge of the foil. It cut through the dimness like a blade to the far wall. His uniform lay in a green heap in the corner, his badge coincidentally gleaming at him like a beacon from the top of the heap. His hat and gun belt lay on the ladder back chair by the door where he had thrown them when he came in just a few hours ago and his dusty boots were tumbled in a random stack on the closet floor, as though too tired to stand up straight. For a few minutes he lay there on his back, hands behind his head, thinking, watching the dust motes dance like fireflies in the sunbeam.

It had been a long shift. By the time they had brought the first group back to the highway and waited for the Detention Officers, another group had crossed almost down to Horizon City. There were only four of them this time, and they weren't stopping for coal nor water as The Real Diehl had put it.

It had been well after dawn before Diehl and Ken had finally caught up with them and they had scattered in four directions almost as if by plan. Fortunately, “Wings” had been up and kept them all spotted. Still, though, it had been nearly 1:00 p.m. before they could go home. Diehl had never got his supper and he was cranky about it, too.

When he arrived home, Ken had found an envelope taped to his door. In it was a note from Kate, asking if he'd like to come down that evening at six for a spaghetti supper. In fact, she pretty much took it for granted that he'd say "Yes" since she'd written that she'd expect him then and he should come prepared to eat heartily.

Conflicting emotions! All he'd wanted to do was sleep for about ten straight hours, but food might lead to . . . other things and there are things sometimes more important than sleep, or even food, to a young man. And, he recalled, he'd not had a home-cooked meal in four months or more. So he heaved himself out of bed and headed for the bathroom.

Showered, shaved, and smelling of Old Spice, dressed in loafers with white socks, chinos, and a short-sleeved madras shirt, he knocked on her door at six sharp. She answered, looking distinctly and calculatedly female in a short, black dress under a frilly apron, wooden spoon in hand. Small diamond earrings sparkled under a cascade of auburn hair that fell nearly to her shoulders and a tiny silver cross flashed at her throat. Red lipstick dressed her full mouth, but she'd not troubled to cover the light spray of freckles across her nose and cheekbones. Her green eyes sent a message that said "welcome" even better than the words she spoke. She gave him a kiss on the cheek, then as she stepped away from him and turned to go back to the kitchen, he saw that high heels shaped her calves and behind.

Over supper they chatted easily, mostly about their jobs and how they had come to be where they found themselves in their lives now. They had covered the same ground in New Mexico, but now they offered more and delved deeper. She spoke without pain of a boyfriend gone wrong, and he of never having had a serious girlfriend despite thinking there must be one out there. He found she was 24, which surprised him. He would not have thought her older than himself, but he found it didn't matter.

He told her the story of Diehl and the snake. She reacted with glee, revealing the same off-center sense of humor he had, which *did* matter.

Finally, Ken laid his silverware across his plate and then folded his napkin and put it down beside the plate. The table was littered with the remains of a meal well done and fully enjoyed. Spots of sauce spattered the checkered tablecloth around the tureen that had held it. Of the food, only a heel of bread remained on the red napkin that lined a wicker breadbasket and a few errant strands of spaghetti lay unclaimed in the clay-colored pottery serving bowl. A near-empty wine bottle with an inch of dago red left served as a tombstone to the remains.

Leaning back in his chair, he smiled across the small, round table at Kate. Their feet, now without shoes, touched slightly under the table, almost, but not quite, by accident.

"Kate, I haven't had a meal like that in, oh, I can't remember when. Who'd guess the Irish could fix better spaghetti than the Italians?

"La, sir, how you do go on," she replied in a faked Scarlett O'Hara accent, head slightly turned away and eyelids batting shamelessly at him. "It was nothing. But we're not done. Won't you have coffee and some fresh apple pie?"

"Have you no mercy, woman? I'm stuffed; that's the first home-cooked food I've had since June. But bring it on, for I won't cry uncle to a woman."

With a direct glance at him she said, "We'll see," then headed for the kitchen, giving him a flounce of her hip to think about while she was out of the room.

And think about it he did. *What is going on here?* he asked himself as he moved from the table to the couch, lighting a Chesterfield as he went.

He pulled up a large ceramic ashtray to easy reach on the heavy, carved coffee table. The girls had apparently bought some furniture for themselves, he thought, for the low table appeared to have been hand-made in Mexico. He looked around and saw that behind his head an arrangement of three impressionist pictures of flowers and sky hung to brighten the white wall. The far wall had been painted a pale blue and spray of red silk flowers in a clear glass vase provided a bright dash of color atop a small table under a mirror. The couch he was sitting on was cream-colored with a muted floral print, and the other chair in the room was a love seat, apparently the other piece of a set with the couch.

I've never met anyone so easy to be around. She flirts shamelessly, but there's that undercurrent of—not flirting at all, I guess. She's so, so . . . enchanting.

That's funny. I don't believe I've ever used that word before. But I suppose that goes with thinking about someone that you've never met anyone like before – there's a sentence that's about as confused as I am.

A new record dropped on the turntable and Johnny Mathis began singing *Chances Are.*

Now that's too damn strange. It's gotta be coincidence, but really . . .

He sat on one end of her couch, slouched with the back of his neck on the back cushion, hands pushed deep into his pockets, legs thrust out straight, cigarette dangling from his lips. He looked at his feet, glad that he'd pulled clean socks from the drawer and specifically checked to make sure they had no holes in them.

"Penny for your thoughts," Kate said as she came back into the room with a tray bearing two cups of coffee and spoons, milk and sugar, and pie on two plates with forks. She set the tray on the table in front of the couch and gave him a smile that would have warmed the heart of a troll. "How do you take your coffee?"

"A little of both, please," he replied as he sat up. "And I was thinking about socks, if you must know." He grinned back at her, both of them picking up on the unintended double *entendre*. He stubbed out his cigarette.

"Socks, huh," she said as she sat beside him, tucking one foot under herself, showing a delightful amount of leg above the knee while doing so. "A likely story from a man. And what should a girl think about a man who thinks about socks after a meal like that?" She leaned forward to mix their coffee.

He reached out and gently placed his hand in the middle of her back, really touching her for the first time without invitation. Under other circumstances it might not have been an intimate touch—but here and now, it was. She did not draw away; instead, she leaned slightly back into it.

"She should know that he gives enough of a damn about what she thinks that he doesn't want to do something that will run her off."

She stopped stirring and looked back over her shoulder at him.

"Like that for you, too, is it?" she said in a low, slightly husky voice, her mouth growing softer, the pupils of her eyes widening. "Since you've confessed, I will, too. As soon as I laid eyes on you outside, when you came home from work one night, even before you came back out to swim the other night, I said to Dot 'I'm going to get to know him better.' I really want to get to know you better, Ken. I don't know where this is going, but I'm along for the ride."

She broke the tension by handing him his cup. He took his hand off her back and looked away. His mind didn't leave her though – she could still feel him thinking about her.

"Are we in a hurry to get somewhere with it?" he asked.

"Not as far as I'm concerned," she replied. "Seems to me like we've got lots of time to explore as we go along."

They looked into each other's eyes, each seeking some truth or secret message. Finally, she broke her gaze away with a laugh that was a little nervous.

"Tonight we'll settle for pie and coffee. Exploration will have to wait until we have more time. I don't want to hurry things too much, if you know what I mean."

"I know exactly what you mean. Let's eat."

Chapter 11

It was just before midnight and Saturday night was in full swing at the Cantina Rio Bravo. Colored lights over the bar and in corners reflected off the mirrored ball in the center of the room and lent an air of gaiety not seen in the place at noon, and the whores were younger and prettier. The place roared with noisy conversation and the clink of glasses as drinks were served.

The place was full of college boys from UTEP and New Mexico State University in Las Cruces, many of them too young to drink in the States. There were GIs from Fort Bliss in El Paso where the Army conducted basic training, most of them fresh out of boot camp, and many were on orders to Viet Nam. There was an air of desperation to some of their drinking and the bartenders and prostitutes were doing a booming business. A modern juke box at the back of the room blasted *Jumpin' Jack Flash* through the crowd and half a dozen young men with very short haircuts were lined up in front of it, quarters in their hands. Others danced wildly on the large floor, either with women they brought or with women they bought. Going to Mexican bars with a date was regarded as "cool." Few of the Americans there thought of the cantina as a whorehouse, but really, it was little more than that.

Despite the crowd and frenetic activity the table in the very back corner remained empty, a small sign on it said "Reserved" in English and Spanish. Anyone tempted to challenge the reservation with more than a question was quickly thrown out the back door into the alley, often with a lump on the head or a twisted shoulder. Sometimes they were rolled before they could get out of the alley, for like sharks collecting around the garbage chute of a ship, young, violent predators of the night haunted the alleys behind the bar.

At the top of a staircase against the wall was a narrow, dim corridor, its dirty plank floor lit by dim, bare bulbs hanging on cords from the ceiling. Half a dozen doors, painted gay, bright colors, opened on each side of the corridor and their closeness to each other reflected the tiny size of the cribs behind them. At the end of the narrow corridor was a door. It was a heavy door and the cribs on either side of the corridor there were not used for commercial purposes by the women from downstairs, but as anterooms for two or three heavily armed men. They could look into the corridor through peepholes in their doors and if things did not look just right they could easily kill or capture whoever stood at *El Patrón's* door. They would do this on command from him, certainly, but they also had a great deal of latitude in applying their own judgment. Mistakes were few and regrettable, but bodies were easier to dispose of than *El Patrón*, in his own opinion, would be to replace. People who approached that door did so only after having checked in with a bartender downstairs. The police were paid generously to ignore what went on there.

Inside the room they spoke of drugs—drugs, and ways to pass them across the border, and ways to get them to their markets in Denver and Dallas and Chicago and Omaha and other places throughout the Midwestern United States. Other men had the west coast and east coast markets and, truth be told, *El Patrón* was not really in charge of the Midwest. He was, in corporate terms, no more than an upper-level manager. Others above him made executive decisions and coordinated with other groups. He knew that he was not truly "*El Patrón*" in the larger sense, but he had money and he had power and that was enough for now. If he did his job well, brought his product safely to market and found new markets, he would be noticed. Then he would be given more money and more power. He owned this *cantina* now, both as an office and an income, but it was not his goal.

"So, Tomás" he said to one of his underlings, a nephew, "the thing with Salinas and the *motocyclista* went well?"

Ayala knew the man who called himself Rafael Salinas, knew him from the old times when they ran *pollos* across the same territory where Ayala now smuggled drugs. As had most of the drug smugglers, Ayala had gotten into the trade by taking illegals to the United States. Once the contacts and infrastructure were developed to do that it was only natural to shift into drugs when the demand for the product increased so explosively and men from the south came to the border wanting to send their product to market.

"It must be said," Ayala had often thought to himself, "drugs are much more profitable and far easier to smuggle." A two-pound package carried by one man is worth tens of thousands of dollars, doesn't take a truck to move, and it can be hidden in the smallest and most unlikely places.

It was that old acquaintance that led Ayala back to Salinas when he needed guides, for he no longer crossed the river himself – he was too well known on the other side, there were warrants. He sent his son and his nephew, who were not known to Salinas, to talk with him about getting back into the business. Salinas resisted, naturally, but eventually saw reason when the consequences were made clear.

Salinas did not know of Ayala's hand in the operation. To have told him would have revealed too much, for they had never been friends, just toilers in the same vineyard one might say, years ago.

"*Si, tío.*" Tomás Ayala replied. "Salinas led them as we told him to. He timed it so they would be caught at the old adobe house. Alfonso carried the drugs and hid them there. They left no sign of being inside the building, so *la migra* never looked for anything other than what was in front of their noses: *pollos*."

"*Bueno, sobrino mio.* Good, my nephew. Have we heard from Dallas?"

"Si, tio. Our man watched all night from a hill and when the *pinche migra* took them away he rode down and retrieved the package. He took it out to our car on the highway. It arrived safely in Dallas an hour ago and we have been paid for it."

"Bueno, Tomás, we will do it again next week, but not at the same place. Like a magician, we will do things right under their noses by making them look at other things we show them. We will do what they don't expect to see."

"Now send me a woman, the newest one, that girl we bought last week from the farm outside of Mata Ortiz." He knew of her, for a whorehouse must have whores and they need not always be willing, just trainable. He wanted to see how the training of this one was coming along—and perhaps teach her a new thing or two.

Chapter 12

A week later Ken stood on the green, manicured grass in Jim Pope's back yard on a Sunday afternoon, Dos Equis beer in hand. The smell of new-mown grass was still there, fresh and pleasant. He watched as Jim unwrapped a roast goat. He'd never eaten goat before, but he had to admit that the smells rising from the just-unwrapped meat were mighty fine.

It had been wrapped in beer-soaked burlap and placed on a thin layer of dirt over hot coals in a hole in ground the previous afternoon. Then it was buried and allowed to cook slowly overnight. Pope was unwrapping and shredding it and the aroma was mouth-watering indeed.

A huge iron pot of cowboy beans simmered on a crane over a bed of coals from a mesquite fire built that morning in a back corner of the yard and ears of corn boiled in other pots on Coleman stoves. A table on the porch was covered with salad makings and desserts. Drinks were iced down in a couple of tin washtubs in the shade of a chinaberry tree beside the head-high stone fence that surrounded the yard.

One of the things Ken had noticed about El Paso was how much stone and brick were used as building materials instead of the wood he was accustomed to back east. It had taken him a few days to notice why things looked so strange to him when he got to town, but finally it sank in: no wood construction, or hardly any, anyway. It made sense in such a dry climate, he supposed. A wood house would burn like a campfire.

Saturday morning Diehl had told him that Pope had followed through on his idea for a *pachang*a, and it would be the next afternoon, Sunday. Ken decided sleep was optional on Sunday. He'd catch a quick nap after the early shift and then go to the party. "There is," he thought, "plenty of time for sleep after they throw dirt in my face." He'd asked Real if he thought it would be all right to take a date.

"Hell, yes," he'd said. "Everybody will be there with some woman or another."

As soon as the shift ended he called Kate to ask her if she'd like to go with him to eat a goat. Her initial reaction was to say, "Eat a *what*?" She went on to say that back in Ohio she didn't even *know* any goats, much less eat them.

He explained about a Border Patrol goat roast, where the main dish was a roast kid, called *cabrito.* It was a Mexican favorite, indulged in by many who were close to the culture. "Think of it as a luau with a goat instead of a pig as the guest of honor".

With that thought, she quickly came around to the idea.

Now she stood beside him, face turned to the afternoon sun, coppery hair a blaze of glory around her face. Her tanned shoulders were exposed in a spaghetti-strap dress cut low enough in front to be interesting. It was high enough to be decent, but demure it was not. Pumps with medium heels showed her well-turned calves to good advantage. She was drawing admiring glances from quite a few of the men there and looks that could kill from a couple of the wives who had let themselves go over the years. She was proud and happy to be there on Ken's arm, and it showed.

"Ken," she asked, "what happened to Jim?"

Pope had met them at the front door, given them both a warm welcome and a cold beer and then gone back to the goat. Kate had nearly shown her shock at his appearance, but good manners won out; she exhibited nothing other than a charming response to him.

"What's exactly wrong? I don't know, other than maybe he's just nearly used up. He's been shot at and hit; that probably took something out of him. Mostly, though, I think it's the results of heavy drinking for too long. He was an alcoholic for a couple years before he went on the wagon—got that way by spending too much time working in Mexican bars."

Kate thought that over, a puzzled look on her face. "Why would he do that? I thought he was a Border Patrolman. Do you guys go over there, too?"

"Well," he said, "I don't. But some of the guys still work over there from time to time when we want some specific information. Mostly they rely on informants now, though. The information isn't as good as getting it first hand like the guys used to, they almost lived over there for days at time, but doing it this way doesn't use officers up. Just look at Jim for an example. He came back from the edge, but you see how it left him. Some guys got that far gone and didn't come back." He paused for a sip of his beer.

"Wow! I didn't know. I guess I really don't know much at all about what you do. I thought you guys just stood at the bridge and checked people in and out or something."

"No," he said, and he began to explain. "Those are Immigrant Inspectors. They talk to people who want to come here legally and decide if they can come in or not. And they look for phony documents. We work between the ports of entry to keep people from coming in illegally. That includes smugglers who bring people in and take them to other places here in the States, usually to work. Sometimes to be prostitutes, too, and some of them smuggle drugs as well."

"Well," she said with a teasing grin, "the things you learn hanging around with men who dress like Smokey Bear."

"Just remember," he replied, "we may wear the same kind of hat and we're covered with hair, too, but Border Patrolmen are ten feet tall and bulletproof. You ready to eat, Kate?" Her name felt good in his mouth; he liked saying it.

"I sure am. I never thought I'd look forward to eating a goat, but that smells good, doesn't it?

"Would you please get us a couple more beers while I load up our plates, Kate? I'll meet you at that table over there." He pointed to a picnic table in the deep shade under another tree in the yard, and then he walked over to the table by the cook pit and picked up a couple plates. As he got in line Diehl came up behind him.

"That's some nice-looking girl you got yourself there, Ken. Known her long?"

"Not long at all, Tom. We've had a couple dates; she's really nice to be around, though. Helluva cook, too."

"Well, you be careful or she'll have a rope on you pretty quick."

"Listen up," he went on, "a few of us are meeting to talk after we eat. A lot gets done at affairs like these since we hardly ever get together, what with shift work and all. Jim's got some information for us. Sounds interesting. You turn your girl over to Laura to talk to while we're busy."

"OK, Tom, will do. Where at?"

"Go in the back door and turn right. You'll find Jim's rec room there."

Ken loaded up two plates with *cabrito*, beans, corn, and a salad for Kate and walked to the table where she waited. Laura Pope, a short, attractively plump, intense blonde of forty-something, was already there chatting with Kate. Ken thought to himself that she and Jim side-by-side would make somebody think of Mutt and Jeff.

Kate introduced them. "Laura, this is Ken Travis. He works with Jim from what I gather. Ken, this is Jim's wife, Laura."

Anxious to correct an overstatement of the case, Ken said, "Well, not exactly works with him, ma'am. We're both Border Patrolmen, but I'm not in Mr. Pope's league yet. Nice to meet you. Thanks for having us over."

"You're very welcome, Ken. It's a pleasure for me to have people over who Jim takes to. I'd better go over and help with the food now. Y'all have fun, hear?" Laura walked off to the other side of the yard, leaving Ken and Kate alone.

"She's nice, Ken. I like her. She told me that we'd have to sit and talk for a bit while you men talk about work or something. Is that right?"

"I guess so, Kate. I don't know what it's about except something special at work. I'll tell you what I can afterwards."

An hour later Diehl caught Ken's eye and gave him a come-on wave. Ken and Kate stood up from the table where they had been chatting with several other PIs and their wives and made their way to the back porch, where Ken surrendered Kate to Laura Pope. The two women walked off arm in arm, talking animatedly about whatever women getting to know one another discuss. He met Diehl going in the back door.

"What's going on, Tom? What are we going to do?"

"Patience, son. I don't know exactly myself, but you just sit and watch and you'll find out as much as I do."

They walked into the rec room to find Pope and two other officers whom Ken had seen around the office already there, seated in a semicircle in front of a cold fireplace, drinks in hand. Pope was drinking Coke from a can, while the other two were drinking something brown from short glasses. A bottle of Jack Daniels sat on one shelf of a built-in bookcase beside the fireplace. It was a cozy room with leather furniture and western art and it was full of books, books everywhere. It looked very much like a place decorated by a woman for a man she knew and loved; there wasn't a feminine geegaw or frill to be seen.

Pope looked up as they walked in.

"Travis," he said, "grab a couple more chairs from the kitchen table, would you? We already got the good ones." He grinned. "Last man doesn't stand a chance. Get yourselves a drink if you want." Pope was seated in a leather recliner, while the other two had comfortable armchairs. Ken returned with two ladder back chairs with seats made of woven rawhide. He handed one to Diehl, who set it beside Pope's recliner.

Ken set his own slightly outside the inner circle, backwards and then stepped to the bookcase. “Can I get you a drink, Real?” he asked as he poured himself a light shot of bourbon.

“Yeah, please. I better have one. Jim don’t usually put out the good stuff.” He got a “fuck-you” look in response from Pope, then a smile.

Ken poured a second shot and handed it to Diehl. Then he straddled his chair and resting his arms across the top of the back, settled down to listen.

"Smoke 'em if you got 'em, boys," Pope said as he fired up a Winston. The other men followed suit, Diehl rolling one of his neat tailor-mades, one of the others lighting a cigar. Ken pulled out a Chesterfield and took a light from Diehl’s match.

"Boys," Pope said, "this is Ken Travis. He's brand new here, but Diehl took to him pretty quick." He grinned again. "I don't know what kind of a recommendation *that* is, but we'll go with it for the time being."

Indicating the portly, balding, cigar-smoking man on his right, Pope said "This here's Paul Lamont, Ken. He's in ASU with me. He's got some good contacts on the other side, including about half the Juarez *Judiciál.* You ever need planting, he's your man," referring to Lamont's prior vocation as an undertaker. Lamont kept his hand in at the trade, "dressing out," as he put it, the occasional body at a local funeral home. He intended to return to the trade after he retired and in the view of some officers the event could not come soon enough. That attitude was encouraged by his occasional practice of walking up behind an unsuspecting officer, placing the back of his hand against the side of the officer's neck and saying something like "Still warm, eh? Damn!" He was also known to ask,”You going to let me do you when you go?” That would bring about the predicatable response, which was seldom kind, but which always evoked a chuckle from him.

"This other character over here is Pablo Mejia. He's the Senior Patrol Inspector down at Ysleta. I've already told them your story about what you ran into out at the old *jacal*, Tom. Each of them has another piece that might fit in with it. Pablo, why don't you start?"

Mejia took a deep drag from his cigarette and let the smoke trickle out his nose as he put his thoughts in order. He set his drink down on a table beside the chair, took off his glasses and dangled them from his other hand as he leaned forward, elbows on his knees. He looked pensive as he spoke.

"One day last week one of my guys was working the late shift, two to ten p.m. cruising around. I don't know what he was doing north of the Interstate, he was supposed to be down backing up the line, but it was quiet that night so he was probably screwing off. He saw what looked like a light up on the ridge not too far from the Ysleta cutoff, so he went up to see who was out there at eleven o'clock at night."

"He found a man laying there on his back on a blanket under the edge of a mesquite bush, just staring at the sky. The light Billy saw was him lighting up a smoke."

"He'd got out there on a dirt bike, one of those new Yamahas, a red one. He said he just liked to get out of town and spend a night in the desert now and then. He had what you'd expect, some water and some grub, but he had also a pair of binoculars, too: big ones. Claimed he used them to look at stars."

"There wasn't anything suspicious there, it just seemed a little strange. Billy didn't have anything to go on, so he just left him alone. Billy's not the brightest guy around though; you'd think he'd have at least got a name or written down the license number, but he didn't. Some guys just never catch on to the idea that little stuff can matter, even if it don't look like anything at the time." With that, he gave Ken a long glance.

"Turns out, where he was overlooks the old Gomez place where you caught that bunch last week. It's a half-mile off, but he'd have been able to see anything that went on there. I didn't think anything about it until Padre here called me up a few days ago to ask if we'd had anything out of the ordinary going on. When he did, I recalled what Billy'd said over coffee. I'd bet that that's who picked up the package." He leaned back again, picked up his drink and took a sip, and then threw the butt of his cigarette into the fireplace. He was obviously finished, so he quit talking.

"Thanks, Pablo. I suspect you're right." said Pope. "One guy out in the desert at night is no big thing, but take it with what else we know and it looks suspicious."

"Diehl, after you dropped in I told Paul here what you'd run into. He talked to a couple of his sources on the other side. Paul, what'd you get?"

Lamont ran his hand over the top of his shiny head as though he'd forgotten he no longer had hair and looked around the group before he said, "Well, I sat down with a couple sergeants from the *Judiciál*, bought them a few drinks and left some money on the table. I didn't mention drugs, just asked if there was anything new going on in town. Neither of them had anything specific to say, but they did allow that there seemed to be some new money floating around at higher levels in the *cuartel.* Travis, that's the police barracks over there," Lamont said in an aside to Ken. "You can count on the chief getting a piece of any major action over there. It looks to my guys like maybe the *commandante* is doing a favor for someone new."

"One of them mentioned a name though. He couldn't tie it to the new money and they don't know who he is, just someone who's supposedly moving something across the line. I could tell they were pissed at him, too, 'cause he's obviously not paying off or they'd know who he is."

He reached for the standing ashtray by his side and knocked an inch of rich, gray ash off his cigar into it. "The name is *Halcón.* Sounds like a street name to me."

Diehl looked at Pope, finally saying "Jim, that's got a familiar ring for some reason, but I can't place it. You got a look on your face says maybe you do?"

"Well, maybe. Probably just coincidence, though. Five or six years ago I had an informant over there was pretty good. In fact, you were covering me a couple times when I talked to him, which is probably why the name sounds familiar."

" I don't doubt he was feeding me information about the competition, 'cause I'm sure he was running wets north, but the information was always good. We actually spent a lot of time sitting around some of the bars together, him pointing out the faces that went with some of the names we had. He turned me on to a couple good-sized operations. I paid him pretty good and as far as I ever could tell he was straight with me, as much as a snitch ever is, anyway. His information was so good I swore he could see everything going on, so I called him *Halcón*, Falcon."

"I doubt this is him, though. He's been out of the business for a long time. In fact, he told me he was going to quit after I got shot up; said it was getting to rough for him and he was too old to be that tough any more. I don't have any idea where he went. It just seemed a little strange that Paul came up with that old name while we're checking out the action over there."

"So," Diehl said, "What do we know? That it looks like drugs are being brought in and that a gringo on a motorcycle is part of it. And that he might be providing overwatch while part of the operation takes place. That the *Jefe Judiciál* is on the take, but *mordida* is a way of life for cops over there. Maybe it's in connection with the drug operation. But him being on the take doesn't prove drugs are moving; hell, he might have something on the governor for all we know. "

“And, finally, there’s somebody running around calling himself *Halcón*, which might or might not mean a damn thing. T’aint much to go on, is it?”

“Nope,” Pope replied. “But big cases have been built with less to start on. Let’s just all keep our ears and eyes open."

He stood up and walked over to turn on a brass standing lamp in the corner. The room was getting dim as sunset approached.

"This whole thing's getting out of hand anyway," Lamont opined as he looked critically at his glass and then took a discriminating sip, "and nobody back at Fort Futility seems to give a damn. It's been fourteen years since Operation Wetback cleaned this part of the country up and we're seeing the same problems all over again. ”

Lamont was referring to a Border Patrol operation carried out in 1954. Because of public concern over the impact that a million illegal aliens were having on the labor market and quality of life in the border states, the Eisenhower administration ordered the Immigration & Naturalization Service, the Border Patrol's parent organization, to fix the problem.

So hundreds of Patrolmen and state and local cops had established a cordon running from central California to Corpus Christi, Texas on the Gulf of Mexico. They began a coordinated drive south, toward the border. Over the next two months they arrested quarter of a million illegals and caused a similar number to run for home. Those arrested were sent, with the cooperation of the Mexican government, deep back into Mexico. Few returned immediately. Although there had been opposition from some quarters the operation had had widespread public support. It was regarded as a major success.

"I was putting together this month's apprehension stats today and it looks like we'll bust the thousand mark," he went on. "We haven't seen that since those days."

"Yeah, and this time we've got drugs thrown into the mix," Diehl interjected. We haven't had real shootouts since Prohibition and the rumrunners, but look what happened to Azrak and Newton last year out in California! Running a routine traffic check and they get hijacked, then murdered in cold blood. They thought they were just looking for plain old wetbacks when they stumbled into a load of dope and let the bad guys get the drop on them."

Lamont set his glass down with a firm click. "We all better be thinking in those terms or somebody will get killed here, too."

Chapter 13

Salinas walked slowly along the dusty, gravel road atop the levee on the Mexican side of the Rio Grande a few miles downriver from the downtown bridges. The afternoon sun burned hot through the thin fabric of his shirt. Unlike the river in the downtown area the channel here was not cemented and fenced and there was a broad *vega*, or grassy area inside the levee on each side. Outside the levee there were residential neighborhoods on both sides of the river. Those in Mexico lacked paved streets and lights.

There was an amusement park on the American side, Ascarate Park. Along the east side of the park, outside the fence, ran a ditch with paths on both sides. Ascarate Ditch returned excess water, surplus from what was turned into the fields for irrigation north of the residential areas, to the Rio Grande. The paths that ran along its bank provided a convenient passage to Alameda Avenue a mile north, a major east-west street in the Lower Valley. Alameda was a place convenient to be picked up by a waiting car. Because of that convenience the ditch path was heavily used by *los mojados,* the wetbacks.

The Border Patrol knew all this, of course. Because of it they usually kept a close watch on Ascarate Ditch, but that close watch was not so close when the shifts changed. To cover gaps in coverage during the change of shift along the line the Patrol had some odd shifts, like noon to 8 p.m., or 2:00 p.m. to 10:00 p.m., but the shift consisted of only one or two officers cruising around, trying to patrol miles of river. All one had to do to avoid capture during the changes of shift was watch carefully to see that a roving unit was not around. Even being fleet of foot was often enough since a lone officer usually found it difficult to capture someone unless he ran right into the officer's arms.

At other times, Salinas knew, the ditch was watched closely. And that was why he was going to cross the river and walk up the ditch at six p.m. while it was still light and there should be normal coverage. So he walked along the levee with the afternoon sun warming his back, enjoying the warmth, and thinking.

As he grew older the heat felt better and cold bothered him more. Age, it seemed, was a bad joke that the Lord played on a man. The body grew older and could no longer keep up with the ideas of a young man. And many of those ideas never went away, they just became tempered by experience which would have made it all the more enjoyable to carry them out. Wisdom, it seemed, only came in exchange for aching joints. There was no justice in that, he thought wryly.

But though he might not be so strong as he once was he could still walk, walk for miles, as he had proved the other night.

And would prove again soon, for *Los Malos,* the bad ones, as he thought of them now, had come to him once more, demanding that he guide more people across the line next week. They had come to his home, those men without names, as though to show him that what had happened before could happen once more. So he had decided on this way to discover if Pope was still working for the Border Patrol in El Paso.

He trusted Pope. Pope had never lied to him, always paid him fairly for the information he provided and was always careful to make sure that no one discovered they were working together. In fact, he had let loads of *pollos* go when it appeared that to arrest them would reveal *Halcón's* identity and cooperation. As Pope had said to him one day: there would always be another chance to arrest someone, but death left neither other chances nor choices. Pope knew that death is what surely would follow for *Halcón* if anyone discovered their arrangement.

But Pope also made it clear that he knew how Salinas supported himself: by smuggling *pollos.* And he made it very clear that if Salinas were ever caught he was on his own, that Pope would make no effort to get him out of the charges. Their arrangement together was a thing totally separate from Salinas' own business. Fortunately, the problem had never come up. He'd never been arrested and charged. He had been caught a few times with small loads: twice walking in the desert and once driving. Each time he simply told the officer that he was one of the group rather than a paid guide or driver and after a few questions they sent him back to Mexico with the others instead of taking him to court. One had to be a much bigger fish than just a mere guide to face a judge; few ever went to jail.

Salinas knew that he could work once again with Pope. Pope owed him a debt, if nothing else. For nothing, *Halcón* had provided information about who was behind the ambush in which Pope had been shot. That information had allowed retribution to be carried out. The gunmen paid with their lives at the time of the shooting. And so, later, did the man who sent them after Pope and his partner—he simply disappeared one summer night while visiting the *cantinas*. His body turned up weeks later on a riverbank south of Juarez. A bullet hole in his head told how he had died and a single cartridge case, a .357 Magnum, was found in his shirt pocket. The caliber was rare in Mexico and its presence was taken as a hint from the other side.

After that, though, *Halcón,* too, disappeared. Rafael Salinas became just another man who gave up life on the other side of the law in favor of a more tranquil existence, living on the proceeds of an earlier, wilder life. Since he had never broken Mexican law by what he did, there was no fear that anything would ever come of it at home.

He must speak with Pope face to face, though, to explain what was going on and what he needed. Then they could plan how to destroy *los malos.*

But first he had to find Pope. This way, being caught like any other *mojado,* wetback, and then taken to the office, seemed the best, safest way. He certainly could not just use his Border Crossing Card to cross the bridge, then drive or catch a bus to the Border Patrol office. The card was useful, but not this time. Since he had no criminal or INS record he had obtained it without trouble years before. It allowed him to pass back and forth legally for brief periods, as long as he stayed in a border state.

It had served him well in the old days, allowing him to drive a car across the river to pick up the loads of *pollos* on the U.S. side that he delivered to the north. He had always crossed with Dora, his wife. She would walk back across the bridge carrying his card, so that if he were caught it would not be found to identify him, to betray his real name rather than whichever one he chose to use on that day. As long as no fingerprints existed with the FBI under his true name and as long as it took two weeks for fingerprints to be checked, as it did in routine cases, he had been safe. *La migra* usually did not detain smugglers long enough to find out what sort of record they had. By using a new name every time he had always been safe from identification.

No, he could not just go straight out to the Border Patrol office. He might be seen entering the front door by others already there. It was best to go in through the back door, along with a few others under arrest. Once inside he would persuade the officer processing his paperwork to take word back to Pope that they should talk. Then, as was common in the usual course of things, he would be taken to Pope's office, where they could speak in private.

As he walked along he thought of his past and what it was that put him and Pope on opposite sides of the law in the United States.

What was it, he wondered, that made the *yanquis* guard their border so jealously? Why were their laws so hard? After all, what was a border anyway, particularly when it separated into two parts country that had once been one? A shallow river? A barbed wire fence in the desert? What was the point? Texas, New Mexico, Arizona, California; all had been Mexico once.

Those he took north were looking for work. Those who hired them were looking for workers. In nearly every case that he took someone north, there was a job waiting for him. Where was the harm in that?

And if the Americans were so serious about their border, why did they not do a better job of guarding it? Any fool with eyes and a bit of patience could be assured of getting into the country. All one had to do, if he didn't wish to hire a professional to guide him, was walk across the river and catch a bus. Or, if one had the money, he could go to the airport and buy a ticket. One might be caught several times, but there was no penalty, not even a fine, only a day in the lockup, then a ride back to the bridge, to be sent back to Mexico to try again. Certainly within three or four tries, one would make it to Denver or Dallas or wherever. It was a curious thing indeed, this border.

But the border had provided him with a good living and he had harmed no one in earning it. He had always been honest with his clients, done his best to get them to where they wanted. Unlike some, he did not pocket the money, then leave them on their own miles out in the desert, or leave them afoot in some small town when they stopped for gas. It had been an honest living; he'd hurt no one with what he did. Now, but for *los malos,* he could enjoy its fruits in peace. He would see if he could not recapture that peace and inflict a *venganza*, a vengeance, upon them in the process.

Finally he arrived across from the amusement park. As many did, he sat down on the dirt bank of the levee. Most did it to wait for dark or change of shift and to watch for *los patrulleros*. It was early though, only five o'clock. The evening shift might still be at their coffee, so he could not be sure there would be anyone waiting yet to snap him up along the ditch bank. He would wait. Patience, he thought. There is so much to be had with patience. A young man just doesn't understand that; everything must be in a hurry.

Soon, though, a green and white car with round blue and gold decals on the doors drove south on the other levee. An officer looked long at him and he knew that they knew he was waiting to cross. So they would go out to Alameda Avenue, then down another street and wait for him to walk up the ditch bank. That was how it was done. The only ones who got caught were the foolish ones, or the blind. And those who wished to be caught.

He waited another fifteen minutes and then walked nonchalantly down to the riverbank, acting as one who is just out for a stroll. It was all just part of the game of course. It fooled no one, but certain rules and practices must be observed.

He sat for a few minutes on the bank, then removed his shoes, tied their laces together and hung them around his neck. Rather than take his pants off he rolled his cuffs up to his knees, for the river was low this time of year and he could cross without getting his pants wet if he walked carefully.

Stepping off the shallow bank into the river he felt the soft mud ooze up between his toes. He hoped he would not step on a broken bottle, for that was the most dangerous part of this crossing: the trash people threw in the river. Farther down, below Ysleta, where only fields and desert bordered the river, Border Patrolmen sometimes threw bottles into the river and then shot at them for target practice as they floated along. He supposed they didn't care if someone cut himself while trying to reach their country, but he wished very much not to be one who did. The river was dirty and cuts often got very bad if done in that water. Some drank it, but not he.

Carefully shuffling his feet on the bottom, he made his way the hundred feet across the river. Once on the other side he ran across the *vega* to the base of the levee. He stopped there, rolled his cuffs down and put his shoes back on. Then he crept up to the crest of the levee and looked carefully over it, as did those who wanted to avoid capture.

Seeing no one, he scuttled quickly across that high ground, then quickly down off the levee. He came immediately to the path and began walking north, the noise and lights of the amusement park already a presence in the dusk to his left.

He had gone no more than a few hundred yards when suddenly a young man with a badge rose up from the brush in the ditch ahead of him. "*Parate, hombre*," he said in a voice with a slight quaver as he climbed up the bank and walked to Salinas.

"Ah, another young one," Salinas thought to himself. "He did not wait until I had passed to speak and show himself and to climb up out of the ditch. I could have turned and run away before he could catch me. Or jumped on him if I were younger."

But since the young man was part of the plan, Salinas stopped as he had been told. And because the young man had a gun and because he appeared nervous, Salinas raised his hands as well.

The young man, a very young man, approached Salinas slowly. In Spanish that was so bad it hurt the ear, the officer told him to put his hands behind his back. Then he put shiny handcuffs on his wrists—they were too tight and Salinas winced, but he did not speak.

"Jonesy, I got him!" the young man yelled with excitement. It was always this way when a new group of *patrulleros* came back from their school, Salinas thought. Soon, he knew, it would become normal for them; just the usual thing, and they would become a part of the game along the border, the contest between the wetbacks and the Border Patrol.

The man named Jones rose up from the brush some yards ahead, in just the place to cut off a run for the neighborhoods if the young man had done as he should and waited for Salinas to pass before speaking.

Salinas listened as Jones told the young man that he had fucked up and how. "A useful phrase, that," thought Salinas. "It addresses so many failings in just a few words."

The young man stood there silently, flushing red visibly even in the evening light.

"Now," said Jones, "are you going to frisk him, or just stand there with your thumb up your ass and your mind in neutral? The operation doesn't grind to a halt because you caught your first tonk."

The young man came behind Salinas and ran his hands inexpertly up his sides, then down the insides and outsides of his legs. Salinas, who had been frisked before by experts, knew that if he'd had a gun or a knife truly hidden the boy would not have found it. He'd not touched the small of Salinas' back at all, or the front of his pants or crotch. Salinas knew men who carried guns and knives in all those places because they know how easily a casual search would miss them.

After watching the search Jones gave a grunt of disgust and said "Goddam it, kid, I *know* they taught you better than that at the Academy. Were you asleep that day, or are you just stupid? A bad frisk can get you killed. Watch me. I don't want to have to show you this again."

Jones stepped up behind Salinas and gently ran his fingers around Salinas' beltline, being careful of sharp objects that might be there, then patted the front of his pants. He ran his hands down his spine and butt and patted his pockets. Finally, he ran his hands up the inside of Salinas' legs, giving his crotch a firm feel. When he was done, Salinas felt that he indeed had been searched.

As Jones stepped back Salinas took the opportunity to ask, in his most polite terms in Spanish, if the cuffs could not be loosened a little bit.

The older officer understood him; the younger one did not. Jones looked more closely at Salinas' wrists in the twilight. He could see that the cuffs were biting deep into the flesh.

"Jesus God, boy," he said to the younger officer. "He hasn't done anything to deserve that kind of pressure from these things. You want to play get the last click on the cuffs with someone, wait until they've done something bad." He pulled out a ring of keys and loosened the ratchet on the cuffs a few clicks. Then he used a stud on the key to double-lock the cuffs so that they would not tighten themselves accidentally, such as when Salinas leaned back on them in the car.

"Es mejor, viejo?" he asked. "Is that better, old man?"

"Si, Señor, gracias," Salinas responded. He saw no reason to reveal to them that he spoke English very comfortably. It was a rare skill among Mexicans of his class and he sometimes found it very useful to understand more than they knew.

They walked silently back up the ditch bank toward Alameda Avenue, then turned onto Ben Swain Drive, where the Border Patrol car was parked. Jones unlocked the car and eased Salinas into the back seat behind the boy. He slammed the door and walked around to the driver's side.

As he got in and fired up the old Plymouth he said, "Lonnie, he's an old man and he's cuffed, but whenever we've got someone in the back seat of one of these unsecured sedans I want you sitting sideways in your seat and watching him every Goddam minute. It's your job to keep them off the back of my neck if they go crazy and to keep them from shooting or cutting either one of us. You don't *ever* let your guard down around these people. Ninety-nine percent of them are harmless, but if you handle a thousand a year, and you probably will the way things are going, there will be some bad actors in the group and you don't know who they are. At least once a year we find a gun or knife floating around the back of a car and that means that some dumb shit in the front seat screwed the pooch on his frisk, then got lucky that he didn't pay a price."

Salinas understood every word and he knew that Jones was right. He knew many bad men who would kill a *patrullero,* a patrolman, without remorse if they were given the opportunity. And carelessness created opportunity.

"Yessir," the young man replied. " Mr. Jones, are we gonna write him up at the bridge, or take him back to the office?"

Salinas noticed that "Jonesy" had gone away as a form of address after the chewing-out. "Young men are strange creatures," he thought. "So anxious to be liked and accepted and so quick to retreat when the old dog turns and snarls." He thought how the young man had nearly rolled on his back and presented his belly to the older officer a few minutes before.

"We'll take him back out to the office," Jones said. "I hear that Padre Pope has something going on that might be interesting. He'll be going home soon and I want to catch him before he does. You can process this one while I talk to Jim, then we'll take him to the bridge when we come back out."

"Luck," thought Salinas. "Good luck in the affairs of men is as important as skill." He decided to speak of Pope to Jones, but in Spanish. He did not want the young man to discover too much. The young, he knew, often talked too much in too many places.

"Señor Jones," he said, going on in rapid Spanish, "do you speak of *Señor* Jaime Pope, a tall, lean man?"

"Si, viejo. Es el mismo hombre. Le conoce a el? Yes, that's him. Do you know him? *"*

"I knew him slightly years ago," Salinas continued in Spanish. "I wondered if he still lives. How does he fare now?"

"*Asi, asi,* so-so, *"* Jones replied. "Why do you ask?"

"I knew of his shooting back then. I tried to help him afterwards. I wonder if I could ask a favor of you?"

The boy broke into the conversation. "What's going on? What are you talking about?"

"Just hang on, kid. Maybe I'll let you know when I figure this story out. Meanwhile, just listen up and practice your Spanish comprehension."

Then to Salinas he said, "You can ask a favor and possibly I will grant it. What do you wish?"

"I would have you go to *Señor Pope* and say the word *Halcón.* He will understand it and will have questions. Or if I can ask even more of you, take me back to see him. And since you seem to be a man of experience and discretion and this young man probably is not, I would also ask that you not reveal all this to him just yet."

"I understand, *viejo,"* Jones replied, "and I even think I understand something of what is going on. You will let this young man who has not yet gained his experience and discretion execute your paperwork. While he does that I will speak to Pope."

They drove up McRae Boulevard to Montana Avenue, then the few blocks west to the sand-colored, one-story cement block building that was the Border Patrol office. The lights were out in the Sector Headquarters part of the building on the street side but things were in full swing back at Station One.

Once in the back parking lot they all got out of the car. As they walked in the back door to Station One and past the desk officer, Jones said to his young partner, "Hastings, take this guy in and get his paperwork going while I go back and talk to Pope. Don't let anybody get eager and haul him back down to the bridge and VR him before I say so. That clear?"

"OK," Hastings replied. "No VR yet for this one. I got it."

Chapter 14

Jones knocked on the painted, steel door of the Anti-Smuggling Unit. He hoped Pope was still there. It was late for the day shift, but Pope often stayed late, trying to make sense of all the information he had, to draw it all together into a pattern that would allow action.

"Come in, dammit! It's open," Jones heard through the door. Obviously, Pope was not in the best of moods, but then he seldom was when at work. In his middle forties, he had already begun to suspect that his efforts and sacrifices through the years were to no effect, but it was not in him to quit trying.

Jones pushed the door open and walked in. He found Pope sitting at his desk, heels up on the top, ankles crossed, with hands laced behind his head as he stared at the perforated, suspended ceiling. Jones figured he'd either been napping or thinking, and he'd bet it was thinking.

"Evenin' Padre, . . ." Jones began, but Pope cut him off.

"Jones, if you came in here to piss me off, you're off to a good start. What the hell do you want?" Jones had been around a few years and Pope knew him to be a competent officer, but they certainly didn't know one another well enough to encourage familiarity of that degree. The nickname was something that Pope didn't even especially care for from his close friends. Besides, he had a reputation to maintain.

Pope sat up at his desk as Jones grabbed a chair from Lamont's desk and turned it to face Pope as they spoke. He fished a Kool out of his pocket, then his lighter as he sat down.

"Sorry, Jim. It just slipped out, you know?" He flicked his lighter and lit up the cigarette.

"Uh-huh," Pope said as he reached into his shirt pocket. He brought out a pack, found it was empty, and crumpled it with a mild oath. Throwing it at the trashcan and missing, he muttered, "Just about par for the course for the way things have been going today."

"Let me have one of those godawful coffin nails you smoke." Pope rummaged in his desk drawer, looking for a book of matches as Jones extended the pack, one cigarette shaken partially out. Finding matches, he took the smoke from Jones and lit up. As he shook the match out and dropped it in the ashtray he blew the smoke out from deep in his lungs and asked rhetorically, "Gawd, these things are awful! How does a body stand the menthol?"

"Now I don't suppose you came in here to waste my time and annoy me. God knows I can do that on my own. I've been sitting here the whole damn day going through field reports, apprehension reports, informant reports and every other damn thing I can lay my hands on and I still can't work out what's going on. So you might as well add to the confusion for me."

"Well," Jones started, "one of the new kids and I were down around Ascarate Ditch a while ago. We saw an old man just sitting on the other side like they do before they come in. Just waiting there."

"I figured he'd wait until dark and that's what I told the kid. I thought I'd show him how to lay in on somebody, so we went out to Delta Drive and around to those streets on the east side of the ditch. I took him down to the ditch and showed him how to lay in and wait. Normally we'd see him about early dark, so I told the kid to stay down in the ditch until he passed by and then come up behind him. That way I'd be in front of him and we'd have him trapped."

Pope interrupted, "Jones, I think I remember how to catch a wet, so save the lesson for your partner."

"Well," Jones went on unperturbed, "the tonk didn't wait. Sure as hell, not twenty minutes later, here he comes, waltzing down the ditch in broad daylight, just like he wanted to be caught."

"Incidentally, that Hastings kid is dumb enough to eat gourds," Jones went on. "Doesn't listen worth a damn and he's not too sharp at figuring things out for himself, either. He popped up on the guy long before he should have. Even that old man could have turned and run away from the kid and probably beat him back to the river by the time the kid got out of the ditch. But he didn't even try. Just threw his hands up like he was in some western movie and stood there waiting."

"So what's your point, Bill?" Pope asked as he took a drag on the Kool, then shuddered. "I know you didn't come in here to give me an appraisal of some trainee."

"Well," Jones went on, "it looked a little fishy right off the bat, too easy, but I didn't think much of it, you know? Just another wet doing something dumb. But then when we were shaking him down and loading him in the car I noticed he seemed to be paying attention to what Hastings and I were talking about, and in the car, too. I think he speaks English, but doesn't let on."

"Jesus Christ, Jones!" Pope said exploded. "Would you please get to the point? This has been a long day and I'm fixing to pack my bags, saddle my nag and ride outa here." He stubbed the cigarette out in a flat, brown glass ashtray that had already seen heavy use that day. Ashes spread around it on the gray linoleum desktop like a dirty snowfall.

Okay, okay, Jim. Here's the deal. He really gave himself away when I told the kid I wanted to come talk to you about some things I heard you're working on. You know: find out what's going on?"

"When he heard me say your name he asked about you; said he knew you back before you got shot. Said I should come back here and say the word *"Halcón,"* that you'd know what it was about. I figure he's an informant wants to talk to you."

Pope shot up out of his chair as though he had grown nettles in his pants. His face showed the closest thing to excitement that Jones had ever seen him display.

"God damn!" he roared. "Do you have him here? Please tell me you didn't VR him down at the bridge."

"Nope," Jones replied. "He's right out in the squad room. Hastings is processing him. I just hope the old man hasn't died of the pain of listening to Hastings' version of Spanish."

"Well go get him right now, please, Bill. I really want to talk to him—he may pull a bunch of things together for us. If he's who I think, you just made my day and all is forgiven. If the kid's generated any paperwork, get it back. I don't want this guy on record, even under a phony name."

"Uh, sure, Jim," Jones replied. He'd never seen Pope so animated before and didn't quite know how to react other than to give the man what he wanted. He took a last drag on his smoke as he stood up, butted it out in the ashtray, and walked out the door back to the squad room.

"Hastings," he called as he entered the squad room, "wrap it up and come with me. Bring him along."

Hasting replied, "I can't, Jonesy. I'm not even done with the I-213 yet, much less the other stuff."

"Dammit, Lonnie, move it! Pull the 213 out of the machine, shove it up your ass and set fire to it if it'll help you move along, but bring the guy here! Until you know enough to think, just do what you're told. Do I have to draw you a map? Now come on."

Grumbling, Hastings yanked the apprehension form out of the old Underwood typewriter, crumpled it and dropped it in the trash. He resented throwing away the effort that had gone into painstakingly getting answers to the questions on the form in his labored, halting Spanish, then carefully entering the information on the form with two fingers on the keyboard.

It was especially hard because no strikeovers were ever permitted on the paperwork; the Station Senior was a fanatic about it. Every error had to be laboriously corrected with whiteout on the original and each of four carbon copies. Lonnie knew that up front in Sector they had a machine that actually copied stuff. You just laid your original on a sheet of special paper, put them together in a machine, punched a button out came a copy of the original on the special paper. He'd never seen one work, but it sure sounded like a good idea, way better than using carbon paper and correction fluid.

Jones led Hastings and Salinas back down the hall to the ASU office. He opened the door without knocking to find Pope still at his desk, this time with a dog-eared manila file folder open in front of him.

"Come in," Pope said with a smile. "Bill, you and Hastings sit over there at Lamont's desk." Then in Spanish, "*Señor* Salinas, please sit here." He motioned to an armless chair placed beside his desk.

He went on. "Hastings, this is all new to you. You don't have a clue what's going on here. And when we get done, you probably won't be much better off since it's going to be in Spanish. But I want you to just sit there and be quiet; don't say a thing. And when we're done I'll let Jones decide how much to tell you. Is that clear? Just sit there and pretend you're a gravestone."

The way Pope spoke demanded attention. It was not loud and it was not profane, but Hastings knew that failure to take heed would bring about consequences he didn't want to explore, so he just said, "Yessir. I understand. I'll be real quiet."

Pope went on in Spanish, addressing Salinas.

"It's been a long time, Rafael; how goes it?" He referred to the folder in front of him. "It's been six years since we did business. What brings you to us today?"

At that, Hastings silently took note that "Rafael" was not the name the man had given him at the typewriter – he started to speak, but remembering what Pope had said, he bit the words off. He wondered how much else he'd been told was a fairy tale.

Salinas, recalling that he and Pope had been nearly friends, replied by telling him of the deaths of Dora and his daughter and son-in-law, and how he was now caring for his grandchildren. It was important that Pope understand about his grandchildren, for that was what brought him here today.

"Did your recovery go well," he finally asked, for he had not seen Pope again after the shooting in the mountains.

"The bullet broke my hip," Pope replied, "and it was months before I could walk again. It still hurts now when the weather changes, but it gets me around."

"And the man who sent them after you; I understand he is seen no more?" Salinas asked. It was formed as a question, but the tone said that he knew the answer. And it reminded Pope gently that he still owed Salinas a debt. It would be a point of honor to repay it now that it was being called in. And Pope would do so, if he could.

"He is seen no more, nor is he heard from," Pope confirmed. "He disappeared shortly after the shooting. I hear they found his body later. But it is no loss; he was a very bad man."

"Yes, he was." Salinas confirmed. They both knew what had happened to the man, but neither would ever admit to the knowledge.

Then, deciding that it was time to move on to the point, Salinas continued.

"He was certainly not the last of the bad men, though. There are others now in Juarez equally bad, maybe worse. There is a new business of smuggling drugs, heroin. People have been killed over it and others forced to help smuggle the drugs."

"Do you know these people, Rafael?" Pope queried. "Can you tell me anything about who is behind the smuggling? Or when it is to take place?"

"Not very much yet, Jaime. But I will help you find out." Then he went on to describe the kidnapping of his granddaughter.

"One day a few weeks ago I was at home. My grandson had arrived from school at the usual hour, but Angela, my granddaughter was late. She has 17 years now and is naturally noticing young men, so at first I thought perhaps she had stopped to chat with one on the way home. There is a small store on the way where the young people stop for a soft drink and to talk. They are always there after school."

"As the hours passed I began to worry. When it was nearly dark and she still had not returned I searched for her. I began at the store, where a clerk told me that she had been in and had sat around with several other students, then left alone. I walked along the way that she would go home but found no sign of her, nor anyone who recalled seeing her that day. Finally, I returned home."

"When I got there," he went on, "I found two men waiting outside in a car. They called to me, so I went over to speak with them."

Pope interjected a question: "Did you recognize either of them, Rafael? Had you seen either of them before?"

"No," Salinas replied. "I have not seen them before, but I recognize their type—they are the hard men who do bad things for other men. And one of them, the driver, had a familiar look, as though I might have known him before. But he is too young to have been a part of my old life. I wrote their license plate number, though. It was a big Ford, nearly new. It was blue."

He took out his battered wallet and extracted a dirty piece of grocery bag with a number written on it in pencil. He laid it carefully on the blotter in front of Pope.

"I presume you can still trace those—you have the contacts in the *Judiciál*?"

"Yes," Pope replied. "But we must do so very carefully, for the same people who would tell us about the owner of the license would lie to us about it and tell the owner himself of our interest if the money were there. And if it involves drugs, the money is certainly there. Yes, we will have to use our most trusted contact, for if they discover our interest, the finger will certainly point at you."

Salinas went on. "They told me that they had Angela. To prove it, they showed me her shoes and schoolbooks."

"What did they want, Rafael?" Pope asked. "They weren't after money from you. And if all they wanted was a woman, she would not have come back to you. She'd have just disappeared like others have. It must have been something else."

"They wanted me to carry drugs into the United States," he replied. "I have never done that before and thought I never would, but . . ."

“So you did it,” Pope said. “I don’t blame you. I can’t honestly say that I would not have done so myself under those circumstances. Did they release her when the job was done? Did they hurt her?”

“They used her, *Señor* Pope, both of them, more than once. They kept her for two days. And they threatened her.”

Here, Salinas, a tough old man who had seen and done much in his life, nearly broke down. He did not weep; his understanding of manhood did not allow that, but his eyes misted over and his voice broke slightly.

“They told her that she would be taken to a whorehouse and put to work for the rest of her life. Then they released her on the streets downtown in Juarez. I don’t understand the timing, but when I came home after being processed at this office she was there. Someone must have told them that I had carried out the job, so they released her while I was still here.”

With that last statement, something clicked for Pope.

"You were arrested when you smuggled the drugs, Rafael? Were you brought here? When was it and what name did you use?

Salinas told him that it had been the previous week and admitted using his Salinas identity, but changing his date of birth.

"Hastings, you go out there and find that I-213 for me. Look for the name Salinas in the current month folder at the Station One desk. Now!"

The tone brought Lonnie to his feet like a jack-in-the-box and he was out the door in an instant.

"Now, Rafael, do you know who caught you that day?"

"Oh, yes, Jaime. He did not recognize me, but it was *Señor* Diehl, your old partner. I was surprised to see him out there. I had never seen him in uniform before, but it was him; I saw his nametag. And some young man who is no doubt just back from school like the one here now."

Hastings came back into the room, carrying the carbon copy of the paperwork executed when Salinas was arrested. He handed it to Pope, who glanced at it.

"Sure enough," he said. "There're Diehl's and Travis's names as apprehending officers. This gets better and better. We're gonna take this case somewhere. We've got an in, guys. We've gotta play it very, very carefully, but we can get into this one."

Salinas, now among people he would trust as much as he could trust any *gringo*, was not afraid to reveal that he spoke English. Pope knew it anyway, and as for the others, well, it didn't matter now. It appeared he would be working with them all.

"*Señor* Jaime," he said in English, the respectful title interjected to underscore the seriousness of what he was about to say, "I understand that you want to get into this organization. I appreciate your concern for my safety as well. I hope these other gentlemen share that concern, but I must tell you all that I have a personal motive in this."

"I will do whatever you say to help you, but money is not my pursuit here, nor is justice. I seek revenge. I will avenge the treatment of my granddaughter. Finding those who actually hurt her is important, but just as important is finding and punishing the man who sent those other two to bend me to his will by using her. He will suffer for it even if I must die to make it happen."

"Rafael," Pope replied, "you've got to do what a man must, but I have to tell you that we will not take part in murder; we will not help you do it."

"Whatever I do," Salinas responded, "will be done in Mexico. I will commit no important crime in the United States. I will not endanger you or any of these officers. All I ask is that you not stand in the way of what I must do."

"*Bueno*, Rafael. We understand one another. Now let us speak of how this thing came about, the delivery of the drugs into my country."

Hastings leaned back in his chair and stared at the ceiling, a blank look on his face. Suddenly, he felt overwhelmed. The afternoon had started out with simply grabbing a wetback fresh from the river, which seemed exciting enough to him.

Now he was confronted with a part of the job he had never expected. It was men who kidnapped and raped and would commit murder and others who sought what was clearly to be bloody vengeance. And Pope apparently accepted it all as routine, a normal course of affairs.

Jones was not an unperceptive man. He noticed out of the corner of his eye the stunned look on Hastings' face.

He remembered his first brush with reality on the job. What a shock it had been to watch helplessly as half a dozen young border bandits across the river savagely beat a lone man who was waiting for dark before crossing, hammering him with rocks before kicking him into unconsciousness, then robbing him of what few possessions he carried. It had been clear that the beating was done for their cruel pleasure; they could have had the man's money and *triques* with far less violence.

He had wanted to cross the river and help the man, even to fire a shot in that direction to distract the bandits, but his partner had forbidden it. The older man explained that what happens in Mexico happens in Mexico and nobody from this side may interfere. The river is more than water; it is a line that must not be crossed. To illegally enter that country with a weapon, even with the best of intentions, would bring about dire consequences. What would happen, he had asked, if Jones had had to shoot someone to save himself? How would he explain that to the *policía* if they arrived? Especially since the *bandidos* were undoubtedly giving the police a cut of what they stole.

So Jones learned the hard lesson: what happens in Mexico must be allowed to happen in Mexico. Most of the time, anyway. Sometimes, under the proper circumstances and with a great deal of planning and thought, one could make things turn out right. But it was rare and only to be tried by those who really knew their way around the land and the culture. Officers like Pope, for instance.

He would also never forget that those same young *bandidos* came to this side of the Rio Grande to prey and that they would do to him what they had done to others. They would kill him if possible for the pleasure of adding a *patrullero's* scalp to their belts. He intended never to give them opportunity.

He came out of his reverie of recollections in time to hear Pope say "These men who told you they had Angelita; what did they tell you to do?"

"First, they made it clear that they would sell her to a *casa de putas* somewhere I would never find her if I did not obey. There was no room for me to argue so I said I would help them. I ventured one question. I asked why they came to me since I was no longer in the business of smuggling and I had never smuggled drugs."

"They told me only that someone knew how well I could take people through the desert and that I would be leading five people. After that, they told me to go to the Cantina Rio Bravo early the next afternoon where someone would get in touch with me and tell me what to do."

Pope prompted him to go on.

"So I went down there about three o'clock. I sat down with a *cerveza* and waited. Within just a few minutes a young man, he appeared to be hardly more than a boy, really, came to my table and told me to follow him. "

"He led me into a back room. The young man from the car, the one who looked familiar, was waiting there with three other people; one of them was my grandson. I don't know how they got him; he should have been at school, but there he was."

Pope held his hand up to stop the narrative.

"Rafael, do you know the names of the others? Especially the young man waiting in back?"

"I know only first names, *Señor;* his is Tomás. The boy who took me back there is Alfonso." Salinas replied. "And my grandson, of course."

"No matter, *hombre*," Pope said. "We'll find these things out in good time." He started to speak to Hastings, but Salinas continued.

"I believe the young man in the room and the boy who took me there are related. The boy called the other one *"primo",* cousin."

"Well isn't that interesting. This begins to look like a family affair, doesn't it? Hastings, go back out there and find the 213s for those people and bring 'em back here."

"Uh, Mr. Pope," Hastings said, "if I don't know their last names how can I find the paperwork?"

Pope, suddenly confronted with this startling degree of ignorance and lack of thought, could only stare blankly at Hastings. Jones sat there looking at Pope with an amused half-smile on his face, as though to say, "I tried to tell you."

Then, with a direct gaze and speaking very slowly, with long pauses between sentences as though to one of limited intelligence, Pope said, "Well, young man, what you do is go out there. Go through all the paperwork done on the day *Señor* Salinas here was caught. Did you notice what date that was when you brought it to me? Did you bother to read it as you walked back here? Or were you just strolling along playing pocket pool and dreaming about your girl back home? To save you the embarrassment of answering that question I'm going to give this 213 back to you for reference."

He picked the I-213 up from his desk. Hastings, face flushed once again for yet another chewing out, stood up and extended his hand to take it. Pope withheld it while he went on.

"Once you find *all* the paperwork from that day, you go through *all* the I-213s looking for those that show Diehl and Travis as arresting officers. Pull them all out. There should be four more to go with the one in your hand. Do I need to write that down for you?"

"Uh, no sir, I don't think so, Mr. Pope."

"Good, good. That's encouraging, Lonnie. Now, just in case there are more than a total of five, what should you do?"

Hastings looked painfully thoughtful. "Uh, bring them all back to you?"

"Lonnie," Pope said as he handed the document to him with a strained smile, "that's one of the right answers. Understand, it's not the best right answer. The *best* right answer would be to select all the paperwork for Diehl and Travis that showed the same time of apprehension. Not the best answer, but it'll do. Go."

Hastings fled, the back of his neck aflame once more.

"Jesus Christ!" Pope muttered. "Where do we find 'em?" Then more clearly, "Jones, he may be trainable, but you got a job cut out for yourself."

Then to Salinas, he went on, "What happened in that back room, Rafael?"

"Tomás, the young man who seemed to me to be in charge, said they would drive us all down to the river near Ysleta. Once they let us out of the car it was up to me since I know the ground, but I was to cross your drag road immediately after your evening shift went home."

"He described the old adobe *jacal* to me. I knew exactly what he was describing and how to get there. Years ago we used it as a resting place sometimes; there was still water in the well then. It is only short walk from there to the highway that goes to Carlsbad, but he told me to go no farther than the *jacal*."

"Hmmm . . ." Pope mused. Then he asked, "What was special at the *jacal*, Rafael? Why were you waiting there?"

"*Señor Jaime*, I didn't understand then, but now I can guess a few things."

"The boy with us actually carried the drugs. The young man who was there gave him a package when we left the building; it was only about the size of a brick and clearly not heavy. I knew what it was, of course. During the hours we were together, especially while we were walking in the desert, he made several comments that made me believe it was intended that we all be caught."

"And why would they want you to be caught, Rafael? " Pope asked.

"Obviously it was intended that we hide the drugs at the *jacal*. The boy hid them right away under some of the fallen bricks when we got there. What I believe now is that they knew if we just kept going your men would look around the *jacal* to work out the trail and might find the package, but if we were there when you came and if we all split up and ran you'd be so busy and excited that you'd never look further. You'd just put us in your vehicles and leave. And they were right.

Chapter 15

October 7, 1968

Dear Mom and Dad,

I suppose that you guys are already seeing fall in the air, but down here it's still summer. I'll sure miss the fall colors and hunting season up there. It's cooling off a bit now, but that means it's only in the 90's during the day, not over 100. At night it's, down into the 50s.

Overall, I like it lots better out here. I guess I'm a westerner at heart; the hat and boots feel natural to me. The desert can be beautiful, too. Dawn and dusk are pretty spectacular sometimes. There's lots of color on the mountains when the sun is low.

We're catching hundreds of wets. SEptember was a record month for apprehensions—over 1,000 here in El Paso alone. It's usually the peak month anyway, as they come in for the harvests. They work mostly in fruit and vegetables all over the west, and cotton, too. Other places along the border are having the same thing; nobody's seen anything like this since the early '50s.

I helped out on a field raid on a big crew picking cotton up towards Las Cruces this week. There were about sixty people out there working, and about a third of them ran when they saw our rigs. We caught most of them, though, since we had an airplane up to spot for us.

It took a while, though. They don't usually keep running, just until they find a place to hide. That's "lay up" in Border Patrol talk. The airplane can see them, though, or at least where they're hiding out, and guide us in.

The esprit de corps of this outfit is terrific. Not everyone has it, but most of the guys are proud to be here, doing a job they believe in. Nearly everyone works harder and longer than he has to, despite all the mixed signals from Washington (they call it Fort Futility out here.)

Mom, don't worry about me. This job is not nearly as dangerous as a lot of work. Mostly it's just dull sitting around, watching the river and waiting for someone to try to come in, but every once in a while you get to chase someone, or track them across the desert. Then it's really fun. I can't wait to do some of the other operations.

I've got a girlfriend, or at least I think she is. We haven't come right out and said it that way yet, but she's pretty special, and it looks like she sees me that way, too. We're spending a lot of time together. She's really cute and a great cook. If I keep seeing her, I'll weigh 200 pounds when I get to come home.

Now I have to hit the books to get ready for class tomorrow. AS much as I hated and avoided studying at college, it's funny how I don't mind it here. Probably because I know now what it's for: it matters. Our five and a half month exam is in two weeks. We don't have to pass this one, but if they don't like us, a failure is an excuse to get rid of us. The ten-month is do or die, though, so I have to work hard to get ready for it.

Love,
Ken

p.s. boy, is there some old equipment here. My gun probably was in the trenches in WWI, and this typewriter isn't much newer.

Chapter 16

El Patrón sat on the edge of the bed, pendulous belly supported by his thighs, elbows on the knees of his spread legs. Sweat beaded his brow and his penis hung limp and sticky between his legs.

He turned slightly and delivered a backhanded slap across the breasts of the naked young woman crying silently behind him.

To her he said: *"Tu eres puta ahora, mujer.* You're a whore now, woman.*"*

"You may not like it now or ever, but whore is what you are and you work for me. Your life will be easier if you are a good one and you will show you are a good one by pleasing me from time to time. That means you had better learn to put some life into your legs and lips and not make a man do all the work!"

He slapped her again. Not hard enough to bruise or in a place to mark her face, but painful never the less. The blow brought a sob from her, the first sound she had made since she had been brought to him an hour ago. She rolled away, burying her face in her hands against the wall. She made no further sound, but her shoulders heaved slightly again and again. A bleeding Christ looked down from the crucifix hung over the head of the bed.

He pulled on his pants and shirt, slipped on his loafers and walked out into his office. His nephew still sat watching television where Ayala had left him when he took the girl back into his bedroom. Tomás had heard all that went on—the door had remained open and the sounds had had their effect on the young man.

"Perhaps I can teach her something, *tío,*" he said. "May I have her now?"

"You are too young to teach her much, but you may have your pleasure with her. Get her out of my bedroom first; take her back to her room. Don't mark her, or hurt her so much she cannot work tomorrow. Skilled yet or not, she has to start making money for us. Lock her in there when you are done. She still has enough spirit to try to escape. Once we have broken her, once enough men have had her, she will no longer try, but now: *Quién sabe?* Who knows? "

She lay listening in the next room, waiting, hating them and what had happened to her and what she had become. Ayala and several others had raped her half a dozen times in half as many days and she could feel her self-respect and will to resist weakening.

Even more than that, she feared what was to come. The future held nothing for her. She could not return to her village—ever. It was not her fault that she had been kidnapped and sold, but she was soiled now and no decent man would have her as a wife. She would always be an object of scorn if she ever went back there.

But she knew life no other place. Her village and her family were all she had ever known and she had no skills. A silent scream wracked her as desperation overtook her once more. She felt she was losing her mind. She had to escape somehow, or die. Then Tomás came in and the agony continued.

Chapter 17

Rafael Salinas sat alone at a table in the rear of the Cantina Rio Bravo. It had been just him and the bartender and the heat until a few minutes before, when a young woman had come slowly down the stairs. She had walked to the bar and taken a seat on a stool by the cash register.

A boy had brought a message to his home the evening before, telling him to go to the bar at noon and wait. He had been on time, but by now his Tecate had grown warm in the can as he waited to be taken to the back room. The dim corner where he waited was as cool a place as a man was likely to find in Juarez that hot day in the middle of October. The sun lit the street like a welding arc and it hammered down on the outside walls, heating the building like an oven. The overhead fans stirred the stale, hot air across the sweat on the back of his neck.

He watched the young woman with interest. She was dressed like a whore, with breasts nearly spilling out over the top of her gaudy dress, its short skirt slit almost to the waist, but the clothes sat ill on her; she was not accustomed to the mode. The circumstances forced only one conclusion about her, but he found it hard to believe she belonged here. She could be but very little older than his granddaughter he thought, eighteen at the most. The dim light kept him from seeing her face well, but she sat with her hands in her lap, slightly hunched, as though in fear.

The bartender never strayed far from her, and when he spoke to her at all it was with an appearance of quiet menace—she did not look up at him to respond. They exchanged a few words as the bartender stood there polishing glasses with a soiled rag before he nodded almost imperceptibly in Salinas' direction. Shortly afterwards she got up from her bar stool and walked slowly toward his table as though she were going to her own execution. She walked stiffly, slowly, and her gaze was fixed on the floor. She came to his table and stopped across from him, eyes fixed on his can of beer. "Would you buy me a drink, *Señor?*" she asked in a small, hesitant voice.

Salinas had spent time, far too much time he sometimes thought, with the real professional women in his younger days, back when passion drove so much of his life. He knew them and their ways well. This was not such a one as he had come to know in the years before and he almost laughed aloud at her uncertain timidity. He choked off the laugh, though. To laugh, he knew, would only add to her obvious anguish.

"*Ciertamente. Que toma asiento.*" he replied. "Certainly. Have a seat." He pushed the chair next to him out with his foot and motioned her to it. It was a natural gesture for the circumstances, but it also placed her with her back to the bartender. He would not be able to see her face, or hear what she said.

"*Mesero*!" called Salinas to the bartender. "*Dos Tecates aqui, por favor.*"

The bartender pulled two cans from the cooler under the bar. He punched them open and walked them over, dripping ice water on the floor. There was no glass for the lady.

As he set the beer before her he casually placed his hand on her shoulder. Someone not watching closely might have failed to notice how hard he squeezed her shoulder as he did, fingers on the nerve under her collarbone. And he might not have noticed her wince with the pain. But Salinas did and with that he knew the whole story. A willing whore need not be abused to assure complaisance, but one not yet broken to harness must be kept in fear of pain, of what will happen to her if she does not act her part.

With that, he could see the very reality of what would happen to his granddaughter if he did not comply with the demands of *los malos.* She would be snatched from the street, just as had been done before, but this time they would make good on their threat: she would be sold to a whorehouse somewhere, never to smile again, and he would die without knowing where she was.

He gave the bartender two dollars and the man walked away carrying the unfinished, warm beer.

Salinas picked up his fresh beer and ran the cool, wet can over his forehead. "It's hot, isn't it, *guapa*?" he said as he pushed hers within her easy reach. She nodded her head up and down, eyes still fixed on the table, hands in her lap. He pulled a pack of Faros and a book of matches out of his shirt pocket and extended it to her. She silently shook her head no.

He lit his, shook the match out and dropped it in an ashtray. He placed his elbows on the slick Formica tabletop and then with both brown, wrinkled hands grasping his beer, he leaned slightly toward her. He glanced over the top of her head at the bartender and saw that he was sitting on a stool by the cash register reading a copy of *El Diario.*

In a normal voice he said: "Look at me, *chica.* Let me see your face." She continued to look down at the table, so he reached out and gently put a finger under her chin. She raised her head slightly and lifted her eyes to glance at him.

"Look at me," he said again. Then dropping his voice he went on, "If you don't look at me, if you don't act like you are entertaining me, they will hurt you again and they will keep hurting you until you do. So look at me and talk with me."

"*Si, Señor,*" she said in a soft voice as she lifted her face fully to look at him. She was young, indeed, certainly not yet hard. She could never be called pretty, but her olive skin was clear and unmarked by cuts or bruises. It shone with the irrepressible glow of youth and her hair was clean and brushed. Close up now though, the fear and pain showed in her eyes and etched her face.

"They have not yet forced drugs on her," he thought. "A wonder. But they certainly will if that is what it takes to break her."

As she looked at him his age was obvious, and it was disarming. She thought of her grandfather back on the *ejido* near Mata Ortiz, and missed him.

"Who are you, girl?" he asked. "What is your name?"

"My name is Luz Ortega," she replied, and then looked away. She had no desire to entertain this man, no matter what he said.

"Luz," he repeated. "A beautiful name. It calls to mind the soft glow of moonlight on a bright night." He wanted very much to put her at ease. "I am Rafael."

She looked quickly back at him, eyes wide, surprised by the soft words. They were the first kindness she had encountered since the men had taken her from the side of the road near her village as she walked to town from the *ejido*. She was determined not to respond to anyone though, so she looked away once more. If they killed her, so be it. Nothing would be worse than the life she foresaw.

"Luz, talk to me." Then, trying to draw her out; "How old are you?"

"I have seventeen years," she replied. A bit of youthful vanity showed through when she added, "but I am told that I look older."

" Where are you from, girl? A small farm somewhere?" Her awkward steps when she came to his table had led him to glance at her feet and he had noticed that they had been forced into the shoes she now wore. Feet that seldom wore shoes grew wide and flat and often had a hard time fitting into anything but the widest of shoes. It was as plain to see on her as it had been on many of the *pollos* he had smuggled into the United States years before.

"Si, Señor," she responded. "I am from an *ejido* near Mata Ortiz.

Salinas forced a loud laugh, although the conversation did not call for it. She was startled and offended. She believed that he found her rural, farm background laughable, so she withdrew back into the shell she had begun to crawl from.

"Pardon me, Luz," Salinas said quietly to her with a smile. "I want the man behind the bar to think that you are amusing me. If he believes that, he may not take you away and there is still much I wish to hear from you.

A shadow fell across the room as someone came in through the open front door, blocking for a moment the bright shaft of sunlight that fell through it. Salinas looked up to see a vastly mustachioed, well-groomed man walk up and speak to the bartender. He wore an embroidered white shirt, with square tails hanging outside his pants. A bulge beneath it betrayed a pistol in his belt. His demeanor was arrogant.

"Pinche chota," Salinas thought. *"Judiciál, ciertamente."* Fucking cop, certainly from the Mexican Federal Judicial Police. The shirt told the story. It was a type favored by the MFJP, too expensive for an ordinary cop to spend money on. The *Judiciál*, though, collected high-level money in bribes and payoffs and they could afford such extravagant things. Salinas searched his memory, trying to recall if he had seen the man in the old days. He decided that he did not recognize him. Out of the corner of his eye, he watched the man go straight to the stairs, his conversation with the bartender having taken no more than seconds. Since he had no woman with him it had to be that he was going to see someone already there, and it was clear he had been there before. Salinas made a mental note to tell Pope there was apparently some activity of interest on the second floor, that the back room to which he had been taken before was not the center of activity.

Bringing his attention back to Luz, he asked, "Is this the first time you have ever been away from home?" The question was casual, but he was feeling the press of time. They might come for him at any time and he wanted to establish some sort of bond with this girl first, something that would make her see that he was not interested in using her as they intended. She could be useful to him in other ways though, and aside from that he wanted very much to help her escape what was in store for her here.

"Yes, although I have been into Mata Ortiz many times to sell my tortillas." She went on with some small animation, the first she had shown, "I make excellent tortillas, both of corn and of flour, and I would walk to town to sell them." Her face brightened at the recollection of this homey skill.

Salinas could see that if he continued with care she would open up more and more, but he could afford no more time spent in talking about her background.

"Luz, I believe that you were brought here against your will. Is that correct?"

Shocked at his perception, and frightened by it, she could only stare wordlessly at him. "Could someone see through me so easily?" she asked herself. If he could read her so easily, could the others do so as well? "Will they know that I intend to never give them what they want of me?"

"Luz! Do you want to stay here?" Salinas asked in a low voice.

Slowly, she shook her head back and forth, afraid to answer aloud. She didn't know what all this with him was about. The unknown was frightening, especially when it came atop all the other uncertainties in her life.

"All right, *chica,* I am going to try to help you. I cannot do it today, or even this week, but I will do it. I will come back another time soon and ask for you. We will go to your room then, where we will talk further of what we must do. Until then you hold my life in your hands—you must breathe no word of this to anyone. If I am killed, there will be no one to help you. Until then you must delay things as much as you can, give what you must, but do not give up hope. Now I must leave you and speak to the bartender."

He stood, took her hand with an elaborate, courtly bow, and kissed it as though in jest. *"Hasta la vista,"* he said to her, the Spanish good-bye that implies you will see someone again.

He walked over to the bar and said: "She is a likely woman, young and fresh, but a man of my years needs longer with one than I have today. I am here to meet with Tomás Ayala. I have waited long enough. Go tell him that I leave in five minutes." With that, he walked out the back door and pissed against the wall in the alley. When he returned, he saw the man in the fancy shirt going out the front door. Luz was no longer there. He took his seat again.

Chapter 18

Diaz! Get me Tomás!" Marcos Ayala shouted out to the anterooms. He wanted to see his nephew and see him now. He had summoned Tomás some time before and the young man had still not appeared.

"He is still with a woman," Diaz responded as he put his head through the door into *El Patrón's* office.

"I don't care if you have to drag him in here with his pants in his hand, bring him to me. He must learn to pay more attention to business and less to his dick. Go!"

Diaz went down the corridor to one of the small rooms used by the women for their business. He pushed the door open, to find Tomás Ayala between the legs of a whore, her knees in the air, him pounding away with a young man's vigor. Hardly missing a stroke, he looked back over his shoulder to see who was intruding.

"What do you want?" he asked shortly, pausing in his efforts.

Diaz reached down, grabbed the younger Ayala by an ankle and pulled him free of the woman. "Your uncle wants you. He wants to see you now and he insists that I bring you back with me, your pants in hand if I must. I'd rather face your anger for interrupting your ride than his for failure to do what he says—he pays me, after all. So come along. Or must I lead you by your balls?" he asked with a smile, flexing his hand. A smile, yes, but Tomás knew that Diaz was capable of doing exactly that.

So, with a groan, he rolled off and sat up on the edge of the bed. His erection wilted quickly; he watched it with regret. "And things were going so well," he said. The woman, reaching for a pack of cigarettes on the bed table, was not visibly disappointed.

He reached for his pants on the floor by the bed and pulled them on, then slipped on his shoes. He had not bothered to remove either his shirt or his socks. Standing, he buttoned and zipped his pants. He reached over and took the cigarette from the woman, said *"Vamos,"* and walked out the door. Diaz followed him down the hall.

He walked in to his uncle's office, where he was met with a glare. He took a seat in the chair in front of the desk.

"Yes, uncle. You called for me?"

"I did. Next time I don't expect to call twice—business comes before pleasure. Forget that again and I'll send you back to your mother in the country. I brought you here as a favor to her, not because I thought you would be of any use."

The senior Ayala did not care much for his sister, whom he grudgingly supported, and even less for her son, who spent far too much time doing exactly what he had just been dragged from.

"I could", he thought, "buy a *hacienda* if I charged him for the use he makes of the women."

Family was family, though, and obligations must be met.

"Salinas is out in the bar," he told Tomás, his temper clear in his voice.

"He has been waiting while you pleasured yourself. Now he has told Pablo that he will leave in a few minutes if you do not come out to speak with him. You should have been out there long ago. Go and tell him what I told you we expect of him this time. Go. Now! Then come back and tell me how it went."

"*Si, tío*", he replied. Then, without daring another word, he left. He went down the stairs, to find Salinas standing at the bar.

"A good thing you came," Salinas said. "I was about to leave."

Still stinging from the rebuke from his uncle, Tomás said angrily, "Do not think, *viejo*, that you can do anything other than what I tell you. You will do exactly what I say or you will suffer. Now come with me."

He turned sharply and walked through a door at the end of the bar into the back room. Salinas followed. He found four men there, and the boy from before, Alfonso.

He nodded to the boy, who grinned at him in return. "We travel together once more, it appears, *joven,"* he said to the boy.

Tomás walked around the desk at the back of the room, leaving Salinas standing in front of it. Opening a drawer, he took out a sheet of paper, covered with near-illiterate scrawls. Salinas could not read word of it upside-down. And probably not had it been handed to him, either, what with it being so badly written.

Tomás, though, apparently could read it, for he began to tell Salinas what he was to do, referring to the page continuously.

"At midnight we will drive you and five other men out to the border near Mount Cristo Rey and leave you there. You all will walk west on the Mexican side of the fence to the monument that is five miles out." He looked up.

"Is that clear so far?"

"Of course," Salinas replied. "I know the area very well. If we go north from there we will cross their border road immediately. Just east of there is another sand road that leads north. It passes a windmill and stock tank, then goes on to the river."

Tomás replied, "Listen to me!" His face grew red and his voice became shrill. "I am the one who knows what is going on and who gives orders! Just shut up and listen."

Salinas bit off a harsh response and did exactly that. There was no point in doing otherwise, but he took note of the disrespect and added it as one more item to repay.

"You will go no farther than the *tanque,* the tank. There, you will wait as you did at the adobe house, until *los patrulleros* come. Then you will all run, allowing yourselves to be caught after some effort on their part.

"After you have been taken back to their office and the papers done, and after they have sent you back across the river, you will return here."

He went on, "You will remain here this afternoon until we take you away."

Salinas asked, "Must we remain in this room, or may we wait in the bar?"

"You may all return to the bar, but do not leave. And make no phone calls. And Salinas, remember who is in charge here."

Salinas returned to the bar. After looking around and still not seeing Luz, he approached the bartender.

"Where is the girl who was trying to get into an old man's pants a while ago? Luz, I think she said her name was. A woman who would undertake such a job is to be admired. I would have her now since it seems that I am to be here for a while."

The chance to talk to her further was unexpected. He had thought he would be sent away until later, but when fate sent opportunity only fools let it pass by, he believed.

"We sent her to her room after you left," the bartender said. He went on sarcastically, "It seems that your rejection of her brought more grief than she could bear, for she began to weep when you left. Perhaps knowing that you are here will comfort her. I will have her brought down for you. Ten dollars will buy an hour of her time for whatever you can do," he said with a leer. "You will pay me now."

"I will pay you when she comes," Salinas replied. "I won't give you money for the time it takes you to make her presentable for me. When she arrives, you can have it. Now, give me a Tecate." He threw ten pesos on the dirty counter.

"You will have to buy one for her, too," the bartender said, trying to maximize the profit from the deal.

"You will give it to me for her for the sake of my good will," Salinas replied with a smile of ambiguous meaning, "or I will just go in the back room and take a nap and you'll get nothing at all."

Grumbling, the bartender took out two cans, punched the tops, and handed them to Salinas. He picked up the change on the counter and turned to the register without a word.

Salinas picked up both cans and went to his table. As he walked over, he thought with a smile that he had not lost his skills for dealing with people.

Chapter 19

Jesus, but it's hot for October!" Diehl said as he lifted his feet off the floor of the Scout and put them on the transmission hump next to the shift levers for the four-wheel drive. He shifted his butt around on the cool cushion he sat on. The nylon mesh and coiled-spring pads weren't really cool, but at least they let the air circulate behind your back and butt and kept you from sweating through your clothes there.

"This floor is hotter than hell's brass doorknobs. You know why, Ken? It's because the over-educated, over-paid automotive engineer who designed the son of a bitch put the exhaust manifold right behind it, about three inches away."

The passenger's floor of the Scout was just a piece of sheet metal with the exhaust manifold close on the other side of it.

"One day last summer Larry Wilson brought his wife's meat thermometer out here to see just how hot it gets. One hundred and sixty degrees! You could cook meat on that. And what does the Service do? It orders more of the little bastards. Shit!"

Out the windshield the sunglare reflected off the hood, making both men squint behind sunglasses dark as lumps of coal. Mirages shimmered on the horizon as they drove west along the border fence drag road and dust devils spun up from the hot sand. Small creatures hid from death on wings, while a hawk watched with a disdainful turn of his head. He had chosen his next meal, for his circles were getting tighter and tighter. The cleanup crew floated effortlessly above them all, the buzzards. Something had died somewhere close by, for the deathsmell overpowered the scent of the heated brush and sand. Soon the buzzards would land. The ever-present dust in the Scout rose from the floor to clog their nostrils. The sun was halfway down to the horizon; sunset, when it would finally cool down, was still three hours off. Diehl took his arm off the windowsill and took a drink from his jug.

Here, from El Paso west to the Pacific Ocean, the border was no longer the Rio Grande, but simply an imaginary line in the desert marked by three strands of barbed wire and a tall cement monument from time to time. The river flowed down from the north, through the middle of New Mexico, not becoming the border until it reached the west side of El Paso. That fact had fooled more than a few Mexicans into entering the U.S. before they thought they had. They left Juarez following the river upstream, looking for a good spot to cross, not realizing that they were already in the U.S. once they left town.

"Yeah, it's hot all right", Travis agreed, "but I can take this a whole lot easier than I can down at the Academy. The humidity off the Gulf down at Harlingen is a killer. I'll take this dry heat any day."

"Hmmph!" Diehl responded. He took another pull from his water jug and then took out the makings for a cigarette. "Wait until next summer when you're here instead of down there. This is hot for October, but it's still only 90 or 95 and the sun’s not quite as high as it is in July or August. Take a day in late June when the sun's straight overhead and the only shade is under your hat and the temperature's over 100. Then tell me how bad 90 degrees feels down there. Take a right on this trail up here."

Travis ground a downshift to first gear, cranked the wheel over, and headed north. The sun shining through the open window onto him felt like someone had lit a campfire in his lap.

"Hold it! Hold it, dammit!" Diehl yelled as he dropped the half-built smoke into his lap. "Coyote! He's out there on my right about 60 yards or so, a little ahead. You'll see him when he gets to that open spot out there."

The spot he meant was clear to Travis because Diehl had shucked his long-barreled Smith revolver out of his holster and pointed it out the window in one smooth move while he spoke.

As he watched, the coyote loped out into the open space and Diehl squeezed off his shot immediately. The animal jumped into the air, fell backwards to the sand, and never twitched.

"Clean shot, by God!" he exclaimed, pleased with his marksmanship. "Ought to have been in the neck, right behind the ears or pretty close. Let's go see."

Ken started to turn the wheel to drive out, but Diehl stopped him.

"Nossir! We're gonna walk out. I want to pace it off. Builds character, y'know? You want to build your character, don't you? If something don't kill you, it's good for you."

Nothing Diehl did or knew surprised Ken any more, even if it was paraphrasing Neitsche in the desert over a dead coyote. The man was a constant source of revelations to Ken.

He opened his door and stepped out into the sand. As he walked away from the Scout he began counting his steps. They numbered eighty-five by the time he got to the animal.

"I don't take much more'n a two-foot stride in this soft sand, Ken, so there's about 170 feet, not quite 60 yards. Not a really long shot, but a respectable one with a handgun on a moving target."

Ken had been raised hunting, where you never left game in the field. "What are we going to do with him, Tom?

"Do? Well, we'll leave him right here, of course. Reason being, he's a varmint. Some rancher will love me for it since this fella and a friend or two would take down a calf in a heartbeat. That might be what we smelled back there."

"That's one reason I shot him. Another is that practice on a moving target is a good thing to do, 'cause if you ever have to shoot somebody it ain't gonna be like *Gunsmoke*, with him standing up straight and tall waiting for you to take your shot. The *hombre's* going to be moving on you and prob'ly shooting at you, too. And you're gonna be scared to death and shaking and your weapon won't be pointed where you think it ought to be. If you survive your first gunfight it'll probably be plain dumb luck. You just gotta hope it's with somebody dumber'n you."

"Last of all, this critter will be somebody else's dinner pretty soon. By dawn there won't be a damn thing left but a hide, hair and a few bones. So it's not a waste."

Ken thought all that over as they walked back, especially the part about surviving a gunfight. When Diehl spoke of such things he was speaking from experience.

"OK," he said. "Thanks."

They got back to the Scout, their shirts sweated through. They pulled out their water jugs. Each took a long pull, then capped them and got back in the vehicle.

"Where we going, Real?" Ken asked.

"There's a stock tank up the trail a ways here. Usually got water in it. Let's go up and see if the windmill's been working."

They drove on for another mile, the sweat drying quickly from their dark green shirts. It left whitish-gray rings of salt under the arms and down their backs. He hated the way it looked, but that's how it was.

This lawman business isn't all that comfortable. They don't tell you about that part. He was beginning to see that while it might be fun, it wasn't glamorous or romantic. Mostly, it was hot, sweaty, outdoor work. So far, he'd been too damned hot and too damned chilly. The only "just right" had been at Station One processing aliens where it was air-conditioned. But air conditioning did not make up for being at a desk indoors.

"That it?" he asked as a steel tank about twenty feet across and three feet deep showed up just off the trail.

"That's the one," Diehl responded. "Pull up back yonder in the brush on the east side. We're going to be here a spell."

Ken drove over to a spot between some tall greasewood bushes, turned the rig around to face the tank, then switched off the engine.

Diehl said, "Let's get out and cut a little sign, see who's been around."

They stepped from the vehicle. Ken fell in behind Diehl, following his path, if not his very footsteps, as they walked to the tank, then around it.

"Hmmm . . ." Diehl said, "looks like a small group was by here this morning sometime." He was looking at a collection of tracks that came up to the wall of the tank. The tracks and a couple of different cigarette butts showed that the group had stood around while at least two of them smoked.

"Most likely they came up here to fill their water jugs, then went on."

Travis asked, "Any point in us chasing them?"

"Nope. They've got a five, six-hour lead on us by now and this trail's easy walking for them. We wouldn't get to 'em before dark; they'd be up along the river, hid out in some village by then and we'd never dig 'em out. No, we're going to sit here a while and see who else comes along."

With that, he took off his gun belt and trouser belt and hung them on a crossbar of the windmill tower. Then he removed his boots and socks. Finally, took his wallet, pocketknife, and cigarette makings from his pockets and dropped them into his boots.

All that done, he climbed into the stock tank and sank down until only his head was out, hat still on to keep his bald head from burning in the afternoon sun.

"Ahhh . . ." he breathed. "Relief. Mighty nice of the old boy who owns this place to put a swimming pool out here for us, huh?"

Ken stood there with his mouth agape, surprised at this midafternoon dip.

"Well, boy, you going to just stand there and sweat, or are you going to come in here? If you decide to come in, hang your gun belt by mine, where we can reach 'em from in here if we have to."

Ken didn't waste any time joining Diehl. He found the water not quite cool, but not warm either—the word tepid came to mind. The water in the tank was warmed by the sun, but apparently the drizzle from the pipe fed by the windmill came cool from deep underground.

The windmill squeaked as the blades rotated lazily in the light breeze and the pump clanked in a slow cadence as the shaft went up and down. He pushed aside some of the green scum on the top and asked: "You ever drink this?"

"Well," Diehl said, "I have, but I don't make a habit of it. Clean enough, except maybe for some cow slobber, I suppose. That mossy stuff kinda puts me off, but get thirsty enough and it's just fine."

With a grin at Ken, then a glance at the trickle of water falling into the tank, he went on, "Or you could just get it straight out of the pipe, couldn't you? I mean, if you didn't like drinking cow slobber and green stuff." Once again Ken felt like an idiot about asking a dumb question.

Fifteen minutes later they had climbed out of the tank. A half hour after that their clothes were dry again, the heat, sun, and dry air having sucked the moisture out of their clothing just as surely as it sucked the moisture out of their skins.

"What we're gonna do," Diehl said, "is wait here for a few hours after sunset to see what goes on out this way. One of us will always be up on the tower here, watching the area all around. We'll likely come up with a few wets walking through, but what I'm really interested in is seeing if there's anybody running around out here after dark on a dirt bike."

"That tower's about thirty feet high and we'll be able to see a pretty good ways from there. If he comes in after dark his headlight will stand out like a hard-on in a convent and we might even hear him. If he lays up somewhere, we'll go see what he's up to, but quiet. You can move quiet out here, can't you? What with it being sand and all?" he asked good-naturedly.

Travis, who'd learned to move quietly in the woods on sticks and leaves, allowed that he thought he could sneak up on a prairie dog if he had to, so some dumbass dirt bike rider should pose no problems.

"Since you don't know the area, if you spot him let me know so I can come up and figure out where he went to ground."

"Sunset's not 'til around 6:30 and it's not full dark for at least a half hour or more after that. The moon ought to be coming up about that time. It was full a week ago, so we won't have but about a quarter moon for light. Not much, but useful."

"We'll stay off the tower during the day so's not to skylight ourselves. He might even be out there now, looking things over and we don't want him to see us doing anything unusual."

You mean like climbing into a stock tank isn't unusual? But he understood what Diehl was getting at.

"What if he's out there now? How will we see him after dark?"

"We know he's not good about light discipline, Ken. He lit a smoke and gave himself away to that PI down in Ysleta last time, didn't he? We'll hope that he does it again, or maybe lights a fire or uses a flashlight around camp. You keep your eyes moving all the time, don't just set and stare off in one direction."

"This whole thing's a guess," he went on. "I don't know that we'll see anything at all. Probably not. But we gotta be doing something out here tonight and it might as well be this."

"Oookay," Travis replied skeptically. "What do we do until dark? We got a couple hours to kill."

"Why, you're the trainee, Ken, so I'm gonna take a nap while you keep watch," Diehl said as he got his water jug from between the seats of the Scout and took a drink.

"Wander if you want, but stay close. Keep an eye on the trail south of us. Any wets will be coming from that direction and I do NOT want them walking up on me while I'm asleep. I told 'em back at Station One that we'd be out pretty late after the shift ends at ten and us old guys need our rest. Wake me up in an hour, then you can catch a nap, too."

With that, Diehl laid his jacket down on the sand in the shade of the Scout, stretched out on it, put his hat under his head for a pillow and went to sleep.

Ken looked at his watch and then looked around at the sunblasted barrenness that is the desert west of El Paso. At 4:30 the hottest part of the day was just past. At dark it would cool off quickly into the 50's. Now though, it was still ninety, or close enough, and aimlessly wandering in the sun was not appealing.

He walked slowly down the sandy trail, back the way they had come, looking at sign as he went. He was trying to learn as much about the desert as he could.

The widely spaced tracks of a jackrabbit were clear. It had obviously been running, perhaps trying to stay ahead of the coyote Diehl had killed. Aside from that there weren't any fresh tracks. Diehl had told him that except for coyotes and rabbits, most of the life in the desert came out at night. By midday the sign they left would be windblown and old. It looked that way now.

He found a patch of shade along the trail that let him sit out of the sun and still be on the north side of a thick stand of creosote bushes. Anyone walking up from the south would be up to his hiding place before they could see him.

He carefully checked the base of the clump of bushes for snakes. He had no desire to be known around the station as the guy who sat on a rattler and got bit in the ass. *That* would get him a nickname, for sure, trainee or not. He wouldn't be able to suck out the venom out and he didn't think his relationship with Diehl had reached the stage where he could count on that from him, either.

He sat down to wait. What little breeze there was came from the west, blowing from his back and across the trail in front of him. He lit a cigarette, knowing that the smell would not betray his presence to anyone approaching from the south until it was too late. He leaned back on his elbows, looking at the pure, blue sky. He exhaled the smoke, letting it trickle from his nostrils and drift slowly across the trail. He loved it, hot and dry or not, he loved the desert and the solitude and the work.

Well, shit! What a dumbass! They may not smell the smoke but they can damn sure see it drifting across the trail before they get here. With that thought, he took one more drag and then butted it out in the sand. He field stripped the butt, scattering the remaining tobacco and then rolled the paper up into a little ball that he threw into the bushes.

What else am I doing wrong? He looked at his surroundings. No shadow to give away his presence. What else?

Tracks! Goddam it, I left tracks in the trail. I shouldn't have been walking there at all. They point right straight at me where they turn off to this bush and anybody with just one eye could see them from twenty yards away. I don't need a partner; I need a keeper. Now what? Those tracks'll show for hours, even if I go back to the rig.

He walked back to the trail, carefully stepping in each footprint he had left before, hoping that to a casual observer it would look as though he had just cut into the trail from out in the brush somewhere. He did the same thing as he walked back up the trail, mostly obliterating the evidence that anyone had walked south at all.

When he got back he found Diehl stretching as he stood up, already awake. Ken noticed that it was 5:30. It seemed that Diehl must have some sort of internal alarm clock.

He told Diehl about the tracks he had left.

"Don't worry about it," Diehl replied. "It would have been better if you hadn't of done it, but likely they won't notice, especially after dark. We're used to tracking and reading sign. Mostly, they don't. They might notice something from time to time, but they don't go around looking for things to figure out. No big deal."

"Now," he went on, "you catch a nap if you want. I'm done."

"Thanks, but no thanks," Ken replied. "Like you said, you old folks need your sleep but I'm still good to go. I think I will eat, though. It's been a long time since lunch and we might be busy later."

"That's kids for you. All appetite and no brains." He pulled out their tricky bags and water and handed Ken's over to him. They sat down in the shade and dug into their sandwiches.

Chapter 20

Goddam it!" Diehl exploded as they drove into the barren patch around the stock tank the next afternoon. "They're beatin' us like a damn drum. Look at that." He pointed at a motorcycle track that came out of the desert and then led north, up the trail, away from the tank.

It was midafternoon. When Ken had come to work at one-thirty to prepare for the two p.m. shift Pope met him as he came through the door and took him straight back to his office.

"I just got a call from *Halcón,"* he said. "He told me that he guided some people in last night and that the same boy who carried the drugs last time was with them. And he had a package."

"Did they go back to that old adobe?"

"No, I don't think we'll see them back there again right away. Not if they're smart, anyway. No, this time they went west on us. From what *Halcón* described, they left the stuff at an old windmill a mile or so north of the line, about five miles west of Cristo Rey."

"Well, shit!" Ken interjected. "Real and I were out there yesterday. We ate supper and then waited until one o'clock this morning for something to happen. We took turns up on the rotor platform of the thing, looking all around to see if the rider showed himself anywhere. Like to froze my ass off but we didn't see a thing."

"That's Diehl for you," Pope said. "He's got a nose for this kind of thing. He didn't really know anything, but he put himself in the right spot. It was just the wrong time. I'll bet they were there not four hours after you left."

"How come *Halcón* didn't call us ahead of time, Jim?"

"He said they made him wait at the cantina after they told him what the plans were. That's not usual, but it doesn't worry me, not yet anyway. I don't think they suspect him; they're just being paranoid. Goes with being a doper."

"Did we catch them like last time? Why did he wait to call you afterwards instead of coming back here to see you?"

"After he called I checked the paperwork. "King" Cole and that trainee LeClaire caught the guys. The narratives on the I-213s didn't mention what went on when they were caught, so I called Cole up and asked him. Sure enough, they were more or less waiting at the windmill and then took off running as soon as the jeep showed up. Scattered real good, he said. They caught all but one of them, loaded 'em up, and brought them in. According to *Halcón*, the one that got away was the mule, the kid who had carried the drugs. I guess he's pretty fast on his feet. He cut out running south and made it back across the line while our guys were rounding up the others."

"*Halcón* called as soon as we VR'ed him." Pope went on. "We don't want him coming back here to the office any more than we can help. We sure don't want anyone to spot him coming back to this office after he's led some drugs in. They'd kill on mere suspicion if anyone saw that, and since at least one in a bunch actually works for the bad guys, it's not worth the chance. No, I told him to always use the phone and if he needs to see me we'll find someplace to meet."

"What I'd like, though," he went on, "is for you and Real to hustle on out there and see what the sign shows. Then come back and tell me what you find. I've already cleared it with the shift supervisor, so you can take off right away."

The door opened and Diehl walked in. "The kid on the desk told me that you'd hauled my partner off by the scruff of the neck as soon as he walked in Jim. I figured something must be up. What up?"

Pope gave him a quick rundown of what he had already told Travis. Then he added one additional bit.

"*Halcón* told me that he's made the main local guy already. Seems that the kid carrying the drugs had a case of the motor mouth while they were walking the stuff in. He said that it is his father who's running things. He didn't say the old man's name, but when he said that, things clicked for *Halcón*."

"Incidentally, Travis", he looked at Ken. "I don't ever want to hear his name pass your lips. Not here, not out there, not anywhere. It could get him killed in a heartbeat. He's *Halcón* and that's all we need to call him."

"Yessir," Ken replied. "I understand."

And he did. Thinking over the last few weeks had made clear to him that he had gotten involved in serious business. It was not a simple game of hide and seek like some of the other guys saw it; it could be life and death for someone. Including himself if things broke wrong sometime.

He couldn't blame his classmates for seeing it that way. It was an easy mistake to make if all you thought of it was that you were chasing farm workers.

He'd had the good fortune, at least he *thought* it was good fortune, to find himself connected to a serious case with serious men and some serious bad guys. He knew from conversations with the other trainees over beers after work that they'd not yet seen anything like what he was involved in. His exposure made him think that maybe regarding himself as a western lawman really did have something to it. He hoped that someday he could live up to the image he imagined. There was so much to learn . . .

"Anyway," Pope went on, "when the kid said his daddy ran things *Halcón* started looking at him pretty good. He remembered that the kid had called Tomás *"primo"* at their first briefing. There's a family resemblance there, he said."

"He's got a great memory. He finally realized why Tomás had looked familiar to him the first time he saw him and why the kid looked familiar, too. It wasn't that he'd seen them before. It was that they looked like somebody he used to do a business with years back. He finally dredged up the name: Marcos Ayala. Does that ring a bell, Diehl?"

"No, it doesn't. Not right off the top of my head, anyway. Let me think."

Pope replied, "Never mind. I've got him ID'ed and I've called for his file. I'd appreciate it if you guys would get on out to the windmill he described. I think it's the same one Ken said you guys were at yesterday. See what the sign shows.

"Oh, one more thing. It doesn't affect you directly, but *Halcón* said he's got a contact inside the place now. Some girl they just brought in who doesn't want to be there. They grabbed her down near Mata Ortiz last week and sold her to Ayala right away. He and his guys have been using her pretty hard but *Halcón* says she's still got some fire now that someone's interested in helping her. He spent an hour in her crib talking to her. She wants out pretty bad and will do anything she can to put the screws to Ayala. She may be useful."

"Good ", Diehl replied. Then turning to Ken he said, "*Vamos.*"

An hour later they were stepping out of the Scout at the *tanque.* "He's not even trying to hide his sign this time," Diehl said.

It was clear he was right. The motorcycle track came from out of brush on the west side of the clearing, straight up to the tank. There, the rider had leaned the bike up against the tank while he excavated a small hole under the edge of the tank, next to the windmill tower. The scattered sand surrounded a hole that could have held a brick. This time Ken could see at a glance that, like the last time, it had been wrapped in plastic. He commented on it to Diehl.

"Good eye, Ken; you're learning. What else can you tell?"

"Well, the early shift caught the wets a little after dawn, same as we did the last time, so we know he was here after that. The sand under this tank is pretty damp, what with it being cool and out of the sun here on the north side. But the sand where he dug out the hole is dried out now. I think he came in here right after Cole and LeClaire caught the group.

Diehl replied, "Good so far. What else can we figure out if that's the case?"

Ken looked pensive for a moment. Then he went on, "The pick-up man probably knows somehow when the group carrying the dope gets caught. Otherwise, he'd be running the risk of coming in too soon, before our guys do, and queering the deal. Worst case, he might come in while they're still here. I think he was watching from somewhere like he did last time."

Diehl asked, "Do you see anywhere around here he could high-point from? Besides this windmill, I mean."

Travis looked around. There wasn't anyplace for miles that gave a view of the windmill and tank. He scratched his head, looked at Diehl, and said, "I'm whipped. I just don't know… "

"You did pretty good, Ken. I'll tell you what I think, and I have an advantage over you to help me there. See, I know that this trail keeps going north, out to the road along the river. You hit that road and turn east, cross the river into the valley, and then you can pick up the old Mesilla Highway. It's the logical way for a couple PIs to go if they have a load of wets to get rid of. They'd either go all the way back to the office, or meet a D.O. out on the highway. Does that tell you anything now""

"Hell, yes!" Ken replied, excited at his mental discovery. "All he has to do is sit somewhere along this trail and watch for our rig to go by with a load of tonks. Better yet, he could wait out on the river road, where our guys wouldn't take any notice even if they did see him."

"Right," Diehl said. "Now you're getting inside a guy's head like you need to. What next?"

"Uhhh, let me think a minute." Ken knew that the answer was right in front of him, tantalizing in its nearness, but the thought wouldn't come.

Diehl helped him out. "Be nice if we knew where he waited, Ken."

"Yeah! Now I got it. We'll go out that way, but just off the trail . . . nah, shit! That's not it; we'd have to cover both sides of the trail and we still might miss it since we don't know how far off it he was."

Diehl could see that Travis was working it out, thinking aloud, so he stayed quiet to see what he came up with.

"The bike tracks," Ken said after a minute. "He came in from the west, but he took the trail when he left. We'll backtrack him; they'll lead us right back to where he waited."

"We'll make a P.I. out of you yet, boy," Diehl said with a big smile. "Let's go. Lock the front hubs and let some air out of the tires; it's pretty deep sand out there and we're gonna need the four-wheel drive."

Ken walked over to the old Jeep and turned the locking knobs as Diehl let some air hiss out of the rear tires. Then Diehl climbed in behind the wheel, pulled the floor levers into low range four-wheel drive, and set off through the brush

"How far is it out to the river road, Tom?"

"Oh, 'bout a mile or mile and a half. I never clocked it, but that'll be about it. We'll know we're getting close when we get to the edge of the cap rock.

"What's that?" Ken thought he knew, but wasn't sure enough to take it for granted.

"There's a hard layer of rock under this sand. They call it caliche. I think it's some sort of soft limestone. Under that is sandstone. The river wears it away as it wanders back and forth. Finally it undercuts the caliche and some of it crumbles off. Where it breaks off it leaves a pretty abrupt edge. It's only four or five feet thick most places, but it ain't the kind of thing you want to run off of in the dark.

Fifteen minutes of grinding through the sand brought them within sight of the edge of the desert above the valley. Diehl left the motorcycle's tracks and drove to the edge of the cap rock. Ken grew increasingly nervous as the Jeep got closer and closer to the edge.

"Uhhh . . . Real," he said as the edge disappeared under the front of the hood.

"Relax, Ken," Diehl said as took his foot off the gas and stepped on the brake, bringing the Jeep to a halt with the front wheels mere feet from the lip. "The edge of this stuff is solid; it won't break away with us."

"You're real sure of that, are you?" Ken said, thinking of the explanation of cap rock that Diehl had just made.

"Well, never has yet, anyway. Don't worry about it," Diehl stated with certainty in his voice.

"Let's sit here a spell and watch the valley. He's likely gone, but you never know what you'll see down there. Did you bring the binoculars?"

"Yeah, I did. At least we got room to keep our stuff up here in this rig. These Jeeps may be old, but there's some room in them, anyway." He reached down under the seat and pulled out a heavy leather case. Releasing the snap, he opened the lid and pulled out a large pair of black 7x50 glasses.

"Look at this," he said, holding the binoculars out to Diehl, pointing at the data plate on the right half, beside the eyepiece. 'Bausch & Lomb, U.S. Navy, 1942.' Good God almighty, these things are four years older than I am."

"Sure are," Diehl replied. "And old as they are, they still work better than you do." He turned his head and grinned at Travis.

"Take a gander down there in the valley. Familiarize yourself with the layout, where the river is and where the roads and highways go. This is a good spot for it, and seeing it from up here, it make more sense when you're driving it."

He reached in back for his water jug and then took a long swig.

"You notice how much of our gear is old stuff—lots of military surplus, too? Goddam cheap bastards in Washington won't go out and get us new equipment. Hell, the outfit drove surplus World War Two jeeps right up into the fifties. This here piece of shit we're in is commercial manufacture, but even so, it's ten years old."

"I noticed that," Ken replied. "Has the Patrol always been equipment-poor?"

Diehl acknowledged that sad truth. "Has been as long as I've been in it. Seems like if they really wanted to control the border they'd give us the *conque.*

Travis looked at him in innocent puzzlement. "I've seen vehicles, and radios, and guns, but I don't believe I've seen any conques," he said. "Are they critical to the operation?"

Diehl gave him a glance, and then began to explain Mexican slang.

"*Conque*," he explained, "is what a Mexican says when he means the stuff to do something with. You know, the necessaries. It's actually two words put together, *con* and *que,* with and what."

"Ohhh," Ken said, his puzzled look changing to an innocent grin, "you mean like the *wherewithal* to do something. Now I see. Thanks." He continued to smile – *conque,* kon-kay, was one of his favorite Spanish words.

Diehl looked at him across the seat for a long minute, and then said, "Travis, I think you just did a mind-fuck on me. You did, didn't you?"

"Oh, no, Real. I'm just a dumbass trainee with such boundless respect and admiration for you old-timers that I'd never do that. Oh, no. Far be it from me. Not ever."

Diehl continued to look at him and finally laughed out loud.

"Anyhow," he went on, "I wish they'd standardize our vehicles. Take this rig. It's got a four-speed transmission, but those Scouts have three-speeds. And all the sedans have automatics. You can get yourself mixed up about what you're driving."

"Hey, let me have those glasses, quick. I think I see something moving along the river down there."

Ken handed the binoculars to him. Diehl looked through them for a bit before he said with excitement, "That's a motorcycle down there along the river – it might be him! Let's go!"

With that, he tossed the binoculars into Travis's lap, bringing a startled yip from him at the unexpected assault on his pride and joy. *Payback for being a smartass, I suppose.*

Diehl started the Jeep, dropped it in gear and snapped the clutch out. The rig shot forward and Diehl let out a scream, "Ahhhh, shit!" as its front wheels dropped off the sheer edge of the cap rock.

Ken shrieked, too, certain that he was about to die a movie-screen death, with the vehicle tumbling over and over in the air before striking the rocky earth to burst into flames. It all flashed across his mind in slow motion as the rig slid forward, pivoting on its frame rails on the edge, front wheels spinning freely. Diehl was swearing loudly. Ken turned his head, eyes big as wagon wheels, to look at Diehl. He saw that Real had his eyes shut tight, with a death grip on the wheel.

The vehicle teetered back and forth once, then gravity took over and the front end dropped on through. At that point Ken closed his eyes and said "Oh, God!" not sure if it was a plea or an oath.

The front end landed with a thump, followed quickly by the rear end. It was not a violent landing and it came far too quickly to have been a long fall. Ken opened his eyes to find that the rig was pointed down a steep sand slope, with Diehl laughing uproariously as he steered down the hill. Obviously, the trick had been done before, because there were visible wheel tracks all the way to the bottom. It was frighteningly steep, but Ken could see right away that as long as the front end stayed ahead of the back end all would be well.

He looked at Diehl, looked away down the hill, and then looked back. "You dirty, black-hearted, evil sonofabitch!" he said. And then he laughed at having been on the receiving end of big-time payback. "I'm going to have to be on my toes working with you, huh?"

"Who me? You wouldn't think I did that on purpose, would you?" Diehl replied, the soul of innocence. "I just stumble through life, trying not to fall down and break a leg and having to be shot. Now let's go see it we can find where he came down the easy way."

Chapter 21

Two hours later they were back at the office, talking to Pope. "So the tracks came up through a cut in the rimrock, really a pretty steep climb," Real was explaining. "Ken here reckons he must be a pretty fair hand to ride a motorcycle up that slope; it's all sand and loose rocks."

"We backtracked him along the ditch bank at the base of the hill to a spot where he could see the road across the ditch. Can't say how long he waited there, but he smoked half a dozen Camels while he waited. The sign looked like he came in there just before dawn. We followed his tracks north along the ditch bank to where we found a spot it looked like he unloaded from a pickup truck close to a bridge across the ditch."

Pope asked, "Could you tell anything about him from the tracks?"

Ken said, “The tracks, both the boots and the tires, were the same as what we saw last week out at the old Gomez place. Same aggressive riding style, too; it's him.”

Real went further, confirming what Ken said, then telling Pope that the truck was old enough that it had an oil leak in the rear end. It had left a noticeable deposit in the dirt on the wide spot beside the road where it had been parked. The front tires looked to be nearly bald, as well. All in all, it was probably the sort of beat-up rig that you saw a hundred times a day along the border. What might draw their attention now was such a truck with a red Yamaha in the back.

He had also seen something that was chilling—there was a print in the dust alongside the tracks left by the truck. It was apparently made by a rifle butt. The size and shape of the imprint in the dust showed it was a small, checkered steel buttplate, probably the type found on a lot of military rifles. It indicated the man had leaned a rifle against the truck while he took a leak in the bushes a step away. And there was a single cartridge, a .223 round pressed into the dirt. Small and high-velocity, it was a very destructive bullet when it struck flesh. It was the type used in the U.S. Army's M-16 and several civilian lightweight rifles as well. The head stamp on the case and the full metal jacket on the bullet indicated that it had been turned out for military use. Its position indicated that it probably rolled out of the vehicle's floor into the dust and been stepped on when the driver got out.

"Now don't that just make your asshole chew holes in your pants?" Diehl finished. "Throws a whole new light on what we're up against. The ole boy ain't hauling that iron around just for fun. If all he wanted was to kill snakes or just protect himself he'd carry a pistol. No, he's got himself a long-range shooter for a reason. I don't think he figures on letting anybody get close enough to him to be threat once he's carrying the dope. As long as he can pass for just being some guy out in the desert on his bike it's OK, but Lord help whoever gets on his trail if he's carrying the stuff. He can shoot it out with 'em and then head for the border just about anywhere he wants. Yessir. The rule is handle with care."

“What do you think, Tom?” Pope asked, “Any way to guess if he has some military connection? Far’s I know there’s not any of that military .223 ammunition in general circulation yet. I think all the stuff in civilian hands is commercial manufacture, no surplus sold off yet. What with the way they burn it up over in Viet Nam it’ll be a long time before we see the government stuff for sale. And since there’s all that basic training going on out at Fort Bliss, there’s a lot of shooting. If he’s a GI that’d give him the chance to pick up a case or two of ammo for his own use.”

Ken was absorbing it all. This exposure to deductive thinking was a revelation. The idea about watching for an old, raggedy truck with a red dirt bike in the back made sense; there were lots of trucks like that around and a fair number of red Yamahas, but together, close to the border? And it wouldn’t have occurred to him to think of a military connection based on one single bullet in the dirt.

With that, a thought came to him.

“Uh, Tom. Can we get onto the base? If we can drive around the barracks and housing areas we might just spot a rig like that in some parking lot or driveway. Get a plate number and see who it is.”

"Now there's a thought," Pope replied before Diehl did. "You'd want to do it in a plain vehicle and wear civvies or he might spot you and get hinky, but it'd sure be safe shortcut to an ID, wouldn't it?"

"Yeah, it would," Diehl agreed. "My guess is that if he is a soldier he's on the training cadre out there. I doubt that a recruit would have a chance or the nerve to steal ammunition, but somebody who was a part of training and demonstration firings . . . that's another deal. Let's do it. It may be that he doesn't even live on post, but it won't hurt to have a look this afternoon. We'll take my truck over and have a look around the base housing and barracks."

Chapter 22

Ken left the office just before midnight that day, intending to go back to his apartment. He thought that if he was lucky he'd find Kate's lights on and stop in to visit, but on the way home he remembered that she was on an overnight to Houston and wouldn't be back 'til tomorrow afternoon.

So he turned around and headed out to a county park where he knew he'd find some of the guys decompressing. He hadn't been down to a choir practice yet, but he'd heard about it.

He drove through the empty park until he found a cluster of cars in one of the lots and saw the glow of cigarettes in the dark. His headlights swept across the park as he turned in from the lane, revealing half a dozen men seated at picnic tables and a few more leaning against the trees.

He parked his GTO and walked over to the picnic pavilion.

"Grab a beer, *compadre*, and pull up a bench," Pete LeClaire called as Ken walked up to the table.

Ken found a washtub full of ice and beer in the corner. He pulled out a Budweiser. "Who's the money man here?" he asked. "Somebody paid for this."

"First one's on me," LeClaire said. "After that I'll take thirty cents a can."

"Thanks, Pete," Ken said. He bent over and picked up the church key tied by a string to the handle of the tub and punched the top of his can. He took a deep swig of the beer and then reached into his shirt pocket for a cigarette. As he lit it he looked around the dark pavilion to see who was there. It looked like there were eight or ten guys and maybe a couple more out in the bushes answering nature's call. There were also a couple of girls he didn't recognize who didn't seem to belong with anyone. He'd heard stories about how a few women would show up to party sometimes and occasionally help a guy relieve a little biological backpressure.

"Howdy, Dunn," he said as he sat down to the man sitting across from LeClaire on the picnic table bench. Dunn nodded once in response and emitted a surly grunt.

"Must be PX beer at this price, huh?" he said to LeClaire. He knew that Pete had been in the Air Force and still had PX privileges that he used to provide the liquids needed at Border Patrol affairs.

"What are you doing here at this hour?" he went on. "Didn't you work the early shift today? I heard you and King Cole caught a bunch this morning out in the west desert just after dawn."

"Yeah, we did. It was noon before we got done, too. I went home and caught a nap, then woke up about six and watched TV for a while. I don't have to work tomorrow, so I grabbed a couple cases of beer out of the closet and brought 'em down here. Ever since the old lady and I split up I can do whatever I want when I want." He took a pull from his can. There was a wistful note in his voice.

LeClaire had come to the Border Patrol from a small town in northern Maine after he'd retired from the Air Force after twenty years. He and Ken had become friendly at the Academy. From conversations there Ken knew that LeClaire's wife had refused to leave Maine when he was hired for the Border Patrol. She'd followed him around while he was in the Air Force, and no way, she had told him, was she moving away from her family again. Pete wondered what he was, if not her family. Ken had no good answer for him. LeClaire wasn't the only Border Patrolman who'd run into the problem. It made Ken glad he didn't have complications like that in his life.

"Tell me about this morning, Pete, what'd you get? Anything funny about it?"

"Cole and I were cutting sign on the border drag road just before dawn and came across the tracks of six out at Monument Five. They crossed and started right up a trail that leads to an old windmill and stock tank. They must have heard us coming, but they were still standing around together when we pulled into the place. Cole said the cigarette butts on the ground showed they'd been there standing around for a while. That was strange; they could have been all the way out to the valley if they had just kept going. Maybe they were waiting for someone."

"Anyway, once we saw 'em they took off in all directions like a covey of quail. We caught five, but one of 'em headed back down the trail and got back to the border before we had rounded up the others. Five out of six ain't bad, though, huh?"

Ken replied, "Yeah, that's pretty good for that close to the border, I guess."

"So what's the deal, Travis?" Dunn asked as he rocked one cheek of his ass up off the bench and farted loudly. "You some sort of fucking intelligence officer now, or something? Hanging around Pope's office and kissing Diehl's ass. You get to work out in the sand hills while the rest of us sit on the line downtown?"

"Dunn, . . ." Ken flared and looked across the table at him, "Aw, forget it." He turned back to LeClaire, but then he turned back to Dunn once more and said, "Steve, you hang around with the right people, pay attention to what they do and say, and do your job and you'll be a whole lot better off. Who knows? You might even turn out to be worth a shit some day."

Dunn sprang up and leaned across the table at Travis, saying "You pussy! I'm gonna kick your ass!" Ken tensed and returned Dunn's glare. He stayed seated, waiting for Dunn to come across the table at him, ready to take him by the front of his jacket and keep him coming until he landed face-first in the dirt.

LeClaire turned to face Dunn and said, "Not tonight, Dunn! Sit down, or we'll all kick your ass just on general principles." Dunn stood there, leaning on his knuckles on the table, before he straightened up with a snort, saying "Later, Travis. I'll be seeing you." Ken didn't respond. He watched Dunn walk across the park to his car, get in and leave, spewing gravel as he did.

"The shithead's been nothing but a pain in the ass since he showed up at school," LeClaire said. "With any luck he won't make probation."

"But he does have a point," he went on. "I got lucky and pulled a sand hills shift this morning when somebody called in sick, but it was the first time I've been out there. You have all the luck. How come?"

"Damned if I know, Pete." Ken replied. "They sent me out there for what was going to just be a day or two of familiarization, but seems like The Real Diehl took a shine to me right off for some reason. We've been partnered up ever since, must be a month now. I know Pope because of Diehl. They're both good guys, and boy, have they got some stories to tell about the old Patrol. Did you know they used to work together across the river, undercover?"

"I've heard some of the journeymen mention the Special Detail," LeClaire responded, "but I didn't know those two had been a part of it. I guess that explains why Pope looks like does, like some skid row alky."

"Yeah," Ken said. "He looks like death warmed over, doesn't he? But Real tells me that Pope gave booze up five years ago. Did it cold turkey, on his own—well, with some help from his wife, I guess."

"Anyway, Pope told Diehl and me about some information about a load of dope that came in last night. He told us that it was dropped at the windmill this morning, so we went out to see what the sign looked like. You and Cole were right on top of it when you caught that group. We think they waited for you, then split up and ran to draw you away from the place. The one that got away was probably the mule."

LeClaire swore long and colorfully in three languages.

Travis went on. "It looks like that load was part of an operation that Diehl and I stumbled onto last month. Pope's putting some of the pieces together. He thinks that all of us out in the field ought to know what's going on or somebody might stumble into it blind and get hurt. You think I'd piss anybody off if I tried to pass the word on to them here tonight?" LeClaire was in his late thirties, older than most of the new officers. He'd been a Master Sergeant in the Air Force and Ken trusted his judgment about people.

"I don't think so, Ken, as long as you just pass along useful information and don't go lording it over them like your shit don't stink. Let me break it to them first, though."

"Hey, everybody!" he yelled. "Come on over here. We gotta talk—this is business. Johnson! Turn loose of that bimbo, pull up your pants and come out of the bushes. He turned to the next table and said, "You women beat it; this has got nothing to do with you. You hear it and we'll have to kill you." The two women in the pavilion started walking out to their car, each still carrying her beer and grumbling. "Jeanette!" one of them yelled over her shoulder. "C'mon or you're going to have to walk home."

Jeanette came out of the bushes, running her fingers through her hair and then tucking her blouse into her skirt as she trotted across the parking lot after the others. Johnson was close behind her, but he turned off into the pavilion.

"Lord, God," he said as he came into the shelter. "They oughta call that woman Hoover. She could suck a gopher out of his hole. This better be good, LeClaire."

The others gathered around and LeClaire began, "Ken here has been working with Diehl out in the sand hills. They've come up with something that he thinks we oughta know about. Hear him out, then we'll piss down his neck if he wasted our time."

That wasn't exactly the introduction that Ken hoped for, but it was all he was going to get, so he stood up and began to talk.

"Some of you guys may have noticed that The Real Diehl has sort of adopted me. I don't know why, just lucky, I guess, but there it is. Working with him has let me see some interesting stuff."

"Anyway, to make a long story short, it looks like somebody on the other side is sending drugs over here."

There was a general laugh from the group. "Like that's news," Johnson said. "I gave up a primo blow job to hear that? LeClaire, you hold him down while I unzip my pants."

"No, there's more", Ken said. "Hear me out; it gets better."

"You better hope so," Johnson growled.

"It looks like what they're doing is having a someone in a group of wets carry the load in with the group. They hide the load somewhere, then the group hangs around it waiting to be found. Once we show up, they run like hell and draw us away from the load. They make sure they get caught, so that the guys who catch 'em have to load them up and haul ‘em out. That leaves a hole in the coverage in that area. Then somebody on a dirt bike comes in and picks up the load and takes it out."

"How do you know so much about it," someone asked out of the dark. His cigarette suddenly glowed brightly as he took a drag, illuminating his face. It was someone Ken didn't know yet.

"Because the first time we know that it happened, Diehl and I were the suckers who caught the group and left the dope behind. Cole and LeClaire were the patsies this morning out at a windmill in the west desert. The sign shows they had no more than left with their bunch when the guy came in on his bike and took a package out from under the stock tank."

“Well, shit, oh dear,” LeClaire muttered, annoyed anew.

"We got any kind of make on the bike?"

"Yeah," Ken said. "We got lucky there. A PI who shall remain nameless to protect the guilty actually talked to him out in the desert near Ysleta last month, the night before Diehl and I caught the group that brought the load in. He was camped out when our guy found him, probably overwatching the drop area. He was riding a red Yamaha DT1. We don't have the plate number or a name. Even the description’s pretty thin; he’s tall, in his late twenties or so. Swarthy; might be Latino, but we’re not sure about that part."

"This afternoon Diehl and I backtracked him from the windmill to a spot by the Mesilla Highway. It looks like he unloaded his bike from a pickup truck there, probably an old one. It was dripping oil and the tires are pretty well used up. We found another spot where he waited for Cole and LeClaire to come down off the rimrock with the wets before he went and picked up the dope. Once he saw 'em he knew the coast was clear for him to go pick up the stuff."

"Diehl noticed something else where the rider parked his truck—this what I really want to tell you to look out for. It looks like he's carrying a rifle, a .223. Diehl found a round in the dirt by where the truck was, like it had fallen out of the truck. There was the print of a steel buttplate, too, where he'd leaned the rifle against the truck."

The men were now listening closely. Drugs were one thing; a smuggler carrying a rifle called for heads-up attention.

Ken hesitated as he pondered whether to mention that it might be a soldier on the bike and that there was an informant involved. He decided that nobody needed to know about the informant but he did tell them about the suspicions of a military connection. An armed man with military training called for a different approach than a couple of Mexicans hiking to Colorado.

"I figured this would be a good place to put the word out. I hope you'll pass it on. And keep an eye open for an old pickup truck driving around out in the sand hills with a red dirt bike in the back. If I saw it, I'd leave it alone and call for help, but that's your call. We don't know anything about him except that he carries a rifle when he goes to work and it's not likely he does it for fun. But if we lay in on the truck, we might catch him when he comes back with the dope."

Chapter 23

Ken walked into the classroom at Sector Headquarters at 7:45 a.m. and took his seat in the middle of the room. The gray floor of linoleum tiles gleamed and the blackboard was freshly washed by alien volunteers from the detention center behind Sector Headquarters. There was a faint smell of Pine-Sol in the air.

He pulled out his Nationality Law book and began to try to get straight in his mind just when somebody born abroad to U.S. parents was a U.S. citizen and what he had to do to keep that citizenship. The law had changed several times over the years. Since you could reasonably expect meet someone on the job who was born any time between the turn of the twentieth century and last week, it was information you needed to have down cold. The Border Patrol had no business messing with U.S. citizens unless they broke some criminal provision of the law, like smuggling.

Pete LeClaire came in and took a seat beside Ken.

"How's it look today, *compa,"* he asked. "Any clearer than last time?"

"Goddam it, Pete, why do they make it so complicated? Good Lord, there's about ten different factors to memorize on this chart. Father citizen or mother a citizen, or both are citizens. There's about three 'born on or after' dates. Then there's the 'lived in the U.S. for *X* years before whatever birthday to retain citizenship.' If I don't get it settled in my head soon I'm gonna bust that five and half month exam for sure."

Pete smiled widely at him. He was one of those fortunate people who can look at a matrix or grid of facts and repeat it back with his eyes closed.

"Tell you what, Ken. The Spanish irregular verb conjugations are kicking my ass. Why don't you come on over to the house and we'll go over all this stuff a couple nights this week."

Ken, to whom Spanish came easily, agreed.

The other fifteen men in the class trickled in one by one. Steve Dunn arrived, apparently still angry because he glared at Ken and muttered, "Fuck you, Travis," as he walked to his seat in the back of the room.

Ken grinned at him as he replied, "And fuck you twice, Dunn."

Mr. Lopez came in and walked straight to the blackboard. As usual, he picked up the pointer, but this time he turned sharply and pointed it at Dunn.

"Mr. Dunn, give me a brief discourse on the concept of waivers of deportability. What are the most common waivers you, as a Border Patrolman, are likely to encounter?"

"Uhhh," Dunn began, "anyone who is found deportable can apply for a waiver of the order and be allowed to stay in the U.S." His voice tapered off as he expended the sum total of his knowledge.

"Mr. Dunn, " Lopez said, fixing him with a hard stare, "the past weeks have shown me that your comprehension of the law is apparently an inch wide and an inch deep, a mere trickle of thought and knowledge. If you do not increase it to at least the scope of the Rio Grande, which is only a small river, you are going to fail your five and half month exam in spectacular fashion this month. That very day you will find yourself on your ass outside the front door of this Sector Headquarters. Is that an acceptable outcome for you?"

Dunn resentfully grumbled a low "No, sir," which apparently satisfied Lopez, who replied, "Then see that you improve your work—you don't have long. I will help you however I can, but the work is yours to be done."

"Sir," one of the other trainees said, "why are there immigration laws at all? I mean, I understand what we're supposed to do on the job and all, but *why?"*

As in every class since a cave man taught flint-knapping, students will try to lead an instructor astray into fields not on the day's lesson plan. The best of teachers recognize those digressions as an opportunity to teach, not just to instruct. Lopez was a good teacher.

He walked in front of his desk and leaned his buttocks back on the edge of it, the palms of his hands thrust down on the desk. His torso leaned toward the class. It was as near to a casual posture as any of them had ever seen him assume, but the position still demanded attention. He looked intently at them all before he said "Mr. Hanson, that is an excellent question, one not covered in the syllabus at the Academy or here. That course of study is structured around the 'hows' of doing your job. But your question is one that deserves some thought, believing as we do that we are a nation of immigrants."

Here, he smiled as he said, "You are a lucky bunch, for it has been your good fortune to stumble upon a man who has given the issue quite some thought. It is an issue that ninety-nine percent of the people in this country, when they think at all about immigration, do not understand. For the sake of brevity I am going to reduce it to its essentials and let you fill in the blanks."

Here he began to tick points off on his fingers. He spoke in clear sentences and full paragraphs, not wandering, in total command of his subject.

"Overall, the laws are intended to protect the country. You will no doubt have noticed that a substantial portion of your law books defines who *may* come to this country. Anyone not in a class defined by law as eligible to enter *may not* enter the United States. For instance, a foreigner may come here as a tourist, but before we let him in he must prove that he actually *is* a tourist, not someone intending to stay here."

"Furthermore, even someone who is allowed to come here may be required to depart on his own, or may be forcibly deported, for any number of reasons. You will notice that another section of your law book goes on at great length defining what those reasons are."

"But your question was: why do we exercise control like that at all?"

"First, the laws are intended to protect the national security and public safety. People who would do ill to the nation or its people are not allowed to come or to stay; Communists, for instance, or others who would overthrow our government by force. Criminals may not come, nor may aliens stay if convicted here of serious crimes. By their conduct they have shown that they are unwilling to abide by a set of laws designed to ensure a peaceful, orderly society. They have no place in ours."

"Second, the laws exist to protect domestic labor. An excess supply of foreign labor in the country has an adverse effect on wages and working conditions. The law of supply and demand applies to labor as surely as it does any other commodity. You may reduce it to this thought; as sweat becomes more available, it becomes cheaper. People who come from Mexico, for example, are willing to work for lower wages, and in worse conditions, than people who have grown up here.

That means that American labor must be willing to settle for less if they are to compete successfully for jobs. And, I must add, they are losing the battle."

"And finally, the law is intended to protect public health. People with contagious diseases typically may not come here. There are exceptions for temporary visits for treatment and for the immediate relatives of resident aliens and U.S. citizens. We have diseases under control here that are epidemic in other places, tuberculosis, for instance. It is common in Mexico; Border Patrolmen, because they are so often in contact with infected people, should pay attention to their own health."

He paused and looked around the room again. The class seemed to grasp this simple concept, so he said, "Now, let us get on with the day's work. Your exam approaches quickly."

"Mr. Travis, let's talk about citizenship at birth."

Chapter 24

Full of steak and red wine, Ken leaned back in his chair. Once again, they were seated around the table's corner from one another, and they felt close. A yellow candle in a glass holder burned at the far corner of the table, making patterns on the white tablecloth through the wine in their glasses. He watched the flicker of the soft light it cast on Kate's face as she finished her medium rare T-bone. She had, Ken thought, a healthy appetite.

She glanced up from carving what remained of her steak from the bone and caught him looking at her. She smiled widely at him and then put a small bite in her mouth. Finally, she swallowed it; as she reached for her wine she said, "This was a great idea, Ken. I'm glad you thought of it."

He and Kate had come once more to the *posada* in Cloudcroft, but this time she had managed to get two days off to coincide with his. They'd taken a single room when they arrived that afternoon and each knew what that implied. Although they had not spoken of it, each knew that the other was ready. It was time.

They'd eaten well this first evening and were now waiting for dessert. For the first time there was some small tension between them. Or perhaps it was just unspoken anticipation.

"So anyway," Ken continued, "we waited out there until one a.m. and didn't see a darn thing. And cold? I should hope to tell you! Sitting up on top of that windmill in the dark with a medium breeze blowing and the temperature probably in the high forties? Up north I've sat outside on a deer stand when the temperature was near zero and haven't been that cold. 'Course I was dressed for it then. That desert cools off fast once the sun goes down and a windbreaker on a night like that just isn't enough. I'll bet we saw a fifty degree temperature spread that day."

He wasn't comfortable talking to anyone outside the Patrol about the details of what they were actually doing, so he changed the subject.

"Tell me," he went on, "what's happening in the world of aviation?" She'd been gone for the last three days and both felt the separation. They had been seeing a great deal of each other for the last few weeks, but her flights and his shifts had kept their contacts brief. And not yet intimate.

"Well, I spent those three days in Dallas covering for one of the other girls there who's been sick, but you knew that. She's better now though, so I'm back. I'll be making an overnighter to L.A. day after tomorrow. Same old thing, I guess."

She looked pensive, then went on, "Lots of the girls become stews looking for the glamour of flying around, but there's not much glamour involved as far as I'm concerned. Being honest with myself, I have to admit that we're mostly airborne waitresses who spend a lot of nights away from home. They train us to deal with crash situations and cabin emergencies, but of course none of us ever wants to go through that! It pays pretty well though, compared to most women's jobs, and we do meet some interesting people."

"And", Ken said, "you might find a pilot to marry." He was fishing.

"Lots of the girls do," she replied after she chewed her last bite a little longer than she really needed to. "In fact, that's another reason some of them take the job—husband hunting. Pilots are supposed to be a good catch, you know? They earn a lot and have to stay in shape, so most of them look pretty good. And they tend to be smart."

She'd considered her comments and they had the effect on Ken she desired. He knew he wasn't the only fish in the sea and now he knew that she knew it, too. He'd better not take anything for granted.

"Oh!" she said. "There is one thing new. The airline has hired its first male—well—I don't know what to call them . . . anyway, they do what I do, but they're men. The company calls them flight attendants but some of the girls and the pilots call them ball-bearing stewardesses. " She blushed, visible even in the soft light, and then she giggled. It was a charming reaction Ken had not seen before.

"Well isn't that something, now?" Ken responded with surprise. "I hadn't heard anything about that. You wouldn't think it'd be a job a man would want, would you? I mean, why would a man want to be a waitress—that's woman's work, isn't it? I don't suppose they're looking for husbands, huh?"

Mildly stung by the "woman's work" remark, Kate responded sharply. "It won't always be woman's work, Ken! And maybe even someday you'll see women up in the cockpit. We're not dumb, you know? We could do it, too. Lots of women flew during the war, ferrying airplanes around. Even across the ocean. I read about it."

He was surprised by the vehemence of her remarks. Caught aback and not knowing exactly how to respond, all he could do was smile at her and say, "Well, if it ever happens, I'm sure you'll be one of the very first. I think you're darned smart. And beautiful, too."

Their desserts arrived, *flan*, bringing a merciful close to the uncomfortable exchange. They looked at one another and smiled.

"There are lots of things to find out about each other, aren't there?"

"You can say that again!" he replied as he gratefully took the first bite of his custard. A mouth full of *flan* didn't have room for feet.

They spent a few minutes in silence, finishing their desserts. Then he asked, "Want to go sit by the fireplace for a while with a Mexican brandy?"

"I'd love that," she replied. "But I never heard of Mexican brandy; I thought brandy was French."

"Nope, not necessarily. You're thinking of Cognac, which is brandy from a particular part of France." He pushed back his chair, stood, and stepped over to pull hers back for her. She stood and he draped her cardigan across her bare shoulders, then she took his hand. "It's named after that region of France, like they name wines. Brandy is just fermented and distilled fruit juice from anywhere. Usually, if you just say "brandy", you're talking about grape juice. They actually make a lot of it in Mexico. Some of it's pretty raw, but we'll have the good stuff."

They walked slowly across the nearly empty dining room. Her high heels clicked slowly on the rust-colored tile floor. It was a very sexy sound to Ken, who loved women in high heels.

They stopped to admire an old wooden mission-style chandelier that hung heavily from black iron chains in the center of the room. Its candles had been replaced by squat, dim bulbs long before. The whole place might have been lifted from the days of the *conquistadores*, with tile floors, adobe walls, and *vigas* supporting the roof.

"Can you imagine what it was like in those days, to be Spanish here and lord of the universe?" she asked as her gaze took in the room.

"Yeah," he said as he led her through double doors into the bar, "they had it good, but they were mighty hard on the locals. Sometime in the late sixteen hundreds, around 1680 I think, the Indians revolted and chased them out of here for a while. Everyone from Taos south grabbed his hat and hit the road back to Mexico, hoping to get there with his hair. In fact, one of our guys actually found an old iron Spanish breastplate, armor, you know, out in the desert after the wind shifted a dune. And there's a legend of some gold they were carrying hidden back up in the Organ Mountains outside Las Cruces. 'Course, that's all part of the White Sands Missile Range now, so nobody can go look any more."

On the far side of the bar a fire burned bright in a man-high fireplace built of native stone in a corner. A massive, round, wooden table, low, and carved deeply, stood on an Indian rug in front of it. The table was surrounded by deep leather chairs and sofas. They stood before the fire holding hands.

"Anyhow, about this brandy. I recall reading somewhere that it was actually invented in Spain, way back when the Moors controlled it. Moorish alchemists distilled grape juice trying to come up with medicines. One thing led to another and next thing you know, they're producing brandy for fun in Spain and France. Neat, huh? Moslems aren't supposed to drink alcohol, but they invented brandy."

They took a seat on a sofa placed close enough to the fireplace that they could feel the warmth of the snapping *piñon* fire. Ken leaned back in a corner of the couch and stretched his feet out on the hearth. He draped his right arm on the back. His pale blue western shirt was starched and crisp under his dark blue wool western jacket. The crease in his whipcord twill pants was sharp and his Nocona dress boots glistened like obsidian in the soft light from overhead. He was fed and had his girl by his side. She sat against him, hip to hip, her head on his shoulder, her hand warm on his thigh. He was well satisfied with himself and his place in the world at that moment.

"How do you know so much stuff, Ken? I never knew anybody who knew so many things."

The waiter came over to ask if they would like something.

"Dos vasos de aguardiente Azteca de Oro, por favor", Ken said; two glasses of Golden Aztec brandy, please. He was pleased to be able to show off his Spanish.

The waiter bowed slightly and responded, *"Si, Señor*", with grave courtesy. He walked back behind the bar.

"Shoot, Kate, I don't know. I just read things and they seem to stick. That is, if it's useless information. Ask me something about nationality law, for instance, or algebra, and you'll find out I don't know much at all despite a lot of study."

The waiter returned quickly with two glasses of the spirits on an antique silver tray that he set on the table in front of them. He left the bottle, knowing that young men with young women often appreciate having a bottle at hand. Ken signed the bill.

Ken leaned forward and picked up a glass for himself and handed the other to her. “Here’s to us,” Ken said, as he offered his glass in a toast, “wherever it may lead.”

She clinked her glass against his and said “Amen.”

Each took a sip, savoring the smooth fire of the drink.

"Mmmm . . ." Kate purred after she let it trickle from her tongue and down her throat. “That's really good. I don't usually like straight liquor, but this is soooo good. It's like wine with more bite to it. And it builds such a nice, warm fire in my tummy!" She dropped her head back on his shoulder, holding the glass in her lap.

"Mmm-hmmm," Ken replied, the thought of a fire in her tummy building a fire in him. “I liked it the first time I tried it, down at the Academy. There was a bar out on the beach at South Padre Island where we used to go. We'd sit outside and watch the surf on the Gulf and eat shrimp 'til our stomachs rose and fell with the tide. We'd drink beer with the shrimp, and then finish off the evening with brandy and a cigar while the sun went down. It's a mighty fine way to pass an evening.”

"Better than this, Ken?" she asked, fishing a little herself.

"Honey," he replied in a soft, fond tone, giving her shoulder a gentle squeeze, "I've never had a better evening than this one. And I don't expect I ever will unless it's with you some other time. Best of all, it's not even over yet, is it?" He buried his nose in her hair and breathed the clean scent of it as he kissed the top of her head.

She leaned forward, turned slightly toward him and looked at him across the top of her glass. She tossed off what remained of the drink, and then said with a slight gasp, "No, it's not. Not even close."

She reached for the bottle, poured herself another two fingers, and then added more to his glass.

"Let's finish these off slowly," she said. "Then it'll be bedtime."

Ken reached to her and placed his hand gently on the side of her head. He caressed her cheekbone several times with his thumb and then he passed his thumb lightly across her lips. Finally, he cupped the back of her head in his hand and pulled her face to his. He kissed her gently, his lips barely touching hers, but staying there long enough to taste her. Pulling back enough to see her eyes and little more, he said, "I can't wait."

From the bar the waiter watched with envy. He silently wished the young man good fortune—he was certain the wish would come true.

Finally, they stood and walked down the hall to their room.

****

Ken opened his eyes as he slowly returned to this world and the present from that far-away, timeless place Kate had taken him. He would have sworn his soul had left him in a long, glorious surge that carried it into some secret place within her.

He lifted himself up on his elbows and looked down at her face beneath his. It was lit by the remains of the fire in the corner of their room and by soft moonlight through the window. Her eyes were still closed but there was a small, sweet smile on her mouth. She opened her eyes and looked into his. He fell into their unplumbed depths. Then she said, "Wow!" She said it quietly, but the word carried a depth of sentiment that Ken felt to his core.

Sometimes words fail; all he could do was say "Wow" back to her. Then he lowered himself gently down on her, still supporting his weight with his arms, but allowing their bodies to touch completely.

As he lowered his face to kiss her neck he heard her whisper, "I love you, Ken."

He told her the truth in turn: "I love you, too, Kate."

Chapter 25

Luz found the knife while sweeping her room in the morning. She'd pushed the broom under the bed, swept it from head to foot and it came tumbling out with a hard rattle, bumping to a stop against the wall by the door. At first, she stared at it as though it were a snake, wondering where it had come from.

She glanced at her open door, hoping that no one else had seen it. Then she reached for it hesitantly, as though it might strike at her.

Stopping to think, she stood up and closed her door. They were forbidden to have weapons and she knew she would be beaten to insensibility if it were found on her. But she wanted it. She didn't know yet how she could use it, but it was the first chance she'd had to do something for herself. So she leaned over and picked it up.

It was a folding knife, long, with black plastic grips and chrome furniture at each end. Turning it over and over in her hand, she could see a single blade folded into the handle. There was a button on the side, and small sliding catch beside it. She had seen a similar knife in the hands of her cousin back on the *ejido;* he had bought it on a trip to Chihuahua City. He loved to make a great show of taking the knife out of his pocket and opening it. She knew if she pushed the button the blade would fly open.

So she took it in her palm, holding the handle awkwardly, and pressed the button with her thumb. Nothing happened. She pressed again, and again, nothing. She looked the knife over and realized that the small catch must be there to lock the button in place so that it would not open the knife while in a pocket. She slid the catch down and then pushed the button again.

The blade leaped out of the handle, jerking the knife from her gentle grip as it clicked into place. It landed point first on the wooden floor, its needle point sinking in and holding it upright. It stood there quivering with silent menace.

She pulled it from the floor and examined the long, slim blade. She ran her finger across the edge and found it keen. She was a farm girl and no stranger to knives. She had killed and cleaned countless chickens and hogs and *chivas* back home and she knew this blade could be counted on to cut deep and easily.

She pressed the button again and folded the blade back into the handle. She pressed it once more and watched the blade flash out, holding it more firmly this time.

Then again. And again. And again. And a small smile grew larger with each deadly click.

Finally, she pulled the top of her blouse away from her bosom and slipped the knife into the soft hammock of her brassiere. She no longer felt helpless.

Chapter 26

"You know, Kate," Ken said over the remains of the fried chicken supper she had fixed for them as soon as she had returned from her overnight trip to L.A. "The outfit really leaves me wondering sometimes."

"Why's that, hon," she responded as she stood and picked up their plates and silverware to clear the table.

"Look, I know I'm a newby and I don't have what they call the "big picture", but it seems like nobody running the office really gives a damn about putting a system together that would make us more efficient."

He stopped to light two cigarettes.

"As long as we catch a few more wets than we did the year before everybody in management is happy. It doesn't seem to matter to them how we could do it better, just that we show some activity. It's all so damned haphazard."

"Hmmm . . ." she replied as she filled the sink, then came back to the table to pick up the glasses and serving dishes.

"Take a few days ago, for instance. Diehl and I got some good information for Pope, part of what could turn out to be a big drug case. It's the sort of thing that ought to be put out to the troops quickly. Not only might that help us catch the bad guys, but also there's an officer safety angle involved. So how do we get the word out? Any other cop shop would bring it up at a shift briefing, but not here, oh no. We don't have shift briefings. So it's gotta circulate by word of mouth."

"Why don't they have shift briefings?" she asked as she walked over to take a puff from the cigarette he had lit for her. She put it down in the ashtray, reached out and touched his face and then walked back to the sink. Ken stretched his legs out and put his hands behind his head, then went on.

"I don't know why we don't. There are a lot of things like that here in El Paso. For instance, most of the supervisors don't make vehicle assignments. That extends how long it takes us to get out of the office while the guys argue over who drives what. And lots of them stop for coffee on the way out and on the way back, so you've got both shifts down at Sambo's at the same time. Between that and the vehicle shortage, there's hardly anybody down on the river for a couple hours at change of shift and the wets know it. The supervisors don't seem to give a damn. In fact, some of them are right there at coffee with the troops You put parts of two shifts of Border Patrolmen in there and the Southern Pacific Railroad Police – they wear green uniforms, too – and it must look to the taxpayers like there's nobody minding the store. And they wouldn't be far wrong, either."

He stopped and took a drag from his Chesterfield. She looked particularly good from this angle, he noticed, the uniform skirt fitting smoothly over her trim backside and her legs shaped by the low heels she wore for work. He felt a stirring in his loins, but put it aside for the time being.

"Of course, it gives guys from one shift a chance to pass along info on what they're seeing to the next shift. Not as good as a shift briefing, but it's something, anyway."

She looked over her shoulder at him. "That doesn't sound very good to me." She gave him a playful grin and said, "As a taxpayer I am distressed, I tell you, distressed and dismayed. What else went on while I was gone?"

"Diehl and I took a drive through the housing out at Fort Bliss looking for a truck that might be a part of this thing. No luck, though, at least not on one pass through the base. For all we know, the guy was off post or something. Or doesn't even live there Anyway, word of mouth is a pretty haphazard way of doing things."

She put the last of the dishes into the drainer to drip dry, pulled the plug to let the wash water out of the sink, and then took off the rubber gloves she'd worn and tossed them into a basket under the sink. Turning gracefully, she walked over to the table where she took a final puff on her cigarette and stubbed it out. Then she sat down in his lap, arms around his neck.

"I thought about you a lot last night," she said softly into his ear, giving the lobe a little nip. "In fact, I woke up in the middle of the night thinking of you." She gently stroked the back of his neck with her fingertips as she leaned her forehead against his and looked into his eyes. "There was this itch I needed to have scratched, if you know what I mean." She pulled her face back and grinned at him, giving him a big, lewd wink and grinding her bottom into his lap. The evidence of his interest was clearly there.

"Oh, yeah?" he said. "Does it still itch?"

"Yes," she replied with mock solemnity, nodding her head. "It does. It itches real bad now. It got worse and worse as the day went on. In fact, I think I might just die if it doesn't get scratched pretty quick."

"I'm always ready to help a damsel in distress." He kissed her, then wrapping an arm around her shoulders to support her, he looked into her eyes as he ran his hand gently, slowly up the inside of her leg to the top of her stocking, to the warm flesh of her inner thigh. Her breathing deepened as he unsnapped the garter he found there, then petted the soft skin. He gently extended his fingertips upward.

She closed her eyes and he felt her tremble. She dropped her head to his shoulder. "Please, Ken—now?" she whispered. "Hurry."

He slipped his arm under her knees, and with the other still cradling her shoulders, stood up and carried her to the bedroom.

Chapter 27

Tomás Ayala sat in the back corner of the Cantina Rio Bravo waiting to hear from Gary Thompson, the *motocyclista.* The remains of a half-eaten plate of *huevos rancheros* was shoved to the far edge of the table and a near-full cup of coffee gone cold was stacked on it. He had no stomach for food.

By now Thompson should have picked up the drugs and delivered them to the truck stop and called to say it was done. But there had been no word and Tomás's stomach felt as though he had swallowed hot tacks. He poured himself a second shot of tequila to calm his nerves.

Would this be the first time they lost a load? He hoped not, for he had recruited another guide for this trip, to use in place of Rafael Salinas. Salinas, he thought, was becoming too independent. He didn't just listen to instructions and do what he was told; he spoke back. Perhaps having someone else guide the drugs in would make him understand his place.

He had done it on his own, telling his uncle nothing of the change of plans. If things had gone wrong . . .

Just as his nerves were about to run away with him Thompson came in the front door, looked around as his eyes adjusted to the dim light and then walked back to Tomás "I don't know who the dumb cocksucker is you hired to guide this load, Ayala, but he needs shooting!" Thompson exploded as he dropped a canvas gear bag on the floor with a thud. He pulled a chair out and sat down, then reached into a shirt pocket and pulled out a cigar and a match. He bit the end off the cigar and spit it into the corner and then lit the stogie and called to the bartender, "*Bacardi, mesero; un doble.*"

Tomas's stomach fell like a stone dropped into a well.

"What happened, *mi amigo*?" Ayala asked in broken English. Thompson's mother was a Mexican-American woman who'd married, so she claimed, a sailor based in San Diego. The man had disappeared while Thompson was very young, leaving nothing but a memory in his mother's mind. He had grown up in the *barrio* in San Diego and his Spanish was good, but he indulged Tomás in his efforts to speak English.

"The dumb sonofabitch was over an hour late coming up the trail from Monument Three. I was sitting up on the high point watching for him. When he came the Border Patrol was right on his ass and Alfonso didn't have time to get to the culvert to hide the load. I saw him throw it into the canal before they got caught, but the *migra* got all four of them together, no split-up or anything else.

Ayala's heart sank and his stomach turned over at the thought of what his uncle would do to him. The suppliers weren't interested in excuses; they wanted cash money. And they would have it, or else – "*plata, o plomo*", he thought, silver, or lead.

It would have to come from his uncle's pocket, and his uncle would get it from—"Me," he said to himself. The future looked very bleak indeed, that is, if he had a future at all. He knew that his uncle had had others killed over less.

Thompson watched Ayala's face melt as he slid down in his chair, both hands clutching the glass on the table in front of him. Tomás' eyes closed and his face broke into a sweat despite the cool air circulating through the bar from the front door. Ayala opened his eyes and took a deep drink of tequila from the glass. He poured another. He realized that the man across the table might be the one who ended his life.

Thompson silently watched Ayala's reaction with interest. He had not yet told Ayala that he recovered the drugs from a weir installed at a culvert downstream from where Alfonso had thrown them in. For all anybody knew they were floating down the Rio Grande by now.

When Alfonso came back he'd tell his father that he'd had to toss the load and that it was fault of the idiot who had led them in. His father would let Alfonso off the hook since it wasn't really his fault.

"And it wasn't my fault, either," Thompson thought. Nobody could blame him for anything. Nobody knew he'd ever gotten even a sniff of the load.

He had a powerful lever over Tomás Ayala at hand—or he could just keep the drugs himself, sell them somewhere far away. They'd never know. It would probably cost this asshole his life and certainly the dumb shit that was guiding the load today would die. He didn't owe them squat, though. Dead or alive, they meant nothing to him. But alive, at least this one could be useful.

"What's your life worth to you, Ayala? Ten thousand? Twenty? Everything you have? Everything you ever expect to have?"

Ayala looked up, mixed emotions passing over his face as quickly as flickering movie frames.

"Why do you ask, Thompson? What do you know?"

"I know that you hired a new man as a guide," Thompson replied. "I know you hired him. I suspect that you didn't tell your uncle about it. And now the load's gone and everybody will know your man lost it. It's your fault it happened. If you can't come up with the money for it I'd guess you're going to die."

He tightened the screws a little more. "Maybe I'll be the one to pull the trigger—somebody will."

Ayala blanched, but said, "My uncle will protect me. It's a family thing. My mother will see to it."

"You really want to bet on that, Tomás? Or will he give you up instead of the money? You might just disappear and momma will never know what happened." He stopped and took a sip of his Bacardi and a deep puff of his cigar. He examined the tip, and then went on.

"That was big load; maybe he doesn't have enough money to pay them. What do you think *they* will settle for if he doesn't? They'll think he ripped them off. He'll have to give them something to show his good faith just to get credit to go on and pay them back. My guess is that he'll give you up to show his regrets."

Ayala knew it was all true. Thompson knew how things worked. It was hopeless. He was as good as dead.

"Tomás, I'm going to save your sorry ass. But it's going to cost you. It's going to cost you five thousand dollars today, right now, and a cut of your share for the next year—ten percent off the top. And I might ask a favor now and then. Nothing hard, you understand, but it will be important. I don't expect you to even think of saying no."

Ayala sat up straight. Suddenly this was business, a proposition. "I don't have five thousand dollars. I don't even know where I could get it today. Would you take two thousand today and a promise of the rest by the end of the week?"

"Tomás, I'm sorry; I was just fucking sure you had it. Well, too bad, but I need five thousand today from you. If you can get it by the end of the week I'll bet you can get it today. If you can't, we'll sit here and wait for Alfonso come back and tell your uncle all about it."

"No, no," Ayala said, nearly frantic. "I think I know who I can call for it today. Just wait here while I call."

"I think you better hurry, Tomás. We never know when Alfonso will come in, do we? You probably ought to be ready to make a little arrangement with him, too."

"Wait," Tomás said, a sudden thought coming to his tequila-addled mind. "How are you going to help me? When you first said it I thought you were going to lend me money, but now I'm going to give money to you?"

"Well, Tomás, it might be that I have some drugs on my hands that I'd be willing to sell you cheap. I mean, since we're *compas* and all, asshole buddies. If you took them to your uncle it might make things easier for you. *Verdad?* He'd think you got them back somehow after Alfonso tossed them. He might still be mad but he probably wouldn't kill you."

The light dawned for Tomás. Suddenly he realized what must have happened.

"You! You took the load! If I tell my uncle that, I'll be in favor with him, a hero, and he'll have you killed."

"Tomás, think. Stir that shit in your head that you call brains and think. Why would he believe you? Especially when Alfonso, his own son, tells him that he had to throw them in the canal to keep from getting caught with them because you fucked up. No, I don't think that will work. But we can give it a try if you want." He stood up as if to go.

Tomás knew he was well and truly on the hook. This man held his life in his hands and he had to cooperate.

"How do I know you have them?" he asked.

"Because I'm telling you I do." Thompson responded. "I don't have them here, but when you show me some money and agree to my terms I can get them for you. But now? You don't have any idea where they are. Your miserable fucking life depends on getting along with me before Alfonso shows up, doesn't it?"

Defeated, Ayala said, "I'll do it. I'll do everything you say."

Thompson knew that he had what he needed for success with the Ayalas.

"Good, Tomás; that's what I like to hear. Now you go round up that cash."

Ayala rose. He stood there unsteadily, rocking back and forth, looking at Thompson. Finally, unable to come up with anything else, he said "*Bueno*", turned, and walked to the phone on the back wall. As he walked away he was trying to figure out how to get back at Thompson, but his mind wasn't working well at all.

Thompson watched. He leaned his chair back against the wall, feet in the chair next to him. He took a deep puff from his cigar and threw his shot of rum back into his throat. He poured a shot from Ayala's bottle of tequila into his glass.

"That little motherfucker will try to get ahead of me again," he thought. "I'd better nail his feet to the floor over this or I'll have to be looking over my shoulder forever."

He considered how best to do that. He came to the conclusion that Tomás would have to go. An idea came.

Ayala spent ten minutes on the phone. His posture as he leaned against the wall and his gestures showed he was pleading. Obviously, it was not going well. Finally, he hung and walked back to the table.

"A woman is bringing the money," he said.

"That figures. How long will it take?"

"She told me she would be here in half an hour."

"You'd better hope she gets here before Alfonso does, Tomás, because unless I have money in hand I'm not going to stop him from going right up there to see his daddy about this*; sabes?"*

"Yeah," Tomás replied. "I know." He reached for the bottle and poured himself a shot of Sauza, which he tossed back. Then another. And a third.

They sat there in silence, staring at each other, each assessing the other's vulnerabilities.

A slim, well-dressed woman in a tight, white dress and spike heels finally walked in. In her early twenties, blonde, with bright red lipstick, she was striking. She looked as out of place in the Cantina Rio Bravo as a rose in a cesspool. She walked straight back to Ayala, certain of where she was headed—apparently she had been here before. She stopped in front of him.

He looked up at her and asked, "Nadia, *querida mia,* do you have it?"

In colloquial gutter Spanish that belied her classy appearance and showed her to be Mexican despite the blonde hair, she said *"Si, pendejo. Aqui está."* With that, she tossed a small, cheap plastic purse into his lap. It landed with a solid thump.

It was a good shot. His hands flew to his crotch and he breathed deeply and painfully for a moment, looking at her with malice. Standing to strike her, though, would require too much effort in his condition.

"I never want to see that ugly thing again," she spat, pointing at his crotch. "Keep it in your pants and stay away from me." She turned and walked out of the *cantina.*

"A little lover's spat, Tomás?" Thompson asked. "It looks like it's all over."

"The *puta* used to work here," Tomás said. "I bought her and put her in an apartment and bought her clothes. She had only to see me and this is the thanks I get."

"Tomás, it looks like she just gave you five thousand dollars, enough to save your life. I'd say she just bought herself back." He poured Tomás another shot of tequila. "Here," he said as he pushed the glass back across the table. Liquor, he knew, would be an ally. "This'll help take the sting out of it. Now give me that money."

Ayala handed the purse to him. Thompson opened it and found it stuffed with hundred dollar bills and a handful of peso coins. He counted the bills: fifty of them. "Tomás, we got the start of a deal here. The first thing I want you to do now is give me the key to that woman's apartment. I know you got one, so don't hold out. Then tell me where she lives."

Ayala, now far gone under the influence of too much tequila soaked up over the last hour, fumbled through his pockets before coming up with it. "Here," he slurred as he passed it over. "She lives in the apartments three blocks down the highway from the Plaza de Toros. Use her hard. And watch her closely—she will steal from you."

Thompson placed the key with the bills, folded the cash, and tucked the items into his hip pocket. The purse and the coins he threw out the back door into the alley behind him. The jingle of the coins drew the attention of a shoeshine boy on the street nearby, who scooped it up and ran.

Mere minutes later, Alfonso came through the front door. He took a seat at the table, glaring at Tomás. He spoke with ill-concealed fury—he was *El Patrón's* son, and despite his youth he could take liberties in the way he talked to others.

"That *cabrón* you hired—he fucked up and made us late. He couldn't even find his way from Monument Three to the river. We didn't cross the border until dawn and the *patrulleros* were on us right away. I had to throw the drugs in the canal or be caught with them—now they're gone. This is your fault. What are you going to do about it?"

Tomás, very drunk by now and too overloaded with troubles to care, dropped his head on the table and slept. Alfonso looked at Thompson, a question in his eyes.

Thompson stood up and spoke. "Alfonso, we need to go see your father, I think." He bent and picked up his war bag and started up the stairs.

Alfonso looked from him to Tomás. Then he stood up and followed him.

*****

Thompson and Alfonso Ayala sat in Marcos Ayala's office, in the chairs in front of his desk. The elder Ayala was leaned forward in his chair, arms thrust forward, hands locked together, almost reaching across the desk. His face was red with rage.

"You lost the load?" he roared at Alfonso, slamming his doubled fists down on the desk. Thompson bided his time calmly. It was not yet time for him to speak.

"No, *Papá*," the younger Ayala responded. "I did not lose it. I had to throw it away when the Border Patrol came upon us too soon. I threw it into the main canal and it sank there. If I had not done that I would have been caught with it and you would now be without the drugs or money, or your son.

"And how," Marcos asked, still dangerously furious, "did it come to pass that the Border Patrol caught up with you so soon? You should have been at the place to leave the load long before then."

"*Papá*," Alfonso began to explain, "the guide became lost as we walked from Mount Cristo Rey out to the crossing place. Then, after we crossed the border, he turned the wrong way. We walked miles farther than was necessary and it cost us much time."

"Salinas will pay for his stupidity," Ayala declared. "And I will have the money for the load from him before he dies."

Turning to Thompson, he asked, "And what do you know of this, *gringo.* Do you have anything to say?" Ayala was looking for someone to vent his rage on, and Thompson felt that he was sitting with a scorpion in his lap. At any moment it might lash out.

"Patrón, . . ." he began, but Alfonso interrupted. *"Papá,"* he said, "this one had nothing to do with it, although he must have seen what happened on the ditch bank. He was surely watching, as he always does, and we were close to the place. He can tell you when we arrived." He, too, was anxious that his father's rage not descend on him.

Thompson began again, "*Patrón,* it was full daylight, nearly eight o'clock, before Alfonso and the others arrived in the area. I could see them walking up the ditch bank with *la migra* close behind them. When Alfonso heard the jeep he threw the package into the canal immediately, but he had no chance to run."

Ayala looked long and hard at Thompson and finally said, "And why did you not try to recover the drugs, *gringo?* You know where they went. Do you have so little loyalty to me? Or perhaps you did just that. Perhaps you hid them somewhere."

Thompson broke out in a sweat, the knowledge that the drugs were in fact in the bag at his feet making his blood run cold. If necessary, he could pull the AR-15 from the bag and kill these two—but that would ruin his plan and perhaps get him killed in the process.

He called up the cold nerve and willingness to gamble that had served him so well in the jungles.

"*Señor,*" he replied, dropping his eyes in respect, "you know that I am loyal to you. I have killed for you and smuggled other loads before. I went to the ditch and looked, but the package sank, as you would expect. The water is swift. I could not linger there or I might have been found by the Patrol. They would think it strange that I was searching water like that. It has surely been carried away by now, lost to us."

"Very well," Ayala replied after searching Thompson's face for what seemed like an eternity. "Now we will see to Salinas, for I must pay for that load somehow. Perhaps he will have enough money; perhaps not, but we will see. He knows those hills, though, and if he delayed you then it was treachery on his part, deliberate, and he must die for it after he watches his precious grandchildren go first."

"*Padre,*" Alfonso said. "Wait. Salinas had no part in this. He was not there. It was a new man."

"What he says is true, *Patrón,*" Thompson interjected, wanting to leave no doubt who was at fault and who should pay for the mistake. " I was watching and I know what Salinas looks like. He was not there."

The elder Ayala was stunned to silence, but he quickly regained his voice. He spoke with quiet menace. "What do you mean, new man, *mi hijo?* Where was Salinas? I chose him because he is reliable—we insure it. And he knows his way everywhere out there in the sand."

Alfonso explained. "*Papá* it was a new man that Tomás hired in the plaza, a *coyote* who usually smuggles *pollos.* I have never seen him, but Tomás said he knew him and that he knew his way through the desert. Tomás does not like Salinas; he thinks he is too independent. He says he might betray us some day. I thought he told you."

"No, my son. He told me nothing, nothing at all. He took it upon himself to do this and it will cost me more than I have. I must find some way to satisfy the others. Both of you go now—let me think."

Chapter 28

An hour later Tomás Ayala, still in a stupor at the table in the bar, was aware of being picked up by the arms and carried out into the alley. He was thrown on his face onto the back floor of a car and covered with a blanket. Someone sat on the seat, feet on the back of his neck. It was not comfortable, but the liquor did its work; he passed out again.

Later, he awoke slowly. Before he opened his eyes he felt constrained. His hands wandered, seeking the source of the constraint. They found walls. He smelled dirt. He opened his bleary eyes to see that he was in a hole in the ground, which struck him as odd—his last recollection was of sitting in the cantina. "What happened," he wondered, his mind still fuddled with drink. As he stared at the sky a face appeared at the edge of the hole, then another on the other side. He looked from one to the other and recognized Diaz and Thompson and where he was. Diaz spoke. "*Amigo,* you fucked up once too often. Now your mother will have to wonder where you went. *Adios.*"

The faces disappeared behind hands holding pistols. He opened his mouth to protest, but no words came. There was a sudden bloom of fire, then nothing more. Thompson turned away from the hole and picked up a shovel as Diaz took a small camera from his pocket and snapped a picture of Tomás' body in the hole. The flash clearly lit the holes in his face and the spattered blood. Thompson threw the first spade full of dirt onto Tomás' face, filling his still-open mouth and the shocked eyes. Diaz snapped another photo. Then he picked up spade, too, and went to work. Soon they were driving back to the Cantina Rio Bravo. Thompson thought with pleasure of how he would soon drop in on *la rubia*, the blonde. She didn't know it yet but she would be looking for someone to pay her bills

Chapter 29

Diaz let Thompson out of the car on the corner of Calles Ugarte and Mariscal, near his apartment. He watched Diaz drive out of sight and then walked into an alley. He walked six blocks the other way, away from the apartment they knew about. His past had taught him never to rely on a single hole; he had another place, a hideout that none of the group knew about. There, he could keep most of his guns and money and now, the dope. It also gave him a place to run to if things went south, as they often did for men in his business. It was little more than a closet, but its shitty location just west of downtown Juarez meant that it cost him almost nothing. A little extra to the landlord bought his silence and himself information about anyone coming around and showing an interest in the place.

He hadn't spent a night there yet; in fact he went there as little as possible to avoid giving it away should he be seen. He didn't intend to be there tonight either, but he wanted to get the heroin out of his war bag—good luck can only go on so long. So far no one had wanted to look in it, but that could change in a heartbeat.

He walked down the dark, urine-stinking hall of the old building, the wooden floor sagging with each step, past the owner's apartment, to the stairs at the rear. One floor up, on the front corner of the building, was his place. He took out his keys and opened both locks, the one in the doorknob and the deadbolt he had installed himself, along with a reinforcing two by four screwed to the doorjamb. Pushing the door open only a couple of inches, he reached around it at floor level and felt for the wadded-up gum wrapper he had laid on the floor there when he closed the door. It was still there—no one had opened his door since he left. Or if they had they knew the trick too, and he was in deeper trouble than he expected.

He closed the door and locked it. He stepped into the tiny bathroom stopping in front of the rust-stained sink with its dripping faucets. Two faucets there may have been, but both flowed cold water. The cubicle contained only the sink and a filthy toilet missing its seat; anyone wanting a bath took his chances in the tub down the hall. Despite all the time he'd spent crawling through the mud and jungle, and crapping in holes in the ground, Thompson was too fastidious to use any of the fixtures except the sink to wash his hands, or to take a leak in the toilet. At least it flushed.

Taking a screwdriver from his bag, he loosened the screws holding the cracked mirror in place on the wall – he had taped the crack on the back side to hold the mirror together. Behind it was a place where he had cut the cheap wallboard away, creating a hole nearly as big as the mirror and four inches deep. It held ten thousand dollars—his bailout money—and a Browning Hi-Power and a box of 9mm ammunition. The pistol was courtesy of the U.S. Army, a tool used by assassins in the Phoenix program in Viet Nam. There was no serial number on the piece and the barrel was threaded to accept a silencer. The silencer lay in the bottom of the compartment. The set was an unintended gift from a Lieutenant in Viet Nam who had made the mistake of leaving it in his hooch one night when Thompson was scrounging for anything he could use.

He took the package of heroin from his bag, and from his hip pocket, four of the five thousand dollars he got from Tomás. There was just enough room for it all in the compartment. The key to the blonde's apartment he put on his own key ring.

He wedged the drugs and money in place, then put the mirror back, being careful not to scratch up the screw heads or wall or mirror around them.

He took three steps across the bedroom and opened the small closet by the bed. He reached back to the war bag he'd dropped on the bed and pulled out his AR-15. Although he hadn't used it this day, weapons maintenance was a daily part of his life, so he sat down on the sagging bed with the piece across his lap. He removed the long magazine from its well in front of the trigger guard and pulled the charging handle to clear the round from the chamber. With his little finger, he felt in the chamber to make sure no round was stuck there. Then he stripped the rounds from the magazine to relieve tension on the magazine spring and then reloaded it. Finally, he set the safety and he was ready to field strip the weapon. Pulling the retaining ring to free them, he took the handguards off the barrel and then pulled out the pin that held the upper and lower receivers together as a unit. That let him swing the lower receiver down, out of the way.

He pulled the bolt housing out and then the charging handle. With that, he could remove the cotter key from the bolt housing and remove the bolt itself, then get the firing pin out of the bolt.

All of these he carefully wiped down, then he ran a patch through the barrel before he put it all together again and reloaded it. He could do it in his sleep, or more likely, in total darkness if necessary.

He placed the rifle and the extra magazine from his bag on the closet shelf. A spare .45 pistol hung on a nail driven into the wall and a jacket hanging on another nail had a thousand dollars in one pocket. Anyone tossing the room would expect to find something, so he offered it to them, a sacrifice, so to speak, to distract them from the bathroom.

He pulled his everyday pistol, a chromed Colt .45 auto, from his waistband. He took out the magazine, cycled the action to eject the round from the chamber and then slipped each round out of the magazine to relieve the pressure on the spring so it would not take a set. After cleaning the weapon he reloaded the magazine, slid it into the butt of the pistol and cycled the action once more to chamber a round. He set the safety, dropped the magazine, replaced the remaining round, and pushed the magazine back into the butt, bringing the pistol back to full capacity. He slipped it into his waistband cocked, just behind his right hip under his vest. He never used a holster; they were hard to get rid of if you had to ditch the weapon. The bag, now containing only his camping gear and other odds and ends, he dropped onto the floor of the closet.

Finally, he pulled the stainless steel Smith and Wesson Bodyguard from the top of his boot. He opened the cylinder –all five rounds were there, his last-ditch defense. He slipped it back into the top of his boot, stood, and opened the door.

Done there, he stepped out into the hall, replacing the gum wrapper inside the door as he left.

He left the building by the back door at the foot of the stairs, into the alley. He walked for three blocks in the alley before he allowed himself to come out onto Calle Mariscal, where he turned left to make his way to Avenida Juarez and the Cantina Rio Bravo.

The neon lights along Avenida Juarez were gleaming as night fell and he could see his breath in the evening chill. His down vest felt good, but he knew he'd have to start wearing his old fatigue jacket over it after dark soon—winter was almost there. The vest would be enough during the day, but nights would go from chilly to cold.

He entered the cantina through the same back door that he and Diaz had hauled Tomás out through just hours before. The bartender looked around at him and Thompson pointed up the stairs, lifting an eyebrow in question. The bartender nodded and pressed a button under the bar. Thompson went up the stairs two at a time, anxious to see *El Patrón.* He intended, before the day was out, to be Tomás' replacement. From there—who could tell?

He waved to the eyes he knew were watching through peepholes from the anterooms then knocked on *El Patrón's* door. Diaz pulled it open and motioned him in and then returned to his chair in the farthest corner in front of Ayala's desk. From there he was behind anyone who spoke to *El Patrón* and *El Patrón was* out of the line of fire. That made Ayala feel very good indeed, secure.

Thompson took the chair in front of Ayala's desk and waited for *El Patrón* to speak.

"Well, *gringo*, Diaz tells me that you had no problem pulling the trigger on Tomás. In fact, he said you smiled?"

"*Patrón*, with all respect due to you and your family, Tomás was an idiot, and stupid, too. Your father's brains obviously came to you, leaving none for your sister to pass on to him. He would have caused us nothing but trouble and cost us too much money in the future, just as he did this time. He drank too much, he put too much money up his nose, and he spent too much time pleasuring himself with the women. A killing was the best way; it was necessary."

Ayala, like anyone else, enjoyed having his decisions confirmed. He smiled at Thompson's words and his trust in Thompson's reliability and judgment went up.

There was a knock at the door. Diaz rose and opened it. The bartender stood there, his hand on Luz's shoulder.

"You called for her, *Patrón*. Do you still want her?"

"Yes," Ayala replied. "Put her in the bedroom and get out of here. I will get to her later."

The bartender led her to the bedroom and gave her a push toward the bed. She went over and sat down as he closed the door behind her. She immediately went over and sat with her with her back against the door. She could hear every word. She would tell Rafael everything she heard; she knew he would be back for her and would know what to do.

"*Patrón,"* Thompson went on, "you must now find someone to replace Tomás, *verdad*? Someone who will pass along your orders and see that they are carried out well. And take care of things if they don't go just right."

Throwing all his chips on the table, he went on, "I want to be that person. I have shown I can be trusted and you know the quality of my work. I am always there, ready to do your bidding."

"What you say, *gringo*, is true: I must replace that *pendejo* Tomás. But why should I give you the job? You are not of the blood, a *mexicano.* Perhaps Diaz there should have the job. He is family."

"*Patrón*, I admire Ramón; he knows that." Here, Thompson knew, he must tread carefully. Diaz was of Ayala's family and, more to the point, he was seated behind Thompson.

"He is strong as a bull and as loyal as a good dog. You can count on him absolutely. But I think even he would admit that the job calls for more thinking than he cares to do." He avoided saying that he thought Diaz probably had a hard time figuring out anything more complicated than how to tie his shoes.

He heard Diaz stir behind him and the hairs rose on the back of his neck. He looked over his shoulder and was relieved to see Diaz' hands still in his lap and his face a normal color. The man was apparently not sensitive about his limitations.

Ayala rocked back in his chair, locking his hands behind his head, staring intently at Thompson, thinking. Thompson knew what Ayala's thoughts must be. Ayala would think hard about allowing someone to live who so obviously coveted power. Thompson's words had been a life or death gamble.

Ayala continued to stare at Thompson, apparently in deep thought. Finally, he said, "Go now, both of you. Thompson—you come back tomorrow morning and I will give you my decision."

With that, Thompson and Diaz both went down to the bar. They took the table in the corner together and each ordered a beer.

"*Señor* Gary, you have *cojones* like a bull to ask that of *El Patrón.* You know that if he decides against you he will have me kill you. Did you consider that?"

"*Por supuesto,* Ramón. Of course. I thought about it all the way back to town after we did Tomás. Life is always a gamble, though. You cannot win if you don't put chips on the table: *verdad? El Patrón* must replace Tomás and I am the best man for the job. If he gives the job to me I will need help though, from a man such as yourself. You would find it rewarding. Can I count on you?"

"You can count on me until the time *El Patrón* tells me to put you in the ground, Thompson. He is family and I will always work first for him. Until then, though, yes."

"*Bueno*, Ramón. Since he has not yet told you to do that, we can drink together. *Mesero,"* he called to the bartender, *"una botella de Sauza!"*

Thompson knew that for now, he was safe. But as soon as Ramón left the table, so would he, and he would not spend the night in his known apartment. Perhaps he would go find the blonde who had abandoned Tomás. Coming back here tomorrow to hear Ayala's decision would be a risk, but unavoidable. He would come well armed, loaded, cocked and ready.

Chapter 30

Ayala pushed open the door to his bedroom to find the girl naked on her back on the bed, apparently awaiting his attention. While she showed no pleasure at his coming, neither was she cringing or crying, or covering up as she had in the past. He was pleased to see that he was making progress with her.

He undressed completely and lay down beside her, a hand on her breast. He kneaded it, then the other for a while before dropping the hand to rub her stomach and other places. He noticed a hard set to her mouth. She showed no pleasure, but her pleasure did not interest him: her compliance was what he wanted. And he was getting that.

"Touch me," he said. She rolled her hand, which lay at her side, outward. She found him hardening. She began an inexpert squeezing and he slowly came to full size.

Finally, he mounted her. She pulled her knees up to assist him, wanting it to end soon. The old man's words made her realize that the only option was pain—that they would keep inflicting pain until she did what they would have her do.

It was over quickly. He rolled off her, satisfied, satisfied with the feel of her and with her attitude.

"You are learning, *chica*," he said when he had regained his breath. "A little more effort towards eagerness and you will be very good at it." He pointed to a door in a corner at the foot of the bed and told her to get a cloth to clean him. She opened the door to a small bathroom, where she ran water in the sink to dampen a dirty cloth that lay wadded there. She sat on the edge of the bed and cleaned him quickly and with no great gentleness, but she was careful not to hurt him. She knew what would happen to her if she hurt him.

He stood and dressed. Knowing that there must be a carrot to accompany the stick, he took twenty dollars from the roll in his pocket and dropped it in her naked lap.

"You earned that, *chica.* Continue this well and more will come to you."

She concealed her disgust and promised herself that there would be very little opportunity to earn more whore's money. One way or another she would escape or die, now that she had the means. If she were to escape, though, she would need money. Only the thought of help from *Señor* Salinas kept her going now.

He turned and walked out of the bedroom, leaving the door open. As he walked out, he said over his shoulder, "Wash yourself then get out of here."

She rose from the bed, wishing there were a window to open to air out the stink of him. In the bathroom she took a new cloth and washed herself carefully. The one she had used on him she threw into the trash, wanting never to touch it again. She hoped she could avoid pregnancy until she could escape.

As she stood there watching him through the door, she saw him stop at his desk and pick up some papers and a gun from a drawer. He slipped the papers into a pocket and the gun into his belt. Then he turned to a door behind his desk, opened it, and stepped through into a—closet? She had seen the door before and assumed it was a closet, but when he closed the door behind himself and did not come out, she decided that it was an exit from his office. She wondered where it went.

She washed her hands over and over again and then dressed. She was thankful that she'd had the delay before he came in that allowed her to hide the knife in the clothing she dropped into the chair beside the bed. She would have to sew a small pouch into the waistband of her skirt as more permanent place to keep it. She put the knife back into its hiding place in her brassiere, willing to put up with the discomfort for the sake of having it near.

She stepped into the office and found no one there. Looking around curiously, she saw a room of modest dimensions, with walls of cheap brown paneling, poorly hung. It was furnished with a desk and swivel chair, four straight chairs in front of the desk and along the facing wall and a small safe behind the desk. In one wall were doors leading to the hall and the two guardrooms and another into the closet behind the desk. A picture of a bullfighter executing a *pase mariposa* hung next to the bedroom door and a small air conditioner mounted in a hole in the wall rattled away. It was all lit by a single bulb in a cheap fixture in the middle of the ceiling and a lamp on the desk.

The doors to the guards' rooms were closed tight. It was clear now why, on several occasions, she had seen Diaz come out of Ayala's office, summon the man from each room by the door, and then go downstairs. Now she understood why she didn't ever see Ayala leave—they got the car while he went out through his back door. She didn't know why he would leave her alone there now, unless he believed that she was so tamed that she would do nothing against him.

Gathering all the courage she had, she walked over to the door behind the desk and holding her breath, she opened it. It was empty. There was one blank wall on the left and hooks and a rod with several coats and other clothing hanging from them on the other side. Straight ahead of her was another door. It had no handle, only a deadbolt with a small knob. She placed her ear to the door and listened. A door slammed faintly, as though down a hall. She listened for several minutes more and heard nothing at all.

She had to open the door to find what was there, but the thought filled her with terror. Finally though, knowing that she would need the information if she were to escape, she turned the knob and pushed the door open a crack. She peeked through, then opened it further and put her head through. There was just an empty staircase leading down to the left, and to the right, a window that looked over the bright lights of a busy street—night had fallen while she was in the bedroom. At the foot of the staircase was another door that she knew must lead to the alley. Having freedom so close tempted her to run, but there was nowhere for her to go. She had no money except for the twenty dollars she had just earned. And who knew what waited outside? Certainly, she could not leave and go to the police, for they were not to be trusted by a young woman all alone in town.

So she closed the door once more, locked it again, and returned to her room. She prayed she would get a chance to talk to *Señor* Salinas soon.

Chapter 31

He awoke quickly, aware that he had slept through the dawn. The room was already flooded with light flowing in like molten gold through the east-facing window. It reflected off a mirror and back onto the bed, illuminating it with a hard, yellow light. He looked around at the unaccustomed surroundings of a woman's bedroom—it was full of feminine clutter and scents. There was no alarm clock, which told him something about her lifestyle. A heap of dirty clothing covered a chair in the corner, which told him even more. The light fell through an open door into the bathroom, where it illuminated the rainbow array of bottles and jars and cans on the sink and top of the toilet. A trashcan under the sink overflowed a cascade of crumpled tissues onto the floor.

She lay naked next to him on her side, partially under the sheet, head resting on an upstretched arm, one leg pulled up, knee bent. Her eyes were open and she was looking at him with a perfectly neutral gaze. He wondered if she had slept at all.

The bright daylight did her no favors. Her hair was tangled and oily and the dark roots showed. There were dark circles under her eyes. He could see the stubble in her armpit and that her skin was coarse, with large pores showing on her cheeks. Her lipstick was smeared with the night's activities and the makeup that had survived the night did a poor job of concealing the flaws in her appearance. He recalled that her fingers were thick and short and her thighs heavy. The odor of their sex permeated the bedclothes and through it he smelled her own scent, a musky smell, the sort of smell mushrooms make. It was not a clean smell, but neither was it unpleasant. The classy appearance she projected in the bar the day before was gone; apparently it had been seen there strictly in comparison to the surroundings. But she would do. For now.

He had found her place with no difficulty, a second-floor apartment in a small, flat-roofed, green building just off Avenida Triunfo de la Republica. It was close to the Pronaf, a government-built tourist shopping area, a convenient place for her to seek out clients. And as Tomás had said, it was just down the road from the bullring, which also drew men.

A few questions of idlers leaning on cars on the curb in the neighborhood and a five-dollar bill had pointed the way to her building. A blonde like her was a rarity, particularly living alone, and many knew of her. Finally another five-dollar bill had opened the mouth of one who pointed to the small apartment building and a unit on the second floor.

Five doors opened onto a porch that ran across the front of the second floor, with a railing of ugly, rustyblack iron bars. Using the key, he opened the door to number seven and walked in. She showed no surprise at seeing him, only a slight start when he came in without knocking. She looked at him from the couch where she sat watching soap operas on a small television and simply said, "Tomás will no longer need the key, I suppose."

It was a statement, but with an element of question to it, so he replied, "Tomás won't be around any more." She understood the finality in the statement.

She took him to bed, where she performed as would be expected of a professional, with great skill, feigning eagerness and making all the sounds of unbearable passion. She was no cook and there was little to eat in the apartment, but afterwards she fixed burritos of flour tortillas and canned refried beans. They drank beer and finally went to bed again.

His first move when he awoke was to reach for his pistol on the nightstand. It did not appear to have been moved in the night, but no matter if she had picked it up; it would have been useless to her. He reached under his pillow and retrieved the magazine he had taken out before he went to sleep. His hands mechanically performed the rest of the loading drill and then he set the safety and put the pistol back on the table with a round in the chamber and the hammer cocked.

He picked up his wallet and opened it; all his money was there. He looked at her silently. She said, "Did you think I would rob you in your sleep? Where would I go? What would I do when you awoke and found your money missing? Could I kill you while you slept? Why should I do that? You are about to become my man, I think. And what would I do with your body?" She smiled a smile no warmer than the morning air. He nodded and continued to look at her. His silence led her on. He began to dress as she spoke.

"My name is Nadia and I am your woman now if you wish it and if you have the money to pay for it. Pay the rent, buy me food and some clothing and a small gift from time to time and you will always find me here for you in the night. The days? The days belong to me and I will do as I wish."

He pulled on his socks and pants, then his shirt. He reached into one boot and removed the Smith & Wesson Bodyguard there. Her eyes widened slightly; she had not seen that one before. He put on the boots and dropped the little five-shot .38 revolver into the top of the left one, on the inside. He went into her bathroom and took a folding toothbrush from a pants pocket and brushed his teeth. He was fastidious about his teeth; he intended to have them for a very long time. Then he splashed his head and face and combed his black hair, a gift from his Mexican mother, straight back.

Now, he was ready once more to face the day.

"Yes," he said, "you will be here at night for me." He peeled three hundred dollars of Tomás' money off the roll in his pocket and dropped it on the night table.

"That will take care of the first month. Don't ask for more. And be here tonight. We will celebrate."

With her whore's expert eye for cash, she had watched as he took the bills from his roll. She knew to the dollar how much he had put down. It was enough and slightly more. She could easily estimate how much was left. She wondered where the rest of Tomás 's money was. She didn't ask that, nor what they would celebrate; she just said, "I will be here."

"If you don't have food for breakfast tomorrow, get some today. I like to eat when I get up. And one more thing. Don't ever come to the Cantina Rio Bravo again and never say my name to anyone."

He went to the kitchen and noted the number on the phone on the counter and then he turned and without another word, stepped out the front door of number seven onto the deck. He stopped and carefully looked up and down the street. There was nothing to attract his attention. All the cars were either moving or empty and no one was hanging around the curbs yet. He didn't think anyone knew where he had spent the night, but you stayed alive by being careful. He looked at the day.

It was morning-cool and the sun, still low in the east, lit a few high mares-tail clouds from below. They indicated a change in the weather, probably a cold front tonight. If he spent the night out he'd better take a liner for his sleeping bag; it would be cold.

He walked down the flight of stairs on the front of the building to the sidewalk. He didn't like that, the exposure and the lack of another way out. He would move her eventually, but it would do for now.

He walked to his truck, a ten-year old Ford, parked in a vacant lot two blocks away. It was not locked. Since he had nothing of value in it and since anyone wanting to determine what might be there would just break a window, he never locked it.

But it might be stolen; it would be a desirable truck for some rural *rancho,* so he did take the distributor rotor out when he left it. He opened the hood, replaced the rotor, then closed the hood and got in. It was the same thing he used to do in 'Nam. Jeeps didn't last long over there, either, if they could be driven off.

It was still far too early to go to the *cantina* to talk to Ayala. He would not arrive from his house outside of town until mid-morning, or even noon. You never knew with him. Thompson had never been to the house but he had heard about it from Diaz. A fine house, but not palatial, Diaz said. Certainly not a *hacienda.* He would have to find out more, especially how to get into it if he needed to. Thompson already thought of Ayala as roadblock to advancement. He thought he would have to take Ayala out of the picture at some point and the prelude to removal was knowledge of the target.

But first, he had to survive this day. With several hours to kill, he would get something to eat. So he drove across the Cordova Bridge to El Paso. At that hour of the morning there was no traffic and a bored inspector waved him straight through without a word. A left turn onto Paisano Boulevard took him downtown.

He parked in the lot at the Greyhound station on San Antonio Avenue and walked up the street to the Paso del Norte Hotel on El Paso Street. The big bronze front doors opened into a vast, high-ceilinged lobby with elegant columns, mahogany woodwork and an ornate Tiffany stained-glass cupola. Just inside the door he stood and looked around, enjoying the feel of the place. It had been built back when money in Texas meant cattle, not oil, and back then good hotels were grand places.

He had stayed there several nights after he was discharged. It had been convenient to get to Juarez from there, but in the end it cost too much, so he moved across the river.

His leather boot heels beat a sharp tattoo on the marble floor as he strode across the lobby to the coffee shop. He might be out of the Army, but when he walked, he still marched.

A good breakfast and several cups of coffee while he looked at the El Paso Times set him up for the day. He snorted when he saw that the Baltimore Bullets had beat his home team, the San Diego Rockets. The Rockets were only playing .500 basketball for the season. Thank God for the Supersonics and the Lakers; they kept his guys out of the cellar.

He left money for the bill and a generous tip on the table. Out in the lobby he turned left into the men's room to drain some excess coffee. When he came back out the shine boy was just unpacking his gear from the drawers under the footrests of his stand in the foyer. Thompson took one of the two chairs on the shine stand and put his feet up on the footrests.

"Ain't seen you around for a while, suh," the shine boy said to him. "Everythin' all right, I hope."

"If it got any better, boy, I don't know what I'd do. Make those things glow, hear?"

"Yessuh. Tony Lamas deserve a good shine." With that, he pulled the cuffs of Thompson's tan twill slacks up over the tops of the boots and began daubing black polish on them.

"You won't get any of that stuff up on the stitching, will you?"

"Nosuh. I knows how to treat a good boot; you know me. I been doin' this since back befo' th' wah. You jus set easy."

As Thompson watched the man bring the good leather up to a high, glistening shine thoughts of the encounter to come with Ayala ran through his mind. They brought the same exhilaration, the same tingle in the groin, that the prospect of a mission used to bring in Viet Nam. The thought of being dead by dark focused his mind and made the surroundings seem—what—brighter? He wondered if those years of his life would shape his every thought for the rest of it.

The shine boy had been popping his buffing rag across and around the boots with a syncopated beat that was as musical as tap dancing. He gave it a final snap, then said "Theah you go suh, lookin' like mirrors," as he dropped Thompson's cuffs back down.

Thompson felt expansive. He gave the man two dollars for a fifty-cent shine and said, "Keep the change." He walked back across the lobby and out to the curb. Standing there watching the street that had become busy while he ate, he lit a cigar and thought there was something fine about breakfast in a great hotel, followed by a cigar and a fresh shine on an expensive pair of boots. It makes a man feel ten feet tall, with a foot-long dick and balls enough to fill a bucket. "That," he thought, "is just how a man wants to feel before he goes into action." He walked back to his truck. "It would be smart to be on the scene first, instead of walking into a situation," he thought, as he opened the door. He started it up and drove across the Santa Fe Street Bridge to find out about the rest of his life.

He parked two blocks away from the Cantina Rio Bravo. This time, he did not disable the engine, for he might have to leave in a hurry. Before he walked away from the truck he looked around carefully, but there was nothing special to be seen. At midmorning, there were the usual vendors who had just opened their shops that sold cheap leather goods, *piñatas,* fake Rolex watches, and other worthless trinkets to the tourists. A few beggars were already seated cross-legged on the dirty sidewalk, taking possession of their spots for the day. The tourists would not show up for a while yet.

He entered the *cantina* quietly through the alley door. Except for the bartender reading the paper, the place was empty. He didn't notice Thompson until he pulled out a chair at a table in the corner by the door.

"*Hay cafe fresco*," he called. "Is there fresh coffee?"

The bartender looked up with a start and recognized Thompson. His expression told Thompson nothing special.

"It's an hour old." He reached for a cup under the counter and filled it from the pot at the end of the bar. Thompson walked over and got the cup. Leaning on the bar, he asked, "Is *El Patrón* upstairs yet? Or Diaz?"

"Not yet; nobody. Maybe in an hour or so."

"I'll wait, then." He took his coffee back to his chair in the corner and sat.

When he saw the bartender engrossed once more in the newspaper, he eased the small revolver from his boot and placed it in his belt in front of his left hip. The big .45, he took from the small of his back and held in his right hand in his lap under the table.

Caution and preparation, he thought, were the keys to survival.

Chapter 32

Salinas came into the Cantina Rio Bravo late in the afternoon, looked slowly around the busy, noisy barroom, but he did not see Luz anywhere. He pushed his way to a place at the bar, ordered a Tecate, and asked about her. The bartender told him that she was upstairs and then pushed a button to summon her.

A few minutes later she came slowly down the stairs, stopping halfway to look the crowd over. Salinas caught her eye and motioned for her to go back upstairs.

He turned to the bartender, who had seen the exchange and threw ten dollars on the counter. "I will be with her for an hour," he said.

"Not for ten dollars, *viejo,* not at this time of evening." The bartender went on, obviously enjoying this payback for Salinas's exchange with him of a few days before. "When it is busy like this, you will pay twenty dollars for her time. Or be happy with a half hour. But who knows what someone as old as you can do in only a half hour? No, you'd better give me another ten."

Salinas peeled another ten-dollar bill off the thin roll in his pocket and dropped it on the bar. As he turned away, he said with a smile, "She's worth all of it to an old man."

Now they sat on the bed in her room, talking. Both were in their underwear in case someone should open the door unexpectedly. The recent events of her life had moved her beyond modesty and he was too old to worry about it. She told him what she had seen upstairs and what she thought about the way Ayala departed from the place.

"Do you think," he asked, "that it would possible for me to get into that office? Perhaps through the back door?"

"I don't think so, *tio.*" It was a source of comfort to her to call him "uncle" now. He did not object.

"The door has only a knob on the inside and a keyhole on the outside, no handle or knob. It opens outward. He must unlock it and pull on the key to open it. Or perhaps he never comes back that way. And I do not know how the door at the bottom of the stairs is locked."

"I will leave the bar through the alley and look at that door as I go past. Perhaps I will be able to tell what kind of lock it has and how it is opened. Would it be possible for you to look from the inside, or even to let me in through that door?"

She shivered with fright at the thought of the chance she would have to take to do that. Then she said, "Yes, I will do that, if we can discover a way to do it. But for me to get there, he must leave me alone in the room again. He has never done that before and I don't understand why he did it this time. But I will try."

She thought about it further, motioning him to silence when he began to speak once more. Finally, she came to a sickening conclusion. She would have to control an encounter, or several, with Ayala. She would have to act as though she wanted to become his special woman. That would be the only way she had any chance of controlling the timing of encounters with him and thus be able to coordinate a plan with Salinas. Yes. She had to make him do things her way.

She explained all this to *tio* Rafael. He didn't like it, but she reminded him that it was he who told her to give what she must to stay alive. She could do this; could do it if she knew there was a future beyond it.

"When you get out of here," he said, "you will hide at my house with my granddaughter for a few days while I make arrangements to take you to *los estados unidos*. You can start a new life there. I still know people in Denver who will give you a safe place to live and who can help you for a while."

It was as though a door full of light had suddenly opened for her in a dark room. Perhaps there was a future after all. She did not have to go back to her village, ashamed of who she was and what she done. Perhaps, after all, she would not have to grow old alone and scorned. With help in the United States, who knew what could be?

"Do you really think that can happen, *tio*? Is it possible?"

"Yes, *guapita*, I think it can happen. But first we must get you safely out of here. We have but a few minutes left now. Let us begin a plan."

By the time he left, they had an outline. And she knew that she could do with Ayala what must be done.

*****

Salinas left and when the bartender called for her to come and get to work with the customers, she told him that her period had started. He cursed and told her to never mind.

She never thought she could say that to a man, but in terrible situations you discover you can do things you never thought you would. Despite her plans with *tio* Salinas though, doubts crept into her mind as she lay in her bed in the dark.

She had been raped by force many times now by Ayala and his men, but just yesterday she had, for the first time, not resisted when Ayala demanded it of her. She complied because she didn't want to be hurt any more. She had not thrown his money back in his face. What did that mean about her? She had accepted the money because she needed it. She complied with his demands and accepted his money because she was desperate. Didn't that make a difference in what she was?

If it did, how, then, was she any different from a woman who became a prostitute from hunger or some other desperation? Should she die first?

She had never had to think about such things before. It had all seemed so easy when she was at home. She committed small sins, she confessed to Father Domingo, and he absolved her. Now though, she didn't know if she could ever confess the things she'd done.

Less even would she be able to confess what she planned. She had not told *tio* all of her plan for fear he would try to discourage her from it.

It all went through her mind in an unending circle of thoughts, like a puppy chasing its tail. But two thoughts were always at the center of the circle: revenge, and escape. The more she thought of those two things the less the other things seemed to matter. Yes. She would do whatever it took to make him think he had broken her to his will. Then she would lead him to where she needed. Finally, she slept.

Chapter 33

Ken stopped at Kate's apartment after class. He saw her first through the front window as he walked up to her apartment. The window was open and he could hear Creedence Clearwater Revival playing *Suzie Q* loud on her stereo. She was dancing barefoot around the room, flicking her dust rag across every horizontal surface as she moved gracefully from place to place. He stood there watching her movements, enjoying her coordinated gracefulness, wishing he could move so well.

She saw him through the window, and without breaking step, she danced to the front door to let him in. She was in high spirits, not a bit embarrassed about having been watched. She threw her arms around his neck as he came in and gave him an enthusiastic kiss.

He invited her up to his place to watch the sunset and have a drink. Then they'd go out to supper. "I've heard invitations like *that* before," she said with a happy smile. Nevertheless, she washed her hands, slipped on her shoes and walked hand-in-hand with him up to his place.

She had not been to his apartment before and she was curious to see how he lived.

She was pleasantly surprised. She'd only known a few bachelors well enough to go to their places, and they had all kept a pretty sloppy house. Her brother was a perfect example. As long as he could find a place to sit down without having to move something, the place was good enough for him.

Ken's apartment was neat: not fussy, but neat. The furniture was mostly furnished-apartment modern, with Formica tops, thin cushions, and skinny, round wooden legs. He had his own disreputable but comfortable overstuffed armchair by the front window. A book was open on the table beside it, with a coffee cup there too, and an ashtray with only a couple of cigarette butts in it. The coffee table in front of the couch was strewn with a few magazines, as though tossed there from the chair after having been read. There were outdoor magazines, gun magazines, and the Playboy that seemed an obligatory publication for young men. A bookshelf full of paperbacks and old college texts was against the far wall. Over the couch there was a triptych print of willows in a Japanese garden that probably came with the apartment, but on a wall where it could be seen from the chair there was a decent print of Charles M. Russell's *Paying the Fiddler*. The little TV was on a rollaway stand in another corner.

He went into the bedroom to change clothes, asking her to get him a beer and mix herself a drink if she wanted. She opened the refrigerator with some trepidation, afraid of what horrors she might find, but there was just milk and orange juice and a few apples. A box on one shelf contained the remains of a pizza: pepperoni, mushrooms, and green peppers, she noted for future reference. The delivery slip taped to the box showed that it was just two days old; it still looked edible.

There was a six-pack of Dos Equis on the bottom shelf. She got one out, found the church key in a drawer by the sink, and popped the top off for him. She found bottles of bourbon and rum, and one of brandy, in a cupboard beside the refrigerator. Since she'd developed a taste for brandy on their New Mexico weekend, she poured herself two fingers of Martel, noticing that it was Cognac, not just brandy.

She went back in the living room and set their drinks down on the coffee table, then turned to pick up the coffee cup and ashtray. His book caught her eye, so she picked it up with a delicious sense of innocent spying to see what he was reading. *Fate is the Hunter*—the title sounded more interesting to her than what the dust jacket blurb revealed, a novel of pilots and flying. That told her something about his interests that she hadn't known before, though.

She set it back down as she'd found it and then took the cup and ashtray to the kitchen. She found the trashcan under the sink and dumped the ashtray and then she washed out the cup and put it in the dish drainer with his breakfast bowl and spoon.

As she turned from the sink, he came into the kitchen in cowboy boots and jeans, buttoning a heavy, blue flannel shirt with headlight snaps. He had a green sweatshirt clamped under his elbow. She enjoyed the look of him in those clothes, tall and lean and western. Even though she'd been raised in Ohio, she found the western look very masculine.

"Did you find the booze, Kate? There's some Cognac in the cupboard over there." He motioned with his chin in the direction of the cupboard as he tucked his shirt down into his pants. "It's the real French thing. I bought it for you since you seemed to enjoy the Mexican stuff."

"I found it and took some, thank you, but I haven't tasted it yet. Your beer is out on the coffee table. I took care of your ashtray and cup; I hope you don't mind."

"You can drop by and clean up here any time you want, but I'll warn you, I don't pay much." He grinned and handed the sweatshirt to her. "You'll want this out on the deck; it's cooling off pretty quick now."

She shrugged into it and pushed the sleeves high up her slender arms. They fell back down immediately. It hung on her like a nightgown, far too big, but she liked how it felt; something of his wrapped around her. They walked through the living room and picked up their drinks and then continued out onto the balcony, where they sat down.

They watched the sky run through its bright palette of colors as the sun set. His feet were propped up on the rail and his steel chair was rocked back on its rear legs. He held the beer in his lap and a fresh cigarette burned in the ashtray by his side. It was sweater weather by this time of afternoon and dark would be on them soon. He hated to see the sun go down so early. For no good reason he could think of, he was feeling melancholy. Maybe it was just the season.

Kate was seated in a chair beside him, one leg crossed over the other, one arm crossed under her breasts, the hand cupping her other elbow. She was wearing jeans, with his Border Patrol sweatshirt over her blouse. As much as he had seen of her, and, he thought with a smile, he'd seen all of her, it was the first time he'd seen her in jeans. They looked good on her. His mood improved at the thought.

"How was class today, honey?" she asked.

"I find myself appalled at the depths of my ignorance of nationality law—that's putting it politely, of course," he said. "The word dumbass also comes to mind."

"I stopped to talk to Mr. Lopez after class to see if he had any study suggestions. He told me I'm doing better than I think and to never mind trying to figure anything out, that's there's no rhyme or reason to it. I should just memorize the tables and apply them logically. So I will. I'm going to get with Pete

LeClaire—you met him at Jim Pope's party—a couple nights between now and the test next week and see what I can do."

"I'm sure you'll do just fine, Ken. What are you doing for Thanksgiving next month? Going home?"

"I can't do it this year; the leave schedule is already filled up with officers senior to me. There won't be any vacation time for me on major holidays for a while, I guess. I'll probably be able to take off on Washington's Birthday or Columbus Day, or something like that. What are you doing?"

She quickly decided that she wasn't going back to Ohio after all; she hoped her folks would understand. She really wanted to fix him a holiday dinner, so she said, "I'll be right here. I was hoping you would be, too, because Dot's going back to San Francisco to see her parents and it would be pretty lonesome. Would you have dinner with me? I'll cook a turkey and everything." She made a mental note to make sure that her schedule allowed enough time to do all the cooking she would have to do.

"Gosh, I'd love it, Kate. I wasn't looking forward to Thanksgiving dinner at some restaurant this year. The thought was making me pretty blue—you're a life-saver."

"It'll be a pleasure for me. I've helped my mother fix dinners forever, but I never fixed a fancy meal for someone I love before. You just don't know how excited I am now." And she really was.

He stood up and offered her a hand out of her chair. She took it and he pulled her up into his arms for a hug and a kiss. They stood there holding one another in the cool evening air, watching the red echoes of the sunset fade in the west.

"Thank you, Kate. I can't tell you how much I'm looking forward to it. I've got to work the early shift from two a.m. to ten a.m. that day, but I'm free after that and I'm off on Friday and Saturday afterwards. Maybe we can spend the whole weekend together. Now let's go find some supper. Italian OK with you?"

It was. Anything would have been OK with her, as long as it was with him.

Chapter 34

October 31, 1968

Dear Mom and Dad,

I PASSED! I finished my five and one-half month test yesterday, so it looks like I still have a job for a while yet. Then comes the ten-month exam, sort of the do-or-die final test.

THe exams take all day, or at least most of it. The first part is a written test about law and all the other things we ought to know how to do. For instance, we have to be able to write, verbatim, about fifteen legal definitions, like "Alien—any person not a citizen or national of the United States." It wasn't till I started studying here that I realized an alien was anything other than a character on My Favorite Martian on TV.

Then in the afternoon we go one at a time before a board of three management officers who interview us for a few minutes and go over the C&E (that's Conduct and Efficiency) reports that the senior guys have done on us every two weeks.

Then we go into a verbal test of SPanish. First we go through the questions we have to ask the wets when we dotheir paperwork, like "What is your name," and

"Where did you cross the border?" There are maybe thirty of them. We have to ask them in acceptable SPanish (darn sticky keys!), then we have to write the answers (that we get in Spanish) down correctly in English. After that, we chat in Spanish for a little while if we can. The only pass\fail part of the SPanish, though, are the questions on this test. The ten-month test is harder. We're supposed to be able to question the alien, not just fill out a form.

They tell you right after if you passed or not, and usually tell you your law grade, too. Anyhow, I only got an 85 in law, but a 98 in Spanish.

I've made a couple of work friends here. One of them, Pete LeClaire, is from Aroostook County. As you might guess, he's a Frenchman, born and raised in Presque Isle. He's retired from the Air Force, which means he's older than me, but I think he's lonesome, so we talk a lot. Coming out here cost him his wife. They'd moved around in the service and she wasn't willing to leave Maine again.

Maybe it's the best thing in the long run, because this work can be pretty hard on a wife. The shifts, the temporary duty out of town and transfers and primitive living conditions in some of the little towns along the border make it hard for a woman. I'm surprised more guys don't end up divorced.

I told you before that they can kick you out the door if you don't pass this test, but usually they don't unless it looks like you're just not going to work out. That happened to one guy this time. He had attitude problems from the beginning so his C&Es weren't very good and his law grade was low. HE's gone now. They told him at the end of the interview to clean out his locker and hit the road. He was gone by the time I got done.

Like I thought, I won't be home for Thanksgiving, or Christmas either. I can't get the time off.

Fortunately, Kate's going to feed me Thanksgiving dinner, so I won't have to eat out alone. As I told you, she's a real good cook. We're seeing a lot of each other; it's pretty serious by now. I think I'm in love with her (I can't believe I'm saying that.)

I'll call you on Thanksgiving. Incidentally, speaking of phones, I just had a new one put in and it has push buttons instead of a dial. They make tones when you push them, not clicks. As far back in the the woods as you all are (grin) maybe you'll get one someday. A dial phone, I mean.

Love to all,
Ken

Chapter 35

Thompson sat in the chair looking at Ayala across the desk. As usual, Diaz sat in the corner behind him. Ayala had gone along with Thompson's idea the week before. He now had Tomás' place in the organization—but it wasn't solid yet.

He got the job only after Ayala obtained permission from his superiors to hire a *pinche gavacho,* a fucking American. They didn't understand why Ayala wanted to do that, but they finally went along with it after Ayala told them he was half Mexican. It was a close call, though. Their first inclination was to kill an American who got that far into the organization.

So Ayala's performance was being closely watched now and he, in turn, watched Thompson. So far, Thompson had carried out just one more job for Ayala since the loss of the last load. He had found and killed the man who had guided it. Misrepresentations or lies or incompetence must be punished, and publicly.

He had done it in broad daylight in the *cantina* where the man hung out. He went in the front door while Diaz watched and provided backup from inside the door. He walked straight to the table where the man sat with five of his friends over beers. He shot him across the table, twice in the chest and once in the head, spilling him backwards out of his chair, leaving a pattern of blood on the wall behind him.

Thompson stood there a moment afterwards, waiting for them to come to their senses once the violence and noise ended. Then, as the powdersmell still hung in the air, he said *"Por ser fulano",* for being a fool. He walked out the back door to the car where Alfonso waited and Diaz simply stepped back onto the street outside the front door. They picked him up on the corner and came back to Ayala's office, where Diaz reported that the job was well done.

Tension was still thick between them, though, and Diaz continued to sit behind him. Thompson knew that he was not yet trusted, that he was still on probation, so to speak. He had to perform, soon.

"*Patrón*, we have used the trick of walking the drugs in several times now. They will have figured it out; I don't think we will fool them again. They will pick up the next load. After the load that Tomás lost it will not be good for us if that happens. I have another idea."

Ayala opened a desk drawer and took out a cigar. He bit the end off and spat it into a wastebasket. Thompson pulled a match from his pocket and leaned over the desk to light *El Patrón's* cigar, hoping he would be invited to have one. He was disappointed, though. Ayala did not invite him to smoke and one did not smoke with *El Patrón* unless invited.

"Tell me of this plan, *gringo.* I believe you are right, but what do you think we should do?"

Thompson didn't like being called *gringo.* He was undeniably *norteamericano,* but he was not white. His mother, after all, had been a *california*, a Mexican native of California. He resented it and he knew it would serve him well if he could get Ayala to stop thinking of him as a *gringo.* He decided to push his recently won advantage.

"*Patrón*, with all respect due to you, please let me tell you that my mother was of the *puro sangre*, the pure blood. While my father was *norteamericano,* I think of myself as of *la raza*. In my heart, I am Mexican. Although I am sure you do not intend it, I hear an insult when you call me *gringo.*"

Ayala stared at him while he considered the thought and the implied request. Finally, he decided that the attitude was understandable—who would wish to be *norteamericano* if he could claim to be Mexican? And while this man was not completely of the *puro sangre,* that was not his fault. He had worked well for them and had earned a level of respect. The request was not, therefore, disrespectful, or unreasonable.

"Yes," he said. "That is fair. Now, Thompson, tell me of your plan."

"Please, *Patrón*, one more request, if I may. In honor of my mother, who raised me, instead of my father who abandoned me, I would like to be called Chavez. It was her name. I would have you call me Gerardo Chavez, *por favor.*"

Thompson didn't actually give a damn what his name was but the change would further his ambition with them and it would tend to cut off any ties of identification by name to his previous life.

"*Bueno,* Gerardo Chavez," Ayala said, exhaling a cloud of fine, blue smoke. "No more favors. Now tell me of your plan."

Chavez explained carefully, making sure that *El Patrón* understood every detail. Life held no guarantees and he would count on treachery and betrayal for the rest of his days. But he wanted to make sure that Ayala could not later claim, if things went wrong, that Chavez had left him in the dark.

When Chavez was through, Ayala thought it over for a long while. Chavez waited, psychologically on the edge of his chair. Finally, Ayala agreed to it.

"*Bueno,*" he said, "we will use your idea the next time; that will be in about two weeks. But Chavez, hear me: you will not kill one of them, not even by accident. That would bring down more problems for us than it would be worth. We play a game now, but that would bring war."

"I don't kill men by accident, *Patrón.* When someone dies at my hands, it is on purpose."

Chapter 36

One afternoon two weeks later Luz lay on the bed, Ayala gasping for air beside her. She had turned her will to the execution of her plan and she had found that by concentrating on the outcome she could do whatever it took to get there. *Tio* Salinas had said to her that if you told yourself something often enough you would come to believe it. So she told herself over and over she could do the impossible things necessary and now she could do them.

She had to gain his trust, or at least make him forget to mistrust her. Over the past few weeks she had become his willing whore, something she had never thought she could do. She came to him with a smile when called, performed eagerly for him, learned the tricks he told her to do. By now, she left him gasping and breathless at the end. But her mind was always focused elsewhere—on the future, on her revenge. This was a part of her life that someday she would lock away in a box in her mind and never think of again.

At first, she had just become more willing with him when he called for her. Then, over the course of a week, she asked to see him a few times. Each time, she presented herself to him in that way women can use that makes a man think of bed, believing it was his idea.

Now she could walk in to see him nearly any time. And she had taught him that her responses were best and thus his pleasure greatest, when there was no one else to see or hear. He had learned to dismiss Diaz and to close the doors to the guard's rooms when Luz was with him.

"Send them away so we can be alone together," she had said one time as she leaned back on the edge of his desk beside him. Her short skirt was pulled high on her thighs and tight across her hips and the arms crossed under her breasts brought them invitingly to the low top of her blouse. She slid back to sit on the desk and her open thighs begged the hand that quickly came. He sent Diaz and the bodyguards away and took her there on the desk. She no longer had to ask him to dismiss his bodyguards.

She was his personal girl now. One day, as they lay on the bed after one of their encounters, she had said that she wanted to be his alone. As she uttered the words, she set about her intimate ministrations to him once more, using all her new tricks, bringing a response he thought was gone with the years. He had to say yes—what man wouldn't?

He was not the first man taken in by a woman's charms, but that is not a thought that usually occurs to a man besotted with lust and satiation.

Chapter 37

He stood up on the pegs and leaned forward over the handlebars. He gunned the bike up the sand hill, getting some air as he came off the back side and then made a perfect landing, rear wheel slightly first with the tire spinning hard, throwing a rooster tail of sand as it bit once more. It drove the machine forward, the front wheel light on the ground. A weight shift back, and a slight tug on the handlebars as he twisted the throttle and the front wheel came up. He wheelied along, enjoying the sense of power and control.

Finally, he throttled back, pulled in the clutch, and rolled to a stop on the sand road he had followed out into the desert. The Franklin Mountains stood high in the sky to the east, their western faces being painted in reds and oranges by the evening sun. The clear sky was still bright blue, but it would be dark in an hour, and chilly. Through the river gap in the mountains he could see the eastern horizon going black. He knew he had better scout out his overwatch location while there was still enough light to see.

He shifted the rifle strapped across his back to a more comfortable position, checked the seat behind him to make sure that his bedroll and war bag were still firmly in place, then sped off across the sand to the edge of the rimrock.

The place was easy to find, a point jutting out from the rimrock with a clear view of the valley below. He had seen it from the valley, when he stood down there looking for a spot with a clear view of an area along the foot of the cap rock. He needed a high, concealed position with an open field of fire on the section of road he was interested in. There had to be clear escape route, too, back to Mexico.

In short, what he needed was a good sniper's hide, for he was treating this as just that sort of mission.

He stopped well short of the edge of the rimrock, climbed off the bike and leaned it into a greasewood bush. The paint on the tank showed that it wasn't the first time he'd treated it so casually.

He lifted the rifle strap over his head, extended the collapsible metal stock and leaned it against the bike and then he unstrapped his war bag from the back seat and threw it on the ground. He unzipped it, and after digging through all the gear packed inside, he came up with a pair of binoculars that were on Army records as having been lost in combat overseas.

Binoculars in hand, he walked over to the lip and looked down. Just as he'd thought. He had a perfectly clear view of the gravel road as it approached the railroad tracks. By laying up under a greasewood bush by the lip he would not silhouette himself against the skyline in the morning as he watched the action below. Now, though, he carefully scanned the whole area around and along the road, looking for any unusual interest being shown. Satisfied that there was none, he turned away from the edge to walk back to his Yamaha.

A smile crossed his face. Working terrain in the desert to your advantage was much simpler than trying to set things up in the jungle. It was harder to hide yourself, of course, but here in the U.S. he could hide in plain sight since he belonged here. All he had to do was avoid looking suspicious and never get caught with a load. And he never intended to—prison wasn't in his plans.

He pulled a ground sheet from the war bag and spread it next to the greasewood bush he'd selected to lay under. Unrolling his sleeping bag, he threw it down atop the groundsheet, then wrapped a shop rag around the receiver of his rifle and slipped it under the edge of the ground sheet. Out of sight, but never out of mind. He'd lived too many years with a rifle in his hand for it ever to be out of mind.

He stretched out on his stomach to watch the area until dark. For an hour he lay there absolutely unmoving, still as a lizard on a warm rock. His body never moved but his eyes never stopped.

He'd learned patience long before, back in 'Nam. Two tours there as a sniper, a very good sniper, had taught him patience, for sometimes to move was to die. On one mission he'd laid up on a hillside above a village for thirty-six hours, never even scratching his nose. Ants crawled up his sleeves, a cobra had slithered by a yard away, and he'd pissed in his pants to avoid moving. Finally the target showed up and from eight hundred meters he'd reached out and made the touch.

Then he'd spent another whole day just lying there while they beat the bushes all around him. They had no luck, although one of them had nearly stepped on him. He'd taken the precaution before the shot of laying down what would look to them like an exit trail from a place he could have shot from. They finally followed that out and away from him and eventually gave up. He could have harvested another of them once they returned to the *ville*. He was tempted, but that wasn't part of the mission.

As he lay there under the greasewood he thought of things. His mind turned them over and over, while his eyes and brain functioned in another channel, seeing, registering, and assessing.

"Life is good," he thought. He liked his work now. He'd never felt more alive than he did in 'Nam because he'd known that he could go from living to dead in a split second. There was a lot to be said about a little lower level of excitement as you got older, though, and the life he'd led made twenty-eight seem plenty old.

They'd made him come home at the end of his second tour. At first they put him in the training cadre at Fort Bliss, teaching recruits how to shoot. He'd been good at it, too. Finally, though, they'd discharged him with a phony excuse.

Thompson slowly moved his hand to his right temple and rubbed the scar from a shrapnel wound taken in a mortar attack during his second tour. Sometimes it gave him headaches.

An Army shrink told him that he had become "unstable", whatever in the hell that meant. What did "stable" have to do with being sent out to crawl through the jungle and elephant grass to find a spot where you could kill someone in cold blood with a twitch of your finger? The doc said that he was supposed to do it, but he wasn't supposed to enjoy it. And he wasn't supposed to brag about it to all the kids in the barracks.

"Shit, why shouldn't a man take pride in something he's good at?" he thought.

So with nothing else to do and nowhere else to go, he'd gone over Juarez to hang around the cantinas. There was always a market for a shooter; all you had to do was find the client.

So he'd talked to anyone who seemed interested about his background. He never said he was looking for a job; he just spoke of what he used to do. Finally, at the Cantina Rio Bravo one night, an ugly, tough-looking Mex sat down at his table to talk. By the time they were done there was a rough understanding. The Mex had told him they'd be talking to some people first, but if he was still interested he should come back in a week and have a seat at the table in the back corner. The

Mex went on to say that if he was lying he'd better not ever be seen in Juarez again. In fact, it would be a good idea to move to Canada if he was lying.

That had been six months ago. Since then he'd killed two people for them right away. The big Mex had come along to watch the first one, a job on a snitch. It was up close and personal with a pistol, where you look into the eyes and watch them widen and the mouth open to say "NO!" as he realizes what's about to happen. Then, two rounds in the breastbone from his .45 automatic and another in the ear as he lay on the ground and it was all over. The big Mex had been satisfied, even happy.

For the second he'd been on his own, a mid-range rifle shot on a Mexican cop who refused to listen to reason from the boss. The *chota* had ignored advice about not being in certain places at certain times and refused money, too, a stupid decision.

It had been out along the levee east of town. Thompson remembered with professional satisfaction how the cop had slumped over the wheel as the bullet through the open passenger window exploded his head, blowing brains and skull and blood in a bright spray out the driver's window. It had been a decent shot, about a hundred and fifty yards on a fast-moving target. The car had veered off the levee, crossed the *vega* with the dead man at the wheel and dropped into the river. It never even made the papers.

He'd successfully run half a dozen loads of drugs for them, too. The first few were right across the border on his bike, the others picking up loads that had been toted in with groups of wetbacks. That was a good scam, he thought. Misdirection of the enemy was always a good trick. In fact, tomorrow's load would catch them off balance, too. The distraction would be close to where the last load had been, only a mile or so from the windmill, and it was only two days after the last one, far sooner than any had been before. Before that, they'd always waited weeks and moved them miles away from where the last load had been. This one should take them by surprise. He had to admire how *El Patrón* did things; he understood how they thought and used it against them.

He was coming to be trusted, trusted as much as a *norteamericano* would ever be trusted by a bunch of Mexicans. There were bigger things in his future. He wouldn't always be a technician for them; he'd get into the chain of command sometime and make some real money. People might have to be removed, but if he was going to move up there had to be a hole to fill.

With the arrival of full dark he rose and went behind the bush, out of view from the valley. He opened his war bag and pulled out a small sheet metal stove that folded up to the size of a box of kitchen matches and a can of Sterno. Folding his long legs, he easily dropped into a cross-legged sitting position, unfolded the stove and took the lid off the can of Sterno. He lit it with his lighter and watched, entranced, as the alcohol gel burned with a flickering, pretty blue flame. He slipped it into its compartment below the stove's grill and set the stove back under the overhang of the bush to conceal the slight glow from the flame.

He poured water from his canteen into a tin cup that he set on the grill. It would be hot enough to make coffee in a few minutes.

An Army LRP ration in the cargo pocket on his pants leg held food enough to keep a man going for a day. The brown plastic envelope held a big packet of freeze-dried spaghetti and meatballs and packets of crackers and jelly and a small, hard fruit bar. He opened the crackers and spread the grape jelly across them. As he chewed the cracker he thought that Lurps would never be confused with gourmet food, but they were a vast improvement over the old C-rations.

Leaning back on one elbow and turning his face to the sand, he struck his Zippo again and lit a Camel, cupping the lighter and the glowing coal of the cigarette in his hand. It had been a mistake a few weeks ago when he didn't shield the flame and it had drawn attention to him that he really didn't want. The green-shirt had been stupid, though, and easy to convince that all was innocent. Fortunately, he'd had his rifle out of sight then, too.

The rifle, a Colt AR15, was a mixed blessing out here. He liked it a lot. First, it was a duplicate of the M-16 he'd trained with in the Army before he became a sniper—the only difference was that this civilian version would not fire fully automatically. He had to pull the trigger for each shot. It was short and handy and he could fire it quickly up close with the stock collapsed. Or he could extend the stock to full length and use the sights. With that, he could drop a man five hundred yards away. With the twenty-round magazine and semi-auto capability it let him lay down so much fire that he could break contact and run while the other guys kept their heads down. Free ammo was a good thing, too. He'd stolen so much of it from the base while he was still on the cadre there that he could shoot as much as he wanted to keep his eye in. Having it was a comfort; it gave him a sort of warm, secure feeling that nothing else could.

On the other hand though, carrying that kind of rifle around out here might make someone pay more attention to him than he wanted. All things considered, though, having it was OK. He wasn't the only one who went shooting in the desert, so having it along was not suspicious by itself, but best if nobody saw it; that way, it wouldn't occur to them to ask questions about it.

The water boiled just as his cigarette burned down to his fingers. He field stripped the butt and then took up the cup and poured the water into the dried spaghetti and meatballs. Coffee sounded good to him, so he filled the cup again and set it back on the burner.

He stirred the ingredients in the plastic bag into a rust-colored mud with a spoon from the ration bag and began to eat. He no longer noticed if the stuff tasted good or bad; it filled him up and that was all he needed.

Once more, the cup of water boiled. He tore open a packet of instant coffee and poured it into the water, licked most of the last of the spaghetti off the spoon and then gave the coffee a quick stir. Long before, he'd quit noticing the taste of his rations in his coffee. He lit another cigarette from the Sterno and then put the lid back on the can, snuffing the flame.

Cross-legged, he sat there enjoying the feel of the smoke in his lungs and the taste of the coffee on his tongue. He tilted his head back and spent a few minutes looking at the stars overhead as he drank his coffee. Venus was low and bright on the western horizon, which still showed just a hint of the sun's glow.

"It's all bullshit," he thought, oblivious to the change of mood that had come upon him since he set up camp.

With that, he snuffed the remains of the Camel out in the sand, tossed the dregs of the coffee into the bush, put the trash into the plastic ration bag and buried it under the bush. He rolled into his sleeping bag, looked at the stars for a minute, and was asleep. He knew that he'd awaken before dawn, as always.

Chapter 38

The Real Diehl and Travis walked into the Denny's Restaurant on Mesa Street on the west side of El Paso. They were looking for a snack and cup of coffee on the way out to the sandhills to work a late evening shift, eight p.m. to four a.m.

"You know, Travis, I gave up sportfucking a few years back; it just wasn't worth the effort and expense any more. Now I got a friendly woman who I can drop in on from time to time. She cooks me a couple of good meals, like dinner and then breakfast, and she warms things up, if you know what I mean, and it's mighty convenient. But there's a young lovely here who makes me question the wisdom of my chosen path. Sometimes clean living and righteous thoughts ain't what they're cracked up to be. "

They stopped just inside the door and looked around before Diehl headed for the short leg of the L-shaped counter. He slid into one of the swivel stools. Ken took one next to him.

"Ken, look yonder down there and see the proof that God loves men, 'cause he made things like that for us." He nodded his head in the direction of a raven-haired girl of twenty-something who was reaching up to the high, stainless steel counter to retrieve a ready order from the kitchen. Her raised arms pulled the front of her white waitress's uniform tight across her full bosom and the skirt rose high, revealing shapely calves, and thighs clear to the garter snap at the top of her stockings. She apparently had not yet given in to the sexless, newfangled pantyhose he had run into a couple times."Don't she just make your heart go pitty-pat, Ken?"

"She is a vision and that's a fact, Real," Ken replied, enjoying the view. "I take it you've been here before." He picked up the menu and looked for breakfast.

"Well, I do come here about once a week, just for the food, of course, but there's nothing says a man's got to eat in unpleasant surroundings, is there?"

The girl placed the order in front of a man seated down the counter, then came on up to Real and Ken, snagging the coffee pot as she came past the hot plate. They turned their cups right side up. Ken still had his face in his menu; he'd missed supper, and his stomach thought his throat had been cut. Food was foremost in his thoughts.

"Good evenin' Mr. Diehl," she said as she poured the two cups full. "You here for your usual?"

"That I am, Sylvia. I'm feeling like a high-roller tonight, though, and since my partner here is buying, throw a little ice cream on it this time."

"Apple pie a la mode it is, then." She turned her gaze on Ken and asked, "What'll it be for you, stranger?"

Ken looked up from the menu into an oval face framed by black hair that curled softly around her ears and stopped at her collar. Her smiling mouth was generous, the lips full, and the white teeth gleamed as she smiled at him. The flawless, creamy skin, high cheekbones, and a pert, perfect nose combined to make it a lovely face, but looking into her deep violet eyes struck him dumb. His mind went blank. Thought stopped while he looked at her with his mouth open, words in his brain running in circles, waiting their turn.

Diehl spoke up, breaking the silence by saying, "Sylvia, this speechless character is Ken Travis. He's new to town, but I expect you'll be seeing more of him in the future."

Ken snapped out of his trance, embarrassed. He looked at Diehl, then back to her. He still said nothing.

Her gaze was speculative, amused. Some beautiful women are oblivious to their effect on some men and others aren't. She wasn't and she got a kick out of the impact she'd had on this one—it was beyond the usual.

"Well, Ken, I hope to see you in here often. Are you here for the food tonight, or are you just keeping Mr. Diehl company?"

Ken realized that he was still looking at her over the top of the menu.

"Uh, make it two scrambled eggs, bacon and sausage, hash browns, pancakes, and a tall orange juice, please," he said, never taking his eyes from hers.

She reached out and gently took the still-open menu from his fingers and put it back in the rack. "One Grand Slam and orange juice," she replied as she jotted the order on her notepad. "Anything else?"

"Uh, nope. Well, keep the coffee coming."

She turned and walked back down to the service counter, the medium-high heels on her waitress shoes and short, tight skirt accentuating sleek hips and a butt round as half a soccer ball and just as firm.

"My God, Real! You only come here once a week? I may never leave. What is somebody who looks like that doing behind the counter here? I didn't see a ring. Does she have a boyfriend? Wonder if I can kill him."

"She makes an impression, don't she? Most guys get pretty taken with her, but I gotta say I never saw one hit as hard as you were. I was afraid your mouth was gonna draw flies, hanging open like it was. Thing is, you ain't seen the best part—watch when she gets my pie."

Ken watched as she moved around the counter, taking and delivering orders, pouring coffee and joking and laughing with the customers. She was good at her job and every man who came into the place, and it was mostly men who came in at that hour, took a seat at the counter. Booths went begging and the other waitresses more or less wound up leaning against the service counters, talking to each other and taking care of the occasional couple who came in and did take a booth.

Ken's order came up and she brought it and the coffee pot to them.

"Here you go," she said as she slid Ken's order in front of him and warmed up their coffee at the same time. "Pie a la mode coming up."

She turned around and set the pot on the back counter and then slid open the door to the pie cooler, a horizontal, glass-fronted cabinet mounted high over the counter on the back wall. Stretching tall and standing on her tiptoes, she reached high to the second shelf, where the apple pie was. Her short skirt rode clear up past the tops of her stockings, to reveal the bare backs of her thighs, then a small slice of the pink panties that hugged the lower curves of her butt.

Ken's jaw dropped open once more. This time there was a predictable male reaction; he didn't know if he'd be able to stand up without embarrassment.

She brought down the pie tin, cut out a slice, put a generous scoop of ice cream on it and then slid it gently to Diehl. Then she turned around and went through the whole operation again to put the pie back.

When she was done she turned to Diehl and said with a knowing smile, "You sure do like apple pie, don't you?" She knew, it was clear. And she didn't mind.

"Yep, I sure do, honey. Thank you kindly," Diehl responded. Ken, who had managed to close his mouth around a forkful of eggs, had nothing to say, so he just nodded.

A few minutes later Ken had paid the bill and left a tip that was more than generous. As they settled into the Scout, Ken said, "God-damn, Real! I try to be a gentleman and admire women for all their virtues, but I gotta tell you I coulda pushed open the front door on the way out without raising a hand and not banged my nose. That is one hell of a woman. Those eyes of hers, she could raise a hard-on on a dead priest. And speaking as an ass man from way back, I will testify that her butt is dead solid perfect. Do you know if she's spoke for?"

"I thought you were the next thing to spoke for yourself, Ken. Man like you, next thing to married, he shouldn't be looking around at other women like that."

"I may be spoke for, but I'm not hog-tied yet. Kate's a terrific woman, but oh, shit . . ." A massive hormone flood was under way and the little head, given a chance, would lead the big one down the road.

"She's a student out at UTEP, working her way through school," Diehl told him. "I don't recall what she's studying, exactly, but it's one of them courses like psychology or sociology or something. Believe she graduates this year. I met her boyfriend one night in there when he got back from a football game. I mean, from playing in a football game. He's some sort of defensive back and he's one big boy. I 'spect he could pick you up by the ankles and rip you in half, was he of a mind to. I think I'd try real hard to keep from putting that thought in his mind, myself. We chatted friendly for a while, but I'm not trying to get into her drawers, so to speak, and he could see that. You just remember: a little pussy never hurt nobody, but chasing it can get you hurt. I'd hate to have to educate another trainee."

Ken filed that information away, but he'd be dropping in to Denny's again.

Chapter 39

Later, they were slowly driving north up Highway 260, up the valley towards Mesilla, looking at one ditch bank or another for fresh sign of groups walking north when Diehl slowed and said, "Well, look at that, would you. Sometimes even a blind hog finds an acorn."

There, on a ditch bank on the other side of the canal was a truck, an old Ford as near as they could tell in the dim light of evening. The sun had set a half hour before and it was nearly dark. The air was cooling quickly, bringing out the night smells and their windbreakers felt good with the windows open. There didn't appear to be anyone around, but it was possible that someone was down in the field on the far side of truck from them.

"We're gonna go have a look at that truck and see if anyone's around. If the driver's there, we're gonna ID him and see what he's up to."

"Ok, Real. What do you want me to do? I'd rather have you tell me now how to handle it than to try to figure it out myself once we're there."

"This here'll be another lesson for your collection of experiences, Ken. I'm gonna stop up here for a minute. You take the binoculars and see if you can make out a license plate number and get some details on what the truck looks like. Write it down and call it in; tell Sector what we're doing and where. We've got to drive on up here another mile or more to get to a place to cross the canal and come back down the ditch bank. If he happens to leave before we get back at least we'll know who was here."

He coasted to a stop at the side of the road and Ken stepped out with the big binoculars. Looking back, he could just make out the license number in the fading light, the white letters visible against the black background. The binoculars were bulky, but he was grateful for the wide fifty-millimeter objective lenses; they gathered a lot of light.

"Definitely a Texas tag, white on black. Looks like PCT 247," he said to Diehl, who wrote it on the palm of his hand. " I think it's some shade of gray, maybe primer; might be pale blue, though. Looks like it's probably a late fifties model. The right front fender's got a ding in it about the size of a football. That's all I can tell now." He got back in the Scout as Diehl rolled, anxious to get up the road and back before the truck left.

"We're gonna approach this thing like it's a Doberman with a toothache, Ken. We'll stop short of the truck and you'll walk up to it yourself. I'll be alongside you, but down in the field at the foot of the ditch bank. We've got about a half moon tonight and it's pretty bright, but the shadows'll be deep there; anybody in the truck won't see me worth a damn, if at all. If somebody's got a hard-on for us I want 'em to have to work to get us both. Reason I want you up on the road is that you can concentrate on one thing: the truck. I'll be looking at it, but at everything else, too. I'll have you covered good."

"You walk up with your gun in your hand, but down by your side. Once you're satisfied it's OK go ahead and put it away, but the rule is, when in doubt, haul it out."

Ken was suddenly tense and confused. It wasn't so much that he couldn't remember the specifics of what Diehl was saying about this situation, but he needed to learn the concepts so that he could apply them in the future, some time when he didn't have someone there to hold his hand. There was a lot of tactical data to absorb in what Diehl had just told him.

"And don't be using your flashlight when you walk up. The dark is your friend. If he lights you up with his headlights, you get the fuck off the ditch bank and down with me like right fucking now, you hear? Don't wait around to hear shots, 'cause if he lights you up you're there like a target in a shooting gallery. Better to have your friends saying "Didn't he look silly diving off of there," over coffee than "Didn't he look natural" as they carry you along by the handles.

Ken thought it over. It made sense to him, assuming that he had to walk on the ditch bank road at all. So he asked Diehl why.

"Reason I want you up there and me down here is to split his attention and throw an element of uncertainty into his thinking. A good man with a gun out in the dark could take out the two of us real quick if we were side-by-side and up on this narrow ditch bank, and that's how we'd have to be. But if you're up here and I'm down there somewhere he can't see it kinda limits his options, you might say. Uncertainty is the enemy of any plan. You write that down, hear? Think about how to confuse the other guy whenever it you can."

Diehl turned left off the highway onto a low wooden bridge across the canal and then immediately made another left at the other end of the bridge onto the ditch bank. He turned the headlights off as soon as he was on the narrow track that ran along the canal and then stopped.

"Give Sector a call now and tell 'em what's up and where we are. We're about a half a mile up highway 260 from where it swings northwest out here in the Valley. Make sure they understand, but don't get 'em excited or anything.

Ken picked up the microphone. After a couple of calls, the Sector radio operator responded and took the message.

"We're going to sit here for a couple minutes and let our eyeballs adjust. It takes about twenty minutes to see real well in the dark but even just a couple minutes helps a lot. Night like tonight, we'll see damn well. Trouble is, so will he since he's already been out here for a while. We best just hope he's not even around."

"Like I told you, the dark is your friend. You want to learn to love it like a warm, fuzzy blanket. At night you should be thinking about light all the time, how to use it and how to keep yourself out of it. Watch out for getting backlighted—that's where you silhouette yourself against a light somewhere."

Christ, almighty, is there no end to what he's gonna dump in my head? I can't remember all this.

"Take tonight. We got a piece of moon, and the stars are out. Right now it's kinda hard to see things, but if you're down in the field beside the ditch bank and somebody walks along it above you he'll have the stars and moonlight behind him and you'll see him real good. Same thing goes if it's house lights or the highway in the background. Know where the light is. Shadows are another thing. A medium bright night like this, once your eyes adjust, you'll think you can see a lot, and in the open, you can. But stuff in shadows just disappears, unless it's light-colored or shiny. You find yourself hiding in a shadow, you take that badge and name tag off."

"We're going in here slow and quiet, with our eyes wide open. Keep your window down so you can hear—and if it makes you feel good, keep your door open a crack so you can bail out quick if a shitstorm develops."

Ken rolled his window down and then pulled the door handle, letting the door open just bit. Someone long before had removed the bulb from the dome light at just such a time, so the interior stayed dark. His heart was racing and his mind was keeping up with it. *This isn't like a law class; this could be life or death. Is this what terror feels like?*

"Don't close your door when you get out, OK? No noise. And hang on a second after you step out; I need time to get out and around the back of the rig and down the bank," Diehl said as they rolled slowly to a stop. He stayed off the brakes to avoid having the brake lights come on.

The Scout finally stopped completely, fifty yards from the old pickup truck. Ken stepped out onto the dusty track and stood looking intently at the truck, searching for any trace of movement. His senses and his nerves were on edge. He looked just to the side of the truck, knowing that things were more easily seen from the corner of the eye after dark. There was nothing—and he'd have felt better if he'd been able to see someone there.

Visions from the shootout in *Bonnie and Clyde* flitted across his mind's eye. The final scene, with Warren Beatty and Faye Dunaway doing death's ugly dance as the Texas Rangers' bullets cut them to doll rags in their car was all too vividly still in his mind. He'd seen the movie just before leaving home to go to El Paso and that scene had nearly made him change his mind about joining the Patrol. He felt the nervous sweat start in his armpits. Like icy fingers, it trickled down his sides to his waist, causing him to shiver. *Oh, God,* he breathed to himself, he hoped it was to himself, *don't let me fuck up.*

He could hear traffic on the Interstate three miles away and the sibilant whisper of an airliner high above. The stars were little brilliant pinpoints overhead and the moon was just above the eastern horizon, casting long, deep shadows westward from the bushes. A light breeze penetrated his jacket, making him shiver, and it carried the scent of a field latrine to his nose. He noticed how cold the flashlight was his hand. He heard Diehl's soft footsteps pass behind him, then a slight scrambling sound as he went down the bank.

He looked down and to his right, trying to see into the deep shadows below him. He could see nothing there but apparently Diehl could see him, for a harsh whisper came from the void: "Don't for crissake look at me! You might as well shine your light down here. Watch the goddam truck!"

Embarrassed once again at another boneheaded trick, Ken jerked his head around and began to walk slowly toward the truck. Diehl's whisper came out of the dark once more: "Your revolver, goddamit."

Wanting to sink into the ground, Ken passed the flashlight from his right hand to his left, unsnapped the safety strap over his .38 and pulled it from the holster. He stopped to gather his wits and took a long look again at the truck. There was still no indication that anyone was around. He began to walk forward, gut churning and knees wobbly, his vision narrowed until he saw just the truck. He stopped again and breathed deep to calm himself. He shook his head.

Stress brings tunnel vision, he reminded himself. *Gotta keep my eyes open.* He looked at the truck, then scanned slowly right and left.

He finally reached the front fender and stopped, unsure where to go from there. *Better check out all around it.* He slowly walked down the driver's side, taking a close look in the open window as he passed by and then into the bed.

Diehl was alert and amused as he watched Travis's actions. So far the kid was doing OK, controlling his nerves, thinking things out as he went. Diehl didn't really expect any problem; the driver was probably miles away. Even if he was close there was no reason that he should start something – probably. It didn't hurt to be careful, though, and it was great training opportunity for Travis. Being prepared was the key to survival in a world where guns were tools.

Ken completed his trip around the vehicle and then softly said, "It looks all clear to me, Real."

"I think I'll just stay right here until you make sure there's nobody under the thing, OK?"

"Awww, shit!" Ken sighed aloud. He bent over and looked beneath the truck. As he straightened, Diehl scrambled up the bank. "I'm sorry, Real. I really fucked that up, didn't I?"

"You didn't do bad, Ken. You controlled yourself and you kept thinking. Instincts are the important things; technique will come with more experience. Now let's see what we got here. Don't turn on your light."

Ken released the pent-up tension in his chest with a long sigh. The sound brought a smile to Diehl's face. Learning to control your nerves was no easy task when it might involve life or death—your own. It didn't matter that perhaps only you thought it was life and death; the effect on your nerves was the same.

There was a reinforced two by ten plank in the bed, and some ropes. Marks in the dust barely visible in the faint moonlight showed that a motorcycle had been unloaded from the bed.

"I'd bet a year's pay that this is our boy, Ken. Did you notice that open window?"

"Yeah, I did."

"Well, let's see if he left the registration in here. We don't want to open the door. If he's out there somewhere it'll catch his eye if the dome light comes on."

Diehl shrouded the lens of his flashlight with four fingers, leaving just a tiny crack between two of them for the light to shine through. He put the light in through the open window and low inside before he turned it on.

There, held onto the steering column with a couple of small springs, was a plastic envelope with a clear window. The registration was visible in it. Ken looked over Real's shoulder.

Real turned his head to Ken and said, "Prob'ly only one of us really needs to look at this thing, huh? How 'bout you turn around and keep your eyes open for business out in the weeds. We don't need nobody sneaking up on us, do we? And split out a little bit; O.K?"

Without a word, but aching inside yet again, Ken turned around and stepped to the tailgate to maintain a lookout. He knew he should have thought of it himself.

Diehl quickly committed the information to memory, and then turned off his light.

"You go 'round the other side now, Ken, while I keep watch. You saw how I used my light, didn't you? Do the same thing to have a look in the glove box."

Ken did, but found nothing there but a book of matches. He turned them over to see where they were from—the Cantina Rio Bravo, he saw. He mentioned it to Diehl, who grunted, "Figures."

"OK," he went on. "Let's get out of here. I'm satisfied this is our guy and if he's out there riding the desert this time of night, it ain't for fun. Something's probably coming in the morning, just like the other times. But this time, we'll be waiting for him when he gets back here with it."

Chapter 40

The bullet smashed through the windshield between them. It narrowly missed Cole, who was driving, but it filled LeClaire's eyes with shards of glass, leaving him blinded and moaning, face buried in his hands, doubled over in his seat. Gary Cole was more fortunate—he was wearing sunglasses. He'd been shot at before and he knew exactly what had just happened.

He cut the wheel hard to the left and dropped off the steep, four-foot high bank into the hardpan desert floor at the base of the grade. As soon as he knew the Scout was not going to roll over he threw the gearshift into neutral, rolled out the door onto the ground and then scrambled over to the base of the road grade for cover. The shot had come from ahead and to the right and the bank provided the only cover around. The Scout had coasted to a stop a few yards away, with LeClaire still in the killing zone.

"Get the hell out of the vehicle," he screamed at LeClaire as he crawled up to the top of the berm and took a quick glance over it, revolver in hand. "Don't give him another shot at you!"

Pete, still unable to see, but able to feel the door handle, fell out the door and landed on his face in the dirt. He rolled back under the rig, the only cover he could find while blinded.

Cole scanned the hillside ahead of them in quick glimpses while LeClaire tried to cry some of the glass out of his eyes so he could at least see well enough to get a shot at someone up close. The excruciating pain continued despite the effort. He was totally blind and out of action.

Cole popped his head up again, hoping not to give the gunman a long enough look at him to get a shot. He cursed an outfit that would send men out to do this kind of work with no long arms or walkie-talkies. He was helpless in the face of a shooter with a rifle and he couldn't even call for help without using the radio in the jeep. All he could do was die, if that was what the rifleman had in mind for them. The lack of a follow-up shot to kill LeClaire when he had been most vulnerable, though, made him wonder just what the shooter had in mind.

He waited, looking in every direction as far as he could see. If the shooter exposed himself Cole could make a long shot that might save their lives. He knew he could hit a man at fifty yards with his revolver and hit close enough to make him keep his head down at a hundred and fifty. But the hillside was way out of range and that, without a doubt, is where the shot came from. He looked at the Scout. There, in the tailgate, was the exit hole from the bullet. It had gone through the windshield at about eye level and exited the tailgate at butt level. That indicated a plunging shot, which could only have come from high up on the hill.

He chanced another look. Again, nothing.

It was only a matter of thirty feet or so to the rear end of the Scout, thirty wide-open feet. Once there, he'd have concealment and some cover. But getting there . . . He had to move, though, for he knew that if the shooter moved just a short distance to his own right he'd have Cole's position against the road grade in enfilade and could take him out at his leisure.

He crawled along in the cover of the grade, breathing caliche dust and smelling his own fear, until he was even with the rear end of the Scout. Then saying to himself, "Feet, don't fail me now", he gathered his legs under himself and sprang across the gap. "How could thirty feet be so goddam far", he thought as he was in the open. He dived and slid under the rear bumper, then crawled deeper under the Scout.

"LeClaire! How are you doing?" He could hear LeClaire whimpering ahead of him and Cole wondered if he'd been hit.

"I'm fucking dying up here, Tom. I'm blinded—can't see a goddam thing with my eyes full of glass. I don't think I'm shot, though."

Another bullet slammed into the radiator and stopped against the engine with a solid WHANG! A gout of water flowed from the radiator with a hiss of steam and a smell of antifreeze. The sound of the shot came a split-second later. They weren't going anywhere, now.

"Hang in there, Pete. I'm going to see if I can get to the radio without getting my head blown off. If I can, I'll call for help."

He slithered forward under the rear axle, collecting black grease and dust on his uniform from the filthy bottom of the rig and then to the left until he was under the driver's door. He did a quick mental calculation of the angles involved and decided the rifleman wouldn't able to see him as long as he stayed below the level of the top of the dashboard. Fortunately, the mike was clipped on the dash down at the level of the driver's right knee. He had cursed that location many times after banging his knee on it, but now he was pitifully grateful that it was there.

He peeked out from under the Scout, past the left front tire. He couldn't see the area on the hill the shot probably came from and that meant that the shooter couldn't see him either. Unless he'd moved, of course. "Well," he thought as he slid warily out from under the Scout, "they told me there'd be days like this."

He crawled a little farther out and then sat up behind the door. Rising to his knees, he leaned across the driver's foot well and grabbed the microphone. He dropped back to the ground with it. He'd been shot at before and anyone who said it wasn't terrifying was lying through his teeth. You had to go on and do what had to be done, though, at least take someone out with you. So far, he hadn't gotten a round off. But then, he hadn't been hit yet, either, so he was still in the game.

The channel knob was already set to the repeater frequency and that meant everyone on the net in the Sector would hear what he said. He keyed the mike and waited for the repeater to cut in, and then he spoke, his voice shaking with stress,

"El Paso, El Paso, this is H-463, Cole and LeClaire. We are under fire on the road to Lizard Siding. We are pinned down and cannot move. LeClaire is injured and out of action, but it's not life threatening. We need help now!"

He thought about the tactical situation, for he knew whoever came to help would be in deadly peril unless they approached safely.

The radio was silent.

"Sector, sector. Answer, goddamit, we need help."

The radio operator finally responded. "Unit calling, repeat, please. I was out of the room."

"Sector, H-463. We've been shot at!" The stress came through clearly in his voice and he stammered slightly. "We, we're pinned down, pinned down by a rifleman just off the road right below Lizard Siding. Can't move without exposing ourselves. I mean, we're just below the siding. He's up on the rimrock. LeClaire has glass in his eyes and can't see. I'm OK."

"We gotta have help! The shooter is ahead of us on the rimrock just above where the road crosses the siding. Nobody can approach this position. Whoever comes to help will have to get at the guy from behind. I don't know if he's alone or not."

He let the button on the mike go and waited for a response.

The radio spoke again, with the stuttering drone of an airplane engine in the background.

"Cole, this is Wagner. I'm over at Santa Teresa now, but I'll be there in five minutes or less to have a look at what's on the hill. Keep your head down." Super Cubs, low and slow, could easily be hit by ground fire, but it was a gamble you had to make when another PI was in trouble. Wagner shoved the throttle forward and climbed to five hundred feet as he headed southwest.

The radio traffic degenerated into a babble of voices, each trying to talk over the other. Finally there was a break and the Sector operator took control again.

"All units hold your traffic. We have emergency in progress. The Chief Patrol Inspector is here now."

"Cole," the Chief said, "What's going on out there? Do you really need help?"

"Yes, goddamit, we really need help!" Cole was still stressed, but his thinking mind was taking control again. "We're pinned down by an asshole with a rifle. No place to go and he can potshot us whenever he gets ready," he yelled into the microphone.

"Calm down, Cole. No need to talk like that on the radio. What can we do for you?"

Squatting beside the Scout with nowhere to go, Cole pulled the mike away from his face and stared at it, wishing he could reach through the thing and grab the Chief by the throat.

Just as he was about to make a sharp reply he hesitated. Did he hear a motorcycle starting? As he listened he heard it come fully to life with a two-stroke sputter, then wind up through the gears, each upshift sounding a little fainter.

Wagner came up on the channel.

"I'm right behind you, King. Where'd the shots come from?"

"Christ, but I'm glad you're here, Wings. I think the shooter's up on the rim, just to the right of straight ahead of the Scout. I just heard a motorcycle pull out, though—might have been him. Don't pick up an ass full of lead checking it out."

Wagner rolled to the right and dropped the nose to pick up speed. The throttle was already ball to the wall and had been since he left Santa Teresa. He roared over Cole with the airspeed needle past the red line on the airspeed indicator that marked 153 miles an hour, the "never exceed" speed. A fast target was harder to hit; he just had to be careful not to tear the wings off. He glanced down as he passed over the Scout and gave Cole a quick wave out the open window of the aircraft.

Then, his head on a swivel, eyes seeking out any trace of a man on the ground, he zoomed to the face of the cliff formed by the cap rock, then up and over it. He saw no one there, but a quarter-mile ahead he could see a rising dust plume, extending straight toward the border. He began to chase it.

He swung wide to the right of the speeding motorcycle, intending to get ahead and come straight back at it. He could see, though, that the rider would be across the border before he could complete the maneuver. "Border be damned," he thought, "there's nobody that matters out here to see." He flew on, level at two hundred feet, flat out at 130 miles an hour.

He looked back over his left shoulder at the landscape and the bike's position and decided that the time was right. Pressing the left rudder pedal and twitching the stick between his knees to the left, he stood the plane up on one wing. The nose began to drop as the wings shed lift in the turn and as he rolled out of the turn, direction reversed, he dropped the nose even more. A thin moment before impact with the ground, he brought it out of the descent, headed straight for the rider. Wagner, in a berserker's blind fury, intended to take the man's head off with his prop and never mind the mechanical consequences—you didn't let somebody get away with shooting at a Border Patrolman if you could help it.

Thompson, concentrating on riding the bucking, screaming motorcycle flat out across the rough desert floor, had not seen the aircraft until the wings flashed the sun back at him as it was in the turn.

"What the fuck . . .! He's not supposed to be over here!" Now he could see it headed straight at him. As he watched, it rose slightly to clear a mesquite bush, then dropped back again, wheels almost on the dirt. His eyes widened. He'd never given a thought to anyone pursuing him. He figured they'd still be hunkered down behind their rig, hiding from the next shot they expected. The airplane was a surprise.

As he cursed, he could suddenly see the pilot's face through the arc of the spinning prop. CLOSE! He bailed off the speeding bike into a mesquite bush. Momentum carried him through the bush, the stiff branches tearing his clothing to shreds and ripping his skin painfully. The plane roared over his head, close enough to touch. He came to rest in the sand on the other side of the bush, looking like he'd been sewn up in a bag full of wildcats. The bike continued on for another thirty yards before it crashed into a bush of its own.

As he climbed away in a turn, Wagner looked back over his shoulder to judge his handiwork. He began a circle two hundred feet up. The man stood on wobbly legs and tried to unsling his rifle.

Wagner, seeing that he had done all he could for the guy today, turned away, back once more toward the border. As he flew, he called Sector on the repeater and advised them that the shooter had made his escape back to Mexico. It appeared, he said, that he was an Anglo riding a red dirt bike.

Throttling back as he approached the siding, he drifted low and slow over the place. He could see Cole and another officer loading someone, LeClaire, he presumed, into the back seat of a Border Patrol sedan. The cloud of dust raised by its arrival still hung in the air. He began to orbit overhead.

When Cole was free to talk Wagner called him on the radio.

"What's up now, King?"

"Jonesy is going to run LeClaire into the hospital to clean his eyes out and take care of them. He's got a pretty good load of glass in them. I'm going to take a walk up to the rim and have a look around. Why don't you land that Tonka Toy of yours and go with me; see how the other half lives. I want to go look over where that asshole was shooting from."

"10-4. I'll be right there."

Chapter 41

Wagner made another low pass over the site to assess an open area next to the road as a landing strip. Normally, he'd land on the road, but then he'd block Jones's exit route. The hardpan next to the road looked good enough for a Super Cub, so he extended out to the west, made another steep turn and headed in, throttled back almost to idle, sideslipping hard to kill altitude and speed. He straightened out at the last second, touched down fifty yards from the vehicles and rolled out with the rumble of the wheels drumming through the aircraft's fabric and frame. He loved the sound of a rough-field landing; days like this were real flying.

Taxiing up to the road, he used his remaining speed to turn the airplane sideways to the road and then pulled the mixture control back to idle cutoff. The engine coughed and died as the fuel ran out and as the prop ticked over to a stop he flicked the magneto switch to "Off". He dropped the lower half of the folding door and stepped out onto the wheel and then down to the ground. He pulled a smoke out of his pocket as he did.

Cole met him under the wing and shook his hand. "I owe you, my friend." Cole said. "I'd still be huddled down there, waiting to get shot, if you hadn't showed up. And Jones couldn't have come in to pick up LeClaire. He's hurting pretty bad, eyes are all chewed up."

"Nothing to it, King. Just wish I could of done something better to the guy." As they walked up the hill he went on to explain how it had worked out. "He'll be hurting son of a bitch if he went through that bush like I think he did. What I could see of him, he was covered with blood and the bike was a good ways off. I decided not to hang around after he began unloosening that smoke pole he carries, though."

"You're smarter than I thought, then," Cole said with a grin. "Hang on here a minute."

They were at the point where the road began to climb up an arroyo to the edge of the valley. Cole looked west along the lip and saw a place that was a likely spot for the shooter's nest. They continued on up the arroyo, then across towards the place.

First they saw the inbound and outbound tracks made by the motorcycle. As they stood there looking they heard the grinding noise of a Scout crawling through the sand in four-wheel drive. A minute later the rig came into view from the northwest, Diehl at the wheel, Travis looking pale beside him. It had been a fast, then rough trip getting there.

"Sorry we didn't get here in time for the excitement," he said as he and Ken stepped out onto the sand. "We were over by Santa Teresa and had to come the long way round to try and get in behind the guy. You OK, King?" He looked his fellow officer up and down.

"Yeah. My asshole won't unpucker for a day or two, but I'm not hurt."

"I know what you mean, man. You never get used to it, do you?"

Cole, who had been in Korea too, said back, "I damn well never did and I don't care if I ever get any more chances to, either!"

They followed the motorcycle tracks over to the edge of the cap rock. There they found the hideout under a bush, a convenient spot that overlooked the road. Diehl knew an ambush point when he saw one.

"Look at that." he said. "It's a perfect setup on the road. Anybody on it would slow for the curve and then couldn't accelerate forward out of the kill zone because of it. He's got a wide-open field of fire on them."

"Looks like he spent the night, too." Cole said. The traces left by a ground sheet were clear, a slight man-length depression in the sand showed where a sleeper might have lain on it in his bag.

"Looks like he ate – awww, shit. Look at this."

They all stood and stared at what Cole had found. Under the edge of the bush, beside where the rifleman had apparently fired from, was a circle drawn in the dust. A circle with a smiling mouth and a nose drawn in it and for eyes, two .223 cases stuck down into the sand.

"Well, I'll be go to hell," Wagner said. "Did you ever see the like of it?"

"Nope," Diehl said. "But it's the guy we've been looking for fer sure. You said the bike was red and look at this boot track—it's the same one we saw over at the windmill and out at the Gomez place. I think we found his truck last night over on the old highway. We laid in on it all night, expecting him to come back with a load of drugs, but it looks like he might have had something else in mind."

"He's screwing with our heads. I don't think he meant to kill anyone; I think he was trying to scare us out of this place."

"Well," Cole said, "I gotta tell you, he's just about done it for me. He could have had us easy through the windshield. With me driving directly towards him it was a straight-on shot. The same for LeClaire. After I got off the road and out on the ground he still could have had LeClaire and all he'd have had to do was work his way along this lip for a hundred yards and he'd have had a clear shot at me again. But he didn't. He just left this little gag and rode off into Mexico. Shit and goddam. It's gonna be hard to drive around out here any more."

"We better leave this place alone for now," Diehl said. "The FBI might actually come out and have a look, maybe pick up the fired cases to check them for fingerprints and such." The FBI was responsible for investigating assaults on federal officers, but it was taken as an article of faith that they wouldn't do anything unless blood was drawn or bones broken. They'd probably just accept an incident report from the Border Patrol on this and file it away.

They walked back to Diehl's rig and then drove down the hill, Cole inside with Diehl, Wagner riding one fender and Ken the other, rather than sit in the tiny, caged back end. There, they found four more Patrol vehicles and a wrecker for the Scout. The wrecker was pulling out, front end of the wounded Scout in the air. The shift supervisor and the Station Senior, Henry Roland, were standing beside the Roland's car, a new Chevrolet sedan, leaning back on the fender. Another pair of Patrol cars was parked by the airplane, the occupants walking around looking disappointed that they'd come to late to participate. They'd learn.

"How you doing, Cole?" Roland asked.

"I quit shaking a little bit ago, Hank, but it was a mighty intense few minutes there." Cole could be familiar with Roland. They had been Academy classmates years ago and Cole knew Roland too well to be awed by his position.

"What are you doing out here at eight in the morning, Diehl? I thought you were supposed to get off at two a.m." Roland asked.

Diehl brought him up to date with the story of the truck and then Wagner told him about the results of his violation of the air space of the sovereign state of Mexico.

"Good work," he said when he had heard the stories. "Elliott, Harris!" he called to two of the two men over at the airplane. "Get on over to Highway 260 and find an old Ford pickup parked on the ditchbank. Don't get too close, but you watch it until somebody comes out and relieves you. If anyone tries to drive it off you stop him, but be careful. And as of now, you don't have any reason to arrest anyone, so approach with caution, but get an ID."

Then, turning back to Diehl, he said, "I don't think we'll see him today. Do you?"

"Nope," Diehl replied. "Wings, you said he looked pretty chewed up by the brush, didn't you? And his bike crashed? I think he'll get back to Juarez the best he can. He may figure the truck's too hot to try to pick up, at least right now."

"I agree," Roland said. "We'll watch it all day just in case he has a case of the stupids, but I'm not counting on anything. We don't have the manpower to watch it any longer than that."

"Diehl, you said you got a name and an address off the registration. Write it up as an intel report and give it to Pope, along with this whole story."

"Boss, Travis and I will drop by the address on the registration on the way back just to see what it looks like, see if anyone's home. Pope will want to know more than just an address and it's on the way anyhow."

"OK, you do that. Let me know, too. Cole, if you're sure you're OK you head on back to the office and write this up as an incident report. I want it on my desk before you go home. The Chief's already asking questions."

"That Dutch son of a bitch would be asking questions instead of showing up, wouldn't he? I don't suppose one of them is "how are the men," is it? Why isn't he out here now? " Cole asked bitterly. "I'm calling for help and he wants to chew me out on the radio for getting excited and swearing. Asshole!"

The Chief was known to be a bureaucratic creature, more concerned with career development and public relations than operations and the troops. Their attitudes about him showed they knew where they stood in his version of the world.

"I know, I know," Roland replied, holding up a hand and shaking his head ruefully. "But we gotta play the game. Just get me the report today, and then take tomorrow off as a mental health day. I'll fix the schedule to show it as administrative leave for you; no charge to your vacation time."

"Thanks, Hank. I appreciate that." He went on, "Wings, are you headed back to base now? If you are, I'll catch a ride with you instead of tempting fate with this yahoo." He motioned towards Diehl with a thumb and a smile. Diehl was known for an ability to keep his passengers on the edge of their seats and the old vehicles contributed to the thrill.

"Sure. Come on," Wagner said as he walked toward the airplane.

"Chicken," Diehl said. "See you back at the office—maybe. I'm gonna watch you tempt death here." He put a foot on the bumper and stood up to sit on the hood. Ken took off his jacket and then leaned back on a fender beside him, the sun warm on his face, arms crossed on his chest. It felt good to be a part of all this, doing a man's work, being a part of the camaraderie.

Wagner let Cole fold himself into the cramped back seat of the Super Cub and then climbed into the front. He pulled the lower door panel up into place and latched it.

He pushed the mixture knob to full rich, cracked the throttle, and turned the magneto switch on to "Both". Sticking his head out the window and looking around, he called "CLEAR!", then after waiting a second he hit the starter button. The prop jerkily spun twice before the first cylinder fired, then the engine caught and ran smoothly. Wagner watched as the oil pressure stabilized and then did a magneto check by switching first to "Left", back to "Both," and "Right", then back to "Both". The engine RPM dropped slightly with each change to a single magneto, and then came back to normal when running on both, idling at eight hundred RPM. As Diehl listened to the engine, he thought, "The cars may be pieces of shit, but they sure keep the planes in good shape."

Satisfied with what he'd seen on the gauges, Wagner shoved the throttle in halfway, touching the right brake and pressing the right rudder as he did. The little airplane pivoted around its right wheel and pointed west. Without a pause, Wagner smoothly gave it full throttle. It accelerated swiftly, tail coming up almost immediately in the prop blast, then in two hundred feet, its 150 horsepower Lycoming engine pulled its 1600 pounds off the ground. Wagner climbed steeply as he circled back over the cars. Both men gave those on the ground a wave out the door.

Diehl climbed down off the hood shaking his head and smiling. "It is", he said, "a mighty fine day."

He and Ken loaded up and headed back to town.

Chapter 42

So we went by the address out just off Fred Wilson Boulevard east of McComb, by Fort Bliss," Diehl said to Pope. "It's a house, a widow lady owns it and lives there alone. She's German; married a GI and came over here after the war. He was killed a couple years ago over in Viet Nam, but she stayed here. Her folks were all killed in the bombing during the war. War's been pure hell on that woman."

"She had a lot to talk about with us, with coffee and cookies, no less," Ken interjected as he pulled a package of Chesterfields out of his pocket.

Pope reached into his desk drawer for a smoke and came out with an empty Winston package.

"Ken, let me bum a cigarette, would you?" Pope asked.

Ken extended the package and with a shake of his wrist, slid one halfway out for Pope.

"I'd rather get lung cancer from this unfiltered weed of yours than to suck on one of those soggy homemades Real rolls up out of horse shit," he said as he took it. "I had one of Jones's KOOLS the other day and thought I'd hit rock bottom, but I wasn't thinking of your partner here."

"Goddam it, Padre," Diehl said with forced vehemence, "You've been flogging that empty pack of Winstons around to my certain knowledge since 1964. Hell, the colors are even fading. When are you going to break down and buy some of your own? Ken, next thing you know he's gonna ask you for a light and a punch in the stomach to help him with the first drag."

“Fuck you, Real,” Pope said with a smile at his friend as he reached into the drawer and came out with a book of matches. “Now, what did you find?”

Diehl went on, “God, but I love your shining temperament, Jim. You’re an example to us all. Anyway, she rents out her garage back of the house to a man to store his motorcycle, so she says, a nice young man who used to be a soldier. She doesn't know anything about the motorcycle except that it's red. He comes around in his blue truck and picks it up sometimes. He's usually gone all night. Other times he leaves the truck and rides off for just a few hours. She said he came by yesterday afternoon and took it away and hasn't been back since."

"That name you got off the registration isn't much use, Tom," Pope said. “There are a lot of Steve Smiths in the world. I don't suppose she had written him any receipts or anything with another name on them?"

"No such luck," Diehl replied. "That's the name she knows him by."

"So it looks like that's a dead end, huh? Unless we want to lay in on the garage until he comes back. If he comes back."

"Well, not exactly, Jim. See, we asked her if she'd let us into the garage to have a look around. She was happy to oblige, just gave us the key, so we checked it out. Found a couple of worn-out knobby tires and some two stroke oil out there that point to a dirt bike." Diehl went silent, as though finished.

Pope waited patiently, then knowing Diehl well enough to read him, made a come-on gesture and said, "Let's hear the rest, goddam it. I know there's more."

"Well, Jim, we found some personal items out there. It looks like he’s storing some things there he didn't want to keep wherever he lives. And it looked like he'd cleaned out his pockets before he went on a mission and left the stuff there. F'rinstance, there was a wallet and a set of dog tags hanging on a nail in the wall. Best of all, there was a file full of his military records, all we'd ever want to know about him, including a couple photos. We hit the jackpot."

Ken sat on the corner of Lamont's desk, a big grin on his face, pleased to be a part of this.

"Well, who the hell is he, Tom?"

"Turns out he's an ex-GI name of Gary Thompson. Did a couple tours in Viet Nam as a sniper that may have fucked up his head. The DD214 in the folder shows he got a medical discharge about a year ago out here at Bliss. Reading between the lines of some other stuff, it was a psychological thing."

"Anyhow, he came back from overseas last year. He was on the training cadre here like we thought since then, right up until his discharge." He paused for a last drag on his cigarette.

"Any other addresses show up in there, Tom? Next of kin? Where they send his disability check to? Any names of people out at Ft. Bliss who might have a line on him?"

"He wanted his checks to go to a P.O. box downtown when he got out. Nothing in his papers to show any different now. Ken, what was that box number and his unit at the base?"

Ken pulled a small, dog-eared, sweat-stained, green notebook out of his shirt pocket and flipped through it to the information.

"The box number is 1367 at the main Post Office. At the time of his discharge, he was attached to the First Training Brigade out there. They let him go on December 2 last year. Next of kin is his mother, Juliana Chavez out in San Diego."

"That sounds like he might be Chicano, doesn't it, Ken?" Pope said. "Might explain what he's doing working with a bunch of Mexican dope smugglers."

"Yeah, it does. Among other things in that paperwork was a skills inventory the Army got from him. He speaks Spanish as a native. He'd be right at home with them."

"OK, boys, are you holding out any other surprises?" Pope asked.

"Well, Jim, there were a couple cases of .223 ammo there, but that's no surprise. He had to be keeping it somewhere. What we didn't find, and I wish we had, is any indication of where he's living. There was a book of matches in the truck from the Cantina Rio Bravo over in Juarez, but that just ties him to Ayala's group. And we already know that. That dive is just a half-assed whorehouse; nobody lives there but the girls. You remember it from when we used to work over there?"

Pope just grunted in response, so Diehl went on.

"I guess we gotta find some way to lay hands on this guy. Catch him with the gun and don't get killed ourselves doing it and we probably got enough to give to the FBI to file assault on a federal officer charges. We gave 'em a couple of fired cases from where he shot at Cole and LeClaire. If we catch him with the gun, then the Bureau can do a chamber analysis on the brass and tie those shots to that gun. That is, if we can get the Bureau to do it even once we hand the whole damn case to them."

Pope looked thoughtful, and then he said, "You guys know that the search you did at that garage was illegal, right? So nothing you found there can be used as evidence against him. Ken, do you know that?"

"Nossir, I didn't. I figured we had permission from the owner, so it was all right. Why wasn't it?"

"Tom, you knew it, didn't you? Explain it to him."

"Yeah, I knew it. But at this point I'm more interested in taking the son-of-bitch out of action before he kills someone than I am in dotting all the i's to prosecute him. Ken, the lady may own the place, but as the renter, he's the one who has to give permission to search the place. Jim's right."

"Doesn't matter at this point, though," Pope said. "You didn't get anything out of that garage that matters yet as far as prosecution is concerned. All you did there was get a true name and some irrelevant background. We don't care what name he's going by, though; we're after a guy who pulled the trigger and never mind what he calls himself – Steve Smith will do just fine. You got that name and his address from a clean snoop through his car window. With that, you have reason to check out the address and question the lady there. She ties him to the truck, so you know you got the right place. Now it's a matter of laying hands on him and for the case, the best place is right there in the garage. Find him in there and you have grounds to search it."

Diehl look pensive. Ken looked puzzled, a state he'd spent a lot of time in recently.

"Jim," Diehl said, "do you think we could get Roland to authorize having somebody reliable from each shift kind of hang around here for the next day or two? We didn't tell the lady much, but we did tell her that we would like to talk to the guy. She agreed to call us when he shows up and not tell him. I'd hate it if she called and nobody went out there to sack him up. I'd like to hang around now, but Ken and I were up all night and we're pretty well whipped."

"Yeah, I think we can work something out with Hank. You guys go get some sleep and I'll talk to him. I wouldn't be surprised if he leads the charge if he's here when she calls—he's not one to sit around when things are happening. Give me a call later on and I'll let you know what he said. But sleep fast, boys" and here he grinned, "because if she calls, somebody will respond, but you'll get called out, too. Nobody's going to wait for you to show up, but you'll at least want to be here when he's brought in."

Chapter 43

So, *gringo* . . . ah, pardon me," Ayala said as he and Chavez sat in his office that afternoon. "We agreed you would become Chavez, didn't we? Not the *gringo* Thompson. How did things go out there? It looks as though you have suffered some damage. I hope that does not indicate things did not go well."

"My part of the plan did not go exactly as I anticipated, a small crash on the motorcycle, but the lure worked. All the Border Patrolmen on that side of El Paso went to the shooting, as cops always do—like flies to shit. We could have driven a truck across the line at Monte Cristo Rey and they would never have seen it. Afoot, our man should have entered easily and Alfonso should have picked him up without interference in Smeltertown. I am surprised that he has not called you yet to say so, since it took me several hours to straighten out my motorcycle's front end and ride back here."

"He did call, from Las Cruces. He not only called, but he is on his way back with Diaz. They tell me that things went just as you predicted. They sat there in Smeltertown and watched the *migra's* cars go flying by, headed west, with their sirens going. None gave a thought to what might be happening behind them. Our man crossed the headgates immediately afterwards and came straight to them as though it was a stroll around the *plaza*."

"Then the load got to the truck stop without a problem?" Chavez asked. "That is good news." And it was good news for him, as well as for the organization. It would have gone hard with him if his first plan had failed and cost them another load. But *El Patrón* had not waited for Diaz to return before he received Chavez, so apparently this success secured Ayala's trust. Ayala would see him alone now.

"What went wrong for you out there, Chavez? Could it have endangered our effort? The line between success and failure is often just a small thing."

Chavez started slightly as the door opened behind him. Paranoia was a part of his life and he was uneasy as Alfonso came through the door, Diaz right behind him.

All was well, though. Alfonso was beaming at having been part of a new, successful operation. Diaz, as usual, though, looked like death waiting to find a place to settle. *"The man is a psycho."* He never thought that it takes one to know one.

"Bueno, bueno, bueno," Alfonso exclaimed as he came in. "Once more we make fools of them! The drugs will be in Albuquerque late tonight and in Chicago tomorrow evening."

He looked directly at Chavez, and then said with wonder, "What happened to you? You look like you were attacked by a wildcat."

"I was about to explain to your father, Alfonso. This will save me having to go through it twice."

"No plan ever goes without small incidents. In this case, I paid the price for not knowing that one of the Border Patrol pilots is a madman. Our operation was never endangered. I knew of their aircraft and even thought that I might be seen by one after the shooting." Here, he lied. He had never considered an aircraft at all, but it would not do to give away that lack of thought to them.

"But even if one saw me, what would it matter? A man in an airplane can't catch you; he can't identify you. All he can do is call someone on the ground and by that time, I would have been into Mexico, beyond their reach."

"Well, what happened," Ayala asked.

"I was riding away from where I fired, intending to get into Mexico, then ride far to the west to cross back into the United States. Then I would go back to my truck as usual."

"Instead, though, this madman of a pilot pursued me across the border. He flew straight at me, so low he nearly killed me with his airplane. I have no doubt that was what he intended. There was no choice but to jump off to save my life. When I did, I landed in a bush . . ."

At that, the other three burst into laughter. It fell slowly away, choking off little by little as the vision of a man flying through a thorny bush faded.

"The motorcycle ran into a bush of its own and is damaged in the front end. I straightened the legs out enough that I could ride it back to town, but they must be replaced before I can ride it again."

"What of your truck, Chavez? Where is it," Ayala asked.

"It is parked on a ditch bank several miles from where I fired. Anyone who sees it will just think it belongs to someone tending to a field. There is no reason that the *patrulleros* would be suspicious of it—they have no idea that I use it."

"You must get yourself cleaned up, Chavez," Ayala said, "and have your wounds seen to. Have one of the women see to your needs—all of them. While that is being done, Alfonso here will find some new clothes for you. Then he will take you back to your truck."

"Thank you, *Patrón,* thank you very much. I appreciate your generosity."

Turning to Alfonso, he said, "If you would, find a pair of Levis for me and a western shirt, one with snaps instead of buttons." He handed the boy a twenty-dollar bill. "The jeans should have a thirty-two inch waist and the same in the length. The shirt should be a size large. Long sleeves, in blue, if you can.

Then he stood and stretched hard, trying to ease some of the cramps and pain that were developing in his joints and muscles.

"I will meet you downstairs in two hours, Alfonso." He turned and left.

The three of them sat quietly before Marcos Ayala said, "What do we think now. Can we work with him?"

"*Papa*," Alfonso said, "he is ambitious. We can use him, we can let him run operations, but he is not family. I do not think we should ever trust him. Probably, he would never betray us to the *yanquis*, but he will step on any of us at any time it suits his purposes. He has no loyalty but to himself."

"There is reason for thought there, Alfonso." Turning to Diaz, he said, "And you, Ramón; what do you think?"

"I think I should kill him now, or as soon as we can replace him. His ability to operate in *los estados unidos* is valuable to us, but we should find someone to take his place then put him in a hole before he harms us."

"*Bueno*, hombres. I agree. We will begin to look for a replacement, but we will continue to use him and his plans when they make sense to us. Then, after we no longer need him . . . But take no action against him until I say so. Watch him closely without letting him know that we do so".

"*Si, Patrón,"* they both assented.

Chapter 44

A few hours later, near dark, Alfonso and Chavez crossed the border on the Santa Fe Street Bridge in his father's van. The damaged motorcycle lay flat in the back end.

"What if the inspector sees this motorcycle in the truck, Chavez? I do not wish to spend time in a *gavacho* jail."

"It won't happen, *joven.* In the first place, the inspector will probably only look at us and ask us where we are from. I have my retired military ID to show that I am an American and you have your border-crossing card. They won't look at us twice. And even if they do, it is clearly damaged; we will tell them we are bringing it over to be repaired. "

"But what if there is a lookout for it; what then?"

"There will be no lookout, *amigo.* The Border Patrol and the men at the bridges hardly talk to each other and even if they do, it takes days for information to be passed along. Calm yourself. Just go where I tell you."

A half hour later they pulled up at the end of the driveway that led to the garage that Chavez rented.

"Help me unload the machine, 'Fonso, but stay here while I take it to the garage. If a woman comes out to see what is happening, remember that she knows me as Steve Smith. It should stay that way." They walked to the rear of the van and opened the double doors and pulled out a long plank, which became a ramp to ease the motorcycle down. Quickly, he had the motorcycle in the garage while Alfonso sat in the van's open back end and smoked. As he closed and locked the garage door he smelled the sauerkraut she had cooked. He could see the flickering glow of her television on the curtains of what he knew was her living room window beside the driveway. Even though the window was closed against the evening air that was growing chilly, he could hear theme from *Hawaii Five-0* pounding away. The curtains parted and she looked out. She waved at him and he waved back as he walked out to the van. She turned away from the window and picked up the phone.

Alfonso and Chavez turned right onto Highway 54 and drove north. They crossed the Franklin Mountains on Trans-Mountain Road, dropping down into the Rio Grande valley at Canutillo. Once into the valley they drove south on Highway 260, past the truck, looking carefully around for surveillance. In the dark it was hard to tell, but there was no indication of interest in the vehicle.

"We'll play it safe, Alfonso. Go on a couple miles, then turn around. Coming back, slow down at the next curve and I'll roll out. And I mean slow, damn it, no more than about ten miles an hour, you hear?" He reached up to the overhead light, removed the lens and bulb, and then tossed them into the glove box.

"What are you going to do, Gerardo?"

"I'm going to hide for a few minutes. After I get out I want you to pull over and stop somewhere close to my truck. Get out and open your hood, then close it and drive away. Go home. If anyone is watching, they will come stop you. If they do they will be suspicious, but since none of them know you, they will let you go."

"I don't like that, Chavez. Why should I be bait? Suppose they grab me?"

"They won't take you in—you have a border crossing card and there is nothing illegal in this van to cause them to arrest you. Now act like a man and do what I tell you."

Ten minutes later Chavez was lying on his belly beside the road, watching as the young Ayala stopped a quarter mile away. Very quickly, he drove away again. Chavez watched him out of sight as he drove down the long straightaway, listening for the sound of an engine starting to disturb the silence of the evening. The van drew no attention.

He crossed the road in a low crawl. It was dark, with clouds across the face of the sliver of moon and he was no more than a flitting shadow. He crossed the dry canal bed and then crawled across the ditch road. For the same reasons Diehl had the night before, he kept to the low fields beside the ditch road as he approached the truck. He was utterly invisible to any watchers.

From under a bush a hundred yards away, he spent a half hour watching and listening. Nothing.

All his guns were on the other side of the river in Mexico and he hated being unarmed. He would be over here for a day or two, until he had his parts and the motorcycle was fixed, and he needed a gun. He hadn't wanted to cross with Alfonso while armed; that would have been trouble for sure if they had been searched, so he left them behind. He felt naked on this side of the river without one in his belt and that is why the truck was important to him.

He crept up to the base of the ditch bank, and then crawled up the bank to the truck and then under it. Lying in the dust, with the gravel digging sharply into his back and the drive shaft invisible just inches from his nose, he ran his hands along the underside of the body until he felt an oilskin-wrapped package wedged into a pocket formed between the body and frame. He pried the package loose and unwrapped it.

With a .45 auto in his hands once more, he stood up beside the truck. He felt ready for anything that came along, now.

But still, nothing. So he took his keys from his pocket, climbed up onto the slick plastic seat, started it, and drove away. Nobody cared. Often, caution and effort are wasted, but they are necessary nonetheless. He would spend the night in a motel, then go to the Yamaha dealer first thing in the morning and order the fork tubes he needed.

*****

The next morning, Hank Roland came into his office. As usual, it was covered with an accumulation of paper that seemed to breed itself overnight. The third item down was a note written in pencil on a three by five index card. It was from the Station One desk officer who worked the evening shift the day before. It said: "Sir, some woman called last night and said a guy dropped a motorcycle off at her house. She said Mr. Diehl would be interested." There was no further information, nor indication that any had been solicited. Roland shook his head. He would speak with the young man about gathering complete information and passing it along timely. He would speak at length with him. It was a never-ending process.

He picked up the phone to call Pope and tell him that they had missed the boat, this time, anyway.

Chapter 45

I hope she left the house like Hank told her to when she called," Diehl said quietly to Ken as they stepped out of the cruiser at the end of the alley that ran behind the German widow's house. He knew he had to take a moment calm Ken down.

As Diehl spoke, Ken eased the slide of the old Winchester Model 97 back slightly to look for a round in the chamber. He knew he'd loaded it as he ran out of the office, but still . . . There was one there, ready to go, and four more waited in the tubular magazine under the barrel. *It'll be enough – if I do my part.* He left the hammer in the half-cocked position, as close to a safety as the old shotgun had, and then he unsnapped the safety strap on his holster.

"Listen up, Ken," Diehl said on as Ken walked around the car to his side. He put his hand on Ken's shoulder and looked into his face as he spoke. "You did good the other night but this time is for real—he's there, and we can figure he's got a gun. Your asshole is gonna quiver as we get closer, and you'll think you're gonna puke." He went on. "Your vision's gonna tunnel down—it'll seem like you're looking through a tube and you won't be hearing a damn thing. Stress does that and it can get you killed. So make yourself look around and listen. 'specially to me."

"Yessir." *Oh, shit!* Reality sank in as thoughts of the consequences of failure blew through his mind like a storm that turned his excitement into fear. Nothing in his life had prepared him for life or death as more than a figure of speech

At eight a.m. the widow had called and told Hank Roland that the man was in her garage again, working on his motorcycle. Roland had passed the word to Diehl, who was winding up an early shift with Travis. Roland grabbed LeClaire and another two men who had just come in for the day shift—they put together a quick and dirty plan and then headed out to the widow's place. Now, it was about to happen.

"You ready, now, Ken? Got your head right?"

"Yeah. Let's go do it."

They stalked down the alley, staying close to the board fences and backs of garages that walled it in. Their feet kicked up small puffs of dust. Ken's right hand choked the grip of the shotgun like a vise as it hung by his side.

Diehl walked down the other side, in the low morning sun. His shadow against the wall got taller, then shorter as he detoured around gray steel garbage cans and junk cars and bicycles. Ken carefully stepped around a pile of beer cans, but a small patch of gravel crunched under his boots. They were on opposite sides of the alley—if Ramos was going to get them both, he'd have to work for it.

Despite the cool morning air, sweat broke out under his arms and soaked his T-shirt. He shifted the shotgun from hand to hand and wiped sweaty palms on his pants leg. A shiver rattled him slightly.

Ken's stomach growled as his nose picked up the piquant odor of chorizo and eggs with salsa cooking for someone's breakfast. His eyes flickered with every step, constantly looking for cover in case things went to hell. Each step became harder to take. With harsh, silent words about the fate of cowards, he forced himself to keep walking. He brought the shotgun up across his chest, left hand on the slide, right thumb on the hammer.

At the fifth garage Diehl stopped and put his ear to the boarded up window in the back wall and listened for a moment. As he turned toward Ken his gold badge flashed bright in the sun. He nodded twice, and Ken stepped softly across the alley.

Diehl whispered, "She said he was working on his motorcycle out here. He's in there; he just swore in Spanish."

Ken nodded his understanding. His mouth was cotton-dry; he couldn't have worked up enough spit to drown an ant.

"We'll go in quiet and easy through that gate over there." A twitch of his thumb indicated a head-high wooden gate in the fence between the garages. "Then we'll go around front of the garage, me in front, you behind. If the door's open I'll keep movin' to the far side but you stop as soon as you can see inside."

Ken nodded; he didn't trust himself to speak. His guts twisted, and he was glad that he'd gone to the bathroom back at the office. *What the hell ever made me think I wanted to be a lawman? I never thought it'd be like this!* The thoughts of

Bonnie and Clyde came back to him again. Somehow, he had to drive those images from his mind or they would paralyze him. But still, it seemed all too real.

"When we get to the gate I'll squat and open it while you cover me over my head through the crack. If he shows up, point that thing right straight at his face and I'll do the talkin'. If he's got a gun in his hand you blow a hole in him right fucking then, right where he stands; got it?"

"Yes, I got it." His knees quivered and he could hear the tremble of fear in his whisper.

"Once we're through that gate we don't know what we'll find so we got to play it by ear. Stay alert and think. If I go down you keep shooting until he quits movin'."

Oh, sweet Jesus! Fearful images flashed through his mind.

A car door slammed in another garage. After a moment the engine started and the car backed out to the street. A dog barked at them from the back yard of the house across the alley. A woman shouted at it to shut up. He could hear the morning news on someone's television and he prayed he would not be an item on the evening edition.

It sounds so damn normal now, but here we are, maybe going to have a gunfight. Like a volcano about to blow up under the town and nobody knows about it but us. Pay attention, goddamit! he told himself silently as he took a deep breath and attempted to control his nerves. *Look around. Listen!*

Diehl nudged him with his elbow as he stepped over to the gate. He squatted there with his .357 Magnum in his hand, thrust forward slightly. Ken stepped up behind him and put the shotgun to his shoulder, pointed high, waiting for room to lower it to firing position as the gate opened. Diehl looked up at him and mouthed the question, "Ready?"

Ken nodded. Diehl put his hand on the latch and pressed the lever. The latch bar lifted with a slight click. Ken pulled the weapon in tight to his shoulder and put his thumb on the hammer, ready to cock it. The smell of Diehl's sweat rose to him. He felt better knowing Tom was nervous, too, and he wondered if Diehl could smell him.

God, but my hands are sweating. I'm going to have to wipe this thing down good when we get back. Pay attention, goddamit!

Diehl pushed the gate gently and a dry hinge squealed. Ken jumped. It sounded loud as a siren in the quiet morning air. Diehl stopped and waited. There was no reaction from inside, so after a moment he pushed again. The hinge groaned slightly in protest, but then the gate swung silently open. Ken dropped the barrel of his shotgun level above Diehl's head and swept it quickly side to side. *Muzzle should always follow eyes.* He repeated the trainee's mantra to himself once more: *Please God; don't let me fuck up!*

Clear. Diehl stands. Lift the muzzle. Follow him. Step out wide. Open a clear line of fire. Not too far. Stop at garage wall. Listen. Nothing. Creep to corner. Get ready. Step around corner. *Oh, shit! The door's standing open! We can't see in. He could see us through the crack.*

Diehl moved fast around the end of the batwing door with Ken close behind. Diehl went wide to the other side of the opening, pistol pointing at something inside. Ken stopped short, looking over the gun sight into the dim garage.

And there he was, crouched by the front wheel of a dirt bike with a wrench in each hand. And a .45 automatic tucked in his belt over his right kidney. Ken's gut tightened. Thompson was looking at Diehl with a startled expression. Ken thumbed back the hammer of the shotgun as he swung it to his target. It made a noticeable click that drew Thompson's attention.

Thompson turned his head slightly, just in time to see Ken's finger drop to the trigger. The grim, unblinking eye of the muzzle stared at him, pointed straight at his face. He didn't move, but clearly he was thinking it over—there was no look of submission on his face.

"Try it and die," Diehl said, his tone flat and cold as a winter day in Kansas.

Thompson waited a further moment before he said, "Not this time." He didn't move.

"Ken, if he drops one of those wrenches I want him dead before it hits the floor, *sabes*? Understand?"

"Mmm – hmmm. I can do that," Ken replied. He was surprised at how calm he felt. The muzzle was steady as a rock and he realized he was no longer scared—wound up, intense, focused, but not scared. He was in control of himself. He was doing what he should—he was okay. He felt the pressure of his finger on the trigger and he knew, *knew* he could pull it if he had to. The realization made him feel good; it was like he'd passed some sort of test.

"OK, Thompson, here's what we're going to do. I say "Move" you put those wrenches down together. Keep your hands on the floor when you do. Then prone out and lock your hands behind your head. Nothing else; understand?"

"Yeah, I got it. Your partner over there's not going to shoot me when I put 'em down, is he?"

"I don't know him very well. Prob'ly not."

Thompson grimaced, but he didn't move.

"Travis, you understand what's about to happen?"

"Yeah. He's going to set the wrenches down and stretch out on his face."

"He does anything but that, shoot him. Don't wait for me and don't warn him. Kill him."

"Got it."

"OK, Thompson—move."

Very slowly, the man bent slightly further over. As his hands touched the floor he opened them and the wrenches dropped with a dull clank. He hesitated a moment, as though thinking it over. He looked at Ken and saw him lean slightly forward, as though anticipating the recoil of the shotgun. So he put his knees down, and then his knuckles. Finally he slid out on his belly, turned his head to one side, and clasped his hands behind it.

Ken breathed out; it surprised him—he'd been holding his breath.

Diehl moved wide around Thompson, then up to his side. He stayed out of Ken's line of fire. Ken paid careful attention to every move, taking mental notes. He turned the muzzle away slightly as Diehl knelt with one knee in the middle of Thompson's back. Diehl pressed the barrel of his revolver firmly against the back of Thompson's neck as he lifted the .45 from his belt and tucked it in his own. He holstered his revolver and pulled Thompson's hands around and cuffed them and then began to pat him down. He took a Buck folding knife from a pouch on Thompson's belt and then he found a bone-handled switchblade in a hip pocket.

"Don't you know these things are illegal? You could go to jail for having this." He gave the gunman a mocking grin as he dropped the knife into his own pocket. Finally, he pulled him to his feet.

Thompson looked at him and said, "*Cabrón.* If it had just been you I'd have taken you." Diehl ignored the insulting word. "Maybe. Maybe not. But if it had just been me, alone, I'da deserved it for being stupid." Diehl took him by the arm to lead him back to the car. "A fair fight means your tactics were bad."

"Ken, you follow two steps back. He does something squirrelly, butt stroke him across the back of the neck with that thing. He does something to me, scatter his brains."

He took Thompson by the cuffs and led him down the driveway to the street. Ken gently lowered the hammer on the shotgun to the half-cock notch, and carrying the weapon at port arms, he followed them from fifteen feet back and a step to the left. His knees felt weak and wobbly as the adrenalin drained from his system—it wasn't a gunfight, but he'd survived his first armed encounter. He'd done all right. He ran it all through his mind again. He especially remembered how he'd picked up on his target right away and how the barrel had never wavered as he kept it pointed at Thompson.

As they came out from between the houses green and white sedans sped down the street from each end of the block, jerking to a halt bumper to bumper in front of the driveway. Henry Roland climbed out of the first one, with Pete LeClaire getting out the other side.

"Elliott, Randall," Roland ordered the other two agents, "load this guy up and take him back to Station One. Put him in my office and sit with him, and I mean sit right there with him, until I get back. Do not put him in the tank with the wets. Keep him cuffed and no damn trips to the bathroom. We won't be long. Is that clear?"

Sixty seconds later Chavez was in the back of one of the sedans, a PI beside him, and the car pulled out. They all watched it out go out of sight down the middle of the narrow, two-lane street crowded with parked cars.

"Now we got him, how are you going to play this, Diehl? There's no authority for you to arrest him for assault on a federal officer unless the assault took place in front of you. He's off the streets for now like we wanted but we're going to have to take the case to the FBI. They'll write the report the U.S. Attorney will see."

"Boss," Diehl replied, "it's like this. We came out just to interview him about finding his truck out there. When we came up to the door he reached for the pistol in his belt and that's an assault right there. Ken here threw down on him with the shotgun, which changed his mind about things. That about right, Ken?"

Roland didn't even look to Ken for an answer, but kept his eyes on Diehl. "You think they're going to buy that, Tom? Why'd you sneak up there through the alley with a shotgun?"

"We did it that way because he's a dangerous sonuvabitch who might try to kill us if we give him a chance. And if the Feebs don't want to buy our story, well fuck 'em. We'll drop a dime on him with the other side and let them take care of him. And I hope he doesn't kill one of us first."

Roland thrust his hands into his hip pockets and stared off into the western sky for a while. Then he looked at his feet and dragged the right one back and forth on the pavement a few times, as though erasing something. No one spoke—the wind rattling the palm tree nearby was the loudest sound around. Finally, he looked up at Diehl and said, "Don't make a habit of this, you hear?" He turned and opened his door, causing LeClaire to run around to the other side and get in. He stopped and spoke across the top of the car. “I’ll call the Bureau when I get to the office. You two stay here until they show up.”

He sat down, closed the door. The Chevy left with a chirp of the tires.

“All right, Ken. Let’s go secure that garage until the Bureau gets here with a search warrant. Remember though, if the arrest doesn’t stand up, neither will anything anybody finds now.”

Chapter 46

Although she had become "Ayala's girl", it was neither reasonable nor profitable to expect her to stay upstairs all day and night. So she came downstairs frequently, especially when Ayala was away. Often, she just sat alone at his table in the back corner of the *cantina,* other times she sat at the bar. She was no longer afraid and by now the music and the noise of the crowd excited her. She enjoyed it.

No matter where she chose to sit, though, young men approached her. They were always *gringos,* for young Mexican men did not frequent the *Cantina Rio Bravo* in the evening. It was a place for GI's with a pass and college boys out for an adventure to come to. She was always friendly, but no more than that. Because it was expected, she always asked them to buy her a drink—she had been taught that phrase immediately—and they always did. She would sit and listen to them as they drank and to most of the lonely, young GI's it didn't seem to matter that she spoke no English. They were lonesome and far from home and often had not been near a girl for weeks if they had been in boot camp. The college boys amused themselves by trying to teach her a few words of English, which she quickly learned. A peasant she may have been, but she was not stupid. She was pleasant company for them all and she quickly learned to recognize the shy ones, the ones who would not press her to go upstairs, whom she could invite to sit down. Most of them wouldn't even ask her to go upstairs; they just wanted to pass some pleasant time with someone soft and then to be able to tell outrageous tales of performance in a Mexican whorehouse to their friends back home.

Her status with Ayala entitled her to special protection and that protection made her life in the Cantina Rio Bravo bearable. The few who were persistent were quickly discouraged by the bartenders or bouncers. If they became obnoxious they were jerked out of their chair and thrown out the back door.

But there was always Ayala. She had to keep him satisfied or she would very quickly become one of the working girls again. She tried to keep him satisfied on her own schedule, coming on to him when she thought it would be useful rather than waiting for him to summon her. She had found that draining him two or three times a week was sufficient to sate him. And while it was repulsive, each act never took long and she could get through it by imagining her revenge and life afterwards. Her body was a tool to be used to build a future.

He did not realize how much he had revealed, but Ayala no longer had secrets from her. As some men do, he talked too much after being satisfied in bed and she was often at his side in his office or staying quietly in the adjacent bedroom when he conducted his business. From where he kept the key to his desk to how much and who he was paying off at the *Judiciál* and whom he spoke to in person and on the phone; she knew it all.

As the weeks passed she had deliberately turned cold inside, building a wall between her natural decency and gentleness and her implacable, icy fury, and it was in that fury that her mind resided.

But she was aware of what was going on in her mind and what she could become if she were not careful. So often, after she went to bed she would open a small breach in the wall in her mind, take out some of the memories of the Luz she had been and let them warm her for a while.

Ayala had been gone for several days to Chihuahua City on business. This afternoon she was talking to *tio* Salinas at the table by the back wall. He was well known in the bar by now and since he had bought drinks for them both to satisfy the bartender they were left alone. Now they conversed quietly about her future.

"I think I am ready to go, *tio,"* she said nearly under her breath. "I have money now, over a thousand dollars, and he no longer thinks about me running away. I still cannot leave the bar without an escort, but here I can come and go as I please."

"Are you certain, girl? You must succeed the first time you try or you will be beaten and sent to a house deep in the country, perhaps in Mexico City. From there, you will never escape."

"I must go now," she replied. "I cannot stand much more and I don't believe it will become any easier. He no longer thinks to mistrust me, but the longer

I stay, the more likely I am to betray myself. I can be alone with him whenever it suits me; all I have to do is . . ." Here, she faded out, too embarrassed to say to the old man what she had to do.

"I understand, *guapita.* Only you can say when you must go."

"*Tio,*" she said, "you told me that you would help me get away. What shall I do when I am out of here?"

"*Momentito,* Luz."

He called to the bartender to bring them another round of drinks. She, of course, was getting straight 7-Up and he was being charged for champagne. He drank his usual Tecate. He knew of the overcharge but it was worth it to him because it bought them time to talk. He had told the bartender that he preferred not to drink alone and that she was amusing company.

When they had their fresh drinks, he said, "You will come to my house when you leave here. Do not take a taxi since the drivers all know Ayala and will tell him immediately where they took you if they discover he is looking for you. It is not far to walk, only ten or fifteen minutes for a girl from the country." He smiled at her with that reminder of her past and then told her how to get to his house. She would go out the back door to the alley, then out to Calle Mariscal. From there it was only a few blocks south to Avenida 16 de Septiembre, then right for three blocks. It was very simple to remember.

"You cannot stay there, nor can my grandchildren once you have gone. Ayala's people will quickly remember how we have talked and it will lead them to my house almost immediately. My granddaughter knows of you. I will tell her that you may show up one day and what to do when you do. If I am not there she will take you and her little brother to the house of her aunt a few blocks away. You will stay there together until I come."

"What will we do then, *tio?"*

'From there we will all go to El Paso, then to Denver. You do not need to know more than that. Just get yourself to my house and all will be well."

"But what will I do in Denver, *tio*?" she asked with natural curiosity. "I speak only a few words of English, not enough to get by."

"I have old friends there who own a small tortilla factory. They always need workers. At first, you can live in a small room at the factory; they will not charge you for it. Later perhaps you can find another young woman who will share an apartment with you. Do not be afraid, *chica.* Denver is full of *mexicanos* and anyone who will work hard can earn a living in the United States. You will do well."

"Now I must go. The children will be home from school soon." He pushed back his chair and stood up, then made the same jesting, gallant gesture that he had other times. He bowed deeply over her hand, kissed it, and said *"Hasta la vista, Señorita."* Then he turned and left.

She sat there for a few more moments, elated and terrified at the prospect of what was to come. Execution of her plan would be the hardest thing she had ever done—and what would come after that was unknown.

Ayala would be back tomorrow.

Chapter 47

He came back early in the afternoon the next day. He had driven up from Chihuahua City with Ramón the day before and had stopped at home south of town for the night.

As he walked through the bar to the stairs she could see that he was in a foul mood. He simply nodded at her as he walked by and she knew that it would be best if she waited a while. She went to her room to prepare.

She put on the skirt and blouse she was wearing when they kidnapped her. She had discovered that he liked her old clothes—they reminded him of a simpler time when he was being raised on a *finca* in the country. Her clothing let him pretend that he was still a young, virile *vaquero*, a cowboy, and she a willing peasant girl.

She took care with her long, black hair, brushing it out until it had a healthy shine and then she tousled it slightly, as though she had been doing a peasant girl's work. She wore no makeup, nor did she need any; the healthy glow of her youth reached him well enough. She looked at herself in the mirror in her room and saw a broad face with high cheekbones and a nose wide enough to betray the *indio* in her ancestry. There was a high forehead, thick eyebrows and a prominent chin. Her eyes were a liquid deep brown and her mouth had generous, well-shaped lips made for a kiss. It was a face that wasn't in the least pretty, but attractive nonetheless.

Then she carefully tucked her money and her knife into the pocket she had sewn into the waistband of her skirt and sat back on her bed to wait until he had had a chance to calm down. She packed nothing, for there was nothing she had that she wished to take with her except what she wore—what she had been brought here in.

At four o'clock she stood up and walked to the mirror once more. She untied the drawstring that held the neck of her loose, white cotton blouse high on her chest. She pulled down the neckline and spread it wide on her shoulders. The smooth skin of her chest invited a caress.

Drawing up every bit of courage she had, she walked down the hall and entered his office with but the briefest of knocks. The guards knew she was always welcome.

"*Bienvenidos, querida,*" she said to him as she walked in, welcome back, my dear. "I missed you." It was a lie, of course, but some lies must be told.

She walked around his desk to his side and leaned over to kiss the top of his head. She continued to lean over, supporting herself on the arm of his chair. She knew that he would turn his head to her and when he did he would look down the front of the blouse that had dropped away from her chest. He would see her full, ripe breasts hanging free, topped by wide, brown nipples that were favorite playthings.

She let him have a long glance, and then she stood up and twirled around on her bare feet in apparent glee. Her colorful skirt swirled wide, exposing her calves.

"I am so happy you are back!" she exclaimed. "It is lonely without you here." She gave a tiny thrust of her hips that carried a subliminal message. She looked directly into his eyes as she spoke and she saw his mouth slacken with growing lust.

"Now I will wait until you call for me," she said as she walked toward the door with a motion that no man could quite describe but that any man could feel clearly in his loins. "I know that you and Ramón have business, but I had to come and say hello."

"Wait, *chica,*" he said. "Ramón and I are nearly through. Come sit down." He motioned to a chair by his desk. She sat, pulling her skirt above her slightly opened knees to keep his attention focused.

Turning to Ramón, he said, "Tomorrow another load will arrive from the south and we will have to pay for it. We no longer have credit since the affair with Tomas; we will have to pay cash, $10,000, and it is the last money we have, so I want you here with me when the transaction takes place. Be here at two o'clock. Until then, you may go. Leave Jose and Emiliano in the rooms outside, but close the doors. Tell them not to disturb me; I want to be alone tonight."

Ramón knew that "alone" did not mean *El Patrón* would be without company, but he understood. He had been witness to the screaming fits thrown at the house by that *bruja,* that witch, *El Patrón* married all those years ago. He thought it a wonder that she had not wound up in one of the holes he had dug in the desert over the years. Some women a man should not have to listen to. This one had made *Señor* Ayala easier to be around, *gracias a dios.*

He left the room, locking the door behind him.

She sat there beside him for a short while as he talked on the phone and then she stood up. She knew she had to force the pace for she did not want to be alone on the streets after dark.

"I will wait for you in the bed" she said as she turned away. As she knew he would, he looked up at her. She gave the back of her skirt a flip, revealing a flash of her bare, round, brown bottom. Not wanting to leave things to chance, she had left her cheap, cotton panties in her room.

His voice faded out as his thoughts left his conversation. She heard him bid the other party a hasty good-bye as she entered the bedroom.

She quickly stepped out of her skirt and put it into the chair beside the bed. She was pulling her blouse up over the top of her head when he came into the room. He jerked it off her arms and tossed her onto the bed, where she lay watching him with concealed disgust as he removed his clothes.

He came into her and she put to use all the tricks she had learned over the months and soon he was groaning and gasping his climax. Finally he fell to the mattress, eyes closed, chest heaving.

"You do miracles, girl," he wheezed when he had caught his breath. "In all my life it was never so strong a feeling." She lay beside him stroking his chest and belly, willing him to go to sleep.

And soon, he did.

As she always did afterwards, she stood up from the bed and went to the bathroom to get a cloth to clean him. Never taking her eyes from his face, watching for the slightest flicker of his eyes, she came back to the bed. He began to snore.

She stooped and picked up her skirt and from its pocket she removed the knife. Shielding it in the rag and holding the blade in with her fingers so that it would not fly out with a click, she pressed the button. The long stiletto blade opened against her fingers. She held the button in with one hand and with the other she eased the blade out until it reached its full extension. She let go of the button and the blade locked silently into place. She still watched him closely. Praying to God to forgive her for what she was about to do, she leaned over him. Taking the knife in both hands, she pointed it at his right eye, then from an inch away she drove it in with all the strength her pent-up hatred gave her.

The blade slid through the eyeball and it was slowed only slightly by the eggshell-thin bones at the back of the socket. In an instant, the blade was five inches deep in his brain and the weight she put behind it caused it to twist and stir, scrambling the contents of his skull. He convulsed once with a groan as the life left him and then he was still. Blood ran from the eye socket for a minute, to be soaked up by the pillow until his heart stopped beating. It was done.

She left the knife standing out from his face as she stood back and looked at her handiwork. The pounding bass from the jukebox downstairs echoed the pounding of her heart. It had been so easy, she thought, as she stood transfixed at the sight of what she had done. Far easier to do than she had expected. There was no fight, no screams, he just – died. She threw the sheet up over him, a little tent forming over the knife still standing out from his face.

Then she turned to the bathroom again. She first washed his juices from herself and then his blood from her hands—there was so little of it. And she thought again how easy it had been and how quickly he had died. She splashed water on her face and then ran a comb through her hair. She put on lipstick. Her mind seemed to be unnaturally calm, numb, really.

She slipped once more into her clothes and she put her feet into a pair of her *huaraches* she kept under the bed. Then she went through his pockets. His wallet contained just papers, but a money clip held nearly a thousand dollars, which she took, and a set of keys.

She walked quietly out of the bedroom and into the office. The clock showed that his passion and his death had taken only twenty minutes. So very strange, she thought. Without trying to form the thought completely, she was aware of the dichotomy of the act of creation and that of death taking place in the same bed within mere moments.

Almost in a trance, she walked to his desk and sat down behind it. She still had the keys in her hand. She selected the one she had seen him use before to open the desk, and gently, she opened the drawers one by one. In the center drawer she found the small revolver he carried and his address and appointment book. She placed them on top of the desk. She had never shot a gun, but what she had seen on TV made it look simple and she would shoot before she would be taken again. In the next one she found money in an envelope, a thick bundle of American fifties and hundreds held together by a rubber band. "How lucky I am," she thought without excitement. "It must be the money he would have used tomorrow." She put it with the gun and address book. She would take the book because she knew that *tio* Salinas could use it somehow.

There was nothing else of value, just loose papers, a box of condoms and a bottle of tequila that she left. He had never used a condom with her and she wondered why not. She had heard whispers of them before she was taken away but she knew nothing of their use. It was birth control and birth control was a sin where she had been raised. The discovery of their common use in the cantina had shocked her—just one of the many things she had learned that shocked her. Finally, she could be shocked no more.

She stood once more and looked at the clock. Time had flown; somehow she had spent a half hour at the desk. She knew she had to go now; it would be dark soon.

She stood up from the desk, leaving the keys hanging in the drawer. With gun and book and money in her hand, she opened the door to the closet. Inside she found several coats. All were too big for her; she was just a small girl, but Ayala had been no big man himself, just fat. She knew it was cold outside and she needed pockets, so she took a short jacket from a hook on the wall and slipped into it. The tail hung below her hips and the sleeves covered her hands, but ill-fitting clothes were no oddity in Juarez. The gun and money she put in the pockets, but the book was too big, so she carried it.

Placing her ear to the back door, she listened carefully. There was nothing to be heard at all so she opened it quietly and stepped through and pulled it gently shut behind her. The dim bulb overhead showed her the stairs to the door to the alley. She was so frightened . . .

But she had to go, there was no other choice, so she stepped softly down each step to the door then opened it to peek out. It was dusk and the lights were coming on and there was no one there. To her left a few yards away was the back door to the *cantina,* but it was closed, so no one would see her unless he came out while she was there. Ahead and to her right she could see the corner of the alley with Calle Mariscal so she quickly stepped out and made her way to the street. It was only a few minutes walk to *tio* Salinas's house, she knew. *"Que Diós me ayude,"* she thought; God help me. But she didn't think he would ever help her again; she had committed murder. It was very cold and the wind whipped around her bare legs.

Chapter 48

Ken cruised northwest on Mesa Street, elbow out the window in the cool, fall air, Ray-Bans cutting the afternoon sun that was in his face and Jeannie C. Riley singing *Harper Valley PTA* on the radio. He'd never paid much attention to country music before, but he'd been listening to more and more of it since he came to El Paso. His roommate at the Academy had been a country freak and you couldn't help hearing it out here.

He was feeling ten feet tall and bulletproof after the morning's events with Diehl, capturing Thompson. This lawman stuff was fun, once you got past the nerve-wracking part; made you feel good. Kate was out of town on an overnight run and he was at loose ends for the evening. He thought he'd go prospecting.

He turned the GTO into the parking lot at Denny's Restaurant on the other side of the street. Nearly blinded by the afternoon sun and thinking about things besides his driving, it took the blare of a horn and a chirp of tires braking hard to shake him from his reverie. He shook his head in disbelief at his inattention; he took pride in being a heads-up driver and was impatient with those who did the sort of thing he'd just done. "Bonehead," he said out loud. He pulled into a parking place in front of the windows, glad to be able to find a spot there. He wanted to be able to point it out to her if she seemed interested in fast cars. His GTO was the coupe version, bright Regimental Red and it was waxed to a high shine. Its 360 horsepower HO engine and four-speed made it faster than most anything else around, as a few Chevelle owners had found. Too fast, a couple of cops had told him. Fortunately, the badge in his billfold with his driver's license seemed to be a get out of jail free card, so their opinions had not cost him anything.

After a quick check in the mirror for boogers in his nose or lunch left over in his teeth he went inside and took a stool at the counter – the one in front of the pie cabinet. It had been ten days since he was in here with Diehl and in that time he had not been able to stop thinking about the look of her. He knew nothing about her personality but that could be discovered later; it was too soon to matter, now. She'd have to ride a broom to work to kill his interest at this point. He had already dropped by once by himself after work but she hadn't been there, so he just ate and left without asking about her.

This was his lucky day, for as he took a seat she strolled down the alley behind the counter toward him, coffee pot in hand.

"Hello, stranger," she said as she turned his cup over. "You're a coffee man, as I recall. What else'll it be?" She poured, and then looked up from his cup to his face. His stomach did a flip-flop as he looked into those violet eyes again. This time, though, he was ready for the impact.

"I'm flattered that you remember me after this long. Most times people don't see the face when a uniform walks in, just the badge, so I'm surprised you recognize me out of uniform after all this time."

"Oh, I remember you, all right. You came in with Mr. Diehl. I recall that the cat got your tongue." He blushed at the memory of it, which brought a grin from her. It was a game she enjoyed, and first point had gone to her.

He responded with a direct counterpunch. "Mmm-hmm." He paused and looked directly into her eyes. "Never happened to me that way before, but I can't imagine any man who meets you for the first time isn't struck dumb." *That puts it out there for discussion,* he thought.

"What's for supper tonight?"

She was flustered and she didn't know how to respond—nobody had ever been so direct with her. His tone, and the look that went with it, made clear things that his words hadn't said. She looked him over as she collected her thoughts. She decided not to respond to the personal comment. "Let him wonder," she thought.

"You have a look at the menu and I'll be right back as soon as I get some more coffee poured." She handed a menu to him as she turned to walk back down the counter to another new arrival. It took him a little time to get around to looking at the menu – there was no way a man could look away from that walk.

She was back shortly, order pad in hand.

"What's good tonight, Sylvia?"

"Well, I had a hot turkey sandwich when I came in that was pretty fair, if you don't mind the instant mashed potatoes that come with it. And the chicken fried steak will go down easy if you like fried food."

"You seem like a woman knows what she likes, so bring me a turkey sandwich." He looked directly, frankly, at her again and then gave her his best thousand-watt smile as he slowly folded his menu closed and put it down. She read his look and held it briefly before she turned away.

Well, that's off to an interesting start. He put cream and sugar in his coffee. He stirred it and then walked outside to the newspaper rack and bought an El Paso Times. He'd have preferred to spend the time waiting for his meal by looking at her, but it wouldn't be wise. Instead, he opened the front page to see if Nixon had anything interesting to say about how he would run things once he was inaugurated in January. Maybe he'd wind things up in Viet Nam; Johnson damn sure had made a mess of it; it looked like the Paris Peace Talks would go on forever. It had to end soon; the NVA got its ass whipped back early in the year when it tried a mass attack all across Viet Nam. They couldn't have much steam left. He turned the page.

Over the top of the paper he saw her coming back with his order, so he laid it down on the next stool.

"One hot turkey sandwich. How 'bout some more coffee?" she asked.

"Thank you kindly," he said with another wide smile that wrinkled his eyes as he unfolded his napkin and put it in his lap. "That looks pretty good." The smile was genuine; he was happy to be there and to see her.

"I remember your face, but I'm darned if I can remember your name—is it Kurt, or Carl, or something?" she said as she poured his coffee. "That ought to put him in his place," she thought, "can't let 'em take anything for granted."

"Well, Sylvia, it's something, but it's not Kurt or Carl. It's Ken. But I'll respond to anything you want to call me."

"Ken," she said. "I'll try to remember that next time."

Fortune favors the bold, or faint heart never won fair maid, or something like that. Sometimes he thought he read too much.

"Why don't we make "next time" after you get off tonight? I just polished up my car and you could help me go get some bugs on the windshield. We could take a run up the valley; get a drink somewhere, maybe dance a little."

"I don't get off until ten. There's not much to do at that hour, is there?"

He could think of several things to do but this was not the time or place to bring them up, so he said, "We could just drive, couldn't we? I mean, I like boring a hole in the dark with the headlights, some music on the radio and the stars shining through the windshield."

"That sounds like fun; I saw your car when you came in. It's a GTO, isn't it? I'll bet it's fast. I like to drive fast at night."

His heart leaped – he was in, he thought as he took the bait. "Well, great," he said . . . but she interrupted.

"Tonight's not a good night, though. My boyfriend's going to pick me up when I get off and he wouldn't like it if I was off with somebody else when he came. You wouldn't want to meet him under those circumstances. He's big—and he's real jealous."

Well, shit. "Another night, then," He tried not to let her see his disappointment. He picked up his fork and cut a bite of sandwich that had gone nearly cold while they dueled.

"Game, set, and match," she said to herself, with an internal smile of victory.

"I'll check back in a little bit." She turned to go. With his mouth full, he had nothing to say, so he just nodded picked up his newspaper again.

He polished off his dinner, cold mashed potatoes and all, and drank down the rest of his coffee just as she came back. He put the paper on the counter and asked her to toss it in the trash.

"Want some more coffee? How about a piece of pie? What do you like?" She knew he'd say yes.

"Pie's mighty tempting, Sylvia," he said with a smile, "but think I'll pass on it tonight." He pulled a smoke from his shirt pocket and lit it. "Thanks anyway, but I better scoot", he said as he snapped his Zippo closed. He put a five-dollar bill on the counter. "That oughta cover it all. See you later." He turned and walked out to his car. She watched as he got in, waiting to see if he'd look back. He waved at her as he closed the door, then she heard the big motor fire up with a bark of the pipes.

"Hmmm . . . I guess it was a draw after all. But" she bet herself, "he'll be back."

Chapter 49

She found the gate in the wall along the sidewalk. There were no numbers, but it was the fourth one from the corner, just as *tio* Salinas had described, and there was the little tree, and keg, and chair against the back wall. This had to be it.

But there was no light. The gate was locked. No one answered her calls. The sun had set and the night creatures would soon begin their prowl. She was alone, cold, and frightened. And appalled at what she had done and could never undo. A desire for revenge indulged often leaves the taste of ashes in the soul.

As she was about to turn from the gate to go she knew not where, she looked down the darkening street to see two small figures coming her way. One was obviously a child, the other a woman. She stayed and watched them draw closer. At last, they seemed to notice her, for the woman leaned and spoke to the boy and they began to run.

"Are you Luz?" the young woman asked breathlessly.

"Yes, I am. You are Angela?"

"Yes. And this is Rafaelito. We can't stay here for even a minute now. My *abuelo* told me about you and what we must do. Come! It is only three blocks to my aunt's house. Where is your bag?"

"I brought nothing. There was nothing I wanted."

"No matter, Luz. I took all my clothes and important things to *tia* Dolores's house the other day, after grandfather told me that you might come. I have clothes that you may wear until we can buy some for you."

They walked quickly along the street and the cold wind chilled them and stirred dust up into their faces. The last glow of the sun lit the bottoms of clouds to the west. At the end of the block they turned and crossed the street, heading north toward the river. The sounds of the Santa Fe railroad yard came across the river on the breeze.

They came to a small, flat-roofed house of cement blocks. Only a patch of bare earth and a waist-high wall separated it from the sidewalk, but the dirt yard was swept clean and the whitewash was fresh on the wall.

Angela led them to the door and knocked. The door opened quickly. A short, round, happy-faced woman with graying hair stood there looking at them. She beckoned them in, making little waving motions with her hand as she backed away from the door to allow them to pass. They had just left and she was surprised to see them back, but the sight of the girl with them, told her the story. Rafael, her brother-in-law, had told her all about it.

"Ven'te! Ven'te! Come! Come! *"* She brought them into a tiny room with a cement floor that was the living room. A red, woven wool rug in the middle of the room provided a touch of color. A chair and a couch and single bed pushed against a wall were the only furniture. A picture of a bleeding, crucified Christ painted on indigo velvet faced the front door, and a crucifix hung beside the door. Otherwise, pale blue walls were bare.

She hurried them through the living room and into the warm kitchen, where the smell of supper's beans and onions and chiles still lingered. The children had eaten there, earlier.

She turned and took Luz's hands in her own—her kind eyes showed that she knew it all. "*Pobrecita,"* she said. Poor little one.

Luz collapsed on the floor and she began weeping. Then, as the last bit of her nerve ran out, the weeping turned into great racking sobs as the tension and terror finally overwhelmed her and the knowledge of what she had done and what had been done to her became real for her.

Dolores sank gently to the floor beside her and took Luz in her arms. She pulled the girl to her bosom, rocking back and forth and patting and stroking her head and saying over and over, *"Bueno, bueno. Todo será bien. Que Diós la bendiga.* Good, good; all will be well. God bless you.*"* Angela, who carried some of the same scars that Luz bore, sat down beside them and whispered gently that all was well and they were safe now. Rafaelito sat on a kitchen chair, awed and frightened by the emotion.

Finally, the tears ran out. She fell silent except for an occasional small sob. Then, there in Dolores's arms, she slept. She was, after all, little more than a child. Together, Dolores and Angela got her to her feet and led her to the double bed in the small bedroom that opened off the living room. She would sleep there, Dolores at her side, while Angela and her brother slept in the living room.

They would see tomorrow what the future held.

*****

Luz awoke to the sound of *tio* Salinas's voice in the kitchen, talking to Dolores. She lay in the bed with a warm, safe feeling that she had thought never to feel again. Even when the memories of yesterday washed over her as she came fully awake they seemed like very old memories, and the thought that men were looking for her did not seem real.

"So she is all right, Dolores?"

"Who can say who is all right after what she has been through? She never spoke a word here last night; she simply collapsed. She slept all night like the dead, without so much as a movement. But she is young and she seems healthy."

"Then we must leave as soon as we can, Dolores. Every minute spent here in town is a minute in which we might be found—they will be looking hard for her. Women cannot be allowed to escape, ever. If one succeeds, others will try. No, they must take her again, and make an example of her to the others. They will suspect that I am involved, all the more now if they find the children are gone too, but unless they find her with me, they will probably do nothing. But I must get her out of town."

"How will you do that, Rafael? You and the children have local cards, so you can cross the bridge, but she certainly does not. Where will you take her?"

"I don't know yet. First, I have to talk to her."

He looked up when he heard a small sound and saw her standing in the kitchen door. She was still dressed in what were obviously yesterday's clothes and she held a book and a gun and an envelope in her hands.

He set his coffee cup down and stood up and stepped to her. Reaching out gently, he took the revolver from her and placed it on the counter. She silently held out the book and the envelope for him and he took them, too, and set them on the counter, too. Then reached his hand out to her. She took it and he led her to a chair at the table. She had a vacant look on her face, and neither of them had spoken a word yet.

Dolores rose and took a plate from a shelf on the wall and a tortilla from under a cloth on a warming basket on the back of the stove and put it on the plate.

Then she scooped a ladle of spicy beans from a pot on the stove and poured them onto the tortilla to make a simple burrito. She set the plate before the girl. A cup of coffee followed and Dolores refreshed the cup in front of Rafael.

Luz's face showed the strain of the past months and of yesterday. Her eyes had a distant look, as though she were seeing things not there for the rest of them.

"I killed him". The words fell tonelessly from her lips. "With a knife."

"Madre de Diós! Mother of God!" Dolores whispered as she brought her hands to her breast in a prayerful clasp, a shocked look on the face she turned to the ceiling.

"*Aiiiee; de veras?* Is that the truth?" Rafael asked.

"Si, tio. Es la verdad. It is true. He fell asleep after raping me again yesterday in his bedroom and I took a knife and stabbed him in the eye with it while he slept." She hesitated and then said, "And then I stole from him." She motioned to the objects on the counter and Rafael felt a sense of macabre amusement at her discomfort over stealing from a man she had just killed.

"I am glad, I think," she went on. "But I feel very bad, too. I will surely go to hell, now."

Rafael understood very well the depth of the sense of sin that possessed her and how badly it would be hurting her. Most Mexican girls, especially small-town Mexican girls, were raised in the Church and it shaped their every thought. Especially thoughts of sin.

"Dolores, is *Padre* Mendoza to be found at the church at this hour of the morning?"

"*Si,* Rafael; he will be at the church. He held the early mass today. He will be hearing confessions now. But you cannot take her there, can you? The risk is too great." Dolores understood the girl's need, too.

"I will bring him here. He certainly knows of that evil man, Ayala, and I'll make certain he understands everything. I will wait until the confession time is over before I go to make arrangements for our journey."

With that, he turned to the counter and picked up the book. Flipping it open, he began reading through it, making sounds of surprise and satisfaction.

"I know men who would be very interested in what is in here." He slapped the book shut and picked up the envelope. It fell open and a green blizzard of U.S. currency fluttered to the floor.

"Madre de Diós" Dolores said once more. "That must be all the money in Juarez!"

"It is ten thousand dollars, I think," Luz said. "Ayala was going to use it to pay for drugs that are being brought to him today—I heard him say it yesterday. Some men are coming this afternoon with drugs. I have a thousand more dollars still in the jacket." She walked into the bedroom and came back with the money and handed it to Rafael.

"*JesuCristo!*" he said. "This changes everything. They would pursue a girl who has run and it would go hard for her if she was caught. The death of Ayala would make things even harder, but this," he held up the money, "for this they will turn the town upside-down and people will die."

Angela walked softly into the kitchen, rubbing the sleep from her eyes. Rafaelito was still sleeping on the couch.

"Did I hear you say you killed the man who raped you, Luz?"

Luz looked down at the floor, ashamed at having been overheard. "Yes, I did. While he slept. And then I escaped."

"Good!" Angela said matter-of-factly, shocking her aunt. "It is no less than he deserved for what he did to you." There was vehemence in her tone that came as no surprise to her grandfather, who knew the source of her feelings. Dolores did not know what had happened to Angela when she had been held by *los malos.*

He took the money and put it all back in the envelope, which he handed to Dolores. "Go and hide this in the privy, Dolores. I have to make a telephone call before I get Padre Mendoza. He turned to the girls, and with a stern look he said, "Do not leave this house. Not even into the yard."

They both nodded. Nothing could have tempted them to go outside.

*****

By late morning Luz had made her confession, been absolved, and was given her penance. Like shedding a heavy burden after a long journey, the weight of her sins fell from her. While the agonizing memories remained, she no longer felt damned by what she had done. Faith is a powerful thing.

And Salinas had set up a meeting with Pope at the Paso del Norte Bridge.

Chapter 50

Salinas walked out of the building at the Paso del Norte Bridge to his car, where the children waited. They had crossed a half hour before, Rafael telling the inspector that he had business about a visa inside. The official looked at their local cards, asked a couple of perfunctory questions, then waved them on. Salinas parked in the lot beside the building, being careful to select a spot that was out of the late-morning sun. Leaving the children in the car, he went into the lobby. He gave his name to the man at the reception counter and then took a seat and waited for his name to be called. As he waited, he looked at the crowd in the lobby, but he saw no one he recognized, nor was there anyone obviously interested in him. After a few minutes, a door at the end of the counter opened and an inspector beckoned to him. He found Pope waiting inside the door.

"Thanks, Jesse," Pope said to the inspector. He led Rafael down the long, polished hall to a vacant office that looked out over the parking lot and downtown.

They talked for less than a half hour. Salinas told Pope his version of Luz's tale and gave Ayala's journal to him. When he left, he said *"Vaya con Diós, amigo mio.* Go with God, my friend. I do not believe we will meet again." They shook hands and Salinas went out. He looked around, up at the cloudless sky, at the mountains in El Paso and those south of Juarez, and then he walked to the car and got in.

From behind the wheel of the battered blue and white '55 Chevrolet, he said to the children in the back seat, "*Todo está bien,* all is well," and then carefully backed out of his parking place against the wall. He drove north on Santa Fe Street to Sixth Avenue, where a right turn and a few blocks took them into the barrio of south El Paso. Finally, he bumped over a broken curb into a small vacant lot cluttered with discarded bottles and trash and randomly parked cars. He backed up to the fence at the back of the lot, then just sat and waited and watched.

Ten minutes later, after not having seen anyone interested in him, he got out and made a slow circuit of the car, apparently checking the tires with a gauge he had taken from the glove box. A boy of about fourteen was sitting across the alley, his back to the wall. He watched vacantly, but said nothing. Eventually, he squirted a spray of paint from a can into a paper bag, put it to his face and breathed deeply of the fumes. The red mask around his mouth showed that it was not his first hit of the day. Salinas shook his head sadly. Life along the border could be very hard on the young – there was nothing to offer hope to children.

There was no one else within view, so he opened the trunk. Luz climbed out stiffly. Although the morning was still cool, the atmosphere in the trunk had been close and hot. Her clothing was dusty, and soaked with sweat. She stood and stretched her short body as far as she could and then twisted this way and that. She had shared the trunk with three small suitcases and a spare tire and it was cramped in there.

He took out the suitcases and then reached into the back of the trunk and folded the rubber mat forward, revealing two Texas license plates. He quickly mounted them and then threw the Chihuahua plate into their place and replaced the mat. He had registered his car in El Paso years before, using a phony address. A Texas plate on the highways in the U.S. drew less attention than one from Chihuahua.

Luz climbed into the front seat. As soon as she was seated, she asked him to turn his back for a moment. When he turned back around she handed him the envelope full of cash and straightened her skirt. Modesty, it seemed, had survived after all.

He walked to the *bodega* across the alley and bought a six-pack of Cokes and a dozen tamales wrapped in tinfoil, made by the owner's wife. Some snacks went into the bag as well, and a carton of Old Gold cigarettes from under the counter. The lack of tax stamps showed that they had probably been brought from Mexico by one of the young boys who made a living smuggling cigarettes across the river. Older boys and men bought them at the duty-free store in El Paso and took them to Juarez. From there the boys brought them back, half a dozen cartons at a time and sold them on the street, or to small stores like this one. They could be bought on the street from the boys for less than half of what legal cigarettes cost, or from a store for very little more than that. Every day at dawn a dozen or more of them would try to cross the river, and apprehending a cigarette boy was a minor triumph for a Border Patrolman. Customs regulations called for destroying contraband cigarettes by burning. And they were; one at a time.

As they sat in the car and ate he said, *"Vamos. Vamos a Denver.* Luz, you are family now, *mi hija,* my daughter. Children, together we will go there. We will find someplace to live and I will find a job again. You will go to school and work when you can. We will not return to Mexico for a long time; the men there have long memories and they would kill us for what we have done. But we will become rich, and some day, when all is forgotten, we will go home again. But now, *vamos.* We go."

He tossed his tinfoil out the window, took the last swig from his Coke and threw the can out too. He started the car and pulled out onto the street and then turned right onto Stanton Street, U.S. Highway 62. It led east to Carlsbad. He knew how to get around the Border Patrol traffic checkpoint on the highway at Dell City – he'd done it many times before. By tomorrow night, God willing, they would be in Denver to begin a new chapter in their lives.

"What of the house, grandfather?" Angela asked. "What will become of it? And our things?"

"In a month or so, when they have quit watching, your aunt Dolores will go there and collect the things that matter. Then her son, Julian, will rent it to someone for us. He has papers that show I sold it to him, but he will send the money to us from time to time. But, children, these are things for a man to worry about. You will come with me and I will take care of us."

Angela leaned forward from the back seat and placed her hand on Luz's shoulder and said *"Bienvenidos, hermana mia,* welcome, my sister." Luz smiled and a tear built in the corner of her eye. She tilted her cheek down against the hand and said, "*Gracias, hermana.*"

In the other corner in the back seat Rafaelito began to cry at leaving his home and his friends and at the unknown to come. But all brightened for the boy when Salinas took a chocolate bar from the bag and passed it back to him. After all, how bad can it be, at six years old, if you had sweets and a family?

Chapter 51

Paul, can you get in here right away?" Pope was on the phone to Lamont. "I need your contacts at the *Judiciál* and I need 'em right now, immediately."

He looked at Diehl and Travis and made a face.

"Too much to explain over the phone, buddy. Just hustle on in here. How long will you be?"

Diehl and Travis could hear the outraged squawks on the line, but did not understand the words.

"Skip the goddam shower! I'll pretend you smell like rosebuds, but we need you here right now. It may already be too late."

He hung up and said, "He's on his way; fifteen minutes, tops, he says."

"What are we going to do, Jim?" Ken asked impatiently.

"Just hold your horses until Paul gets here. I'll tell all of you about it then and he can tell me if what I want to do is possible in the time we have."

On his way to the office from the Paso del Norte Bridge, where he had met Salinas, Pope had told the radio operator to call the two of them at home to come into the office. Ken had walked out on a pleasant morning with Kate, much to her displeasure—he tried to explain "duty" to her as he threw on a uniform, but she didn't seem to get it. She had fixed breakfast, waffles, eggs, and bacon, for them in his apartment but he left most of it on the table. It was the first real time they'd had together in over a week and she had been enjoying it. Now she was mad and he couldn't take the time to make her see why he had to go.

Diehl walked out to the coffee vending machine and came back in a few minutes with a steaming paper cup, drops of coffee hanging from the bottom edge.

"I don't know why they don't get rid of that goddam machine. He set the cup down on the desk by Ken. It made a ring. "The stuff tastes like burned shit smells and the machine usually drops the cup in crooked so you loose most of it before you scald your hand sticking it in there to stand the cup up. Goddam cheap outfit."

Pope looked up from the journal that was open on his desk with a quizzical glance. He turned his head and said, "Let me have a smoke, would you, Ken?"

Ken reached for his shirt pocket, happy to oblige, but Diehl spoke up. "Don't give it to him. Let him buy his own." There was no humor in his voice.

That drew another look and a raised eyebrow from Pope. "Who peed in your Cheerios this morning, my friend? Hemorrhoids acting up, or what?"

Diehl glared at him, then looked away. "Just in a shitty mood. Sorry."

They had known each other for a long time; Pope could recognize when something was eating at his friend. "Heard from Louise recently, have you?"

"Goddam it, Jim, I swear you know me better than she ever did. Yeah, she got the day off to a bad start for me on the phone. Wants more money for the girl. Damn, I'll send it; I've never been cheap where Donna's concerned. Louise knows that, but she makes me out to be a skinflint every chance she gets. Woman's got a tongue rougher'n Turkish toilet paper."

There you go. All this time we've been together and I never knew he'd been married. Must have been a dandy of a breakup to make him feel like he does about women. Ken wanted to know more, but he was not going to ask.

"How's the daughter doing, Tom?" Pope asked gently.

"I just don't know any more, Jim. She used to call me from time to time, even a letter once in a while, but I hardly talk to her any more. She's in high school this year, you know?" He turned to Ken. "Travis, I don't usually talk about personal business at work, so anything you hear between Jim and me you forget. I ain't going to be an object of gossip, you hear me?" The look on his face spoke more than his words.

Ken knew he would never breathe a word of anything he heard. All he said was, "Yes, sir," but he was curious. He admired Diehl and wanted to know more about him, who he really was. The way he usually acted, Ken couldn't imagine that he wouldn't be a good father, strict, even stern, but a good man to bring up a kid.

"I think the old lady is running me down to her. Why that woman hates me so . . . you know, I told her once during an argument that I had a right to see my daughter. You know what she said?" Pope looked at him, a question in his eyes. "She asked me what made me so damn sure Donna was *my* daughter." He looked at the floor as he took a long drag on his cigarette, before he went on. "What with them over in Galveston, I can't exactly drop in to take her out to supper or anything to stay acquainted and Louise always finds some excuse to keep her from me when I try to arrange a trip. It's hard, Jim, hard. I miss that girl bad, even after five years. It don't get any easier."

Lamont blew into the room like a chubby hurricane, slamming the door behind him.

"What in the god-damned hell is so important it can't wait for me to get a shower? And am I going to have to blow off watching the Jets this afternoon? Do you fucking believe how they cut the game off short last week, the Jets ahead by four points, a minute to go and some brain-dead idiot cuts off the game to start a fucking movie! *Heidi; Heidi*, for Christ's sweet sake. And then Oakland comes from behind to win! Ought cut the producer's nuts off." Lamont was from New York and he was a rabid Jets fan.

"Paul. Paul!" Pope slapped the top of his desk. "Goddam it, put a cork in it and pay attention! We've got business to do here, confusion to bring to the bad guys. Listen up!"

He went on. "*Halcón* called me a couple hours ago; wanted real bad to meet me right away. We got together down at the PDN Bridge and he gave me this." He held up the journal. "It's got everything in it that you'd ever want to know about Ayala and all his contacts. He's out of the picture, though"

"How's that?" Lamont asked him.

"According to *Halcón*, that young girl he ran into at the Cantina Rio Bravo, the one that Ayala bought, killed him and escaped. Doesn't seem a likely thing for a girl to do, but there it is. She ran to *Halcón* and gave him this book. *Halcón* says he doesn't have any details, but I suspect he's not telling me all he knows, either."

"Anyhow, he tells me that she overheard Ayala talking to one of his bodyguards yesterday afternoon, saying that there's a load coming to his office this afternoon. She saw him lock a bunch of cash in his desk to pay for it. Odds are she actually got away with it, but that doesn't matter to what we're going to do."

Lamont looked pensive. "Ought to be some way we can put that info to use, isn't there? You've been thinking again, haven't you? Why do I think I'm not going to like this?"

"We're going to fuck with their minds, is what we're going to do. And make 'em very suspicious of each other. I want you to call up those sergeants you bought drinks for last month and tell 'em this." He went on to explain the tale

Chapter 52

At two p.m. Ramón Diaz pounded on the office door upstairs at the Cantina Rio Bravo. He was surprised not to have seen *El Patrón* yet today, but then, the new girl had been keeping him very occupied. Now, though, it was time for business. The men from Jalisco would be here soon. He pounded again. The door to his right opened and the guard Emiliano looked out.

"Have you seen *El Patrón*?" Diaz asked.

"No, *jefe*. You told us not to disturb him with the new girl." He smirked. "We heard some groans from the room in the evening, but nothing else." It was hardly unusual that they'd not heard much; the walls and doors had been reinforced when Ayala bought the place and moved in.

Diaz pulled a key from his pocket and opened the door. He immediately smelled the shit and bloody odor of death; he drew a Star nine-millimeter automatic from his belt.

"Come," he said to Emiliano. They walked into the office and found no one in the room. Emiliano glanced into the bedroom and saw a bare foot hanging off the edge of the bed, so he slowly put his head through the door. "*Aiee, chingado*" he exclaimed, "Oh, fuck!" Diaz stepped into the room and saw the small, bloodstained tent over the face. He pulled the sheet back. "The *puta* killed him," he said as he stared at his cousin's ruined face with the knife standing out of the eye. It was a flat declaration, with no element of uncertainty to it, totally lacking emotion. It came out as though he was beyond being surprised by anything.

"We will deal with the body tonight and with her later, but first we have business to finish."

He left the bedroom, closing the door without a backward glance. He sat down behind the desk and opened the drawers one at a time. He went through them again, and then uttered a particularly vile curse. "She has taken the money. I told him he should put it in the safe, but he didn't. Now he has managed to fuck us even in his dying."

He stood up suddenly, shoving the chair all the way back against the wall with a crash. It was the first time Emiliano had seen him display emotion; it was a frightening thing on his face.

Downstairs in the bar, two men had been there for half an hour drinking beer at a table in a corner. They wore fancy, long-sleeved shirts with the square tails out to cover bulges in their belts. They, and two *gringos* in another corner, were the only ones in the bar early on a Sunday afternoon.

They looked up as two large men pushed open the front door, allowing shaft of sunlight in, and a cold draft that raised some dust as it swirled across the floor. They, too, wore shirts with the tails out and one of them carried a briefcase. They looked around and saw the two men in the corner and nodded to them. They expected to see security—it was that kind of business. They went straight back to the bar and spoke to the man there. After he gave them a nod they turned and walked over to the stairs against the wall and went up. The bartender pushed the button under the bar once to alert those in the rooms above that someone was coming.

The two men at the table nodded to each other and stood up together. They walked back to the bar, where the larger one grabbed the bartender by the front of the shirt. He pulled him halfway across the bar, pressed the muzzle of a large, chromed, automatic pistol against the tip of his nose, and said "You must leave now and don't come back. Don't walk: run!" He released the man with a push that rattled the glasses on the back bar when he staggered into it. The bartender slammed through the alley door at a dead run without a backward glance. The other one turned to look at the two men who were holding hands across the table in the front of the room. He lifted his shirt and drew his pistol. He barked, "*Andale, maricones!* Take a hike, faggots." They had seen the interplay at the bar so they took the advice and left through the front door. One of them knocked over a chair in his haste.

Upstairs, Diaz said to Emiliano, "She will have run to Salinas, certainly; she knows no one else. I will go there and bring the money back. And her. Salinas;

him I will leave there." He looked Emiliano in the eye and said, "This is my deal and my business now, Emiliano. Are you with me? Or not?" He did not need to explain the unspoken "or else."

There was no doubt in Emiliano's mind that he was with him; he said so with feeling. Diaz started through the door into the corridor. He heard the buzzer go off behind him but he ignored it.

He recognized the two men he met at the top of the stairs; he had met them when they were here to set up the deal with Ayala. He had hoped to have some time before they arrived but it was not to be. Now he knew that his life had just become much more complicated—he would have to talk fast to keep the deal from going sour. He knew where Salinas lived and he had to persuade them to wait while he went in search of the girl and the money. .

"Ah, *Señor* Benavidez. *Señor* Armendariz. *Bienvenidos.* Welcome. Come, come." He opened his arms to them in a Latino *abrazo* of welcome. They stopped together and stared at him without warmth. Diaz recognized that this would not be a friendly meeting.

He took the arm of Armendariz, who carried the black, sturdy briefcase. Armendariz immediately shook his grip loose, but both men followed Diaz down the hall and into the office.

"*Que tomen asiento, Señores"* Diaz said with a sweeping gesture to the two chairs in front of the desk. They went to the chairs but each moved his chair a foot or two before sitting down in it. Benavidez turned his chair sideways, to keep Emiliano, who was in the corner of the room in Diaz's old spot, in his field of view.

Diaz reached into a desk drawer and brought out the bottle of tequila. *"Una bebida, Senóres?* A drink?*"*

"Where is Ayala?" Armendariz demanded, ignoring the question.

"Alas, he met with an accident last night and will not be able to carry out this arrangement. But I am here to do so." Diaz poured a shot of tequila for himself.

The door swung wide with a crash as two men with pistols drawn came through it—Emiliano had left his security post in the next room and no one else was there. He paid for his mistake when he went for the gun tucked in his belt. He was not nearly the *pistolero* he fancied himself to be and easily, almost contemptuously, the first man through the door shot him twice in the center of his chest. The other never took his eyes or his aim from the men at the desk. Diaz sat there frozen as the silence returned to the room, the bottle of tequila still in his hand, halfway to being poured. The other two never stirred, but their vision flickered around the room, alert for opportunity.

Men shot with a pistol seldom die immediately. Even with the heart pierced, death takes time to find its way to the mind. Emiliano staggered backward to the wall and leaned against it, seeking support against the weakness that was drawing the strength from his legs. A hand tried to reach up again to find the pistol in his belt, but it, too, had lost its strength. It touched the grip but could not close around it. Both of his arms dropped to his sides and his breath rattled in his throat as he tried to speak. The sucking sound of air entering his chest through the holes in his breast was clear to the other five, who were watching him die. Eyes wide open, looking at the other men, he slid down the wall and finally collapsed on his side. He breathed a final sigh and then was silent forever. The man who shot him walked over and took the pistol from his belt, for he knew that only fools and victims leave guns lying around.

There were still five beating hearts in the room and six guns. No one wanted to start a shootout in such close quarters but no mental bets were being laid that it wouldn't happen. Each man was assessing the others, measuring his chances. There was much to be gained by the survivors of a shootout.

The cops held the best cards; they were standing and had their guns out and they had shown they were ready to kill. But they were outnumbered. Armendariz and Benavidez were seated. With their guns under their shirts they were at a grave tactical disadvantage but the briefcase Armendariz held could be a weapon of distraction if he threw it. Diaz was the odd man out. His partner was dead on the floor and his own gun was in his belt against the back of the chair. He knew that unless the situation changed somehow he'd better check to the power and wait for the draw.

"Now to business, *Senóres.*" The first cop spoke to the group. He and his partner were keeping their distance, beyond reach, but within easy shooting distance if it came to that. "It would be far more congenial here if we could have an element of trust. And we believe that we could trust you far more if your pistols were on the floor."

He pointed his pistol at Armendariz. "You first, and only you. Keep the briefcase in your lap but slowly put your gun on the floor and kick it over here."

Armendariz looked long and hard at the two of them, as though memorizing their faces for later reference. It cost him his life, for the first cop shot him in the forehead without hesitation, killing him instantly. He slumped in his chair. Benavidez, recognizing what was to come, went for the gun in the front of his belt. He died in his chair as the second cop shot him in the ear, the round from the .38 Super spattering Diaz and the desk with gore as it exited the skull.

Diaz, smarter than many thought him to be, had immediately thrown his arms up in a gesture of surrender when the shooting started. He thought his chances of survival were slim, but better than if he tried to get his gun out. These cops were good; there was no way to take them but perhaps he could deal with them.

They stared at him over their pistols. His life hung in the balance while they considered what threat he posed to them, or what benefit.

Finally, he said, "I would have it be congenial. I will give you my gun if you wish."

They both gave him a come-on sign, so he slowly stood up at the desk and turned his back to them. He didn't fear doing it at all, for he had already seen that they didn't need a back to shoot at if they wanted to kill—he could not be any more vulnerable than he was. He put his hands behind his head and sat back against the desk, making it possible for one of them to take the pistol from his belt.

When they had it he sat down again, looked at them, and said, "We can deal, I think."

One of them laughed. "What do you have to deal with, Diaz? And who are you to deal, anyway? Where is Ayala? Our business is with him; he has been holding out on us, it seems." He shoved Armendariz' body out of the chair and sat down. The chair was still usable; the bullet he had fired from his .32 automatic did not penetrate Armendariz' head completely. His, he thought, had been, a neat killing. His partner always used too much gun.

He picked up the briefcase. When he opened it there was a single, brick-sized bundle inside, tightly wrapped in plastic. He held it out for Diaz to examine.

"*Drogas, heroina*, Diaz. Where is Ayala? Where is the money to pay for this? In the desk? Or perhaps there is a safe?"

Diaz had seen what happens to someone who hesitated too long in talking to these two so he answered quickly.

"The money is gone. Ayala is dead. I am in charge now. Let me have the drugs and I can deal them for us. Then you will get your money."

The two looked at each other. This was not what they had expected at all—they came believing that Ayala had been holding out on paying them the *mordida,* the bite, the payoff, that went to the police in return for a blind eye turned to illegal activity. The first they had heard of this deal was when their *amigo*, Lamont, had called this morning and told them about it. He believed, they thought, that they would take the drugs and destroy them, protecting his precious *estados unidos* from the poison.

"What happened to Ayala? Have you killed him?"

"No. Come with me."

Diaz slowly stood up, hands always clearly visible as he walked toward the bedroom door. They stood and covered him and the door with their guns while he opened it. When he stepped back they maneuvered to be able to see into the room. When they could see it was clear, they stepped in and one of them pulled the sheet back.

"De veras. Esta bien muerto. Truly, he is very dead." He took hold of the knife and wiggled it a little. There was no resistance, so he pulled it out. He wiped it off on the sheet, folded it closed, and put it in his pocket. He could get five dollars for it. Maybe more, since it had killed someone.

"Who killed him, Diaz?"

"It was one of the girls, sergeant. She was young and fresh and he had fallen for her. He let her get too close to him—a *puta;* imagine that. He kept her with him sometimes at night and last night she must have killed him. She took the money and ran."

"*Estupido!* Stupid! I saw her here once, I believe. To let a whore get so close is stupid. Why do you not have her yet, Diaz? She can't be hard to find. Where can a whore from the country go?"

"We had just found him when those two arrived." He motioned at the bodies on the floor in the other room; "I had just begun to talk business with them when you came in. I would certainly have called you as soon as we were done. I know my duty to the police." He smiled ingratiatingly. "I have not had time to find her yet."

"How much money was there, Diaz? How much did she get away with?"

"It was eight thousand dollars, *sergento,* all that we had. We were putting everything into this deal that we had after the load was lost last month. You know of that, I am sure."

The cop whipped his automatic across Diaz's face with a cat-quick backhand, adding a cut that would become another scar on the face. Tough as he was, Diaz recoiled from the blow. He fell backwards across the corpse on the bed, squeezing a fart from the body. The odor filled the room.

"*Pinche mentiroso!* Fucking liar! Do you think we are stupid? Think! How was it that we knew this was happening here today? We know that there were ten thousand dollars here. We know more than you know. Someone has been talking to the Border Patrol. They told us, *cabrón.*"

Diaz rolled across the body, and then pushed himself up.

"I will get the money. I think I can find the cow and the man who is helping her and bring them both back here." He left unsaid that he would also find and settle with Chavez, who had betrayed them.

"Your problems are your own to solve. We have no wish to see either of them, ever. We will keep the merchandise for one week while you seek the money. When you have it we will sell the heroin to you. If you fail we have other people who will be interested in it. We are giving you this chance to demonstrate that you are smarter than Ayala, but if you fail . . . it will go hard for you. Succeed, and all will be well. You cannot reach us but we will return next Sunday afternoon to see how you have done."

They left with the briefcase. Diaz took a wad of the sheet and pressed it to his cheek to stanch the copious bleeding from his ripped skin. He had work to do, beginning with getting rid of these bodies before they began to stink. He knew he had the answer, whether he found the girl or not. It would just take a little time.

Chapter 53

It was three in the morning on Thanksgiving Day. Diehl and Travis sat in their old Jeep on the south side of the Courchesne Bridge on the Rio Grande, upriver from the ASARCO smelter. It had snowed hard the night before, a rare event in El Paso. The city had shut down for the biggest part of the day, until the sun and temperatures in the forties had uncovered the roads. Ice and snow remained on the north sides of buildings and it was still cold for El Paso; the temperature was down in the thirties and there was a stiff breeze. They kept the engine running for warmth.

"I thought I left this shit behind in Maine," Travis groused. "When I rolled out of there last May I thought I'd seen the last of it. I just hate being cold!" He shifted uncomfortably on the seat. They hadn't been out of the rig since they came on duty at midnight and he was in a bad mood.

"Give thanks on this special day, young man," Diehl said with unsympathetic good humor, "that all the Mexicans are home snug and warm in bed and not out here demanding your attention. You wouldn't want to be out running tonight, would you? Yes, I believe you should count your blessings."

"Kiss my ass," Travis muttered. He knew The Real Diehl well enough now to say that to him, as long as he wasn't serious. Diehl grinned in the dark—the kid had come a long way; it looked like the investment Diehl had made in him would pay off.

"You cooking yourself a turkey for dinner today, Ken?"

The question cheered Travis up considerably, the thought of a full Thanksgiving dinner with Kate.

"Not me, man. I could screw up the recipe for ice water. Kate's fixing us a fancy dinner, turkey, she told me, and all the fixings, just like back home. I'll catch a nap, and then go down to her place about four. What are you doing?" It was in his mind to try to call Kate as soon as he got home and ask her if Diehl could come over, if he was going to be alone.

"Margaret's coming down from Las Cruces to do the same thing for me. She wants to stay through the weekend and I didn't have the heart to say no to her after she said she'd do dinner today. I don't know how I'll do, being around one that long. It's been a while."

"Is that the woman you mentioned the other night at Denny's? The one you can drop in on for a couple of meals and a warm-up from time to time?"

"That's her. Nice lady, as such things go. But even the best of them are still women—they all got their clockwork in backwards. Hey—did you ever hear why everything inside 'em don't fall right out the bottom, what with the way they're built?"

"Aww, Jesus, Real—no, I don't know. And I got a feeling this is going to be something not a woman on the planet would like."

Diehl chuckled as he told Travis the answer. "The vacuum in their heads keeps everything sucked up tight."

Man, does he have a bad case of it . . . His marriage must have been a dandy. No wonder she left him.

"Well," Ken said, "I've had pretty good luck with them so far."

"You're still young. I thought I had it all figured out once upon a time, too. I thought Louise and I were doing pretty good. Decent house and I bought her a nice car every couple years. I tried to listen to her, much as a man can, anyway. Hell, I loved her. Then one day I came home from a three-day detail to Deming and right out of the clear blue, she'd packed up and moved out. And I mean *moved out.* Had a truck come and haul damn near everything away. Hell, she even sold my guns and tools to a hockshop out on Dyer Street. Cost me a bunch to get 'em back. And she took Donna away from me. I'd have died for them; it's a man's job to do. But she wouldn't even tell me what was wrong; she just up and left."

Ken was dumbstruck by this sudden confidence from a man who had, so far, not let much of his personal thinking show to Ken. He couldn't think of anything to say. But it gave him food for thought.

Uncomfortable at having shown a piece of his soul, Diehl changed the subject.

"These seats are just about wore out," he said, as he shifted his butt around on the rump-sprung cushions and moved his legs. Then, suddenly, WHOOOSH! and the rig was filled with a white, choking, impenetrable cloud of dust, apparently from nowhere.

"What the . . .!" Both threw their doors open and rolled out onto the ground, fumbling for their guns. Whatever it was, it didn't feel like good news.

"You OK, Ken?" came from the other side of the Jeep after a few seconds.

"Yeah. You?"

"Yeah, except for I'm laying in about two inches of mud under the ice, goddammit. You see anything out there?"

"Clear over here."

Slowly, carefully, vigilantly, they stood up and looked around, then at each other through the open doors.

"Well, aren't you a sight," Ken said as he broke out in laughter. The dim glow of a streetlight down the road showed that Diehl was mud from his knees to his chin, with big splashes of it on his face. Where he wasn't mud, he was covered with white dust.

Diehl looked down at himself and then scraped some mud off his shirt.

"To quote you, Travis, kiss my ass. You're no beauty yourself, what with looking like a drumstick been dipped ready to deep fry. What the hell happened?"

Ken looked down at the thick coat of powder that coated his uniform. He took his hat off and beat the dust off of it against his leg, and then used it to dust his uniform.

They could see that the inside of the rig was covered in the white powder.

"I ain't getting back in there until I know what that shit is," Diehl announced positively.

Ken picked his flashlight off the seat, and shone it inside.

"Hell, Real, *you* did it. Looky there." He pointed the beam at the transmission hump behind the gearshift. There lay a dry chemical fire extinguisher in its mount, safety pin for the trigger gone, and gauge showing half-empty. "You set it off with your foot."

"Shit and goddam," Diehl swore. "Who the hell would put a fire extinguisher in like that? The damn pin's not on the floor anywhere over here – prob'ly wasn't even there when they mounted it. Some of those guys down in the garage are dumb as a Three Stooges double feature. I'll bet they put it in like that and it's just been sitting there like a little secret surprise."

"Let's head on back to the office. I ain't gonna sit around in the dust, wearing this coat of mud."

"Does that mean I don't get to ask you to tell me why Pope had Lamont call those cops in Juarez the other day; you know; about Ayala's money and the journal? Does he figure the cops are going to go arrest them and grab the dope, or what?"

Diehl looked over at him as he started the rig.

"Boy, you are a cherry, aren't you? Well, you've got it all to learn, and, lucky for you, me here to tell you."

"The idea is that the cops over there will be pretty pissed off about what's been going on under their noses. Apparently, Ayala was moving some dope without paying off and that's a no-no, a big one. They'll go to see him about it. Now he's dead, they'll talk to whoever took over and get their money from him. And it will occur to whoever that is to ask how they knew about it. If you're a doper, the logical answer is that the man who's been out of sight blew them in. They wouldn't figure it to have been the girl. What could she know and how could she tell us about it? But guess who's been in the jug over here for almost a week now?"

"Ahhh-ha," Ken said. *Pretty goddam cold-blooded; they'll probably kill him if they lay hands on him. Do I care?* He found that he had to stop and think that over. *No, I don't. He's a shooter and we're better off with him out of the picture. He bought cards in the game and sometimes you wind up on the short end of the pot.*

He looked at Diehl, who looked back at him with a grin. "Sometimes special measures are called for. But we don't generally talk about it to folks."

*****

Ken shoved the last bite of a piece of pumpkin pie into his mouth and washed it down with the last of his second cup of coffee.

"Kate, honey, that was a meal to write home about. In fact, I will write home about it. Talk about mom's home cooking—she'll be jealous. 'course, she's not that good a cook, though, so the competition's not very tough." He grinned at her and she threw her wadded-up napkin across the table at him.

It had been a great meal and she knew it, and she knew he knew it. She'd made several calls to her mother, telling her why she wanted it to be special and getting advice about what to cook and how to prepare it. Her mother seemed as excited about it as Kate was. She was not at all disappointed that Kate had not come home for the holiday; she understood perfectly.

So Kate had spent hours on Wednesday selecting the just the right ingredients and had started cooking at six a.m. today. She had spoiled nothing; it all turned out perfect.

"You have no idea how much I enjoyed doing it, Ken. Like I told you, I never have done something like that for someone I love. In fact, I haven't loved anyone before enough to want to make something special for him. You're the first one."

"It was a first for me, too, honey. A girl brought me a cookie she made once upon a time, but it was burnt and we were only twelve. Just no comparison, at all. Seriously, it was wonderful—if the way to a man's heart really is his stomach, it looks like you've got mine sewed up. Thank you. Why don't you let me help you with the dishes?"

She had cleaned up the cooking mess already, so there were just the serving and eating dishes to do. As she turned on the water to fill the sink, she said, "No, love, you just sit there and keep me company while I do it. It's woman's work." She turned and smiled at him. The "woman's work" thing had become a joke with them since their first weekend together in Cloudcroft, but she really did seem to go by it. She wouldn't let him lift a finger in domestic chores and he took it for granted that was how it ought to be.

This is pretty wonderful. Guess I can tell the folks I really am in love now.

Chapter 54

Diaz was seated at the desk when the alarm announced with a single buzz that someone was coming up. He knew who it would be, so he walked to the door to open it for them. As expected, he found the two cops at the top of the stairs.

"*Ah, Señor Fuentes, Señor Madrid; Bienvenidos a mi oficina.* Welcome to my office." He had troubled himself to find out about them from contacts of his own and it startled them that he knew their names. Ayala had not bothered to discover who they were; it was enough for him that they were from the *Judiciál* and that money would satisfy them. "Perhaps," they thought, "we should not take too much for granted with this one."

He motioned them toward the chairs in which Armendariz and Benavidez had died so quickly a week before. There was no trace left of them—not anywhere.

"Sit down, gentlemen, sit down, please. How are your families? Fuentes, your son will be a major soccer player, without doubt, and Madrid, your wife, Martina, is of rare beauty, and so young. You must be much man for such a woman."

The two cops looked at each other, off balance. They were accustomed to being in charge, but with just a few words Diaz had shown them the iron fist. They slowly took the offered seats, watching Diaz closely, trying to read his face. What they saw was not encouraging. Fuentes set down the briefcase he had carried in.

"Alonzo," Diaz called out. One of the doors behind the two cops opened, startling them. Diaz, it seemed, was a step ahead of them at every turn. His words had distracted them and they forgot their backs. Alonzo, large and muscular, came through the door. A short, double-barreled shotgun dangled from a huge hand. It pointed almost, but not quite, at the two men.

"You called, jefe*?"* His eyes were locked on the two cops, and theirs on him.

"Unas bebidas por mis amigos, Alonzo. Drinks for my friends. Tequila, the good stuff from my bedroom."

"Now, *Senóres,* to business." When the cops turned their faces back to Diaz, they found him holding a gun on them. "Alonzo is my cousin from Guanajuato. He has much experience in the business, and he will go wherever I go and do whatever I tell him. I have no secrets from him; we can talk freely."

Alonzo returned with a heavy, pottery tray bearing a bottle of Cuervo tequila, limes, salt, and three glasses. The shotgun was tucked under his arm. He set the tray on the corner of the desk in front of the cops and then retired to the back of the room. He sat down in a hard, straight chair, the shotgun across his lap. Diaz slipped his gun back into a desk drawer. Alonzo was always there, in the back of the minds of Fuentes and Madrid.

Diaz poured some liquor into each of the three glasses. "My cousin does not drink, you understand. He always wants his wits about him in case I should need him for some service." He nodded in Alonzo's direction; Alonzo returned the nod with bright eyes and a broad grin. He lifted the shotgun muzzle slightly, as though in salute.

Diaz picked up his glass and raised it. "*Tomen, amigos. A nuestro negocio nuevo.* Drink, friends, to our new business." They each took a glass and brought their glasses together in a toast, but the cops were visibly unenthusiastic. "*Salud, amor, y pesetas,"* Diaz said; "Health, love, and money." He tossed off his drink and they followed his example.

"Now, *Senóres,* we must talk. You have something I want and I have money that you want. Alas, it is not all the money you wanted, but I believe you can be fair about things. After all, it would hardly be just for you to charge me full price for something that you obtained so easily, *verdad?*" He smiled. "Name a price and I will tell you if what you have is worth that to me."

"You were prepared pay ten thousand dollars for the merchandise, Diaz. That seems a fair price, one we agreed on a week ago. Yes, ten thousand . . ."

"No, no *Senóres.* Ayala was prepared to pay ten thousand a week ago. But he is dead and the market has changed since then. I have incurred several expenses and gone to no small amount of trouble. That figure is far too high. Please reconsider."

Behind them, Alonzo stood up, reminding them of his presence. Each of the two shifted nervously in his chair.

Fuentes looked at Madrid, and Madrid shrugged, deferring back to him.

"You said a week ago that you were going to pay eight thousand dollars, *Señor* Diaz. That sounds like a fair price now, since there have been problems for you to resolve. I think that is a good price. Certainly, when you sell it you will make a profit by having bought it at that price. Yes, eight thousand dollars – we will take that."

"No, *Senóres,* I don't think so." Diaz's voice lost all trace of humor, feigned or real. He leaned forward on his arms, folded on the desk. "You are *guzanos,* worms, but taking care of you is a cost of business for me. I will pay you now, two thousand dollars as a token of my good faith. But I will pay you only one thousand dollars for every kilo that comes to me in the future. Ayala may have neglected to advise you of his dealings, but that was between him and you. We, you and I, will have a new business and I do not adopt his debts; is that clear?" He glanced at Alonzo, who shifted his position even further along the wall, giving him a clear shot that would take both of them out with one barrel. They all knew that the cops would not be killed here and now as long as they didn't start anything, but Alonzo's looming presence reminded them of the ever-present threat he represented if they did not cooperate. The pressure was on.

Fuentes shrugged, and said, "Well, we had to try, didn't we? "

"Yes, you had to try. I understand that it was just business," Diaz said jovially, as he came around the desk, arms wide in apparent bonhomie. The two cops began to stand, but as they did Diaz, at the end of the desk, dropped his right arm to the tray and swept the bottle up by the neck. With a full swing of his arm, he slammed it across the bridge of Fuentes' nose, crushing it, and cutting deeply into his brow. Fuentes staggered and fell, clutching his face. Blood ran through his fingers and down his arm, soaking the sleeves of his white, embroidered shirt, ruining it. Alonzo had his shotgun high, in shooting position, controlling Madrid with the twin muzzles. The cop let go of the tail of his shirt, and instead, he reached down to help his partner stand.

Diaz took a clean handkerchief from his pocket and handed it to Fuentes, putting a hand on his shoulder as he did, looking into his face. Although Fuentes could not see yet, he could smell the man's breath and feel it on his face as he spoke almost gently. "That will leave a nasty mark, but it was justice, Fuentes. Let us have no more of that sort of thing, *entiendes?* Understand?"

Fuentes nodded, and they walked to the door with him pressing the handkerchief to his ruined nose and brow. Diaz said, "See the man at the bar. He has your money. And that is where you will get your money in the future. You will not come up here again."

They left, and Diaz heaved a sigh of relief. By using what he had tucked away in places here and there, and calling in debts, and threatening several people to make them lend him small amounts, and enlisting Alonzo, he had scraped together five thousand dollars. He would have gone that high if they had refused to accept two thousand, but they had given in easily. It had not been a bluff, though, and they knew it. Threats backed by facts and action are credible and even crooked cops love their families.

He would have to pay these cops just a few times before the fate they bought themselves by killing Benavidez and Armendariz arrived. The bosses in the south, whom Diaz had told of the murders to explain what happened to the drugs, would see to that. There would be others to pay afterwards, but they would have learned what happens when a *chota* gets greedy. Five thousand dollars was all he had, but he had made it work. Now, he was in business.

There were three things to do. First, business. He picked up the phone to call the buyer in Dallas and tell him the merchandise would be on the way tomorrow—there had to be money in the bank before he could go hunting Chavez. Then, the *puta* and Salinas. There was a lesson to be taught there, too. And if he could recover *that* money . . . what a start he could make.

Chapter 55

The GTO ran through the night, sending thunder rolling across the barren desert. The stars and full moon were bright in the windshield, center stripes were a steady blur and mileposts flashed by every thirty seconds. *Light My Fire* from the Doors blasted out of the radio, the tempo driving them to higher speeds, and the heater made the car an island of warmth for them in the cold night. The speedometer had been pegged at one hundred and twenty miles an hour for the last nine miles, ever since they had passed the Ysleta turnoff from Carlsbad Highway. Now they were approaching a series of curves where the road descended into an arroyo, then climbed out again.

As the first curve, a gentle left, loomed Ken took his right hand off the wheel and dropped it to the four-speed gearshift on the floor. The girl put her left hand gently on top of his, to mimic the shift. She had done it before.

He shifted down to third, not touching the brakes, adding throttle to hold his speed as he eased the clutch out. The tachometer jumped and the power stabilized the suspension as he accelerated through the curve, shifting up to fourth under full power as he entered the long straight to the next curve. He smiled—he had lost no speed in the curve. A quick glance at Sylvia showed a wide grin on her face. Finally, on his fourth try, she had said she'd go for a ride with him. Tonight at ten he'd picked her up after work and headed straight out the Carlsbad highway to a stretch of road with these few curves in it. Curves were hard to find on West Texas highways. At this time of night, the road was empty and the troopers were close to town.

The speedometer stayed just beyond the hundred and twenty mark, as high as it went. A half-mile ahead the road curved to the right a bit more sharply than the last one. He knew from previous trips that some cracked pavement made it rough. At the last second, just as Sylvia began to grip the armrest and suck her breath in fright, he downshifted, letting the engine braking slow the car to a hundred before he stabilized it again with steady throttle. The tires jounced as they went over the rough spot and the rear end felt loose, but the tires held. He and Sylvia slid to the left in their seats as the car tracked around the curve as though on rails. Her squeal of excitement echoed the tires as they clung to the road.

For nearly three miles the road let them roar along at full throttle. Calculating from the tachometer, Ken figured they were doing close to a hundred and thirty miles an hour. He said it out loud and she looked over at him with that same grin. *She's loving this. And I am, too.*

He thought about things running out in front of them, but the biggest thing there might be would be a coyote. There was no telling what would happen if he overbraked, probably a long slide, turning into a rolling crash, so he coached himself to hold the throttle if it happened. It would be noisy and messy and something might break up front, but the worst thing he could do at this speed would be to brake hard.

Ahead were two turns, a left and then a right, both sharp enough to require that he slow down quickly. He analyzed what was coming up.

He was overdriving his headlights severely and the first curve sneaked up on him. Fortunately, the moon gave enough light for him to recognize where he was and he had just enough time to begin to brake, but it was before he had intended to use them, and harder. The rear end slewed to the left a little as the mass of the car shifted forward and unweighted the rear tires. It scared him badly and made Sylvia jump in her seat. She looked at him with her eyes wide, mouth slightly open. He got off the brakes and things straightened out in time for him to set up for the curve. He dropped a gear once more and cautiously powered through it, still fast, but slower than he had wanted.

He flew through a sweeping right-left-right ess and then prepared for the real challenge, a hard right, not a corner, but a curve sharp enough to roll them out into the weeds if he misjudged it.

He slowed to a hundred and ten, braking gently, trying not to upset the car's balance too badly. And downshift. Perfect—he was doing just ninety-five as he entered the curve in third gear, then back onto the gas to stabilize the suspension. The speed felt slow compared to what had gone before, but he knew the curve tightened as he got deeper into it. Sylvia sat up straighter in her seat as she lost sight of the road as it swung to her right around a low hill. "Ken . . ." she breathed, and said no more, but from the corner of his eye he saw her legs stiffen and clamp together.

He had been here many times to do exactly this; it was a great way to decompress after a shift. He knew where the apex of the curve was and as he could see it show up in his mind's eye he began to feed in power. The car accelerated and the back end got loose—he was on the ragged edge of control. When he could actually see the apex he fed in all the power it would take without breaking the rear end loose and then just before he was there he used even more power to encourage the rear end to drift out. It broke loose gently, predictably, swung out a couple feet, and hung right there as the tires spun, searching for traction – a full drift. Too much and he would spin out into the bushes. Too little and the front end would begin to plow, scrubbing the tires ahead despite their angle of turn, understeering them off the road. Sylvia began to breathe in short, panting breaths, hands clenched on her thighs, legs thrust forward, upright in her seat, with her head thrown back.

He worked the throttle gently, adding or subtracting power to tell the rear end what he wanted of it to make the front of the car point in the right direction. With gentle throttle nudges and gentle twitches of the wheel he drifted the car through the curve. It responded like a quarterhorse to the knees of its rider. Finally, he was past the apex of the curve, looking down the straight. He nailed the throttle and all four barrels on the big carburetor opened wide and roared as they sucked in air. The Goat screamed like a banshee and wailed down the road.

"Oh, GOD, Ken, That was WONDERFUL! Stop! Stop, NOW!"

Startled at her words, Ken looked over at her—he was ready to go all the way to Carlsbad. She was pushing herself away from her door, across the console toward him. At over a hundred miles an hour he didn't dare look away from the road for very long but it was enough to see her face in the moonlight. She had a look he'd never seen on a woman's face before . . . eyes wide, lips drawn back from her teeth in something that wasn't a smile—she looked almost like a wild creature.

She reached over the console and squeezed his thigh, high up on his thigh. "Now, Ken, now. Stop this thing now. Pull off the road somewhere." To emphasize her point she reached higher still and placed her hand firmly on his crotch and massaged it. He responded instantly. She felt it and it inflamed her even more.

He braked as hard as he could before he pulled fifty yards off the highway onto a sand trail. He hoped that they would be able to get back out but at the moment he had a wildcat to think about. This was new to him and he didn't know how to respond to such . . . aggressiveness.

As he slowed on the sandy track she peeled her shoes and skirt and panties off and left them laying on the front floor. She pushed herself through the gap between the front seatbacks, into the rear seat. Ken looked over his shoulder at her as the car came to a full stop and he turned off the headlights. She was lying down across the seat, feet against the left side, knees bent and open, sweater wrinkled high on her torso, the top of her head against the right armrest. One arm was folded across her forehead and the other hand was stroking her lower belly as she looked at him. He sat there unable to take his eyes from her, noticing what perfect light the moon provided to see her by.

"Come ON!" she demanded. He mentally slapped himself back to the business at hand.

He'd never get his pants off while he was behind the wheel and he'd never fit through that gap between the seats, so he opened the door and stood up outside. The dome light shone brightly on her. He flipped his seatback forward so he could see her as he hopped on one foot, trying to take a boot off. She had no patience with that.

"God DAMN!" she said and sat up. She reached through the door and pulled him forward by his belt, then unbuckled it and unfastened and unzipped his pants with a speed he'd never have matched. When she had everything down around his knees she dragged him, boots and all, in on top of her, then into herself, pulling him deep.

It was rodeo sex; all he had to do was stay on for a while. And as intimate as a rodeo; it was purely a physical, athletic event. She had her hands up under his shirt, clawing grooves in his bare back. She sank her teeth into his shoulder or neck; he wouldn't know which until he could see it in a mirror. She drew blood from his lip with a kiss that turned into a bite. She drummed her feet against his buttocks and he thought about spurs. Then he could feel it coming for him and as he swelled and burst, she screamed her own climax, thrusting her hips hard at him before collapsing.

Very soon, she pushed him away, leaving him with nothing to do but roll awkwardly onto the floor, then work his way to the door again. "Hoo-HA!" she whooped, throwing her arms up. Then she giggled, "That was GREAT! I told you I liked driving fast at night. Bet you didn't guess it'd get you fucked like that, did you? I did; it always happens."

He sat on the doorsill, breathing hard, with nothing to say, wondering how often "always" was and with whom, and wondering when girls started using that word. He recalled how Kate had blushed when she'd said "ball-bearing stewardesses" up in Cloudcroft. He found that he liked that, that she had been a little embarrassed, now that he had something to compare it to.

When he regained his breath, he stood and pulled his underwear and pants up and secured them. Then he took off his shirt, peeled his t-shirt off over his head and handed it back to her to use to wipe herself off.

"Well, aren't you a gentleman? Cat got your tongue again?"

He didn't respond. Shirtless, with a light sweat dampening his skin, he stood there. The night air raised goose bumps all over him. He looked at the stars and moon and smelled the night as he put his shirt back on. She handed him his t-shirt and he tossed it into the brush. A coyote howled far away and close by an owl hooted to scare its prey into moving.

Now I wonder who's been chasing who. He heard the soft sounds of cloth whispering as she slipped into her clothes behind him and then she squeezed out of the back seat and put an arm around him and rested her head on his shoulder.

"Say cowboy, got a cigarette for a girl?" Her tone was friendly, not intimate, but gentle.

"Sure." He reached across the inside of the car to the glove box and pulled out a pack of Winstons. He had noticed at the restaurant that it was her brand. He opened the pack, lit one and handed it to her before he pulled one of his Chesterfields out.

"Thank you, Ken. You are a sweetheart, aren't you? It was nice of you to have these for me. Are you always considerate like that?"

"You're welcome, Sylvia. I try. And thank you."

She leaned against him again and wrapped her arms around his. He felt her full breast press against his arm. It was pleasant, but it left him unmoved.

"Kind of overwhelming when it happens like that, isn't it, Ken? First time it's been that way for you? It was, wasn't it? I can tell."

"Sylvia, I'd rather not talk about it, not yet, anyway. Yeah, it's way outside my experience, maybe even outside my league. The whole thing was a big surprise. Let that be enough for now."

"No, it's not enough for now. I want you to know that I don't do that with every guy who drops by the restaurant with a fast car and a cute face, but I like fast cars and sex and when the right guy comes along at the right time, well, I'll share." She squeezed his arm and smiled up at him. "This time, it was you. It might be you again the next time, too, or maybe not. If you can live with that, we can have a good time once in a while."

"What does your boyfriend think of that?" Ken looked down at her face, lit by the moonlight. *God, she's beautiful! I didn't know there really were girls like that. I wonder how old she is. I feel like a ten-year old next to her.*

"We're not going nearly as steady as he thinks we are and what he doesn't know won't hurt him. Come on, now, take me home." He walked her around the car to open the door for her. "If I don't see you again at the restaurant I'll know you aren't up for it."

They drove back to town at a legal speed. Neither of them had anything left to prove, or to get any more, and the tension of seduction was gone.

Chapter 56

"They did what!" Pope exploded into the phone. "What is wrong with those idiots down there? Don't they give a shit if that son-of-a-bitch kills someone out here?" He listened to the FBI agent on the other end of the line for a minute. His face turned red and the color crept up over the top of his head, visible even through the thinning blond hair.

"Evidence, my ass. You know damned well that the brass he left at the shooting site matched up with the chamber and firing pin marks on the gun he had in his truck when we arrested him. Everything pointed to him. His truck was parked in the area at the time of the shooting, and the shooter was riding a red motorcycle, and he was working on a red dirt bike when we arrested him. It was him, goddam it. Don't give me that shit about how he claimed he lent the gun to someone that day. Did the U.S. Attorney really buy off on that? Why didn't they even bother to talk to some of us about what happened?"

His face went from red to crimson as the FBI agent went on.

"Yeah, I know what your report said. It did everything but say we made an illegal arrest. A damned good thing it was that somebody made an arrest, anyway. So what did he plead out to? Uh-huh. What'd he get?"

'Bullshit!" He slammed the phone down and swiveled his chair to face Diehl, Travis, and LeClaire, who had come in to find out what happened in court.

"They let him plead out to the magistrate to a misdemeanor at the preliminary hearing. His attorney told the U.S. Attorney the arrest was bogus and that if it went to trial they'd win. They didn't want to take the case to trial because the arrest and search looked shaky, so they let him plead to receiving stolen government property under a thousand dollars, one of the two cases of G.I. ammo he had."

"What's his sentence?" Travis asked.

"The mag said that he'd served his country well in a difficult time and had received a medical discharge because of that service. He said it was clear to him that the defendant's judgment had been impaired by the circumstances of his service. He didn't want to punish him more for such a petty crime, so he sentenced him to time served. He walked out of the courtroom and nobody knows where he is now."

"Well, what about the shooting?" LeClaire asked. He had more than an average interest since he'd been on the receiving end when the bullet went through the windshield.

"The magistrate never heard about it; it was never a part of the charge. The only thing he heard about from the FBI and U.S. Attorney was the stolen property charge. By pleading to that, the whole things comes to an end. The U.S. Attorney avoids a trial and Chavez avoids a chance of going to jail."

Diehl swore. Ken and LeClaire sat there stunned – they'd heard about how things sometimes went in court, but the reality of having it happen to your case was different than hearing about it.

Pope went on to say, "And the magistrate ordered the Bureau to give all the evidence back to him except for the ammo. That means he has his rifle, his two pistols, and the Marshals gave back all his ID and service records when they cut him loose."

"Well shit, oh dear," Diehl swore. "Looks like we're up against it. Now he'll figure he's got a free pass to the circus for sure."

****

Chavez walked out of the jail into the bright sunlight. He squinted his eyes against the glare and looked around. He opened the envelope that contained his money and watch and other personal items – everything was there except the switchblade. The tip of the blade on his Buck folding knife had been broken off. *"Chickenshit bastards."* He knew it had been the jailers; they hated knives.

He saw a café a block up the street. Since he had passed up the grits and baloney they served for breakfast in the jail, he headed that way. A few minutes later he sat in a booth, lighting a cigarette and drinking a pretty good cup of coffee while he waited for his bacon and eggs and toast. He looked out the plate-glass window in front of him and idly watched the traffic go by as he thought about what to do.

"First, the truck, then pick up the guns and take them back to the garage. Then, the woman." His guns were still with the FBI evidence custodian, but the order of the court in his pocket would get them released to him. After he dropped them off back at the garage he'd drive over to Nadia's place and have a serious word with her.

"I'll teach that stupid cunt that when I need something from her I expect her to deliver. She can screw who she wants all day, but when I say "frog" I want her to jump, goddamn it. I'm paying her bills."

He'd called her from the jail to post his bail; she'd reminded him that she'd given Tomás all her money and didn't have any left. He damn sure wasn't going to send her to his stash joint to get the money he had behind the mirror there. He'd never been in jail before and he didn't like it worth a damn, so he told her to call Ayala and see if he would give it to her as a loan to him. She'd said she would, but nothing happened—he'd had to spend ten days there with the perverts and he was not in a good mood about it. He'd slept with his back to the wall and not showered at all the whole time. Educating her and getting his ashes hauled in the process might put him in a better mood.

He shoveled his breakfast down in a hurry, eager to get on with the day. He told the waitress to call a cab for him while he finished.

It came while he was standing at the register paying his bill. He dropped a penny in the cup and picked up a couple of peppermints to kill the coffee taste. He walked out the door, popping the first one in his mouth as he stepped into the cab.

Four hours later he was standing in his secret place, taking the bathroom mirror off the wall.

"Naturally," he thought, "those assholes at the Feeble Bureau of Incarceration took their sweet time giving me back my stuff." At least it was all there and nobody had scratched his initials in the guns as evidence markings. The garage had even been left pretty neat after the search since it was someone else's property, not his. He'd lost ten days and a couple cases of ammo, but aside from that and a bullshit police record, it had come out pretty well. Now, he had to get back in Ayala's good graces and get on with business.

He never crossed the bridge with a gun. That was just begging for trouble, so when he had gone over to work on his bike he'd left what he thought of as his "Mexican" pistols here in the apartment. When he got to the garage that day, he climbed up into the rafters and retrieved his "American" guns, the .45 that he'd had tucked up under the truck and a little Smith & Wesson that he'd always kept in the garage. And then they'd grabbed him. So now, here he was ten days later, back in Mexico picking up some walking-around money and his pistols.

He pulled a thousand dollars from the hole. As he did, he looked at the kilo of smack sitting there. He had to figure out what to do with that, or at least who to do it with. It would have to be someone the Ayalas didn't know, because if they ever heard he'd dealt a key of horse they'd put two and two together and it would all be over for him. He wasn't ready for that yet, not by a long shot. So he probably ought to take it somewhere far away, like San Francisco or Seattle to see if he could peddle it.

After he put the mirror back he went into the bedroom and cleaned all his guns, particularly making sure no one had tampered with them. The telltale at the door had not been disturbed, but you never knew. He pulled and inspected the firing pins to make sure they were intact – putting in a short or broken firing pin was the least obvious way he knew to disable a firearm but still leave it looking normal. Then he looked carefully at each round as he reloaded the magazines. Guns were a good thing to be sure of; they were a real comfort when you knew they were right. Then he loaded the .45 he liked best, put the other weapons back in the closet, and left.

At Nadia's he drove around the block before he stopped, looking carefully at each car, but nothing was out of place. The usual idlers were there, but none of them looked suspicious. Most were familiar faces from his search for the girl's apartment; a couple of them waved at him. He slipped the old truck into the curb around the corner so that she would not see him coming, quietly went up the stairs and entered the place with his key. He could hear the shower running, so he went to the refrigerator to see if she had any beer. Wonderfully, there was a six-pack of Tecate. He took one and then sat down on the brown, Naugahyde couch in the living room, crossed one ankle over the other knee, and waited. The chair gave him a view of the bathroom door in her bedroom. He had time to think as he sat there waiting.

A few minutes later the water went off, so he walked over to the door to wait for her. She came out soon, naked and bent over as she toweled her head. The first she knew of anyone being there was when he grabbed her around the waist and threw her onto the bed – she screamed with fright. The towel and her hair fell over her eyes, blinding her and increasing her terror at the sudden assault. He bent over and took her throat in one hand, slapped her, and choked off her screams and her breath. Her hands ripped at his wrists, scratching him, and her legs thrashed and kicked.

"Be quiet," he said, finally. She went still at the familiar voice; he let go of her and stepped back. Slowly, she reached to her head and moved the towel.

"Why did you do that to me!" she shrieked when she saw him, her voice hoarsened by the squeeze he had given her throat.

"It was a lesson." He took the pistol from his belt, cleared it and set it on the bed table and then unbuttoned his shirt as he pierced her with his gaze. "When I want something from you, you are to treat it as the most important thing you have to do in the world." He took off his boots. "There will be no excuses. I don't want to wonder if you will do it – understand? " He stepped out of his pants and underwear. "We won't need another lesson, will we?" He believed in military-style teaching: lessons, simply taught, with clear consequences for slow learners.

He lay down beside her on his back, arms behind his head, and she began to show that she understood the lesson.

In the late afternoon, as the setting sun spilled its light through her front window, they sat at her small dinette table in the end of the kitchen. They were eating Chinese food she had called to have delivered. He loaded his rice with soy sauce, scooped some up, then speared a piece of sweet and sour pork. As he chewed he looked at her pensively. He came to a decision.

"You will call the *cantina* and ask if *El Patrón will* be there during the evening. "Do not say who you are and do not mention my name. Just say that you are calling for someone who needs to see him about a business matter. Tell whoever answers that your friend knows to check in with the bartender.

She nodded her understanding. "I have the number that I used to call Tomás." She consulted a small book from her purse and dialed the phone.

The conversation was brief. It was no more than what he had told her to say, and a series of questions from them answered by "yes" or "no" from her. Finally, she said, "Yes, he is known there," listened to an answer, and then hung up.

"What did they say?"

"They wanted very much to know who you are; they tried to get me to tell them, but you heard me. I did what you said, but I had to tell them that they know you or they wouldn't have told me anything. You are to go there at eight o'clock and speak to the bartender."

He looked at his watch; it was five-thirty. "We have time for some more of what I pay you for, woman. Come." He walked into the bedroom. Ten days in jail had left him with urges to indulge.

Chapter 57

At a quarter to eight he found a parking place a block from the Cantina Rio Bravo. As he strolled up the block, the cold breeze cut through his denim jacket. He thought he should have stopped at his apartment to get something heavier.

It was Friday night and the neon lights lit the street in bright colors. Traffic crawled by with young men examining the attractions before they decided to stop. It was too cold for them to want to walk far, so they would find where they wanted to be before they parked. The shills outside the doors of the bars and clubs barked at the crowd as the people walked by. The alleys, as always, were dim. Movements like ghostly shadows could be seen down them if you paused and looked closely. Few did, for the alleys spilled a sense of menace into the street like a dark stain and the danger was real just a few feet away from the sidewalks. He was tempted to take his pistol in hand under his jacket and walk down one of them to surprise someone, but he had other business first. Fun would have to wait.

The noise and lights hit him like an explosion when he opened the door to the Cantina Rio Bravo and the place was funky-warm from all the bodies there. Every girl at the bar had one or two men with her; there were no wallflowers tonight. The bartender was attentive. Chavez ordered a beer and lifted a thumb to point at the ceiling, a question on his face. The bartender recognized him and nodded his OK. He pressed the button—three times—as Chavez went to the stairs.

His knock on the door at the end of the hall was answered by two men, one from each door to the right and left. Alfonso Ayala was on his right, with a pistol pointed at his belly. The boy was young, but the pistol made him as old as he needed to be. The other man was a stranger, a very large man with a double-barreled shotgun he held by the small of the stock and the forend. It looked like a toy in his hands, but Chavez recognized the weapon; it was a Rossi Coach Gun and the holes in the ends of the short barrels said it was a twelve-gauge. The exposed hammers were cocked and it was aimed at his throat. That did not mean anything good for him—it was a serious man-killer and it was ready to go to work.

He saw the stock twitch and he tried to move, for he knew what was coming, but too late. The stock of the shotgun smashed into his jaw just below his ear. As the lights went out for him he dropped to the floor like puppet with its strings cut. One of the girls came up the stairs, a client with his hand on her ass right behind her, but as her head came above the landing and she saw what was happening she turned and led him back down to the bar.

Each of them took Chavez by an arm and dragged him into the room. As Diaz watched, silently pleased, they took the pistols from his belt and boot and then stripped him. Alfonso went through his pockets and removed the wallet and keys and other litter while Alonzo tied his arms behind his back with wire and then trussed his ankles.

"Alfonso, get the car and bring it around back. In five minutes we will bring him downstairs."

A few minutes later Diaz stepped through the closet and unlocked the back door to the office. He and Alonzo dragged Chavez down the stairs by his feet. His head made a hollow thump as it hit each of the twelve bare, wooden steps and the skin was gone from the back of his shoulders when they reached the bottom.

Alonzo threw Chavez onto the back floor of the car and got in, his feet in the middle of Chavez's back. As Diaz got into the front seat with Alfonso, Chavez made a sound and moved slightly. A blow to the back of his head from the butt of the shotgun ended that. Diaz turned and said, "Be careful you do not kill him yet."

A half hour later they were within meters of where Diaz and Chavez had buried Tomás Ayala in the desert southwest of Juarez. A fresh hole waited, the pile of dirt beside it making it easy to find in the headlights. Two spades were shoved into the dirt.

While Diaz watched, Alfonso helped Alonzo drag Chavez out of the back floor to the lip of the hole, where they laid him face down. With a push of his foot, Diaz rolled him in. He landed on his back with a solid thump and the air left his lungs in a breathy rush.

He awoke to a splash of water in his face, a stream of water. He shook his head back and forth. The pain lit fireworks behind his eyes. When the stream stopped and he opened his eyes he saw Diaz standing above him, zipping his pants. The two men from the hall stood beside him. The wind moaned as it blew sand over the lip of the hole, into his face. The glare of the headlights created shadows on their faces, eerie against the blackness of the sky behind them. He knew what was to come but he didn't know why.

"Why are you doing this? I have done nothing but serve you well." He tried to shift the way his body lay on top of his bound hands. The dirt burned his scuffed shoulders.

"Fool," Diaz said. "Did you really think that the woman was a secret? Before you had her the first time Ayala owned her. She was Tomás' toy but she was Ayala's tool and now she is mine."

"Am I to be killed over one more *puta?"* Chavez had faced death already too many times to be panic-stricken, and besides, it did not seem real—a haze of pain clouded his mind.

"You will die now for betraying me. I know that you were arrested for your foolish shooting at the *patrulleros,* Thompson. It was a bad idea and Ayala was an idiot to go along with it. The woman told us as soon as you called her when you were arrested—I was there when she called."

"She called because I told her to, Diaz. I asked for your help to get out of jail. I would have come back here."

Diaz knelt on one knee on the edge of the hole and went on as though he hadn't heard. "You told them everything about us; you betrayed us to them, just as I knew you would, one day. We heard all about what you told them—and it is the only way you could be back so soon. We have been waiting for you."

"I told them nothing, nothing, do you hear? They had no case against me. You can find out." He was pleading now. To be killed for stealing the drugs would have been fair. To die for something he never did was not. He tried to think of who might have invented the tale.

"Ayala should never have hired you, *gringo.* I told him you should be killed before you betrayed us. Now he is dead and the business is mine and I will rectify old mistakes. You will die screaming and these men will let it be known how you died as a lesson to others who would talk too much."

"You will certainly kill me, *pendejo,*" Chavez spat at him in defiance. "But you will never make me scream."

Diaz smiled, and as he arose he drew his pistol. He aimed carefully and shot Thompson once, low in the gut. He screamed. As he took a breath to scream again, the first shovelful of dirt landed on his feet.

Chapter 58

Kate stood in front of him, half-undressed, hands on her hips. There were no sobs yet but tears were running down her cheeks. Her face was flushed, and etched with misery. She had returned from her two-day trip and gone straight to his door, stopping in her place only long enough to drop her suitcase. When he answered her knock she had stepped in, dropped her purse and backed him right into the bedroom, unbuttoning her blouse as she went, laughing gaily, ready to give herself to him completely, talking a mile a minute about how much she had missed him. Then she saw the cut lip and the bite mark on his neck and the look on his face and she knew.

She stood there, frozen in shock, hands on the zipper of her skirt. Finally, she could say, “Oh, Ken, oh no, no—not that . . .” as the tears came in a flood.

She reached for the blouse she had thrown onto the chair next to his bedroom door when she came in. Finally, the words came. "I love you Ken, like nobody I ever knew before. I'd have been your girl—I'd have been the best thing that ever happened to you—but I won't be *one* of your girls, ever." A sob broke through.

"Kate . . ." he started to say, but she held up her hands to cut him off as she looked away from his face.

"No, Ken, there's nothing for you to say to me now.” She fumbled her blouse on, giving him an angry glare that was soaked in tears and pain. “There’s nothing you *can* say that will make it all right." She buttoned her blouse and it came out crooked. "Damn!" she swore. But she didn't fix it. She just tucked it into her uniform skirt while she slipped into the shoes she had kicked off in the living room.

"You can pretend you're James Bond and take every girl you meet to bed if you want. That's fantasy, *Playboy* stuff! But I'm the real thing, the *best* thing," she said as she bent to pick up her purse. "If that's what you want, though, you just do it! But leave me out of it. You may have to leave me out of it no matter what you decide; I don't know any more."

She stalked out, shoulders shaking but back straight. She didn't look back.

"Kate, I'm sorry . . ." but he was talking to the empty doorway.

After she left, he dropped into his armchair and stared blankly at the television. It wasn't on and he didn't know how long he sat there. Eventually, he turned it on and watched something for a while, but now he couldn't even remember what it was. Finally, he took a cigar and a heavy shot of bourbon out into the cold on the balcony. He put his feet on the rail and leaned the chair back against the wall, as he had so many times since he came here in September. He set his glass on the low table by the chair and then cut the end off his cigar with his pocketknife. He concentrated on the task more than was called for. His hands shook and he used three matches to get it going. When it was evenly lit and drawing well he took a sip of his drink and stared at the dark sky to the west. Mars was there, bright red, and Venus shone silver just above the horizon. He stared at them. There was symbolism there he couldn't quite grasp.

His heart ached—he'd heard the word before but never understood that it was real. He felt whipped, numb, and emotionally dead. And guilty. He had hurt her, damaged someone he cared for. No. Someone he *loved.* And for what? The thing with Sylvia had been exciting, but it meant nothing to him—but it meant everything to Kate. It didn't matter to her who it had been or that Sylvia meant nothing to him. It hadn't been her, and that was everything that mattered.

He thought about what she had said—he could have her and only her, or as many others as he could find. She hadn't even asked him for forever, just that if she was the one, she be the only one. All the things she had done for him passed through his mind, and how sweet it was when they were together.

Is she the one? Do I even want a one and only and all the complications? Maybe Diehl was right—I better look out, or she'll have a rope on me pretty quick. I do not need a wife to slow me down. Sylvias are easier—but God, I miss Kate already.

Inside, the phone rang and he leaped out of his chair, but when he answered it was Diehl. "Drop your cock and grab your socks, sport. We got work to do—I'll pick you up in twenty minutes." Ken dropped the phone back in the cradle and got dressed. The job was always there.

The Old Signcutter

The Old Patrol

As with most organizations, the Border Patrol's old timers (like your author) remember better days. In the Border Patrol it is the fabled "Old Patrol." In the Old Patrol things were harder. You didn't earn much, the supervisors were tougher, the bad guys meaner, you worked the whole day from "can-see" to "can't see" and beyond, and you provided your own equipment.

But on the other hand, men were taller and stronger and completely fearless. Everyone was a signcutter of note; some could even track a buzzard's shadow across the highway. They could run all day and not break a sweat, arrest ten aliens at once and never lose a one, and bad guys quivered in fear at the mere mention of their names. Naturally, they were all crack shots with anything that went "bang." It was a time when men were men and women were damn glad they were.

It's nonsense, of course. Yes, there is an "old patrol." If you're a Border Patrolman it is made up of you and the officers who put the badge on before you did. Officers who came in after you are the new guys, and the Patrol might not survive their presence. Or so goes the common wisdom. It is within that framework of belief that the following story takes place.

It's 1924 and the Border Patrol has just been established. Two newly-minted managers are out in El Paso hiring the first officers that would put on the badge. A man comes in for interview, and the conversation goes as follows:

"Well, Mr. Jones, you appear healthy enough. Do you own a gun, and can you shoot?"

"Yessir, I do. There are bad men now in coffins who would testify that I can shoot, if they could."

"That sounds like what we're looking for, Mr. Jones. Now do you own a sound horse and a good saddle? You'll be covering a lot of border on a horse."

"Nobody's got a better horse than me. I rode him all the way here from Amarillo with hardly a stop. And tough? He'll run with a tornado just for the sheer pleasure in it."

"You'll do, Jones. Go on out back, get your horse some oats and put him in the corral. We'll get with you when we're done."

And the next candidate comes in.

"So you want to be a Border Patrolman, eh, Mr. Smith? What makes you think you're qualified?"

"Sir, I've ridden these canyons and draws most of my life. I know where the trails and water are and where men hide. If they're out there, I'll find 'em."

"But do you own a pistol and a rifle Mr. Smith, and can you shoot? Some of these are dangerous men we're after."

"Yes, I do, and yes, I can. If it comes to gunplay, I fear no man."

"How about a horse and saddle? You must provide your own, you know."

"Well, sir, I've had a piece of bad luck there. I was riding down here from Alamogordo just this morning and my horse stumbled in a hole and broke his leg. I had to shoot him, but I do have my saddle."

"That is bad luck, Mr. Smith, and not your fault. We have a couple of spare horses and we can let you use one for a day or two until you buy yourself another. Now you go on out to the corral and wait until we're through in here."

So Smith moseys on out to the corral, where he finds Mr. Jones sitting on the top rail, rolling a smoke. Smith climbs up and introduces himself.

"New guy, huh?" says Jones.

"Yup. Just got here from Alamogordo."

"Where's yer horse?"

"Don't have one right at the moment," replied Smith.

"Hmmph!" said Jones. "Back in the *old* patrol we had to bring our own horses."

Printed in the United States
202851BV00007B/34/P

9 780615 184302